MW00883544

Early Reviews for *Swinging Sisters* ~~~

In a world of commercialism, *me first* attitudes, and sagging ethics and morals, *Swinging Sisters* offers a heartwarming step back in time. Not only is the reader amazed at the pluck of the matriarch and her girls in their early musical travels at a time when most women never ventured from home, the reader jumps to another amazing realm when the musicians trade their cowgirl outfits for nuns' habits and a life of service to God. *Swinging Sisters* is an uplifting read for the whole family.

~~~ Nadja Bernitt, past-president Sarasota Fiction Writers;
author of *Final Grave*

An awesome; well-written story.

~~~ Mike Savage, author of the Lake Superior Murder Mystery series
[Savage Press]

In *Swinging Sisters*, Madonna Christensen parts the curtains and gives us a peek at history, specifically, the swing era of the 1930s. Immensely popular, the Texas Rangerettes defy tradition, invading and succeeding in a previously male-domi-nated venue. But the four sisters harbor a desire that none of their fans suspect. What would tempt this talented group to leave show business at the height of popularity? Christensen gives us the most unexpected answer. When their fans find out, it's too late. Whatever your background, this tale will keep you turning the pages.

~~~ Joanne Meyer, author of *Heavenly Detour, Fortune Cookie,* and *The Single Girl's Guide to Murder* [Kensington Publishing Corp.]

I was charmed by the whole story, especially since it's based on true life. If I were a public library librarian, I would highly recommend this book for purchase.

~~~ Joy Sparr, retired librarian

In this time of religious turbulence, it's refreshing to read a most unusual story about faith. Madonna Christensen's *Swinging Sisters* is a lively account of the four Jones sisters' lives. What makes their story unique is that they gave up a successful musical career for one far-removed from the footlights of the stage. Why they, and their widowed mother, chose this new life remains a mystery. But, after reading this book, you might discover some clues and even gain a revival of your own faith.

~~~ E.P. Burke, author of *The Hero of Barryton* and *1959; In Search of Eldorado*
[iUniverse]

Swinging Sisters

Swinging Sisters

Madonna Dries Christensen

iUniverse, Inc.
New York Lincoln Shanghai

Swinging Sisters

All Rights Reserved © 2004 by Madonna Dries Christensen

No part of this book may be reproduced or transmitted in any form or by any means, graphic, electronic, or mechanical, including photocopying, recording, taping, or by any information storage retrieval system, without the written permission of the publisher.

iUniverse, Inc.

For information address:
iUniverse, Inc.
2021 Pine Lake Road, Suite 100
Lincoln, NE 68512
www.iuniverse.com

ISBN: 0-595-33186-6

Printed in the United States of America

This is a partly fictional account of a true story. Real people, places, and events are used fictionally; other characters and settings are entirely figments of the author's imagination and do not represent anyone living or dead. Some information about the Incarnate Word and Blessed Sacrament order was taken from a 1996 booklet celebrating the 400th birthday of founder Jeanne Chezard de Matel, and from the booklet *Extending the Incarnation into the Third Millennium* (1998). Newspaper articles, in whole or part, are used with permission from *Park Rapids Enterprise, San Antonio Express-News, Victoria Advocate,* and *Catholic News Service.* Excerpts from *Oblate Monthly and Word of God Catholic Weekly* are paraphrased. *Hubbard County Weekly, Osceola County Clarion, Las Noticias de Piedras Negras,* and *Bluebonnet Press* are fictional newspapers. Some articles and letters are fictional; obituaries are presented as they were originally written; the Joneses' wedding announcement is adapted from one for the author's parents and one for Linford O'Brien and Marie Foley O'Brien. The wedding shivaree article is adapted from one for Linford and Marie O'Brien.

Front cover photo: The Jones Quartet and instructor Mrs. J. B. Tremblay, circa 1930s. Left to right, Evelyn, Gladys, Hazel, Dorothy; seated, Mrs. J. B. Tremblay

Back cover: sketch by a friend

With respect and admiration for my maternal immigrant ancestors, the McLaughlin and O'Brien clans; and to Martin, Mary, Hazel, Gladys, Dorothy, and Evelyn Jones; and to Sisters Pius, Jude, Genevieve, Catherine, and Dorothy Jones ~~~

Dance as if no one were watching; sing as if no one were listening, and live every day as your last.

~~~ Irish toast

Take courage, my sisters. Let us obey simply and generously, for the obedient will sing a song of victory.

~~~ Jeanne Chezard de Matel, founder Incarnate Word Sisters

A song is a thing of joy; more profoundly, it is a thing of love.

~~~ Saint Augustine

DANCE PROGRAM

▼

Acknowledgments

Thank heaven for little girls; they grow up in the most delightful way ~~~

With love and devotion to my granddaughters: Grace Linnet Buzby, a Tuesday's child filled with grace, and Sarah Catherine Buzby, a Monday's child fair of face. They are my past, present, and future; they bring *ceol binn* (sweet music) to my life.

I get by with a little help from my friends ~~~

For their friendship, critiques, and encouragement, I'm grateful to the Emerald Coast Writers (aka Hotsies); to the writing duo Carrillee Collins Burke and Ned Burke; and to the West Coast (Florida) Writers. Many thanks to Donna L. Singer, Nadja Bernitt, Martha Demerly, Paula Ellis, Madge Williams, and Joy Sparr for manuscript evaluation, and to Mike Altman at iUniverse for his patience and one-on-one help.

For information, photos and other assistance, I thank Jean O'Brien Korum; Diana Robertson Craig; Shawn Hughes; Sister Marian Oleksik; Sister Stephana Marbach; Sister Evelyn Korenek; Sister Andrea Hubnik; Sister Kathleen McDonagh; Sister Elaine Baden; Sister Virginia Sheblak; Sister Mildred Truchard; Sister Rebecca Janacek; Martha Vaerst; Florence Vokes; Elaine R. Hooker; Ethel Conner; Robert and Arlene McCarren; Dorothy McLaughlin Tupker, Georgia Brower Davis; Eileen Wilkins; John Sexton; Diana Rhodes; John D. McLaughlin; Robert L. McLaughlin; Adam Koelsch (*Billboard*); Darryl Hensel and Beth Waller (Hubbard County Minnesota Genealogy Society); Laurie Conzemius and Mary L. Garlie (Park Rapids, Minnesota schools); Scot Walker and Ovetta Brann (*The Victoria Advocate*); J. Myler and Deborah Countess (San Antonio Public Library); and Warren Kahn (Sarasota Music Archives).

Slainte ~~~

Introduction

This tale is based on a true story.

Swinging Sisters is a blend of fact, family history, and fiction, relating the story of the Jones sisters: Hazel, Gladys, Dorothy, and Evelyn, and their mother, Mary McLaughlin Jones. With roots in the Irish famine of the 1840s, the sisters were raised in a Catholic household in rural Minnesota, where religion, family, and music were their mother's trinity.

Upon discovering these cousins through genealogy, I became intrigued with their musical and spiritual journey. My letter to them at Incarnate Word and Blessed Sacrament Convent in San Antonio brought this reply from Sister Dorothy: "It was nice to hear from you. I doubt that I can furnish you with as much information as you might need, but I'll do my best. I should be happy to hear from you as you complete some history and 'roots.' With all good wishes and God's blessing on your endeavors. Sincerely, Sister M. Dorothy Jones."

A few months later, Sister Catherine wrote to tell me that Sister Dorothy had passed away. Through correspondence with the remaining sisters, I pieced together an article about them that appeared in *Catholic Digest, Reminisce,* and *Family Tree Magazine.* After each publication, I received letters and phone calls from people across the country. Some were related to the sisters or knew them as children; others had seen them perform, or wished they had. Clara Skaggs, wrote, "I grew up in a small Texas town about 60 miles north of Dallas. I always wanted to see the Texas Rangerettes, but in the '30s not many had a car or money to go anywhere. I often wondered what had become of them."

My published article in the *Tampa Tribune* somehow fell into the hands of an independent Los Angeles film producer. She contacted me and proposed that I be a consultant on a screenplay she would write based on my material. Although I believe *Swinging Sisters* would make a delightful movie, concern that the story might become lost in a Hollywood version convinced me to retain sole rights to the work.

Those who knew the Jones family should understand that because my information about them came late in their lives, I needed to create fictional situations, dialogue, and characters in order to present the essence of the way it *might have been.* Whenever possible, facts were used. Information pertaining to convent life is general, and might not be exactly as it would have been at Incarnate Word and Blessed Sacrament, but I believe all scenes are typical of the eras they depict.

Why did these five women become nuns, all at the same time? The characters in the book explain, but if their words do not satisfy you, the answer will remain a mystery, like faith itself.

Royalties from the sale of this book go to the Sisters of Incarnate Word and Blessed Sacrament, Victoria, Texas.

Madonna Dries Christensen
3209 Riviera Drive
Sarasota, Florida 34232-4741 [e-mail: Iowagirl1@aol.com]

The Players

Mary Loretta McLaughlin Jones/Sister Pius Jones
Martin Lawrence Jones
~~~ their children ~~~
Hazelbon Martha/Sister Jude Jones
Gladys Julia/Sister Genevieve Jones
Dorothy May/Sister Catherine Jones
Evelyn Agnes/Sister Dorothy Jones
Lawrence Robert Jones

Supporting Players ~~~

Patrick McLaughlin and Mary Callighan McLaughlin ~~~ Mary's grandparents
Lawrence McLaughlin and Martha Burke McLaughlin ~~~ Mary's parents
John, Joseph, Victor, Julia, Anna, Robert, Clem, Alice, Eddie ~~~ Mary's siblings

Sister Pius Miles ~~~ Mary's music instructor
Professor J. B. Tremblay ~~~ Girls' music instructor
Louise Tremblay ~~~ Girls' music instructor/manager

Jerry McRae ~~~ Texas Rangerettes band leader
Willeen Grey ~~~ Texas Rangerettes band member

Doc Walters ~~~ Friend
Sister Joseph Gosse ~~~ Mother Superior
Sister Marian Oleksik ~~~ Sister Genevieve's friend

PRELUDE

Climb every mountain, ford every stream, follow every rainbow ~~~

Sister Genevieve Jones waved to me from the passenger seat of a golf cart with a license plate reading Nun Mobile. The cart careened along a path that meandered around Incarnate Word and Blessed Sacrament motherhouse, past a guest cottage, a vegetable garden, a pavilion and a pool. Beyond the simple, buff colored convent in Victoria, Texas, the Guadalupe River lapped against the muddy banks lined with cypress trees.

The petite nun wore a calf-length white habit with a cowl neckline, long sleeves, and a crimson scapular. The front of the scapular bore a navy appliqué of the order's emblem: a crown of thorns within which is the name Jesus, a heart with three nails in it and the words *Amor Meus* (my love). A navy headpiece trimmed with soft white fabric covered Sister Genevieve's white hair except for a curl across her forehead. The deep blue of the headpiece complemented her blue eyes and the red scapular brought a rosy glow to her relatively unlined face.

We sat on cushioned lawn chairs in the shade of sprawling live oaks strung with garlands of Spanish moss. After a moment of small talk about my flight, Sister Genevieve said, "I've always wanted to have a plane ride, but I suppose I never will. I remember my first automobile ride, though, and my first train ride. I was about eight. Pa put my three sisters and me on the train in Park Rapids. While we traveled to the next stop, he took off in the horse and wagon to meet the train and pick us up. We fancied ourselves very grown up, riding the train by ourselves."

She closed her eyes, seemingly relishing the memory. Returning her attention to me, she opened her fist and displayed a sterling silver medal. I read the inscription aloud, "Minnesota State High School Music Contest, 1926, Violin, Gladys Jones."

"That was me, long ago; a different time, a different place," she said. "I'll tell you about winning the award, and lots more. I confess my mind rambles these days, but maybe you can make sense of what I tell you and put everything in order."

Sister Genevieve settled back in her chair. "I must start my story with Mama. It's as much hers as mine. Whatever I and my sisters accomplished is a credit to her. And Pa, of course. Sister Catherine used to say, 'God orchestrated our lives and Mama set the rhythm and directed us.' Mama called God, family, and music her touchstones, her trinity. They were the most important things in her life, and they became ours, too. She was our teacher, and our inspiration."

Her expression changed from thoughtful to playful; a twinkle glinted in her eyes. "Mama could belt out a song like Ethel Merman. But Mama's voice was nicer to listen to. It was sweet, and pure. I can hear it now."

For it was Mary, Mary, plain as any name can be ~~~

MARY'S SONG

What'll I Do

When I'm alone, with only dreams of you ~~~

As snow storms often do, the Saint Patrick's Day blizzard of 1899 created an atmosphere of gaiety and relaxation at Saint Francis Academy in Mason City, Iowa. The day students were sent home and the boarders were given a reprieve, too, when Sister Pius announced, "After music class we'll call it a day. Mary Loretta, please monitor the rehearsal for our upcoming recital. I'll be in my office." In addition to teaching music, Sister Pius Miles had been principal of the city's first Catholic school since it was built ten years earlier.

"Teacher's pet," Fiona Sweeney teased Mary McLaughlin.

The senior class president denied the assertion with a shrug. Later, after adjourning class, she went to the principal's office and tapped on the open door.

"Come in," Sister Pius called. "So, how did everything go?"

"Very well. I think we know the pieces, but you'd be a better judge of that." Mary faced the window, watching snow swirl and blow and cling to trees and shrubs, creating frosty images on the landscape. From here, it was like being inside a snow globe. "Don't you just love snow?" she asked without turning around.

"Oh, I suppose I did when I was your age. Now it's a nuisance. The bottom of my habit gets wet and soiled. But you girls might take your toboggans from the cellar and go out and get some fresh air."

"That would be fun." Mary continued staring out the window. "Papa won't have gotten his *pratais* planted today. Grandda McLaughlin, God rest his soul, always said if you don't get your *pratais* planted by Saint Paddy's day you might as well forget it."

"I've heard that old saying. Your father will plant his potatoes soon enough and it'll be fine."

Mary faced the nun. "I'll go now and leave you to your work."

"Don't rush away." Sister Pius laid aside a stack of papers. "I've sensed the past few days that you're troubled. What's on your mind?"

Sister's keen perception did not surprise Mary. She did have something on her mind and needed to talk about it. Seating herself in the visitor's chair, she came right to the point. "I think I have a vocation."

"You think you have?"

Mary smoothed the wrinkles from the skirt of her blue gabardine uniform. "Yes, maybe, but how do I know for sure?"

Sister Pius's chair squeaked as she leaned back and fixed her eyes on the transom. Waiting for a response, Mary twisted an auburn curl that hung down the front of her blouse, and then quickly released it. Hair twisting was a childish habit she needed to break.

The principal cleared her throat and gave Mary her full attention. "If you have a vocation, you wouldn't question it. You would know. It's not a choice you make. It's God's. When the call comes, it shakes you to the bone. At least it did me." She pulled her black wool shawl around her shoulders as if chilled to the bone now. "It might seem as if you've made the decision, but you're simply following God's wish. Do you understand?"

"I'm not sure. I know a girl who felt certain she had a vocation and went to the convent but she didn't stay."

"Some girls enter because they're denying the real reason; perhaps running away from an unhappy romance or home life. Other times they hope to please a parent. One young postulant I knew said the calling had nagged at her for a long time, but once she entered the convent, she quickly realized the religious life was not for her. She said she was relieved that God didn't want her."

"Mother wants me to be a nun. She says every Catholic family owes a nun and a priest to the Church."

"With all due respect to your mother, she's mistaken. It's not about owing anything. Sometimes God plants the seed in your mind at an early age and it doesn't germinate until years later. He has other plans for you in the interim. With you, perhaps it's your mother who planted the idea. For me the calling came at seven or eight. I didn't tell anyone for a long time, but I knew I would be a nun or a sister."

"What do you mean? Is there a difference?"

"Technically, yes. Nuns are cloistered, and sisters work in the community as nurses and teachers."

"I never knew that."

"It's not that important to most folks. We all use the same title. But you must understand, the calling is not always a bolt from the blue. It's simply an overwhelming knowledge. It can be as quiet as a sunset."

"A girl back home told me that whenever she goes to confession the priest talks to her about becoming a nun. He told her he's been appointed by the pope to choose boys and girls from the congregation to lead the religious life."

Sister Pius's enigmatic expression suggested to Mary that there might be something to this, but the principal kept her own counsel.

"I'm sure I'd like being a sister," Mary said. "As a child, I often pretended to be one, with my sisters and brothers as students. But I sometimes think I'd like to marry and have children."

"Well, you can choose to be a wife and mother but you're chosen for the religious life. You'd be a fine music teacher, whether as a sister or as a lay teacher. You're my most talented student. A clear soprano voice, a fine pianist and cellist."

"Oh, thank you for the compliment. I owe it all to you."

Sister Pius waved away the comment. "Talents are gifts from God. I've only steered you along. Your parents have, too. They've no doubt sacrificed to keep you in school. I believe you'd be a fine sister, but you mustn't decide on that simply because your mother wishes it. For now, pray that you'll be shown which path to take. By the time you graduate, you'll have an answer. If you're confident then that you have a calling, I'll help any way I can."

"Thank you, Sister Pius. I'm glad I talked to you. I'll start a novena tonight and hope that the answer becomes clear."

"Give it time. Now, go find your friends and have fun in the snow. Life is too short for all this fretting."

Graduation Day

It's a time for joy, a time for tears ~~~

Commencement day turned bittersweet when Mary's father arrived and she learned that her mother was bedridden with another recurrence of the rheumatic fever she'd had as a child. In her place, Papa brought Julia and Anna, who nearly toppled their older sister with hugs and squeals.

Smoothing her white organdy dress, Mary stepped onto the stage. During the ceremony she accepted her diploma, an award as top music student, and delivered her Valedictorian speech.

Afterward, Sister Pius told her accomplished student, "I'm extremely proud of you, Mary Loretta. You've worked hard and earned your awards."

"Thank you so much, Sister Pius. For everything."

"You're welcome. I'm sorry your mother couldn't be here. Your father tells me she's ill and needs your help at home. I'll pray for her well-being."

"Thank you. Well, I guess...."

"You guess what?"

Mary paused again. "That God didn't answer my prayers about joining the religious life."

She knew she had sounded like a petulant child when Sister Pius frowned and asked, "Are you sure? Did you specifically pray you would be given a vocation?"

"Well, no; I prayed for guidance that I would know which way to turn."

"That's what I thought. You were confused about whether or not you have a vocation. And hasn't that question been answered? That your place is with your family?"

"I suppose so."

"So God did answer your prayers. Perhaps not the way you expected. He gave you a job to do, and that job might be part of a greater plan."

"Like what?"

"Mary Loretta; I can't answer that, but prayer will show you the way."

"Yes, Sister Pius."

"Let me know how things are going and if I can help. Don't neglect your music, though."

"I won't. It means everything to me." Mary wanted to hug the nun, but instead she offered a sincere smile and turned away to find her father.

On the way home, Papa said, "Let me see that fine certificate of yours." She held it up; he smiled and patted her head. He never spoke of love to his children, but they recognized his pat on the head as a gesture of endearment.

She no longer felt like a child; she had an adult burden on her shoulders. With a sigh, she said, "Thank you, Papa."

"For what?"

"My schooling. It was wonderful."

"Aye; you did us proud. Your mother will hang the diploma on the wall."

"Probably next to the pope's picture."

They shared a laugh, and Papa said, "No doubt, but it deserves to be there."

After a moment Mary said, "I was selfish in going away to school instead of helping at home."

"No, no, Lass. It's your mother's dream that her children be nun-educated. Now she'll be happy to have you home, to have you singin' and playin' the piano."

"It'll be good to see her. I've missed you all."

Mary leaned her head against Papa's solid frame so he wouldn't see her tears. While he whistled a merry tune and her carefree sisters giggled and chatted, she fell quiet under the realization that commencement was supposed to be the beginning of a new and exciting life, but she was going home to be a house-keeper. What use would her religious and music education be to anyone now?

An Irish Lullaby

A song my mother sang to me, in a voice so soft and low ~~~

Mary had made her appearance into the Scots-Irish McLaughlin clan on the third of March, 1881, a blustery, snowy day. For many pioneers, that dreadful winter became the fabric from which blizzard stories were fashioned for years to come. Mary could almost recite word for word her mother's recollection, her voice soft, reverent, like when she crooned lullabies to the babies.

~~~ The winter of eighty and eighty-one was the worst folks ever seen. The first snow come in mid-October, leaves still on the trees, what few trees we had. We listened to branches snap and fall from the extra weight. Pretty soon just the trunks was standin', like fence posts. It snowed near two days and some most ever' day from then on; the wind howlin' like a banshee and blowin' snow into drifts high as the barn. The animals was in the barn when the storm started, else they'd have been buried. We dug a tunnel to the barn and melted snow to water the stock.

Your brothers had a high old time playin' they was explorin' glaciers. They made caves and forts in the drifts. When your grandmother McLaughlin died in December from the pneumonia we dint know for three days. Nobody could get out here to tell us. The undertaker stored her body in his shed. The ground was frozen and tombstones was buried under mountains of snow.

Scandinavians and old-timers like us was used to harsh winters, but we heard later about an Irish settlement over in Minnesota where folks froze to death in their shanties. They'd fled Ireland's second famine and died anyways. When my time come, your pa and I delivered you. He'd never have made it to town and back with Doc. The first time you saw the light of day and got a breath of outdoor air was when we buried your grandma, your namesake. Mid-May it was.
~~~

Mary had often been told that she danced before she walked and hummed before she spoke. As children, she and her O'Brien cousins, Bridget, Annie, Aggie, and Essie attended community dances with their brothers. Recalling those happy days, she hoped that when she settled in at home the O'Brien boys would let her play with their band.

Happily, they welcomed her. "We need a bonny lass," Linford said. "Folks don't cotton much to our homely Irish mugs. Besides, you're a trained musician. You actually know how to read music."

By fall, with her mother up and around again, Mary accepted a teaching position at Township School #7. Teachers were forbidden to frequent dance halls, let alone play with a band, but a shortage of qualified teachers kept officials looking the other way. Knock wood, Mary thought one night when she parked the wagon next to the barn and left the horse hitched to the cart. "Duke can sleep standing up and so could I," she muttered as she staggered to the house.

Exhausted, but too stimulated to sleep after an evening of raucous music, she rose at dawn, her gray-green eyes aflame from last night's smoky room. While her mother slept, Mary rousted her siblings to the breakfast table and then freshened herself for the day. After scooting the children down the path, she pulled her lithe body onto Duke and prodded him into a gallop. She was burning the candle at both ends, but she loved teaching as much as she did God and music. She needed these outlets in her life.

With few reference books available to rural teachers, Mary drew on family lore to teach history and geography. Her grandfather, Patrick McLaughlin, a storyteller in the tradition of oral historians, the *seanchaidhe* (shawn-a-key), had told her, "Family stories is all the poor has to their names; 'tis all we can leave to our children. I caint read or write but I can hear and see and remember and tell stories."

When Grandda showed her his citizenship certificate with his X next to the signature someone else had written, she offered to teach him to read and write. He said, "I got no one to write letters to. You grandchildren can read to me."

Now gone to his reward, perhaps swapping stories with his hero, Saint Patrick, Grandda's voice always grew melancholy and his brogue thickened when he spoke of *An Gorta Mor*, The Great Hunger. His failing eyes welled with tears when he intoned the names of relatives and friends who died.

"Wee bairns dyin' in their mum's arms, but it dint need be. Aye, t'was blight what done in the *pratais* crop, but the British landlords was exportin' other crops and livestock that could have fed the all of us. They out and out starved us, they did. Blight was all over Europe, even America, but people wasn't starvin' and dyin' like the Irish was. The Brits blamed us, said us ignorant farmers dint know how to do nuthin' but raise *pratais,* that we sat there swillin' whiskey and watchin' the crops rot. Ha, they was the ones with whiskey, not us."

Patrick credited the grace of God that he and his wife, Mary, and two young children survived the hunger. The famine had all but ended when they emigrated from County Armagh in Northern Ireland. Primarily made up of Scottish settlers, Catholic and Protestant, Grandda boasted to Mary, "The city of Armagh was the spiritual capital of Ireland for fifteen-hunnert years. Saint Patrick himself called Armagh 'my sweet hill' and built his first church there."

Mary captured in memory and in her journal the scenes Grandda described about the perilous seven week voyage to Boston in 1850. "Coffin ships, they called 'em. Aye, more than one body was dropped in the sea, more than one boat come apart. They was poorly-built, overloaded, infested with disease and vermin. Filthy dirty, they was. We saw one ship busted up in the water, bodies floatin' about."

He sucked on his pipe, the fire extinguished but the embers of memory still smoldering these many years later. "We heard the streets was paved with gold in America, but we lived in tenements no better than what we left behind. Scorned, we was. Folks called us greenhorns; said we ate from pig troughs. Stores posted signs sayin' no Irish need apply. We took jobs no one else would have, diggin' ditches, collectin' garbage. In some places, men and boys went down in the coal mines and never came out. I made a half dollar a day deliverin' coal to rich people's houses. The way they lived and the way we lived was different as Irish whiskey and the river Liffey."

Mary learned that Grandda gradually saved enough money to move his family to an Irish settlement in Dane County, Wisconsin. He convinced his wife and six children that this voyage by train would be the adventure of their life. "Once out of the city," he said, "seein' the prairie schooners sailin' through tall grass, and the crops, the livestock, the small towns with churches and schools, I knew I'd made the right choice."

Despite its visual charm, Grandda described life in Wisconsin as hard scrabble, with crops lost to fire, hail, drought and grasshoppers. Worst of all, he lost his oldest son, John. "The lad was a baby when we come on the ship, but he was always sickly from the starvation. Died from the consumption when he was but nineteen."

With hard work, faith in God and in the land, Patrick and his family eked out a living for twenty years. Then, having heard that soil in Iowa was even richer than Wisconsin's, the McLaughlins moved to north-central Iowa in the midst of farmland "as green and hilly as the auld sod itself." With a chuckle breaking Grandda's story, he recalled, "Lookin' at the Dougherty plat map, I thought I'd moved back'ta Ireland or died and gone t'heaven. We was among our own: Kelly, Burke, Dougherty, Gallagher, McKenna. And Hogan, Conners, Murphy, Sweeney. Even some McLaughlins, but no kin of ours that we could ever figger out, 'cept maybe years back in the clan."

Now, in this new century, Mary realized that most of her students carried the surnames Grandda mentioned. This history she planned to teach was part of their heritage, too. She must make them feel the stories, as Grandda had for her.

The next day she waited until late morning before beginning her talk about the Great Hunger. Spinning a globe to locate Ireland, she talked about the blight that wiped out the potato crop between 1845 and 1850. She explained that a half million people were unable to pay rent to Protestant or British landlords and were driven from their homes. "They lived in workhouses, where thousands died from starvation, typhus, or cholera. More than a million people died. That's more people than the whole state of Iowa. Imagine that." She knew the children could not imagine it; not even she could comprehend a number as large as a million.

She held up her journal to show them pictures she had sketched with pen and ink to illustrate Grandda's stories. Above her head, the wall clock chimed noon, and the hand ticked downward.

A little girl raised her hand, and Mary called on her. "It's past time to eat, Miss McLaughlin." A chorus of agreement followed but Mary did not dismiss class. The clock's hands settled on twelve-thirty; then climbed upward.

Finally, with the students restless, sighing, and shuffling their feet, Mary relented. "You're hungry, aren't you? How does it feel? Like a knot in your belly?" She looked at the nodding heads.

"All right, we'll have lunch. But while you're eating, remember that the people I've talked about had no lunch pail in the corner. Not a piece of bread, or a nibble of cheese. Only days and weeks of feeling worse than you do now. They weren't just hungry; they were starving, and sick. Some ate seaweed or grass."

A teenage boy mumbled, "I'd settle for grass," and mooed like a cow.

That tickled Mary and she let her pupils go. Her stomach had been complaining, too. Outside in the fall sunshine, while she ate a hardboiled egg and an apple, a blond boy approached. "Miss McLaughlin, you always talk about Ireland. How about the Vikings? My grandpa was a Viking."

Hiding amusement behind a napkin, she said, "Lars, I promise we'll get to the Vikings. Maybe your grandfather would come to school and talk about them."

Lars smiled, showing buckteeth decorated with grape jelly. "I'll ask tonight."

Recalling that the Vikings somehow figured in Irish history, Mary made a mental note to visit Mr. Nordstrom. He was not old enough to have been a Viking, but surely he had information she could use.

Too-ra-loo-ra-looral, hush, now don't you cry ~~~

After a fun-filled hour watching her students exchange Valentine cards and devour the heart-shaped cookies she had brought, Mary called for attention and delivered an announcement that made her voice quaver. "Before dismissal, I must tell you that I'll be leaving at the end of this week."

"Oh, no," came several cries, and a petite girl asked, "Are you getting married, Miss McLaughlin?"

"No, Sybella; my family is moving to Minnesota." She glanced around at her siblings. "That means some of your friends are leaving, too, my brothers and sisters."

"Golly gee," a boy called, "half the class will be gone."

"We do number quite a few, don't we? Seven, plus me. Well, my replacement, Miss Scott, should be able to handle the rest of you with no trouble."

Mary lost not only her students and her teaching job, but the excitement of playing with her cousins' band. All that paled five months later when her mother died. Inconsolable underneath, she stoically accepted the responsibility handed her: surrogate mother of seven, another phase of God's plan.

At home after the burial and then an interminable dinner in the church hall, she slipped off to the grove behind the house to read her mother's obituary in *The Park Rapids Enterprise*:

~~~~ McLaughlin: Died at her home west of town Aug. 15, 1903, Mrs. L. McLaughlin, of Rheumatic Fever, age 49 years. Martha Burke, born at Deerfield, Wis., May 1854, was united in marriage to Lawrence McLaughlin in 1872, and in company with her husband removed to Dougherty, Iowa, in 1876, where they lived until March of this present year when they came to this place to make their home. Thirteen children were born to them of whom ten survive her, eight of this place and two sons in Dougherty. Mrs. McLaughlin also leaves one brother and two sisters in Dougherty and one brother in Boundry, Wash.

She was a truly Christian woman, a devoted wife and mother and loyal friend. She died a peaceful happy death and has gone to receive her reward. The services were conducted by the Rev. John Walsh at the Catholic Church who paid a fine tribute to her virtues. The choir, with Mrs. Lewis as organist, rendered some choice music, especially a solo by Miss Kathleen McKenna. The sympathy of the community goes out to Mr. McLaughlin and his bereaved family in this hour of affliction. We can only commend them to Him who alone can comfort them. ~~~~

Rocking little Eddie to sleep that night, Mary shed tears for her motherless siblings and for herself. Having gone off to boarding school as a teenager, she now realized she barely knew her mother as one adult to another. Home only on holidays and in the summer, there was little time for chatter while the two women ran a household for ten. After graduation, between housekeeping, teaching, and playing in the band, there'd been no time either.

She recalled that her raven-haired, blue-eyed mother had rarely raised her voice, not even when scolding children. "Little ones respond better to a soft voice than a shrill one," she explained to Mary. At meals, she said little, but nodded or shook her head in agreement or disagreement with what others said. She smiled with her mouth closed and lowered her head when she laughed to hide teeth gone bad or gaps where they should have been. "Women lose a tooth for every child they bear," she warned her oldest daughter.

Looking back, Mary thought that her tuition money should have gone for Mother's dental work. But she would have scoffed at that and said education was more important than her teeth. Still, Mary gave in to feelings of guilt. All she could do now was vow to look after the children.

Sister Pius once advised, "Pray that God will show you which path to take." The path was clear; she would not enter religious life or be a teacher or a professional musician. With Eddie heavy in her arms, she understood that it would be another ten years before he was grown. She would be in her early thirties. Was that too old to become a nun, or teacher, or perhaps marry?

Time would tell. For now, the only decision for the morrow, and the day after, and the day after, was what to prepare for meals.

Ma, He's Making Eyes At Me

Ma, he's awful nice to me ~~~

With the first blush of autumn color on the trees, the McLaughlin children returned to school, making Mary long to be teaching. The first weeks of school had always been fun; the students eager and bright-eyed. Alone all day, she tore into fall housecleaning, mindful that things wouldn't stay clean for long. With nine people in the house, clutter was a fact of life.

Then a tenth person moved in, or so it seemed. A new neighbor stopped by to borrow a scythe, and he and Mary's brother, Victor, struck up a friendship. Soon, Martin Jones had his feet under the McLaughlin's table more often than not.

"He's sweet on you," brother Robert said one night after Martin left.

Clem added, "Maybe you won't be an old maid after all."

Mary scoffed at the notion that the young farmer was interested in her. He called her Miss McLaughlin, as if she were the real mother of the family or a maiden aunt housekeeper. But she became alert to his comings and goings, uncertain if she wanted his attention or not. She had enough men in her life right now.

Outside after supper one night, she dug into a bed of snapdragons that had seen better days. Before long, Martin showed up and sat on the porch steps. "Thanks for another fine meal," he said.

"Oh, it was leftovers, but you're welcome."

"The crops look good, don't you think?"

"Papa seems satisfied with our first year here."

"You never know with farming. It's a game of chance." He shifted himself from one step to another, and brushed soil off his shoes. "Yep, should be a good harvest."

Mary looked away and smiled. Certainly he hadn't come to talk about crops. Maybe the boys were right about his intentions. That made her nervous.

"Miss McLaughlin." He cleared his throat.

"Please, I'm Mary."

"Yes, Ma'am. Well, uh, I spoke to your pa. He says it would be all right if I was to court you. If you're agreeable, that is."

Before she could respond, he added, "If you think it's too soon, on account of your mother's recent passin', we can see each other here instead of in public."

Without much thought, Mary answered, "We already see each other here several times a week. How would I know when you're courting?"

Switching from nervous to confident, Martin stood, reached for her hand and tugged her to her feet. "Lass, you'll know. Let's start with a walk to the creek. Bring your cloak. It gets cool when the sun sets."

Embarrassed at his closeness, Mary pulled away. "I'll be just a minute."

Inside, she scrubbed her dishpan hands, noting that two of her nails were broken. Well, Martin probably wouldn't expect her to hold hands just yet. Still, she rubbed in a generous dose of Corn Husker's lotion; it usually worked miracles. While running a brush over her hair, she peeked outside at the slim, wiry man with a drooping mustache and receding hairline. Other girls might not consider him a catch, she thought, but I'm no raving beauty. I'm as plain as my name, and freckled.

She heard her mother's voice saying: There's a lid for every kettle. Were she and Martin Jones a kettle and a lid, a matching pair? Papa called him a likeable lad; the children liked him, and he had an easy-going disposition. Speaking to her mirror image she said, "It looks as if I have a suitor. Another part of God's plan?"

Four years her senior, Martin charmed Mary and, come spring, they approached Papa for permission to set a wedding date. Mary joked, "I'll still look after the house and kids. We'll live here. Martin's here all the time anyway, so nothing will change."

Shaking Martin's hand, Papa said, "You have my blessin', but you'll live on Martin's farm. Julia and Anna are old enough to run this house." Then, focusing on Martin, he asked, "Tell me, was it an Irish proposal?"

"Sir?"

Mary gave Papa a warning scowl. Surely he wasn't going to embarrass her by telling about the Irishman who proposed by asking: Would you like to hang your undies next to mine? To her relief, he chose another old story.

"That's where the fella proposes by askin' the girl if she wants to be buried with his people."

Martin's eyes pleaded with Mary for an explanation. "You know, the Irish being so clannish about kin, they want to make sure they're buried together."

Grinning, Papa said, "Welcome to the family, Martin Jones. Now, you two young folks go take a walk before I change my mind."

Mary slipped her hand into Martin's. "C'mon, let's go tell the children."

For Me And My Gal

And for weeks they've been sewing, every Susie and Sal ~~~

Mary's pre-wedding day emotions ran the gamut from jitters to stars-in-her eyes to guilt over breaking her vow to look after the children. Papa thought Julia and Anna were old enough to keep house, but they were only sixteen and fifteen. And Eddie fretted about his big sister leaving him as his mother had done. Mary's stomach tensed when he looked at her with sad eyes and called her "Mum."

Julia delighted in any chore related to the wedding. Adept with a needle, she offered to pin the hem in place on the gown Mary had made. Mumbling through a row of straight pins in her mouth, Julia ordered, "Stand still or I'll never get this even. You're nervous as a biddy hen with her chicks." She poked several pins into the hem and stood back to check her work. "See what you think."

Mary pirouetted before the mirror propped against the kitchen wall. "Perfect. Now, put on your dress and I'll pin the hem for you."

Anna grumbled, "Why can't I be in the wedding?"

"I told you; because it's a small wedding. You and Alice will hand out favors to the ladies; the lace tussie-mussies you helped fill with dried flowers and herbs."

"How about just me handing them out?"

"Then Alice would complain that she's not in the wedding."

"She's a baby. She's only eight."

Mary sighed. "How can a simple wedding get so complicated? The next thing I know Eddie will want to be in the ceremony."

"Don't let him do anything. He'd mess it up"

Mary couldn't help laughing at Anna's comment. Eddie was not the most coordinated child she'd known.

Anna asked, "When Martin kisses you, does your heart go rootie-tootie?"

"Young lady, where did you hear such common language?"

"From Julia."

Mary wagged her finger at Julia, who tossed her head and giggled

"Do you think Martin's handsome?" Anna continued.

"Well…maybe not film star handsome, but he's pleasant to look at."

"Mama always said handsome is as handsome does. Whatever that means. I think Martin's funny. He teases me and makes me laugh."

"Yes, he's fun. Personality is more important than outer appearance. That's what Mama meant by handsome is as handsome does."

Papa wandered in, threw his cap on a chair and ran his fingers through his wiry copper hair. "Chores are done. What can I do to ready this place for the shindig on Saturday?"

"There's plenty to do. Move the parlor furniture back to the walls and take the rugs outside for a beating. Have Clem do that. He's in a snit about something so he can take out his anger on the rugs. Robert can help. They should store the rugs upstairs so folks can dance in the parlor. Oh, and we'll need to wax the floors for dancing and clean the front and back porches, and…."

Mary glanced through the window at the cloudless sky. "And pray we get a good rain before the wedding so we can all have baths and hair washings in nice soft rainwater." She grabbed Eddie and inspected his ears. "I declare, there are potatoes growing in your ears."

"No, I don't want a bath, Mum," he yelled, twisting away from her.

The parson's waiting, for me and my gal ~~~

Mr. and Mrs. Martin Joneses' wedding announcement appeared in the *Hubbard County Weekly* while they were on their honeymoon. Back home, Mary read the piece to Martin.

~~~~ Jones-McLaughlin Nuptials ~~~ While wedding bells were ringing sweet and clear on July 6, 1904 at St. Peter's Catholic Church, the hands and hearts of Miss Mary Loretta McLaughlin and Mr. Martin Lawrence Jones were joined in Holy Matrimony. They were met at the altar by the Rev. John Walsh, who conducted the ring service, followed by a Nuptial High Mass. The couple was attended by the bride's sister, Miss Julia McLaughlin, and the groom's uncle, Pat Drew.

The bride, the daughter of Lawrence McLaughlin and the late Mrs. Martha McLaughlin, was prettily attired in white crepe meteor trimmed with Irish lace and chiffon ruching. She wore a monogrammed gold locket that belonged to her mother, a white veiled hat, white gloves and shoes, and carried a shower bouquet of white bridal roses. The bridesmaid wore blue *crepe de chine* and a blue picture hat, and carried red roses. The groom and groomsman wore the conventional blue serge suits.

Following the ceremony, a parade of decorated carriages escorted the couple to the farm home of the bride's father, where a bounteous wedding dinner was served by the Ladies Sodality. The rooms were adorned with flowers and decorated in the bride's chosen colors. The couple received many useful and beautiful gifts, and blessings and toasts, such as this one: "May your blessings outnumber the shamrocks that grow, and may trouble avoid you wherever you go."

Miss Julia McLaughlin played a selection of classics on the piano. The bride's cousins, Henry O'Brien, Jr. and his brothers Larry and Linford, provided dance music, including Irish *ceili* songs and sea chanties.

The bride, a graduate of St. Francis Academy, Mason City, Iowa, has taught music to area youngsters since moving here last year. This charming young lady has added to her accomplishments of mind the qualities of a good housekeeper, which will do much to make a happy home. The groom, the son of Mr. and Mrs. John Jones of Decorah, Iowa, is favorably known in this community. An industrious farmer, he and his wife will make their home on a farm south of Park Rapids. We wish the young couple many years of happiness and prosperity.~~~~

"The groom wore the conventional blue serge?" Martin scoffed playfully. "Glad Lottie didn't know the suit was second-hand. She'd have put that in, too. But I like the part about me being an industrious farmer."

Mary didn't tell him that most newspapers used that phrase; brides and grooms were always exemplary folks, as were the deceased when it came time for an obituary. "Listen to this," she said. "Lottie wrote about the shivaree, too."

~~~~ On the evening of July 7, the silence of the countryside surrounding the farm home of Mr. Lawrence McLaughlin was shattered by a crowd of boys and young men carrying tin horns, drums and other noise-making instruments. They had come to shivaree Mr. McLaughlin's daughter, Mary, and her new husband, Martin Jones. After they had expanded some lusty lung power and made the night resound with sundry tin cans, horse fiddles and bells, the father of the bride told his visitors that the would-be victims of their sonorousness were miles away on a honeymoon to Minneapolis. A thirty-cent piece would have darkened the moon for the crestfallen serenaders.~~~~

"I like a good shivaree," Martin said, "but I wouldn't have missed our trip to the Twin Cities for it."

While her husband's flirtatious eyes swept over her, Mary blushed and busied herself rereading the articles. As Martin drifted to sleep on the horsehair sofa, she recalled last week when they returned from their trip.

My Blue Heaven

A little nest that's nestled where the roses bloom ~~~

Mary's brother, Victor, met her and Martin at the depot and drove them by wagon to their box-like farmhouse with no gingerbread frills. A Mankato businessman owned the farm and paid Martin a meager salary to look after the place. What he made from farming was his to keep. "The house isn't much," he had told Mary on the way home. Now he added, "The landlord says I can build on if I want to. He'll pay for supplies and I'll provide the elbow grease." By his own admission, Martin was a better carpenter than farmer.

"Nothing wrong with small and simple," Mary said. "You know what they say: *Mid pleasures and palaces though we may roam, be it ever so humble ~~~*"

"You've got a song for every occasion. Anyway, the house is clean and I stocked the larder the best I knew how. You make a list of what you want and we'll go to the mercantile together."

"I won't know what we need until you take me inside. The house does have an inside, doesn't it? Or is it even humbler than it appears?"

Laughing, Martin scooped Mary into his arms. He stopped on the porch to show her a sign he'd made and hung by the door. "*Ceid mille failte* (Kay mee fall shuh)," he read. "A hundred thousand welcomes."

Feeling at home already, Mary had only a glimpse of the kitchen as Martin carried her over the threshold and moved on to the parlor. "Look here at what the landlord gave us," he said.

On her feet now, Mary blinked in disbelief at the upright piano that covered nearly one wall of the small room.

"It's from Sears Roebuck and cost near a hundred dollars new. The landlord had it shipped here. Said to consider it a weddin' present."

"It's wonderful, and so generous."

Martin twirled the piano stool seat. "I can raise or lower it to fit you. Try it out."

Amused by his excitement, Mary thought: As if I didn't know a piano stool can be adjusted. Before she could sit, Martin tugged on her arm. "Wait, that's not all. I got a used sewin' machine at auction. Fella's wife died and he had no use for it. It's in the kitchen by the window where the light's good."

"A piano and a sewing machine? I'm spoiled already." Mary suspected the spoiling would be short-lived; a layer of furry dust covered the piano and every other piece of furniture.

In the kitchen, she noted mouse droppings on the table by the stove. Mouse traps would go at the top of her shopping list. Pulling off her gloves, she said, "Honeymoon's over. Time to get to work. I'll need cleaning rags and bedding, from my trunk."

Her father had brought over their wedding gifts, Mary's clothing, her cello, and the trunk packed with towels, bedding, kitchenware, and freshly laundered feed sacks. Lifting the wooden trunk's camel back lid, she recalled her grandfather's stories about the voyage to Boston. She often thought she could smell the sea in the trunk, but she had no idea what smell an ocean had. Grandda said that Mary's grandmother wouldn't let her "going to America" trunk out of sight on the trip, and that before she died she said she wanted the expected baby to have it. She knew it was a girl, and a girl would treasure the trunk. It was true; the older Mary got the more she treasured the box made by her great-grandfather.

During the first weeks in her new home, she covered the kitchen table with a sunny yellow cloth; thrust wild flowers into jars filled with water, and dressed the arms of the parlor sofa with her mother's antimacassars. Singing as she pedaled the Burdick sewing machine, she made flowered curtains and hung them to replace the dark green paper shades that kept out the sunshine.

Returning from town one day, she rolled up her sleeves and worked on the walls with wallpaper cleaner, but the smudges the rubbery stuff left were worse than the soiled paper. She yearned for new paper in all the rooms, but it cost two-to-nine cents a roll and she was uncomfortable about spending Martin's money. She had no idea how much cash he had, but certainly not enough to spend on unnecessary decorations for the house.

Hands on her hips, she surveyed the room and told herself: All I need to hide that spot on the wall by the buffet is a large vase. There's a perfect one at Papa's. The one Mother said had been in the Burke family for generations, and always added, "Someone should have accidentally broken that ugly urn generations ago."

Bringing In The Sheaves

We shall come rejoicing, bringing in the sheaves ~~~

Truth be told, Mary looked for reasons to go over to Papa's, be it a vase, a piece of sheet music, or to help Julia and Anna. With Martin in the field all day, she missed the boisterous household she'd left behind; the sound of Papa's whistling, girl-talk with her sisters, the clamor of little Eddie and Alice running wild as river otters, and even the lack of elbow room when Papa, Victor, Robert, and Clem all sat at the kitchen table with their legs stretched in front of them, the chair backs tilted against the wall.

When she saw that the gardens and orchards at both farms were ripe for picking, she asked Julia and Anna to bring their produce to her house. There, in the screened summer kitchen Martin had rigged under the trees along Beaver Creek, the three young women canned fruits and vegetables, singing and chattering as they toiled over the cookstove fueled by twigs and wood scraps.

Emulating their mother, they admired the jars filled with green and yellow beans, dill and sweet pickles, apple sauce and whole apples, beets, carrots, tomato juice, stewed tomatoes, rhubarb sauce, sweet corn cut off the cob, and sauerkraut they stored in crocks in the cellar. Mary kept only enough of the canned goods for herself and Martin and sent the rest home to the McLaughlin household.

Finally, with most of the canning finished, she readied herself for the field harvest. She and her sisters had already prepared some of the enormous amounts of food for the crew. They'd baked dozens of loaves of bread and as many pies and cakes, and had peeled buckets of potatoes from which they made potato salad. Mary lost count of how many chickens she had beheaded, then dipped the bodies in scalding water, plucked the feathers, singed off the pin feathers, and finally rolled the poultry pieces in flour and salt and pepper and fried them in hot lard. The hungry men never cared if the food was hot or cold, as long as there was plenty of it.

The crew would arrive tomorrow, and Julia and Anna would help cook and serve. When Papa brought over the horse powered threshing machine just after supper, Eddie came along for the ride and told Mary, "Mum, I rode a dinosaur." His calling her Mum still brought her almost to tears. He and Martin were asleep now, restoring energy for tomorrow.

After a day of full boil heat, dusk had fallen and the temperature had tapered to simmer. She lingered on the porch, hoping that in an hour or so the house would be cooler and she could sleep easily. The moon, suspended above a silhouette of the barn, had the color and lumpy texture of a muskmelon. A dozen barn swallows swooped out of the golden field bursting with grain, and from somewhere in the distance an owl hooted. Seated in a rocker, wondering how anything could be more peaceful than a farm at night, she said her bedtime prayers and special thanks for a bountiful crop.

At the outdoor dinner the next day, Mary watched with amusement as Julia and Anna turned on their youthful charms. They sang as they walked among the tables, carrying water pitchers and trays of food. Some of the workers were the same age as or not much older than the girls, so there was as much flirting as eating. Tanned from the sun, the bare-chested young men vied for the girls' attention, and each got his share.

Mary never fretted about the competition among farm women as to who could fix the best and biggest harvest meals. So it surprised her to overhear a compliment at church on Sunday. "Why, those sweet young McLaughlin girls laid as grand a table as mine own," Mrs. Conner said. "Their dear departed mother, God rest her soul, taught them well."

"She never even knew Mother," Mary sputtered to Martin.

When school began after harvest, Mary taught music twice at week at the township school. One day it was vocal and the other piano, cello, and clarinet lessons. Much to Mary's dismay, Julia did not return to school. Papa said there was too much that needed doing at home. Still, Julia was clever and had always been a good student so Mary took comfort in knowing her sister had learned the basics: Reading, writing and arithmetic.

Through teaching and playing the organ at church, Mary had a host of friends. She and Martin hosted *ceilis,* parties where everyone sang, danced, or played instruments. When the guests spilled onto the porch and lawn, she recalled a wedding toast: "May your home always be too small to hold all your friends." Happy and content, she considered herself truly blessed.

While doing chores, she kept her ears tuned to the music of the countryside; God's symphony she called it. The horses led off with bells jingling on their harnesses, their thick hooves thudding as they plodded up the dirt lane, their whinnying and snorting as they rested in the barn. Cows bawled to be milked; pigs squealed as she approached the sty with slops from the table; hens clucked and chicks peeped when she gathered eggs. From the crevices of the barn and the haymow seeped the cooing of pigeons and doves, while at a nearby lake, loons yodeled. The windmill kept a steady pulsating rhythm; grasshoppers and crickets hummed and whirred in the pasture, while the crisp silvery-green leaves on the cottonwoods, propelled by a breeze, soughed a whispered tune. Even the silence of prairie grass and golden wheat swaying in the wind was *ceol binn* (kell bin), sweet music.

Rock-a-bye Your Baby

When you croon, croon a tune ~~~

A wet petticoat slapped Mary's face as she hung laundry in a robust October breeze. Untangling herself, she gulped a mouthful of crisp air to quell a wave of nausea. There had been one earlier, and several flutters yesterday. Having had a mother who was with child most of the time, she felt certain that life was stirring in her body.

Seated on the grass to rest, her thoughts wandered to when the McLaughlin household had rarely been without a baby or two. She did not remember when Michael was born; she was only three at the time. Nor did she remember a year later when William Leo was born, and died within hours, but she was ten when seven-year-old Michael fell from the silo ladder and lay dead on the ground.

Mother had ordered the children countless times not to climb the ladder, but Michael was a mischievous lad with boundless energy and up he scrambled. Mary was in the kitchen when her teenaged brothers, John and Joseph, brought Michael to the house and then fled in the wagon to get the priest. While Mother fell to her knees and wept and prayed at the same time, a visiting neighbor woman placed the motionless body on the kitchen table and washed the child and dressed him in his Sunday clothes. Out in the barn, Papa and Grandda built a coffin from scrap wood. Mary flinched each time the hammer hit wood.

After the priest administered Extreme Unction, and Michael lay in his box on one of Mother's quilts, the neighbor woman placed a penny on each of his closed eyes. "If he wakes, the pennies'll fall and we'll see he's not dead. Praise be to Saint Bridget."

During the wake that night, Mary slumped in a darkened niche in the hall-way, from where she heard women keening in the parlor and watched men gather in the kitchen to drink tea or coffee, sometimes laced with whisky. The farmers talked about weather and crops, but in monotone rather than with their usual authority and enthusiasm. Young as she was, Mary recognized that they were simply making polite conversation.

Later, she tiptoed into the parlor, where Grandda sat with the body, another custom to make sure the person was really dead. "I want to say a prayer for Michael," she whispered.

"Aye, *Macushla*. And would ye be too big now to sit on me lap?"

She perched on his bony knees with his coarse gray beard whispering against her cheek. He smelled of tobacco and Sen-Sen, the licorice pellets he always placed on his tongue after sipping from his whisky bottle. Leaning back, she felt his harmonica in his shirt pocket. He always kept it there, ready to breathe a lilting tune from it, but with Michael dead there was no music from anyone. Not a whistle. Not a hum.

She wanted to see Michael up close, to check on the pennies, but Grandda had asked her to sit with him and she would do as asked. At last his hand relaxed and his head dropped as if he'd fallen asleep. Easing off his lap, she knelt by the coffin, her head bowed in prayer.

Finally, bracing herself, she peeked at Michael. The pennies had not moved. They stayed in place all the next day, and the following day when the lid was nailed onto the coffin and moved to the church. During the Requiem Mass of the Angels, Mary imagined the pennies lying next to Michael's head. Not because he had opened his eyes, but because the casket had been moved. Still, for months she had nightmares about him waking and not being able to get out of his box. Gradually, the dreams faded, and disappeared, as Michael had.

Two years later, Mother delivered a tiny girl who was barely breathing. Born unexpectedly, there was no time to fetch a doctor or priest. Papa quickly baptized the baby before the soul left the body. Catherine Grace was buried in the churchyard cemetery with only family attending.

Shaking away the sad reverie, Mary placed her hands on her stomach and prayed she would never lose a child. But she added, "Thy will be done," for a person of good faith did not question God's will.

A meadowlark landed on the clothesline pole. Dressed in a coat of lime, yellow and black, the bird's merry chirp relaxed Mary. Imitating what the bird's tune sounded like to her, she trilled, "I've gotta heap o' work to do, a heap o' work to do."

A million baby kisses, I'll deliver ~~~

Mary's marriage had just passed the one-year mark when, on a blistering hot, humid July afternoon, the thirtieth day, Doctor Peterson delivered her firstborn. After Doc had gone and Julia had bathed Mary and the newborn, Martin hovered over the bed, listening to his red-haired daughter wail. "The lass is gonna be a singer. Did you ever decide on a name? Maybe Jenny Lind after that singer you fancy?"

Mary wrinkled her nose. "A jenny's a mule. I should name her Martha, for Mother, but I'm partial to the name Hazel. It means wisdom, commanding authority. She's already demanding attention. Look, she wants to nurse."

"She sure is little, and bonny," Martin said.

"Bonnie is a sweet name. How about we name her Hazel Bonnie? Wait, that reminds me; I read the name Hazelbon somewhere."

"Hazelbon? That's a new one on me. I'll leave the name up to you."

"All right; she'll be Hazelbon Martha. We can call her Bonnie."

"At least she's not named Pius, after that nun friend of yours."

"Well, that's an idea. Pius Jones is a name that demands authority."

Hazelbon, who gradually became Hazel, not Bonnie, had no competition for her parents' love and attention for nearly three years, when Gladys Julia joined the family. Being the mother of two didn't seem like double work to Mary, except when big sister wanted to help with the baby. That took time, showing Hazel what to do and how to do it. Still, the little tyke was trustworthy, giving Mama a chance to at least slip away to the outhouse to read the mail.

One afternoon, lingering at the parlor door, Mary watched Hazel at the piano. Her miniature fingers plunked away at the keyboard, while Gladys, holding onto the piano stool, her wet diaper drooping, pumped her chubby legs up and down, dancing to the music. Mary sang along, *"and that's a very good sign, that he's your tootsie-wootsie in the good old summertime."*

Martin sneaked up behind and whispered, "Did you teach her to play that?"

"No; she plays by ear. I've been playing the song for her. I must start teaching her to read music so she'll play the correct way."

Gladys climbed onto Hazel's lap and ran her chubby fingers over the keyboard.

"They'll wear it out and we'll need a new one," Martin said, "but it's grand listenin' to 'em play duets."

By the time Dorothy May came along two years after Gladys's birth, followed by Evelyn Agnes another two years later, Hazel was an accomplished pianist and Gladys was striving to keep up. Hazel played the church organ and Mary began teaching her to play the cello and sousaphone. "You have to hold it for me," the petite child behind either instrument ordered, and Mary obliged with pleasure and pride.

The little house bubbled and steamed with the unbridled energy of four girls playing, arguing, crying, whooping and hollering, singing, and practicing instruments. At bedtime, in a ritual that seldom varied, Mary knelt with the girls to hear their prayers. Then they sang together for ten minutes before she tucked them into two beds in the same room, kissed each on the forehead and said, "May leprechauns strew happiness wherever you walk each day, and Irish angels smile on you, all along the way."

"Good night, Mama," they chorused.

Finally, pausing in the doorway she played a silly game they enjoyed. "Who wants me to bake a chocolate cake tomorrow?" Four hands popped up.

"With cod liver oil frosting?"

"No, no," came a collective squeal.

"Who wants to be a world-famous pianist?"

Gladys replied, "I like violin better than piano."

"Who wants to be a nun when she grows up?"

"I do," Gladys quickly answered.

"Maybe," Hazel added.

Dorothy said, "Evie's still a baby but I think she'll want to be a nun." After a pause, "What is a nun?"

Stifling a laugh, Mary promised, "We'll talk about it tomorrow. Sleep now."

Going downstairs, she uttered a prayer of thanks to God for giving her four delightful, healthy daughters. When she related Dorothy's comment to Martin he said, "They're cut from the same cloth as their mother. You gave 'em penny whistles and harmonicas for teethin' rings, now you're pushin' for 'em to be nuns. I think you've always regretted not being able to go to the convent."

"Oh, how can you say such a thing? If I had gone, I wouldn't have you or the girls. I simply wasn't called to the religious life; I was called to this one, right here, and I love every minute of it."

With her ear tuned to a commotion upstairs, she evoked her mother's calm tone of voice and called, "I hear talking up there. Quiet now, and go to sleep."

Gladys whined, "Hazel is pushing me out of bed."

"I am not, tattle tale. You're way over on my side."

"Uh, uh, you're on my side."

Sighing, Mary told Martin, "That's not to say I wouldn't welcome a peaceful convent now and then. If you're going up to bed, you settle things."

Sonny Boy

Climb upon my knee, Sonny Boy ~~~

Mary rolled onto her side and nudged Martin. He grunted; she elbowed him again. "I have something to tell you." Even that teaser didn't budge him so she tried, "I'm in the family way."

His head emerged, his eyes wide.

She laughed. "You look like a turtle popping out of its shell."

"Did you say…another baby?"

"I figure early June."

He planted a kiss on her forehead. "Saints be praised. I might get a farmer after all. This one's a boy. Listen, the Price farm's for rent. It has a bigger house for the same rent. I'll go by there today, check it out."

"Hold your horses. We moved less than a year ago. I don't feel like moving my body let alone a household."

"Don't you worry. I'll take care of things."

"Start by bringing me soda crackers and tea to stop my nausea. And get the girls up for school. I need to lie here a while."

By the time Lawrence Robert Jones arrived, the family had settled into a roomier house. Neither Mary nor Martin attempted to contain their delight in having a boy. "Not that I don't love my lasses," Martin told Evelyn after she wagged her tongue at Robbie, "but now I'm not the only man in the house."

Two-year-old Evelyn soon became as enamored as the rest of the family with "the wee bub," as Martin called him. By Christmas, Robbie was crawling and by the following Christmas, Mary announced that he had the gift of music. The family sat bundled together in a horse-drawn sleigh, a million stars lighting the Christmas eve sky, and the girls singing, "*Over the river and through the woods to Grandfather's house we go ~~~*"

"Robbie's keeping time with his finger," Mary shouted above the chorus.

Martin glanced sideways. "You're movin' his arm up and down."

"I most certainly am not. Look at his long fingers. Perfect for the piano."

"Perfect to wrap around a pitchfork handle or a cow's teat. Come spring I'll get him started on bein' a farmer. Make a man outta him."

After a Christmas day filled with relatives coming and going, Robbie spent a restless night. "Too much commotion," Mary said. "Truth be known, he's a tad spoiled. His feet didn't touch the floor yesterday. You'd think the McLaughlin clan had never seen a baby before."

Robbie continued to be listless, and refused to eat. "Must be coming down with a cold," Mary said. Two days later a cold had failed to develop. When it occurred to her that he hadn't had a dirty diaper for several days, she concluded he was constipated. "Look how his belly's swollen. He's all plugged up."

"Come on," Martin said, "enough of this guess work. He's sick. We're takin' him to see Doc. I'll bring the wagon around."

Mary swaddled the squirming baby in a quilt and called into the parlor, "Hazel, we're taking Robbie to see Doc. You look after your sisters."

"Yes, Mama. We're playing Chinese Checkers."

Gladys came to the doorway. "What's wrong with him?"

"I don't know. Doc will fix him up. Help Hazel with your little sisters."

"I will, Mama. Bye, Robbie." She waved her hand at the sick child.

Robbie writhed with pain when Doc Peterson poked and prodded. "Looks like a bowel obstruction. I need to operate, fast, right here and now."

Mary reached for him. "No; he's only a baby."

"Out of the way. The two of you, in the waiting room. Tell my wife to come in." Before anyone could move, Doc shouted, "Hell, he's stopped breathing."

"For God's sake, do somethin'," Martin yelled.

Doc put his mouth over the child's mouth and blew, pulled away and repeated the procedure, again, again, again.

Mary reeled with dizziness. Her legs quivered. Every bone in her body loosened and she felt her frame come apart.

The angels, they don't do wrong, for they love you always, Sonny Boy

She awakened in bed, with daylight seeping under the window shade. Women's muffled voices drifted up alongside the pipe that ran from the kitchen stove through the bedroom and out the roof. The house is never this quiet, she thought. Where are the girls? Robbie? What am I doing in bed wearing my clothes?

Blurred images swam before her eyes, like slides in a magic lantern show. *A child fell from a silo. Carried inside by two boys. A woman on the floor. Weeping. Small coffin brought into house. Pennies on child's eyes. Coffin closed. Baby on table. Man trying to breathe life into him. He's not breathing. Not breathing. Robbie.*

Pain seared Mary's body as if lightning were running through it. "Robbie," she screamed, and Martin was there, leaning over the bed.

"You passed out yesterday, needed smellin' salts, and a sedative. Must've been powerful. I was wonderin' if you'd ever wake up."

Mary buried her face in her hands. "I wish I hadn't."

"Aww, now; don't talk that way."

Overcome with tears, Mary realized she had not yet cried; she'd been asleep while the rest of the family had been mourning, weeping.

Martin blew his nose. "You have to come downstairs; the undertaker's comin' about noon."

"Don't say it. Don't say why he's coming. Where are the girls?"

"Julia took them to her place."

"Took my girls? She can't have them."

"Of course not. Just for the day. Pull yourself together and come downstairs. People will be comin' when they hear about the baby. We have to be ready."

"Ready? How can we be ready for that?"

She watched her husband leave the room, his arms dangling at his sides as if they didn't belong to him; like that plaster Halloween skeleton the girls had, whose arms and legs hung loose.

People will be coming. They've already come. Who are the women downstairs? They probably found my kitchen dirty and think I'm *sreilach,* a messy Irish woman. Will they understand that I hurried off to the doctor yesterday, leaving chores undone? Good Lord, what does it matter? My baby is…. Mary stopped the next word from forming in her thoughts.

Hearing the back door open and then close, she struggled to her feet and stood on trembling legs at the window. Pushing aside the shade, she watched Martin plod through the snow dragging the Christmas tree, its branches trimmed with clip-on candles, strung popcorn, paper doily snowflakes and crepe paper chains the girls had made. He tossed the tree on a trash heap, kicked it, stomped on it, and finally lit a match and dropped it. Flames erupted; he backed away, nearly toppling the snowman Hazel and Gladys had made. They had carried Robbie out to see it, and wrapped the lopsided figure in an old quilt so it wouldn't get cold.

As Martin approached the house, Father Walsh pulled his carriage into the lane. The men greeted one another with a handshake; each, it seemed, acknowledging the other's role, grieving father and comforter of the afflicted.

Mary knew she must go downstairs; it would be disrespectful to ignore a priest in her home. She took her only black dress from the closet, but it had a white collar. With shaking hands she tried to remove the basting stitches that held the lace collar to the dress. She threw it aside. The faded garment she'd slept in would do for now. This was not a party; it would soon be her baby's wake.

By late afternoon the house overflowed with callers bringing baked ham and fried chicken, pies, cakes, and cookies shaped like Christmas trees, gingerbread men and candy canes. Mary's sisters and sisters-in-law took over the kitchen, offering tea, coffee and dessert to the solemn and polite visitors.

Fleeing to Robbie's room, Mary tucked her face into his quilt, savoring the smell of sour milk and talcum powder mixed with his personal scent. She ran her hands over the wrinkled crib sheet, into the indentation where his body had rested, and noted the dried spittle on the pillow. He'd been cutting molars.

She shivered; the kerosene stove in the corner had not been lit since the last night Robbie slept here. When was that? Last night? No, last night he had been at the funeral home in town, while she had slept soundly, drugged and unaware.

I should be downstairs with Martin, she thought. Earlier, they had clasped cold trembling hands when the undertaker arrived with Robbie, dressed in a blue knit romper with a sailboat embroidered on the front, a white long sleeved sweater and long white stockings and white shoes. Martin had picked out the clothes while she slept.

When Julia brought the girls home, Mary had cowered in the hall, unable to watch or hear their reaction to seeing their baby brother lying in a box as if sleeping. Let Aunt Julia explain, if she could.

Hazel, discovering her mother in the hall, said, "Aunt Julia let us kiss Robbie," and tiny Evelyn added, "He's sleeping," before Julia whisked them away again.

She wished everyone would go to Julia's house. Except for the women in the kitchen; with them here nothing was required of her. Nothing save accepting condolences, handshakes, hugs, and empty platitudes. At least no one suggested putting pennies on Robbie's eyes to be sure he was dead. But it was a hurtful comment that had caused her to escape upstairs.

A neighbor woman had said, "You're still young. You'll have more babies," as if one could replace another. Struggling to understand why anyone would say something so thoughtless, she decided it wasn't as bad as what a woman had said to Mother when Michael fell from the silo. Mother told her when she was older, "Mrs. Wright, she said to me that us pioneer women ought not get attached to our children because so many of them die young."

That night, after the visitors had gone, Mary stretched out on the sofa to spend the night with Robbie. The cloying scent of roses caused her to cover her nose with her wet handkerchief. Where had roses come from in the dead of winter? Perhaps from that hermit down the road who turned an enclosed porch into a greenhouse. He'd once told Martin that the room was solar heated, but admitted he had a wood stove in there.

When she closed her eyes, they felt permanently scalded by salty tears. She didn't expect to sleep, but when a chunk of coal snapped and shifted on the stove grate, startling her, she realized she had slipped into the kind of thin slumber mothers of young children grow accustomed to. As her eyes adjusted to the dark she saw Martin beside the coffin, his back to her. He sucked in a series of sobs and muttered, "Oh, God, why, tell me why." Swiveling around, he sank onto the end of the sofa and whispered, "Mary." Waiting a moment he added, "Lass, come to bed now."

She held her breath; she had nothing to give, not even when he rubbed her ankles and spoke her name again. He plucked a heavy knit shawl off the sofa back, covered her, and left the room. Listening to the stairs squeak as he ascended, she heaved her grief into the cushions.

Somehow the minutes, hours, days and nights passed, and she found herself returning to the house after the burial and the dinner served at the parish hall. Dinner? She couldn't recall eating a bite. For days. Collapsed in a chair, still wearing her coat, hat, and galoshes, she uttered, "The Lord giveth and the Lord taketh away."

Martin lifted her head, forcing her to look into his red-streaked eyes. "I hope you're not going to say it's God's will. You'd have to explain to me how it could be God's will to have the lad suffer and be snatched from us."

Releasing his hold, he kicked an ottoman on his way upstairs. "I gotta change clothes," he said. "There's chores to do."

Mary knew she should follow him, try to comfort him, but Hazel needed attention, too. She huddled in the corner where a week ago a Christmas tree brightened the room, and for the past two days a baby's coffin stood. "Why did this happen at Christmas?" she wailed. "We'll never, ever, ever, have another good Christmas."

Mary held her oldest daughter's rigid body and prayed for an answer that might satisfy a child. All she could muster was, "When death comes, it's a shock to those left behind. It makes no difference if it's Christmas or Easter or any ordinary day. Next Christmas we'll be reminded of this, but we'll think of Robbie all year long. Always and forever."

Hazel pulled away. "Sister Gregory told me Robbie's funeral was the Mass of the Angels and that I should be happy to have an angel brother in Heaven. I said I was happy but that's a big fat lie and I don't care if I have to confess it. This is the saddest day of my life. I don't want an angel brother. I want my real brother. I loved him." She stomped her foot and raised her fists.

"You can still love him, Hazelbon. That doesn't stop."

Mary wanted to stomp her feet, too. Sister Gregory had told her, "We wish to take on half of your family's sorrow so you need not bear it alone," and the other parish nun nodded in agreement. If only it were as simple as wishing, or turning over half the grieving to someone else.

Evelyn crawled onto her lap and said, "Mama's sad. I'll be the baby."

Mary pulled the child against her bosom and sang, "*Hush, little baby, don't you cry, Mama's gonna buy you a mockingbird.*" She stopped; this was no time for music, not even a lullaby, especially not Robbie's favorite about "birdie."

The wind whistled through its razor-sharp teeth and rattled the tarpaper Martin had wrapped around the foundation of the house to ward off wintry blasts. It might protect against colds, but there was no defense against the fury that slammed into their lives and took Robbie.

Stormy Weather

There's no sun up in the sky ~~~

As despair coiled itself around Mary, she lost sight of her touchstones: God, family, and music. When she tried to pray, she became distracted by the remembered sound of Robbie's giggle or, worse, his cries of suffering. She could not bring herself to include music in her life. She welcomed the silence of the dormant countryside; no birds singing, no insects chirping, no animals snorting and squealing, no men's voices in the fields. As for family, with four children under ten, she couldn't abandon them, so she forced herself to keep a sense of purpose.

With Robbie's pain in mind, she accepted the discomfort of having her hands in hot lye soap water, of bruising her knuckles raw on the washboard, and hanging clothes outside while the bitter cold ate through her work gloves.

"You make extra work for yourself," Martin commented when she struggled through the door with an armload of cumbersome frozen garments. "Never understood why you hang clothes out, then bring them in frozen and dry them in here."

"Because the sun bleaches them. Now you know." Sweeping past him, she cracked the arms on an icy shirt and draped it over the wooden clothes rack by the stove. "I need to keep busy. I can't sit around like you've been doing."

"Yeah, well, there ain't much farmin' to do in the dead of winter."

Dead. The word stopped her. Robbie's dead. In the ground; in the dead of winter.

Martin pushed away from the table. "I told your pa I'd fix that door that won't close. Reckon I'll go on over."

Mary rubbed bag balm into the cracked skin on her fingertips, thinking: If only I could rub salve onto my wounded soul and heal it.

"Maybe I'll stay for supper."

"Suit yourself. Probably better than what I'll fix here. The smell of food makes me sick to my stomach."

With Martin gone and the two little girls napping, Mary paced the floor. In the hall mirror, she glimpsed a woman with uncombed hair and dark circles accenting her lifeless eyes. She turned away from the image. Her entire body ached. If she bothered to look at herself unclothed, her skin would most likely show bruises from pain.

A stack of sympathy cards on the buffet reminded her that she must tell Sister Pius about Robbie's death. Sister always sent cards to the children on Christmas and their birthdays. The best way to tell her was to enclose a copy of Robbie's obituary from the paper, dated December 31, 1915. Everyone she knew had given her a copy. She could hardly bear seeing the piece; it was as brief as his life, but she read it again.

~~~~ The little son of Mr. and Mrs. M. Jones was taken sick with estoppage of the bowels the first of the week and died on Tuesday. The child was one and a half years old The sympathy of all goes out to Mr. and Mrs. Jones in the sad loss that came to them the closing days of the year.~~~~

Along with the clipping, Mary wrote:

~~~~ My dear friend Sister Pius: No matter how many times I read this notice I can't believe it's my baby who God called home. It happened so fast. The little lad suffered, crying and crying. I didn't know what was wrong and I didn't know what to do for him but pray. We should have taken him to the doctor sooner. Maybe he'd still be with us. He died on the 29th. Now he's buried near Mother in that cold cemetery. They had a hard time digging the grave with the ground frozen. Good thing the grave was so small.

I've never put in such a lonesome week. I'm just beginning to get my bearings. People say it's better if I put everything of baby's away but I feel better when I see his things around. I don't know how so small a boy can have left such an immense hole in our lives. I suppose I'll get over it sometime. Not even my younger siblings' deaths prepared me for this. I was their sister; I'm Robbie's mother. There's no deeper connection between two human beings.

I must confess I've done battle with God and our Blessed Mother over this loss. I'm flimsy as an autumn leaf clinging to a branch. Unexpected acts of kindness shatter me. The night before the funeral, after everyone had gone, I found the girls' shoes polished and their Sunday dresses washed and ironed. I can't think who might have done that. At the funeral a woman told me she has a son who is nearly grown but has the mind of a child. She said that makes her sad but it must be nothing compared to my sadness. I thought of the old saying: Don't let my sorrow rob you of your own. But I didn't feel charitable enough to speak the words to her. God forgive me, I wanted my sorrow to be the only one that mattered that day, and tomorrow, and next year, however long it lingers. I'm not sure I even recognize that Martin and the girls have suffered a loss. I need your prayers to help me through this. Affectionately, Mary Jones ~~~~

When April Comes Again

When robins return and spring has softened winter's chill ~~~

Mary kept a firm grip on sorrow as winter's frozen shell cracked and spring throbbed to life. The tinkle of icicles dripping from the eaves onto the tin cistern cover used to make her think of xylophone music. Now she closed her ears to it. She turned away from the sight of pale green shoots sprouting through dirty snow. The girls would have grass for their Easter baskets, but Robbie would not enjoy his first egg hunt with his sisters.

When the yard filled with dandelions, so friendly and abundant it looked as if someone had slathered on a layer of mustard, she mourned the idea that this year the girls would have shown their little brother how to blow the wispy white heads off dandelions gone to seed; how to make dandelion stem bracelets and how to split the stems and put them in water, where they curled into tight little knots. She'd passed along this childhood fun to her daughters, and they would have enjoyed the game with Robbie.

Doing her spring cleaning, she crumbled to the floor in grief when she rolled out the piano to scrub the floor and found Robbie's teething ring, his tiny marks frozen in the dried rubber that had once been pliable enough to ease discomfort. She put it in her trunk, along with his clothes, shoes, blankets and toys. Seeing them strewn about had at first been comforting; now they were a constant reminder of his absence.

After finding the teething ring, she draped the parlor carpet over the clothesline and beat the daylights out of it with a wire paddle. Striking at something inanimate released tension, anger, and emotion. Hiding between the folds of the carpet, she lapsed into prolonged sobbing.

But nature's most glorious season, a time of renewal, could not be denied. "Smell the lilacs and the apple blossoms," she said to Papa when he stopped by to check on her well-being. Later, walking with the girls in the meadow, surrounded by a brisk wind, she marveled at how the rampant wild flowers shifted and sifted into glistening prisms of kaleidoscopic patterns.

Seated on the porch steps while the girls romped in the yard, she watched a knot of clouds unravel like strands of white yarn pulled from a skein. Birds twittered as they flapped from the ground to branches in the budding trees, carrying material for new nests. Their gay conversation served as a reminder that her nest had been quiet too long, and, like the clouds, her household had unraveled.

She and Martin barely spoke. It took all her effort to utter even necessary words: grace at meals, disciplining the girls, or answering their questions about school matters. The small talk that, during ordinary times, carried her and Martin through meals had come to a standstill. What did it matter if she told him that the laundry dried quickly today? Or that she'd opened the last jar of dill pickles from last summer's canning? Did she care how many rows he plowed today? Or that Bull Epson still hadn't returned that wrench he borrowed a week ago? What did Martin expect? Everyone knew if you loaned Bull anything, even a dime, you had to borrow it back if you ever wanted to see it again.

As for the girls, Evelyn had reverted to talking and acting like a baby; she even sucked her thumb. She'd never done that, but Robbie had. Dorothy and Gladys tiptoed around their mother, and Hazel had become a bossy big sister. She'd taken over Mary's bedtime routine for the girls. One recent night she heard Hazel ask, "Who wants to start playing music again?" A subdued "I do" came from Gladys and Dorothy.

Mary realized she had never told the girls they couldn't play music, but she had set an example by not singing while she worked or by not plopping down at the piano after supper to play a medley of family favorites.

She must no longer deprive them of music, nor herself the joy they and their music brought her. She needed them and they needed her, to nourish and protect them. She would, with God's help, pick up the banner of motherhood that had been bestowed on her. Martin needed attention, too.

"Girls," she called, "supper in ten minutes. Go find your father. After supper we'll have a family concert and entertain him."

God, family, music, she said over and over. God, family, music, God, family, music, God, family music....

Look For The Silver Lining

When e'er a cloud appears in the blue, remember somewhere, the sun is shining ~~~

The pall that had draped itself over the household did not disintegrate all at once; it frayed and faded week by week. At the end of May, on Decoration Day, Mary and the three oldest girls carpeted Robbie's grave with crimson peony buds. On her knees, Mary blocked an image her mind tried to send of the small white casket beneath the fertile soil, but she couldn't stop the tears that glazed her eyes.

A few yards away, Martin played with Evelyn under a weeping willow tree. When she tumbled onto a gravel lane and Mary dashed over to comfort her, Martin called, "Leave her be. She didn't cry until she saw you comin' to baby her. You can't build a corral 'round these girls."

"Well, watch her then. Don't let her trample on people's graves."

Mary knew she had become over-protective. A sniffle, a sneeze, a cough, and out came the Vick's VapoRub. A scraped knee had her fretting about lockjaw, while the girls complained that the scrubbing she gave the wound was worse than the scrape. She stewed over Dorothy's loose tooth as if it was the first one she'd seen. Martin finally tied a string around the wobbling tooth and yanked it out.

June brought what would have been Robbie's second birthday. Mary and Martin returned from visiting the cemetery to find that Hazel had baked a cake. Mary didn't have the heart to scold her for lighting the oven on her own. Besides, the child was nearly eleven and had probably seen her light the stove a hundred times. The two layer chocolate cake had no frosting and the center caved in like meringue gone bad, but it held two candles side by side.

"I helped stir the batter," Gladys bragged.

"And we licked the bowl," Dorothy added, speaking for herself and Evelyn.

"Do you think Robbie would have liked it?" Hazel asked.

"He would have gobbled it up," Mary answered. "I'll whip some cream to put on it. I have some fresh from this morning."

As summer coursed along into August, Mary contained her fragile emotions and the children were carefree, as they should be, unaware their short leashes were attached to Mama's apron strings. On her knees weeding the garden, she yanked a plump, warm tomato from the vine, wiped it on her sleeve and bit into the flesh. Juice spurted and ran down her arm. With the next nibble, she sucked the juice before biting down.

Leaning back on her heels, she saw that the sky had gone from clear to cloudy, with barely enough blue to patch a Dutchman's pants, as Mother used to say. A half hour later, the wind ceased, causing the windmill to slow its rotation and nearly stop, and the sky had a yellowish haze. "Twister weather," she said to herself. Scrambling to her feet she called, "Hazel, bring your sisters to the cellar."

"Aww; we're playing with hollyhock dolls."

"Now; make it snappy. Bring your dolls if you like."

"I'm coming," Dorothy called, hiking up her bloomers as she skipped along the path from the outhouse.

The other girls sang, "I see London, I see France, I see Dorothy's underpants."

Mary loped toward the dugout built by early settlers. Martin had shored up the inside, spread old carpet on the floor and tacked cheesecloth to the rafters to keep dirt from falling, but particles seeped through. Hazel always complained about the musty smell and claimed it was an Indian burial ground. With a kerosene lantern, Mary checked for rodents, spiders, snakes, anything that might frighten or bite the children.

They scurried into the bunker with their old dog Tapioca nipping at their heels, and sat in a row on the edge of an iron frame cot with a lumpy straw mattress.

Seated on a milking stool, Mary saw Gladys wiggle her fingers on Evelyn's head. "It's a bat," Gladys said. Evelyn screamed and leaped onto her mother's lap.

Gladys added, "When a bat gets in your hair it gets tangled and you can never get it out."

Evelyn screamed again. "Mama, do I have something in my hair?"

"No, and Gladys, stop scaring your sister. C'mon, let's all sing to pass the time."

"I know a song," Hazel shouted. "Lizzie Borden took an axe and gave her mother forty whacks."

Mary grabbed Hazel's arm. "Stop, right now."

Hazel spurted out the rest of the ditty, "When she saw what she had done she gave her father forty-one."

"Hazelbon, you will say the Act of Contrition forty times tonight, on your knees. Make that forty-one times. And I never want to hear that song again."

"Why?" Dorothy asked. "Does it have naughty words?"

"Yes. Now, forget it." Mary snapped her fingers for attention. "Here's a song you all know. *Oh, there was an old man named Michael Finnegan, with whiskers on his chinnegan.*"

The girls joined in but soon grew restless. "It's freezing in here," Hazel complained. "Like a grave."

"How would you know how a grave feels?" Mary asked. "Pull your skirt around you. We've seen you in your undies."

Hazel held her nose and then released it. "Speaking of undies, something stinks. Evelyn must have wet her diaper."

Evelyn slugged her sister's arm. "I don't wear diddies."

"You do at night."

"Girls, girls. Listen, here's an old sea chant." Mary lowered her voice and sang, "*Well, it's Bully John from Baltimore, I knew him well on the eastern shore. Well, it's Bully John's the boy for me, he's a buckle on land and a bully at sea.*"

She applauded herself. "Grandda used to sing these songs. When he came from Ireland he listened to the sailors sing on the ship. *Well, it's been a long time and a very long time, it's been a long time since I made this rhyme. Well, my old mother she wrote to me, my darlin' son come home from sea.*"

"Listen, it's hailing," Hazel said.

Dorothy snuggled next to her mother. "I'm afraid of hail. Should we pray?"

"Prayer never hurts, but don't worry, the hail won't reach us."

"Tell us a story so I don't have to listen to the noise."

"Tell the one about lightning," Gladys added. "I like scary stories."

"Well, let me see, if I remember," Mary said, as if she didn't know every detail. She often wondered about the wisdom of telling youngsters a story that involved death, but it was about family and they'd already dealt with their brother's death, including the funeral, which some relatives insisted they should not attend. Besides, it was a mother's duty to teach her children that Mother Nature could be dangerous as well as benevolent. Here on the plains a tranquil day could suddenly turn deadly with a blinding blizzard, a raging tornado or a solitary lightning strike.

"It was July, eighteen-ninety-two," she began. "I was eleven and my cousin Essie was twelve."

"Did you know her?" Dorothy yelled above the noise.

Mary raised her voice, too. "Of course. Aunt Bridget's and Uncle Henry's farm was near ours. We played together all the time; danced the jig. She was better than I was. Anyway, as Uncle Henry told the story later, Essie was bringing lunch to him in the field. A storm was brewing, like today. She skipped through the field and was a short way from Uncle Henry when a flash of lightning struck her to the ground. Uncle Henry shouted and ran to her, but darling Essie was already home with God. He grabbed her and crawled under the wagon until the storm was over. Then he took her home to her mother and sisters and brothers. We all were heart-broken. I lost my favorite playmate. I cried for days."

Relating the details of Essie's death sparked memories of Robbie. To distract herself, she stood and cracked the trap door and peeked outside. Rain dribbled in; she closed the door and sat down.

"Tell the second part of the story," Gladys prodded. "It starts with seventeen years later."

"Yes, I know. Seventeen years later, in nineteen-aught-nine, Uncle Henry was in the field again, a different field this time. His son, Lin, told us what happened. It was about five in the afternoon when storm clouds appeared. Both men were afraid of lightning because of what happened to Essie. When the first sliver of lightning flashed, Uncle Henry yelled, 'Prairie fire.' That's what he called it because of the way it lit up the sky and caused crops and grass to catch fire. They jumped in the wagon and headed home. Suddenly, Uncle Henry was struck on the back of the head by a huge bolt of lightning that threw him from the wagon."

Mary paused for the gasp that always came from the girls. "The team was knocked to the ground and Lin was shocked, too. But he jumped down to see about his pa, but he was beyond help."

"Was he dead?" Dorothy asked.

"You know he was," Hazel answered. "We've heard this story fifty times."

"I asked Mama, not you."

"Yes, Dorothy; he was dead. The paper said he was 'hurled from this earth to eternity.' Imagine, two from the same family killed by lightning."

Hazel said, "Teacher says lightning never strikes twice in the same place."

"Perhaps so, but this wasn't the same place. It was a different farm than the one where Essie died. Your father and I left Hazel and Gladys with your aunt Julia while we traveled to the funeral. My, it was a sad affair. Uncle Henry was a dear man, admired for his generosity. Aunt Bridget, too, so sweet and kind. She died from cancer about three years later."

"What's cancer?" Hazel asked.

"I don't rightly know, except it causes great pain. Her daughters said she never complained. She put her suffering in the Lord's hands and accepted it."

"Did Robbie have cancer? He was in pain."

"No, Hazel; he didn't have cancer." Eager to move away from talking about Robbie, Mary said, "Even at funerals there can be happiness. Seeing relatives I hadn't seen for years. Cousin Elizabeth, who's my age. Cousin Aggie with her children. Little Maybelle with her long dark curls. She looks so different than you carrot-tops."

The door creaked open, and daylight flooded the snug underground room. "I figured your mother would tuck you away here," Martin said. "Come on out now. Small twister touched down not far from here. Lightnin' sparked a grass fire but the rain put it out right quick."

Following the girls up the stairs, Mary wagged her finger at them. "See, I told you we needed to find shelter. Let this be a lesson to you to listen to your elders."

With that admonition, she sloshed off through the mud to see if her garden had been damaged by hail.

The Happy Wanderer

I love to wander by the stream that dances in the sun ~~~

"Stop fidgeting," Mary ordered as she tied back Gladys's pipe curls with a navy ribbon. She knelt on the floor and redid the red sash on the child's white sailor blouse. "All right; you're presentable. Now stay clean."

Gladys swerved to the open door. "Aunt Julia's coming. Come on, Hazel."

Mary followed her two oldest daughters to the porch, where they watched Julia's spiffy new surrey arrive. "Stay up here until the horse is settled. Your aunt Julia likes horses with lots of spirit. Like herself."

She waved to her sister and, when the dust settled, she told the girls, "Go on now, get aboard. Hazel, look out for your sister. And Julia, don't drive as fast as you usually do."

"Yes, Mother," the young woman teased.

"Have fun, girls. Mind your manners and Aunt Julia."

Aunt Julia turned to her nieces. "Hold onto your bloomers." She rippled the reins across the mare's back and headed down the lane, lickety-split.

Mary could have gone to the movie with Hazel and Gladys, but Julia liked having them to herself now and then. More than that, Mary now had a few hours alone. Martin had gone to help her father with a plow repair and had taken the two little girls.

With everyone out of the way, what should she do first? The kitchen floor needed a serious mopping and, come to think of it, she hadn't made beds this morning. The dinner dishes were still on the table, and with school opening next week, she should look through the girls' clothing and see what needed repair or altering.

A cow lowing in the pasture caught her attention. It looked pleasant out there, green and lush after yesterday's rain. Outdoor chores were more enticing than indoor. Make hay while the sun shines. She would work in the garden.

Lifting her straw hat from atop the dry sink on the porch, she uncovered Grandda McLaughlin's old harmonica. She marched across the yard, pulling a nameless tune from the instrument. The garden lay under full sun, but the mud had not yet dried. She would need her galoshes, and they were back at the house. Too much bother. She veered away and headed for the creek. There would be a breeze there. Why not play hooky for an hour?

Walking at a brisk pace, her legs stirred with vigor. A tawny cat crept from a crevice in the barn foundation, followed by three tottering kittens and then two more. "Come on," she called, and the cat family trotted after her. Looking over her shoulder as she whistled into the harmonica she thought: I'm the Pied Piper only I have cats instead of rats. Well, that's a good thing.

A gray jackrabbit sprinted past, startling two of the kittens. They began playing, tumbling over one another in the ragged grass. Mary separated the balls of fur and put each in an apron pocket, where they squirmed and mewed in tiny voices. It sounded as if they were singing a duet to her music.

Near the stream, a pair of robins bobbed on spindly legs and pulled fat worms from the damp soil. A chubby pocket gopher bolted up on his hind legs, moving his front paws as if he were directing a band. Laughing, Mary said, "All God's creatures like music. It's good for the body and soul."

Well, not all of them. A mud turtle on the creek bank retracted his head as if offended by her tune. Maybe his shell would soften the music a bit and he'd fall asleep. When she sat down, the kittens crawled out of her pocket into her lap, and then scampered off, their skinny tails perked straight up and curled just on the tip. Smiling at their cuteness, she wished the girls were here.

Funny thing, when they were home, she scooted them out from under her feet. When they were gone, even briefly, she wanted them back. When they return, she thought, I'll tell them about all the animals, and they'll tell me about their day.

I Love A Piano

I love a piano, it simply carries me away ~~~

Gladys clung to Hazel when Aunt Julia signaled her horse to a halt in the alley behind Sundquist Cinema.

"This is the movie house?" Gladys asked. "It looks like an old barn."

Aunt Julia explained, "It was a harness shop before Victor's uncle turned it into a theater. It's nice inside. You'll see." Her husband helped her from the carriage and they kissed each other, on the mouth.

Uncle Victor looked strong, and Gladys liked his blond, almost white, hair. She wondered again about something Hazel had told her. Hazel overheard Mama tell Pa that Victor couldn't give Julia any children. But that didn't make sense to either girl because Sister Caroline said God gives children to mothers and fathers.

Aunt Julia led her nieces inside. In a darkened corner, she sank onto a swivel stool and ran her scarlet fingertips across the piano keyboard. Fingernail polish intrigued Gladys; she also admired her aunt's fashionable dark brown gabardine suit. Atop Aunt Julia's crinkly russet hair sat a straw hat with wooden cherries dripping from the side as if they were hanging on a branch.

"How do you know what music to play for the movie?" Gladys asked.

Aunt Julia picked up a stack of papers and spun around to face the girls. "These cue sheets are from the film studio. They list the scenes so the musical director, that's me, can pick appropriate music. You know what appropriate means? It means the right music for each scene. Theaters in big cities have full orchestras but folks here have to content themselves with me and my piano."

Her fingers marched across the keyboard, pounding out a melody that stormed louder and louder before she stopped. "I have to drown out the noise of the projection machine. People complain about the clatter it makes but they don't mind loud music."

Aunt Julia nodded toward a door with an opening like a window, but without glass. "Victor runs the movie in there." She glanced at the watch pinned to her white pleated blouse. "I'm chattering like a magpie when it's nearly time for the movie to begin. Hazel, you've been here before. Take your sister and find a seat."

When they were seated, Hazel read aloud the announcements crawling across the bottom of the screen. "Do not spit on the floor. Do not put gum under seats. No talking during film. If the baby cries, please take him outside. When leaving, please turn up your seat."

"Did Uncle Victor write the rules?" Gladys asked.

"I suppose so. He's the boss."

"I need to go to the outhouse."

"No, you don't."

"Yes, I do. How would you know?"

"Well, I do know they don't have an outhouse. You'd have to use the one in the alley behind the pool hall. Mama wouldn't want you going there. A lot of men hang out in the alley. You'll have to hold it."

Gladys knew the agony of holding it. On winter nights when she didn't want to get out of her warm bed to use the metal pot in the hall, she held it until morning. Even the pot was cold, but it was better than going outside to the "little house." In the morning, the girls all used the pot downstairs behind the kitchen stove, where it was warmer.

"Where do the screen stars go to the toilet?" she asked.

Hazel bellowed, "You dumb cluck. The actors aren't really here." She lowered her voice. "Stop fussing or I'll tell Aunt Julia you aren't old enough to go to movies."

"I am so old enough." Embarrassed, Gladys slouched and kicked the seat in front of her.

The boy in the seat turned and glared at her. "Don't do that." Then he and his friend said, "Cluck, cluck."

Hazel nudged Gladys and offered her popcorn from the bag Mama had sent along. Gladys turned down the peace offering and gnawed on a red licorice whip.

Aunt Julia seated herself at the piano, her back to the audience. Beaded bracelets clinked on her wrists as she stacked sheet music under the oil lamp's glow. Hands poised over the keyboard, she glanced over her shoulder and winked at the girls. Gladys tried winking back but she couldn't master it; both of her eyes closed at the same time.

The screen flickered with squiggles of numbers and letters. Finally, the movie title appeared: *The Perils of Pauline*, Episode Four, starring Pearl White. Hazel whispered the title and the star's name to Gladys.

"Is she Pauline or Pearl or Peril?"

"Her real name is Pearl, but she's acting as Pauline."

"Then who's Peril?"

"No one. Peril means danger. Now hush."

Worried about being called a dumb cluck again, Gladys hushed. Eyes riveted on the screen, she watched the heroine struggle to fight off a band of Gypsies. A handsome young man with black curly hair, sparkly eyes, and a pencil-thin mustache, tied Pauline to the back of his gaily decorated wagon. His swarthy features made Pauline's fair skin and blonde flowing curls seem even paler.

Gladys skimmed her eyes from the screen to Aunt Julia, whose slender fingers flitted across the ivories, like a butterfly dancing on flowers. Gladys's fingers played an imaginary piano in her lap. On the screen, Pauline mouthed, "Help, someone help me," while the words appeared below.

"There's no one to hear you my pretty one," Ramon replied in print, while Aunt Julia underlined and punctuated the sentence with notes that sounded scary to Gladys. The sentences continued to flow while the action accelerated:

How will Pearl get out of this predicament?

Does she have the fortitude to escape the clutches of Ramon?

Does she really want to?

Is she secretly attracted to the dark-eyed stranger?

The words flew too fast for Gladys to catch all of them but she liked the musical sound effects. Dum dah dum dah dah dum, Aunt Julia hammered, so animated that her arm flew up and knocked her hat to the floor. She continued, not missing a beat.

Gladys understood that the heroine had been saved when a posse chased Ramon out of town in his wagon with a sign reading "The End" attached to the rear.

The sconce lamps came on and while the audience cheered, Aunt Julia took a bow and retrieved her hat from the floor in one graceful movement. "How'd you like the movie?" she asked Gladys.

"It was swell, but I liked your piano playing better. When I grow up and you're too old to play, I'd like to work here."

Aunt Julia pinched Gladys's cheek. "Thank you, Sweetpea."

"Can nuns play piano in movie houses?"

"Nuns? I don't know. Why?"

"Because I might be a nun someday. If God lets me."

"I'm sure he'll let you play music if that's what you want. Maybe not in a movie house, but I happen to know that God loves music."

While Gladys absorbed that good news, Aunt Julia suggested, "Let's find your uncle and let him buy us an ice cream soda. I'm about to swoon from thirst."

"Me, too," Hazel said, and followed Aunt Julia out back.

Gladys lingered to look at the theater with the lights on. Maybe it would be fun to be a film star like Pearl White. Or to play music and sing on a stage like those vaudeville people Mama talked about.

But not burlesque; Mama said that was naughty.

Over There

Send the word, send the word over there ~~~

Mary settled into her platform rocker and picked up her mending basket. Next to her on the sofa, Martin leafed through the paper. Sometimes he read to her while she did her mending and they discussed local or national matters. These days it was mostly war news.

Martin had voted for Woodrow Wilson because he vowed to keep the country out of war. Although disappointed in that broken promise, Martin insisted that the family do its duty on the home front. When Mary complained that she couldn't keep all the new regulations straight, he made a chart: No coal for heat on Mondays. No wheat on Mondays and Wednesdays. No meat on Tuesdays. No pork on Thursdays and Saturdays.

"You didn't put down we can't eat meat on Fridays," Mary said.

"For Pete's sake; a good Catholic oughta know that."

"Just teasing, but war rules or Catholic rules, a meatless dinner simply isn't a full meal."

Martin had a heck of a time explaining Daylight Savings Time to the girls, but they enjoyed the new words coined because of anti-German sentiment. Sauerkraut was liberty cabbage, hamburger became Salisbury steak, and dachshunds were liberty pups.

Martin had read Mary an article explaining that the war was a financial boon to many Americans. With immigration from Europe cut off, men found employment and good wages in factories, mining, lumbering, and other industries. Women filled jobs vacated by men serving in the army. Farmers sold mules and horses to the army and used the money to buy new equipment. Despite this, the Jones family's meager income hadn't increased by a dime.

Martin blew a smoke ring at Gladys, on the floor reading the comics. "Martin," Mary scolded, "I've asked you not to blow smoke at the girls. Breathing that poison is not good for them. You neither, but that's your business."

"So you say." He yawned. "Gladdie, is your homework done?"

Nodding, Gladys laid aside the comic strips. "Pa, some kids were picking on Anton Lenz because he's a German. Hannah Bergstrom said the war is his fault. Is that true?"

"Nah, that's crazy. He's just a kid. His bein' German has nothin' to do with the war. Anyway, he's not a German. He's American like you and most of the kids around here. Born in the U. S. of A. His parents have nothin' to do with the war either, just because they came here from Germany. Understand?"

"I guess so. Will you have to go to the war?"

"Nope, your old man's too old to be a soldier."

"I'm glad you're old."

"Yeah, for once, I'm glad, too."

"Hannah says mean things," Gladys continued.

"About you?"

"About everyone. She said Donald Hardin is a half-breed, that his mother's a squaw. She said a squaw is an Indian woman, and that Donald has bed bugs and cooties. She picked on him at recess because I was nice to him. Then she called me Shanty Irish and made a face at me."

Mary glanced up, ready to defend the Irish, but decided to let Martin handle it.

"Hannah needs to learn some manners. Shanty Irish ain't a bad thing. It means poor. Lots of folks are poor and there's no shame in that. Irish people who are better off are called Lace Curtain. When I was a lad, we were called worse than Shanty Irish. It had to do with pig manure but the word wasn't manure."

"Tut, tut," Mary warned her husband.

"Would you need to go to Confession if you said the word?" Gladys asked.

"Well...." Martin twiddled his thumbs forward, and then reversed the motion.

Gladys copied his twiddling. "Venial sin or mortal sin?"

"I reckon venial. Ignore Hannah. She just wants attention."

"Anyway, she's wrong. We have lace curtains so we aren't Shanty Irish. But are we rich?"

Mary chuckled, while Martin answered, "We ain't even close to rich. The other day I found a dime in my pocket and thought I was wearin' some other fella's britches."

"Whose?"

"Never mind. It's a joke. Times are fair to middlin' right now but we never catch up on the bills. You don't go hungry, do you? You eatin' enough spuds? Cuttin' back on meat and bread the way we have to, you gotta fill up on taters. So, anything else on your mind?"

"I guess not." Gladys's response drowned beneath a drawn out shriek from a horn and the toot-toot of a flute.

"Ain't you supposed to be practicing your fiddle?" Martin asked.

"It's a violin, Pa."

"It'd be a fiddle in my hands. I'd be just fiddlin' around with it. You go on and practice. You girls play and I'll pray, that you get it right someday."

Gladys giggled. "You're a poet and don't know it."

She skipped off and Martin resumed reading the paper. "Listen to this. That flu that's been makin' its way across the country has hit Minnesota."

"Oh, dear," Mary said. "Read the story to me."

"No, you'll just start frettin'."

"I have to know what we're up against. What does it say? If you don't want to read it, paraphrase it."

"What the heck does that mean, schoolmarm?"

"A summary, in your own words."

"Well, this writer can tell it better than I can."

"Then read it. You've wasted five minutes arguing with me."

"You win. It says: With the Great War windin' down, Americans are more concerned about the Spanish influenza than the overseas war. The disease may have started in China and spread by travelers. Rumors have circulated that the Germans brought the disease to the United States as a weapon that would rapidly kill thousands. Health officials have concluded that the virus was spread in this country in the spring of 1918, from animal to humans when soldiers at Fort Riley, Kansas, burned tons of manure. A fierce wind brewed a dust storm that, combined with the smoke from Fort Riley, created a stinkin' yellow haze that spread for miles. The mixture stung the soldiers' eyes and nostrils; they began to cough, vomit, and complain of headaches. By noon, more than a hundred soldiers were violently ill."

"Like tobacco smoke. Bad for humans. What else does it say?"

"The disease spreads rapidly where people are closely confined, such as prisons and military camps. Doughboys, unaware they are carriers, board ships for Europe, makin' the deadly virus a global concern. Unlike many illnesses that attack children or the weak and elderly, the age group hit hardest by this influenza is healthy young adults, ages twenty to forty. Early symptoms are muscle and joint aches, high fever, weakness, followed by pneumonia in which the lungs fill with a red frothy liquid. Death often comes within hours of the flu's onset."

Martin tossed aside the paper. "That's enough for me. I'm off to bed."

Mary soon followed him, but she tossed and turned thinking about the influenza. It was true; this concerned her more than the war overseas did. This was an immediate danger, not so much to her children as to herself and Martin.

I had a little bird, its name was Enza, I opened up the window and in-flu-enza~~~

Mary paused while sweeping the porch to watch Dorothy and Evelyn jump rope. Crisp leaves scattered each time the rope hit the ground. Realizing the song they were chanting was about the flu, she called, "Girls, I've told you not to sing that song."

"But why?" Dorothy asked. "What's wrong with it?"

"Never mind. Just don't sing it. There are plenty of other songs."

"Like what?" Evelyn yelled.

Mary paused, thinking. "Here's one. *Playmate, come out and play with me, and bring your dollies three.*"

"That's not a jump rope chant, it's a song," Dorothy called. "*Climb up my apple tree, look down my rain barrel, slide down my cellar door, and we'll be jolly friends forever more.*"

Singing along with the girls, Mary remembered an upcoming verse with the line *I cannot play with you, my dollies have the flu.* She led the girls into a repeat of the first verse and then walked away sputtering, "Flu, flu, flu; I'm tired of it, and frightened."

It somewhat allayed her concern when Park Rapid's officials placed a ban on public gatherings, and when schools and churches closed and the post office and other businesses allowed one person at a time into the building. She cut from the paper an article headlined "Coughs and Sneezes Spread Diseases, as Dangerous as Poison Gas Shells." Preventive measures listed were: Keep the body in good general health. Chew food well. Avoid tight clothing and shoes. Wash hands often. Do not use common drinking cups, water dippers, or towels. Mainly, stay away from anyone with flu.

Mary boiled water to use for drinking, cooking, and sterilizing dishes and utensils. She tore up old sheets to make individual towels for each member of the family, and saw to it that they avoided other people. And she prayed. It seemed to work; no one in the Jones household contracted so much as a cold.

The McLaughlins were not so fortunate. In early October, Mary's brother, Victor, age thirty-two, died at a makeshift hospital at the Duluth Shrine Auditorium where he'd been for five days. He was buried the next day after a graveside service, with only his father and brother, Robert, attending. The men returned to Park Rapids after burning Victor's few possessions, gathered from his room over a cafe where he worked as a cook.

Eleven days later, with the family still stunned by Victor's death, Julia McLaughlin Olson succumbed to influenza. At home, after Mary and Martin attended Julia's private burial, Mary heard sobs coming from behind the piano. "Girls, come out," she coaxed. "We'll pray the rosary together."

"Oh, Mama," Dorothy wailed, scooting out and dragging Evelyn with her. "We're so sorry about Aunt Julia and Uncle Victor."

"I know. I'm very, very sad." With tears for her two siblings momentarily spent, she kept her composure. She lifted six-year-old Evelyn into her lap and hugged Dorothy against her hip.

Dorothy looked up, her eyes red and swollen. "But we're more sadder than you because...because we killed them."

Mary jerked in her chair. "Child, why would you say such a thing?"

The story tumbled out: "You told us not to sing the song about the birdie and we sang it and then Uncle Victor got sick and died and then Aunt Julia died and we're sorry. Will we go to where the devil lives?"

"Oh, no, no, my darling girls, listen to me. I don't like that song, but it has nothing to do with people dying from this terrible illness. Promise me you'll forget the notion that you had anything to do with Aunt Julia's and Uncle Victor's deaths."

Wiping her wet face on her sleeve, Dorothy whimpered, "We promise."

Mary shifted Evelyn from her lap to the floor. "Evie, do you understand that singing a song does not make someone die?"

Biting her lower lip, Evelyn nodded.

"All right, then. Run along and play, both of you, and don't think about this any longer. Just remember your aunt and uncle in your prayers."

When they were gone, Mary covered her face with her hands and wept.

When Johnny Comes Marching Home

They'll give him a hearty welcome then, hurrah, hurrah ~~~

Through the kitchen window, Mary watched orange and yellow leaves flutter in the wind. Soon the trees would be bare and another dismal winter would set in. On the good side, maybe the first frost would kill the flu germs.

St. Peter's Church bell ringing caught her attention. Father Adolph always sounded the bell when a parishioner died. She folded her hands in prayer, certain it was another death from influenza. She soon realized the bell wasn't the slow, dirge-like peal of a death announcement. It grew louder and faster as other church bells rang, mixing into a harmonious chorus.

Martin burst into the kitchen, leaving the door ajar. "Hold dinner. We're goin' to town. The war's over."

"What? How do you know?" Mary poured water off a pot of boiled potatoes and set them aside.

"Eli came by on his way to town. Said there's an armistice."

Crossing herself, Mary peered out the window, as if the war had been unfolding in the fields and had now ceased.

"Let's go. Eli says the whole town's celebratin'."

"But the flu. The crowds."

"Forget that. We haven't been off this farm for a month. The paper says the flu has run its course. I'm goin' to town with or without you. Where are the girls?"

"In the dining room doing lessons. I closed the door to keep it quiet. Just because there's no school doesn't mean they don't have to study. I won't have them getting behind."

"Yeah, yeah, I know, schoolmarm. This is part of history, too. Girls, c'mon," Martin shouted, "we're goin' to town."

"Why?" Gladys asked as she and her sisters straggled into the kitchen.

"I'll explain on the way. You don't need jackets. It's warm today."

"Take a sweater anyway," Mary ordered. "Oh, dear, my hair's a mess. Let me get my turban." She grabbed a knit wrapper from a drawer and stretched it over her hair. Martin propelled her out the door and then marched across the yard ahead of her. "You could at least take time to change out of your work clothes," she called.

Martin herded the three youngest girls onto the bed of his bright green truck with yellow lattice sides. "No standin' up," he ordered. "I can see in the rearview mirror, and your mother claims to have eyes in back of her head."

"Thank goodness they're covered by her turban," Evelyn said.

"Come on, Hazel," Gladys called. "Sit by me."

Hazel shook her head and waited until her mother got into the cab; then she squeezed in next to her. The first-year teenager had refused to ride in the bed of the truck since last week's trip to church. "I was mortified," she told her mother later. "We were bouncing around, holding onto our hats, and the girls were waving to people and singing, *down the road of life we'll fly, automobubbling you and I.*" Hazel spoke the words instead of singing them.

"It was fun," Gladys had said. "You're a stick-in-the-mud."

Mary added, "Sounds like fun to me, too. And beggars can't be choosers. With our car broke down and no money to fix it, your father bartered his time digging a well for a man in exchange for the truck. We're lucky to have it."

Now, as the jalopy rattled along, the ruckus from town drowned out the voices of the three girls singing, "*Come Josephine in my flying machine ~~~*"

A traffic jam had formed at the corner where Martin wanted to turn but the drivers were in a merry mood. They tooted the horns on their vehicles and intentionally backfired them. Someone shouted, "Park anywhere. There's no more room for cars up ahead."

Martin pulled to the side of the road, and the Joneses joined the throng of townsfolk, walking, singing, laughing, hugging, kissing, and dancing in the streets.

Merv Snider had posted a sign on his meat market: Closed for the Kaiser's funeral. He yelled to the crowd, "Someone light a bonfire on the lot by the creamery. I'll bring the meat." He dashed inside and returned with strands of wieners wound around his beefy arms, and packages of bread and rolls carried in his stained apron. Children scooped up dry leaves and gathered sticks from trees, and soon a wiener roast was underway.

Late in the day, Mary and Martin rounded up their giddy girls and headed home. At the table, eating food left behind at noon, the family listened to the celebration in town. Church bells rang, firecrackers pop-pop-popped, and Roman candles sizzled and shot bursts of sparks into a sky aglow with color from dozens of bonfires.

Like the Northern Lights, Mary thought as she watched a pink cloud of smoke swim below the mottled bone-gray moon. Long after Martin and the girls were asleep, she prayed, giving thanks that *the war to end all wars was over.* But the influenza had not ended, and she worried about having spent the day in town with germs floating around. She offered prayers for those whose lives had been touched by the flu and those who still might be.

With the epidemic declared over in June of 1919, it stunned Mary when she read that worldwide deaths were estimated at between twenty and forty million. Of the American servicemen who died during the war, more than half died from the flu rather than from enemy fire.

In her quiet corner of the world, missing two siblings, she shared the anguish of those mourning loved ones abroad and at home.

Anything You Can Do

I can do better, I can do most anything ~~~

Mary lit the oven at dawn, using a corncob soaked in kerosene for kindling. She and Martin had eaten breakfast before his chores, and she had packed the girls' lunches: fried egg sandwiches and jelly glasses of apple sauce. The lunch pails stood on a chair by the door. Beneath the chair a Jack-o-lantern had melted into itself, leaving a shriveled, grotesque face instead of the happy one Martin had carved a week ago. It was time to put the pumpkin in the slop bucket for the pigs, but Evelyn had a hard time parting with holiday decorations.

By the time Mary finished her chores, the sun had reached the kitchen windows on which Jack Frost had etched a filigree lace pattern. She paused to admire the frozen design, its silver threads glittering like icicles on a Christmas tree. Through a clear pane, she looked out into the frozen fields, where haystacks capped with snow reminded her of frosted cinnamon rolls in a pan. There was no time to make rolls now. After the children were gone to school, she had bigger fish to fry. In town, not the kitchen.

Seated at the table with a cup of coffee, Mary picked threads of lint from the skirt of her red crepe dress. The color revived a memory from early in her marriage when she borrowed a red dress from Julia to wear to a wedding dance. When a man began paying more attention to Mary than Martin thought he should, Martin told the Lothario to get lost unless he wanted a knuckle sandwich. Mary barely had time to feel flattered by the other man's attention and her husband's jealousy before Martin told her that men considered red a flirtatious color. "A married woman's got no business wearin' a provocative dress," he said. "Julia's the one ought be wearin' it. She's single and looking for a fella."

The amusing recollection dissolved when four girls tumbled down the stairs, each wrapped in a wool blanket. Their school clothes hung over chairs by the stove, the warmest place in the house to dress. Mary marveled at how the girls were growing; like stairs in size, except that the oldest, Hazel, was the second step, shorter than Gladys.

As always, Evelyn needed prodding. Mary pulled the flannel nightgown over the child's head and slipped a linsey-woolsey dress over the shivering body clad in a union suit. Evelyn propped her butt on a chair and drew on black stockings and hooked them to garters sewn to her underwear legs, front and back. Dorothy and Gladys did likewise, but Hazel had refused to wear long stockings when she became a teenager. That was twelve-year-old Gladys's goal, handing down her stockings to her little sisters. "They make my legs look like an elephant's," she complained now, borrowing the description from Hazel. "No matter how tight I pull them, I can't get them smooth because of the underwear."

"There are worse things than wrinkled stockings," Mary offered.

"Yeah," Evelyn said, "it could be your legs that are baggy. Like that really fat woman who comes to church."

Mary chuckled inwardly at the child's observation, but warned, "Don't make fun of people. Now hurry along, all of you. I'm going to town this morning and I can't leave dirty breakfast dishes. Eat, Hazel. I'm tired of that so-called diet of yours. Once and for all, you are not overweight. If anything, you're too skinny."

"Why're you going to town?" Evelyn asked.

Mary pointed to the wall calendar on which November 9, 1920 was circled in red crayon.

"Oh, yeah, something about the Constitution."

A horn tooted outside. "School bus," Hazel called, leaving her toast uneaten.

Mary glanced out the window at the motorized vehicle. Years earlier, when she taught, there had been a horse-drawn bus to carry students to schools around the county. Now everyone attended town school. The girls had grown up having adults tell them they were lucky to have a bus, and how they had walked miles to school in the rain, sweltering sun, or several feet of snow.

Martin opened the kitchen door from the outside just in time to hold it for the girls on their way out. "Hazel, where's your headscarf?" he called.

"Save your breath," Mary advised. "She wouldn't be caught dead in a scarf."

While Martin warmed his hands atop the reservoir on the side of the stove, Mary said, "I'll be ready to go in a jiffy." She slipped off her coverall apron and hung on it on a hook. Martin didn't seem to notice her red dress, but she thought the color was perfect for today. Red was not only provocative, it was bold, assertive.

"I need more than a jiffy to thaw out." He pulled off his mackinaw and poured a cup of coffee.

"I told you I want to leave early."

"You told me a hundred times this past week. I milked the cows so fast the cream turned to butter before it hit the pail."

"I've heard that joke more times than I can count, usually related to cold weather, not to how fast you milked." She secured her green felt hat to her head with a decorative hat pin, and slipped into her black wool coat.

"Oh, all right. It's a big day for you." Martin shucked off the overall he'd worn over his going-to-town clothes.

"And a long time coming."

"Got your birth certificate?"

"Oh, you. Anyone with one good eye can see I'm years past twenty-one."

"Aye, Lass, ya coulda fooled me."

"Aye, Laddie, sure'n ya can slip into the voice of angels when you need some blarney. Now can we go?"

"Your vote'll count no matter what time you get there. The poll's open till seven." Martin grabbed his coat, hat, and car keys. "Say a prayer that the car starts."

"Already did. For good measure, I stacked quilts over the hood last night."

"Next thing I know, you'll be drivin' and I won't see that car again."

"Now that's a good idea, teaching me to drive."

She was right about the car starting. After a few tries the engine turned over and they chugged down the road. "So, who're you gonna vote for?" Martin asked.

"Haven't you heard? It's a secret ballot."

"Not from your husband."

"I don't recall that exception. Besides, you know who I'll vote for. James Cox, not that Republican Harding."

"Because of the talk about him?"

"Because I'm a Democrat. What talk?"

"You know, that he's a philanderer. That he's got Negro blood."

"Oh, for pity sake. Such gossip. Well, the Negro blood wouldn't bother me but I can't abide a man who's unfaithful to his wife. Anyway, I'm voting for Cox, but it's really his running mate who interests me."

"F.D.R.?"

"Yes, he's interesting and charming."

"Charming? Is that what you girls base your votes on?"

"No, it isn't. And we're women, not girls."

"Girls, women, females, what's the difference?" Martin cranked down the window to signal a left turn and then eased into a parking place near the library. "Hey, look at all the...women. Haven't seen this many together since that get-out-the-vote hen party you had at the house."

"Great; this is a wonderful turnout." Mary stepped out of the car and waved to three friends chatting in front of the building. "You coming?" she asked Martin.

"You go ahead. I'll let you cast the first vote from our household. You don't need me to hold your hand. More power to you, Lass."

The vote of confidence so pleased Mary that she kissed Martin's cheek, right there in front of God and everybody, as Pa liked to say. Then she strode toward the library, where she was delayed by two men.

"What's this world comin' to, lettin' womenfolk vote?" one man heckled.

His partner said, "Women took away our whiskey and now you wanna redecorate our voting booths with frilly curtains."

Mary met him eye to eye. "Last time I checked, Congress was made up of mostly men. It was men who voted for Prohibition, not women. It was men who gave women the vote, and I intend to do that just that. Anything you can do, I can do."

She turned and entered the library under a banner reading: Welcome, Women of Park Rapids, First Time Voters, 1920.

Runnin' Wild

Lost control; mighty bold ~~~

Mary gathered the material in her dress and pinned it above her knees on each side. Whirling the handle on the Victrola she nodded at Dorothy.

From a half-squat position, Dorothy demonstrated and instructed, "Cross your arms and put them on your knees, like this." As the jazzy music emerged from the machine, she continued. "Move your knees in and out and your hands back and forth, like this, and shuffle your feet. Charleston, Charleston, dah dum dah dah dum dah. That's it. You've got it, Mama."

Mary had often practiced the dance while alone, but didn't let on. "Whee; this is fun. Who taught you this dance?"

"A girl in school. Her sister is a flapper."

From the doorway, Hazel called above the music, "Mama, the dishtowel around your neck doesn't have the same fashionable look as a feather boa and strings of beads."

Mary stepped up her pace and nearly collided with Martin coming in the door.

"Hey, what's goin' on?" he yelled.

Dorothy grabbed his arm. "Come on, Pa; I'll teach you the Charleston."

"Oh, no you don't. I can't even walk and scratch my nose at the same time."

The music slowed and ground to a halt. So did Mary; she collapsed onto a chair while Dorothy cranked the machine again and she and Hazel kept going as only young people can.

With voting day under her belt, Mary's independent streak blossomed to Mae West's bosom proportions. She watched with interest and acceptance as Americans, particularly women, cast off not only cumbersome garments but shed conventions, customs, and inhibitions. People were, as a popular song said, *Runnin' wild; lost control, runnin' wild; mighty bold.* Liberated women no longer aspired to the winsome Gibson girl look. They wore pants, bobbed their hair, and raised hemlines to show their knees. Clothing had become skimpier during the war when people were asked to save fabric, and women liked the daring style. Philip Morris tobacco company introduced the Mild As May Marlboro, encouraging females to smoke, in public as well as behind the wood shed.

Still, when she saw the cover of *Harper's Bazaar*, showing America's first bathing beauty contest, with the women wearing skin-tight swimsuits that bared their legs from hips to ankles, astonishment surfaced. "I think of myself as modern," she said to Hazel, "but this might be going a bit too far."

"Don't be a prude. Times are changing. Look around."

"I know times are changing, and I'm not a prude. Look around all you want in Park Rapids. I guarantee you won't see anyone wearing skimpy swimming outfits."

"Jeepers, I just imagined Miss Best, the home ec teacher, in one of those swim costumes. Not a pretty sight."

"This style is not for everyone. I don't mean to be unkind, but especially not Miss Best."

Mary and her two oldest daughters agreed that Jazz was the definitive music of the 1920s, an age about which F. Scott Fitzgerald wrote, "America is on its greatest and gaudiest spree in history."

Hazel devoured the music magazines given to her by Professor Tremblay at school. She often read aloud from them, with Mary and Gladys an avid audience.

"The term 'Jazz' came from Jasbo Brown, a Chicago cabaret musician. Under the influence of gin, he was extravagant and risqué. He made his trombone 'talk' by moving a hat against and away from the instrument's mouth. 'More Jasbo, more Jas,' the audience would request, working Brown into fevered renditions of his music."

Although Park Rapids lay far removed from city jazz clubs, this was the era in which Mary watched her daughters come of age. It both worried and fascinated her as the impressionable girls tried to find their niche in the music world. Their repertoire at social events where they entertained included popular tunes of the day rendered with a jazzy tempo. Mary and Martin were often jarred from sleep when a session commenced in the parlor. Mary's foot would begin moving under the covers; before long she'd slide out of bed, leaving Martin to fend for himself on getting some sleep. If you can't beat 'em, join 'em, became her motto.

I Ain't Got Nobody

And nobody cares for me ~~~

"What's eating you?" Mary asked Evelyn when she plopped onto a kitchen chair and released a heavy sigh.

"Nothing," Evelyn mumbled.

Mary bided her time, knowing an explanation would come. She let her paring knife drop an apple peel into one long strand onto the table and sang an old rhyme: *Apple peel, apple peel, twist then rest. Show me the one who I love best.* Look, Evie, it landed in the shape of an L. Who's the lucky boy?"

"Boy? Ha. No one knows I'm alive."

"Ah, so it's a boy who has you in a snit."

Before Evelyn could confirm or deny being in a snit or that it was about a boy, Gladys called from the porch, "Probably that cute Lee Hurtz."

"Butt out," Evelyn fired back. "Besides, he's a flat tire."

"A flat tire," Mary echoed. "I can't keep up with today's slang."

"It means boring," Evelyn explained.

"Then why do you care that he doesn't know you're alive?"

"I don't care. Gladys brought him up, not me." She sighed again and fumed for a minute. "What I was trying to say is, no one knows who I am. I'm just one of the Jones girls. Like today, two boys were talking about *the Jones girls.* I felt like telling them we each have a name. Mine is Evelyn."

Gladys stepped inside, her violin tucked under her arm. "Do these boys have names? You're complaining that we're always *the Jones girls.* Are they just *the boys?*"

"If you must know, it was Buddy Simpleton and Carl Blockhead."

Mary rapped Evelyn's hand with a spoon. "Don't use disparaging nicknames."

"Buddy Sempel and Carl Block."

"That's better. What did they say that has you so lathered?"

"They were taking about our quartet. Buddy told Carl he couldn't tell those redheads apart. Carl said it was easy; Hazel is the smallest, and cute, with darkish red hair. Gladys is the one with the sweet smile."

"Carl said that? What else did he say?"

"About you, nothing, but when he said Dorothy's name, he wolf-whistled and rolled his eyes and said she's the pretty one. A beaut with nice legs and a curvy figure. He made a girl's shape with his hands."

While Mary tskked disapproval of the boy's freshness, Evelyn added, "Guess what he said about me."

"Just tell us," Gladys said.

"That I'm spunky and funny."

"Nothing wrong with that," Mary and Gladys said in unison.

"Oh, yeah? My sisters are pretty and sweet and curvy and I'm spunky and funny. Piffle on spunky. How does he know anyway? He's a senior. He doesn't know me from a load of coal. He probably meant I'm funny-looking, not funny."

Mary scoffed, "You're not funny-looking. You favor my mother's side of the family and they were handsome people. You look like your grandmother Burke."

"Jeepers, now I look like a grandma."

"I didn't say that. Mother was a young woman when she died and very pretty. Look at that picture of her in the hall if you don't believe me."

Evelyn darted into the foyer and back again. "She's pretty for an old person, but I don't look anything like her. You're just saying that."

"Because it's the truth."

"Well, don't tell Dorothy that boys think she's the pretty one. Not that she doesn't already know it. She's stuck on herself."

"I won't tell her, but Dorothy isn't at all conceited. She's quiet, calm, rarely a complaint out of her. And you're pretty, too. You're still young. You haven't come into your looks yet."

"Or my figure. My chest looks like a pea pod. A couple of bumps showing."

"For Pete's sake, give yourself time. You're still in puberty."

"Eewww, I hate that word."

"It's a perfectly good word, and the correct one. But never mind about bosoms. You have inner beauty."

"Boys don't see inner beauty."

"Nice boys do. Stop worrying about your looks and make yourself useful. Roll out two piecrusts for me."

"I don't know how. Uncle Eddie says if you don't learn to do something you'll never be asked to do it."

"Lord only knows where he got that nonsense. Not from me. It doesn't hold true in this household. I'm teaching; you're learning." Mary flattened a wad of dough and ran the rolling pin over it until it was the size of the pie pan with a bit to spare for the crust. She handed the rolling pin to Evelyn. "Do the other one."

Gladys leaned in to watch. "Looks good, Evie."

Mary tapped Gladys on the head. "If you're finished with the violin wax put it away. The smell gives me a headache. Then put those apple peelings in the slop bucket and take it to the pigs. I know you both know how to do that. And I need the wallpaper pulled off in the dining room so I can paper this weekend."

Both girls gaped at her as if they'd never done chores before. "Keeping busy builds character, and good character leads to inner beauty," she said.

"Do we need to develop our entire character this afternoon?" Evelyn asked.

"You can get a good start. Hop to it. Time's a wasting."

Strike Up The Band

Let the trumpet call, while the people shout ~~~

Mary read and reread the first publicity the girls received, written by her friend Lottie Lund for the *Hubbard County Weekly*, February 22, 1924.

~~~ Victor Olson, owner of Orpheum Cinema, formerly Sundquist Theater, hosted a Grand Opening on Friday evening. Mr. Olson treated guests to a showing of *Orphans of the Storm*, starring the Gish sisters. Prior to the movie, guests enjoyed the music of the Jones Quartet. Hazel, Gladys, Dorothy, and Evelyn are Mr. Olson's nieces and the daughters of Mr. and Mrs. Martin Jones. The young musicians offered a pleasing program, from jazz to popular tunes to chamber music. The late night show did nothing to dampen the band's enthusiasm for another performance the next day.

Beginning at noon and well into the day, the Quartet entertained at Hubbard County Co-op Creamery's first Creamery Day. Costumed in overalls, plaid flannel shirts and straw hats, the music-makers played, sang, and yodeled, while the audience enjoyed not only the entertainment, but a free lunch of cheese sandwiches, milk, coffee, and ice cream. The Co-op hosted the event in appreciation of the patronage received from area farmers and townsfolk. ~~~

Mary nearly burst with pride until her conscience reminded her that excessive pride goeth before a fall. She remembered, too, the tizzy Hazel had been in when the family came home from Creamery Day.

Wagging her finger in Evelyn's face, Hazel shouted, "Don't you ever suggest we wear these hayseed costumes again."

"Whoa, Tootsie," Mary scolded, "you come from a long line of your so-called hayseeds. It's nothing to be ashamed of. This day was for and about farmers."

Looking chagrined for only a moment, Hazel told Evelyn, "From now on, I'll decide what we wear. You're still a child; I'm the oldest and someone has to be in charge of the group." Then she turned on Gladys. "Furthermore, your number with the banjo was not part of the program."

"I played during intermission because someone requested it. I like the banjo; it's fun. The violin is my serious instrument."

"From now on, we stick to the program."

"Girls, girls, it sounds to me as if we have a few wrinkles to iron out if you plan to find other engagements. Maybe I should make the decisions."

"I should be in charge," Hazel said. "I'm an adult."

"Then act like one. We'll work together. I'll handle the money, starting with what you earned today. We'll all decide how to spend it. Maybe on new dresses."

"Money?" Martin asked.

"Yes, the creamery manager gave me a five dollar bill."

"Wow," Evelyn said, "that's a buck and a quarter for each of us. When can we go shopping?"

Still huffy, Hazel headed upstairs, with Evelyn a few steps behind. "Cal Arness said you looked cute as a button in overalls and straw hat. I saw you sparking with him during intermission."

"I was doing no such thing," Hazel yelled before slamming her bedroom door.

"Stop taunting your sister," Mary warned Evelyn.

"She was cuddling with him. I saw her with my own two eyes."

"That's her business. She's nearly nineteen-years-old."

Evelyn segued into a popular tune, "*He's such a delicate thing, but when he starts in to squeeze, you'd be surprised. He doesn't look very strong, but when you sit on his knees, you'd be surprised.*"

The whole family broke into laughter at scrawny Evelyn vamping and rolling her eyes. The song teased Mary's imagination all day and she sang the silly lyrics while working around the house, "*He doesn't look like much of a lover, but you can't judge a book by its cover.*"

Let the drums roll out, let the cymbals ring ~~~

Mary spread a blanket under an elm tree and sat down to read the paper. Inside the house, the four girls and two female cousins were making taffy, shrieking and giggling as they pulled and twisted the goo back and forth between their greased hands. To add to the frenzy, Evelyn had decided to try her hand at the drum set Mary had dragged home that day.

Before long, Martin charged out the back door, hands over his ears. "Have you taken leave of your senses? You had to add drums and cymbals to your instrument collection?"

Donning an innocent countenance, Mary shrugged. "It seemed like a good idea at the time. No one was bidding on it at the auction."

"That's another thing. Where'd you get the money? I ain't got but a handful of change to my name."

"The band earns money I've tucked away. But it didn't cost anything. The auctioneer said I'd do him a favor taking it off his hands. That if he took it home his kids would want to keep it."

"So you did him a favor instead of us. Are you gonna teach them to play it?"

Mary leaned back on her elbows. "I don't know the first thing about playing a drum set."

"Has that ever stopped you? You could make music with a blacksmith's bellows."

"A bellows? If that's the case, I expect I can master drums and cymbals."

Seated next to her, Martin fished a cloth bag of Prince Albert tobacco from his overall pocket and rolled a cigarette. Instead of lighting it, he stretched out and laid his head in her lap, the way he did when they were first married and she brought lunch to him in the field. She stroked his bald head, pale as a fish belly compared to his suntanned face and neck.

The intimate and peaceful moment was shattered by an extended drum roll and clash of cymbals. The commotion startled a red hen settled among the bedraggled geraniums in the window box. With a squawk, she flapped her wings and landed in Martin's lap. "Jeez, Louise," he yelled while Mary laughed. "I'm movin' that contraption to the barn. Anybody who wants to beat on it can have an audience of cows. Come to think of it, why should I punish them? I'll take it to the dump."

He didn't carry out his threat, nor did he need to; none of the girls took to drumming with anything approaching seriousness. Mary tried her hand at it when she was home alone, but that rarely happened. The house nearly always overflowed with the constant tumult created by the girls and their friends. Evelyn's schoolmate, Shirley, stayed overnight so often that Martin called her his fifth daughter. She lived across the street from the Catholic church and, although Episcopalian, she often joined Evelyn at Mass and came home with them for dinner. Shirley set them all to giggling once when she remarked, "My dad says Episcopalians are just dehorned Catholics." Even their special guest, Father Adolph, guffawed.

Life in the Jones household was not all gaiety and music. Hazel had dropped out of school at sixteen to financially aid the family. At first she'd been a hired girl on a neighbor's farm; now she worked in town at Dolores's Hat Shoppe.

The younger girls complained that Hazel was Mary's pet, that she had a knack for getting out of chores. "Why doesn't Hazel have to help with dishes?" Gladys whined one evening.

"She does her part. She's bringing home a paycheck. At night is the only time she has to practice the cello. Sounds wonderful, doesn't it?" Mary waltzed across the room with a mop as her partner. "Hazel has perfect timing."

"No doubt about that," Gladys grumbled. "Whenever it's time to do chores, she needs to practice. As soon as chores are finished, she's finished with practice. That's good timing."

Dorothy added to the complaint, "She picks the biggest instruments to play and then makes us carry them. When she needs the sousaphone, she carries the mouthpiece and we end up lugging the instrument."

Hazel stroked a plaintive chord on the cello. "Be thankful I don't play the harp."

Gladys joked that Hazel had the deepest faith of any of them, and explained why to Evelyn's friend Shirley. "When we were little, Aunt Julia and Uncle Victor had been to California. When they came home Uncle Victor had a pocket watch he'd bought in a pawnshop. Hazel decided she had to have that watch and asked us to pray that he'd give it to her. We told her she better pray to Saint Jude, the patron of hopeless cases. Why would Uncle Victor give her his watch? Guess what, before leaving, he gave it to her. For no reason, he gave it to her. Saint Jude has been her favorite ever since."

Hazel had a litany of prayers and rhymes for evoking help from the saints. When something was lost, she sang, "Dear Saint Anthony, please come 'round, something's lost and can't be found." One of Mary's favorite stories was about the time Hazel hid Evelyn's First Communion rosary, and then made her recite the prayer. While Evelyn was on her knees beseeching Saint Anthony, Hazel *found* the rosary on a windowsill.

Hazel's faith in her petitions to Saints Anthony and Jude became Mary's own during the summer of 1924, when someone dear to her couldn't be found and the case appeared hopeless.

After You've Gone

And left me crying ~~~

Fanning herself with a church bulletin after Mass, Mary noticed her brother Clem's wife talking to Clem's boss. Catherine seemed agitated, so when the man left, Mary hurried over.

"I'm glad to see you," Catherine said. "I'm worried about Clem." She spoke in a low tone; her three young girls were playing nearby.

"What's wrong? Is he sick?"

"No. Well, I don't know. He's not home. You know, the lumbering crew stays at a site all week and sometimes stay over the weekend. Clem didn't come home last night so I assumed he stayed to work. But the foreman said the men all collected their pay envelopes and left about four o'clock. He remembers seeing Clem leave in his car."

Martin joined the women, and Mary filled him in on the situation. "Calm down," he advised. "Catherine, I think you should go home. Chances are Clem will show up before long. He might be there now."

"I suppose you're right. I can't imagine where he's been, though."

With Catherine gone, Martin said, "I can imagine where he is. Off on one of his benders. He's done that before and been away two, three days, so I don't know what Catherine's so excited about this time."

"He hasn't done that for a long time. He's cut back on his drinking."

"Yeah, and he's fallen off the wagon plenty of times. Come on, find the girls and let's go home and have dinner. We'll see how the day plays out."

That evening, Papa stopped by to say there was still no word, and he was going to spend the night with Catherine and the kids. Watching him drive away, Mary said, "This isn't like Clem."

"Aww, it is like him. I keep telling you, it's been only a day."

"A day and a half, since he left work yesterday."

"Okay, a day and a half. Betcha he'll show up at work tomorrow."

Martin sounded sincere; she wanted to believe him. She crossed herself. "I pray he will. You know, he's never had much gumption but he's a good boy."

"He ain't a boy; he's a man with responsibilities." Martin chucked a cigarette butt into the yard. "Reminds me of your uncle Pat. Ran off after his wife died givin' birth and left three kids. No one ever heard from him again."

Mary jerked her head toward him. "Now you're saying Clem did run off and we'll never see him again? And you're saying this runs in my family?"

"Now, now; don't get your Irish up. I didn't mean that. Clem's gonna show up with some cock and bull story about where he's been."

"I hope you're right. But for your information, Uncle Pat didn't up and leave his kids. The way I remember it from Mother and Papa talking, he was heartbroken when Aunt Rose died. He didn't know what to do with a newborn and two little ones. Aunt Rose's sister took the baby to Minnesota. She was nursing a baby anyway and had enough milk for two. The other two kids stayed in Dougherty with a cousin. I don't know if Uncle Pat even had much to say about it. Seems to me they took the kids while he was grieving, trying to figure things out. He left town and that was the last anyone heard of him." Mary hid her face in her lap and sobbed, "I can't bear the thought of never seeing Clem again."

Martin wrapped his arm around her shoulder and they watched darkness fall.

Night passed with no word from Clem, and another day, and another. Days became a week, a month. Hazel's salary paid the rent on Aunt Catherine's house and kept food in the pantry. In town all day at the millinery, she reported the latest gossip to her parents. "One fella said Uncle Clem had been bootlegging whiskey from Canada."

"Absolutely not," Mary said.

Martin scoffed, too. "Whenever someone gets in trouble people start talkin' bootleggin'. That doesn't sound like Clem. But I guess we don't always know people the way we think we do."

One day Hazel sent her employer's young son to the farm to ask her father to come to town. "I'm going, too," Mary said, "and don't tell me I can't."

Hazel met them out front. "Oh, Mama, a body was found near the reservation. The sheriff asked me to come see if it's Clem, but I couldn't go alone."

While the two women hugged and comforted one another, Martin told Hazel, "You stay here in the store; we'll go."

Mary's prayers were answered; the body wasn't Clem. When she later learned that it was a Chippewa who lived on the reservation north of town, she scolded, "Land sakes, scare a person half to death. Can't that fool sheriff tell an Indian from a freckled, red-headed Irishman?"

"He was just makin' sure," Martin said. "Fella appears to have died of natural causes. No sign of any trouble. Probably a heart attack."

Still, stories circulated; with all that drinking at the reservation, maybe the Indian owed Clem money for booze. They got in a fight and Clem accidentally killed him and ran off to hide. "Ridiculous," Mary said. "He's a gentle soul."

Gradually, Clem McLaughlin's disappearance became yesterday's news. Catherine had no choice but to go live with her parents in South Dakota. Hazel purchased train tickets for Catherine and her daughters and brought them to say goodbye to Mary before driving them to the depot. "It's just 'til Clem comes home," Catherine said through tears.

"Of course. I'll send him to you as soon as he returns. After I give that boy a good scolding."

Watching the car lumber down the lane, dust boiling up behind, Mary fingered the locket around her neck. Worn on her wedding day and not often since, she had taken it out of her trunk after Clem disappeared. It had been a birthday present to her mother from nine-year-old Clem. He'd earned two dollars working an entire week for a farmer and had sent away for the locket. Mary recalled the pleasure on his face when he fastened the chain around Mother's neck and said, "The M is for Martha and McLaughlin and Mother."

Clem's whereabouts remained a mystery. Catherine stayed where she was, a grass widow struggling to raise three daughters without a father. Meanwhile, Mary lit a vigil candle for Clem each time she attended church. At home she prayed daily to Saints Jude and Anthony, entertaining hope that working together they would one day find Clem and send him back where he belonged.

In November, when her younger sister, Anna, died from peritonitis from a ruptured appendix, Mary became incapacitated. The siblings she had helped raise were as beloved as her own children and she was losing them one by one.

After Anna's burial, she crawled into bed to indulge her grief. Martin and the girls brought food but she only picked at it. Three days later, Hazel came into the room and said, "Mama, there's talk around town that you've had a nervous breakdown."

Mary came upright so quickly her head spun with dizziness. "Who said that?"

"I don't know where it started but Tillie Jepsen came into the store and asked about you, said she heard about your breakdown. I told her that wasn't so and I asked who told her such a thing. She hemmed and hawed and said she couldn't recall."

"This gossipy old town. Every time a woman feels poorly she's either going through the change or she's had a breakdown. I can't imagine how anyone outside this household would even know I'm in bed. Even Alice doesn't know. Not that she'd tell anyone. She's mourning, too."

"I told my boss you were feeling awful sad about your sister, but how that got to be a nervous breakdown is beyond me. Well, I'm going down to fix supper. Do you want anything?"

"No. I'm too angry to eat. A nervous breakdown, for Heaven's sake."

"Maybe you should get up and around and let folks see for themselves that you're all right."

"When I get up and around it won't be to please others."

"Okay. If you want anything, give a holler."

After Hazel left, Mary dragged herself to the vanity and looked in the mirror. She shuddered at the crone looking back at her. Her hair, a nest of burrs and thistles, had a new ribbon of gray across the top, like a crown. Well, she thought, Jesus wore a crown of thorns and I have a crown of sorrows. I've lost Mother, Robbie, Victor, dear sweet Julia and Anna. God only knows where Clem is. Who's next? Martin? One of my daughters?

Berating herself for daring to compare herself to Jesus, a quote from Saint Francis de Sales ran through her mind. She had memorized it as a schoolgirl.

~~~ Have no fear for what tomorrow may bring. The same loving God who cares for you today will take care of you tomorrow and every day. God will either shield you from suffering or give you unfailing strength to bear it. Be at peace, then, and put aside all anxious thoughts and imaginations. ~~~

She hadn't been shielded from suffering, so that meant she would be given the strength to bear whatever came her way. I'm in your hands, she told God as she combed her hair. Then she dressed and stepped into the hall.

Descending the stairs, she felt an arm on her shoulder. She turned; there was no one there, but a wave of comfort washed over her, like a voice telling her that her daughters would always be with her.

Years later, she would recognize the significance of that silent message.

SWINGING SISTERS

As Time Goes By

No matter what the future brings, as time goes by ~~~

Thanks to Lottie Lund, folks in and around Park Rapids "kept up with the Joneses" through the social reporter's items in the *Hubbard County Weekly*. It became Mary's pleasure to read them aloud to the family at suppertime.

~~~ March 1, 1925

The Jones Quartet had the honor of playing for the conductor of the Minneapolis-St. Paul Symphony Orchestra, Mr. Henri Verbrugghen, who urged them to continue their studies in music. They were further honored when Mr. Verbrugghen played his $35,000 Stradivarius violin for them. Gladys Jones, herself a violinist, said, "It's the most beautiful instrument I've ever seen and the most beautiful sound I've ever heard. Only angels singing would be sweeter music." ~~~

~~~ March 21, 1925

St. Peter's church hosted a potluck supper and St. Patrick's Day *ceili* in the church basement. Entertainment was provided by the Jones Quartet and their mother, Mrs. Mary Jones. The group played a selection of well-known Irish favorites, as well as jazzy tunes of the day. Guests kicked up their heels to the lively music and their happy faces bespoke messages of appreciation for this festive event. ~~~

~~~~ April 20, 1925

Mr. and Mrs. Martin Jones and Lawrence McLaughlin have returned from a visit to San Antonio, Texas, where they visited Mr. Jones's sister and family. While Mr. Jones enjoyed the warmer clime, Mr. McLaughlin found it too warm and dry. Mary Jones exclaimed that the trip was worthwhile if only to see the bluebonnets in bloom. "I've never seen an ocean," she said, "but I imagine it must look something like the acres of bluebonnets rippling across the prairie." ~~~

Although Mary treasured the press clippings about her daughters, the attention they received had a down side. If it wasn't Hazel in a snit about costumes or Evelyn wanting to be recognized on her own, Gladys came home one day behaving like a prima donna.

I have a song to sing, O, I have a song to sing ~~~

Mary glanced up from the sewing machine when Gladys stormed into the kitchen and tossed her books on the table. Dorothy and Evelyn burst in right behind Gladys. "How was school?" Mary asked.

Dorothy and Evelyn chorused their practiced, "Fine."

"Not fine." Gladys pulled a jug of milk from the icebox.

Before Mary could ask the reason, Evelyn explained, "Her bloomers are in a knot about Miss Finn."

"Evie, let your sister speak for herself. Gladys, what's wrong?"

"I tried out for the school musical, *The Pirates of Penzance*, and…." She made a face. "Ugh, this milk is spoiled."

Mary tasted the milk. "It's just warm. Your pa's gone to get some ice."

Evelyn picked up the story her sister had started. "Gladdie's mad because she wanted the part of Mabel, the prettiest maiden."

Dorothy added, "Because Mabel gets to kiss Frederic and Tom Feeney is playing Frederic."

"Girls, please."

"I did want the part of Mabel," Gladys admitted, "but it has nothing to do with Tom Feeney. I told Miss Finn I'd take the part of any of the daughters, but she said I was needed in the orchestra. I told her I could sing as well as play an instrument but she wouldn't listen. She repeated that I was needed in the orchestra."

"I'm sure that's true. With you and Dorothy in Senior Orchestra and Evelyn in Junior…my goodness, I'm proud of you all."

Evelyn butted in again. "When I played one of the wise men in the Christmas program in first grade, Sister Gregory said I did a top-notch job. Maybe your acting was punk, so Miss Finn said she needed you in the orchestra to make you feel better."

"My acting is not punk. I'm on the Declamation Team, in Dramatic Reading. Dramatic reading, in case you don't know, is acting. We won awards at state contest."

Dorothy reminded Gladys, "The team won third place, not you."

"I didn't say I won. I said we, meaning the team."

Mary stepped in. "Gladdie, I'm sorry you're disappointed, but you're a talented musician and you must use that gift as God sees fit. Whether it's in the orchestra or in the play."

"God wasn't picking the cast. Miss Finn was."

"Don't be pert. Teachers are guided by God. Make the best of it and enjoy yourself. We'll all be there rooting for you."

"I'll yodel instead of rooting," Evelyn said. "Yo-de-ladee-yo-de-ladee whooo."

A giggle overcame Gladys. "You sound like a coyote howling."

Within the week, Gladys came home with news that assuaged her earlier disappointment. She'd been chosen to crown the Blessed Mother at the church's annual ceremony on Mother's Day. "You should've seen the look on Jeanette's face," she said. "She'd been bragging that she was going to be picked. I'd rather do this than have the lead in the operetta."

Mary laid aside her mending. "Gladdie; I'm delighted you were chosen but please forget about competing with Jeanette. It's unbecoming and beneath you."

"Yes, Mama," Gladys said. "You're right."

That honor carried her through the year and into January 1926, when she won a sterling silver medal at the Minnesota State High School Music Contest in St. Paul.

Quoting a Twin Cities newspaper, Lottie Lund wrote for the *Hubbard County Weekly:*

~~~ Miss Gladys Jones gave an award winning performance, playing *La Primavera* in E Major from Vivaldi's Four Seasons. The judges seemed to hang on every note as Miss Jones alternated between a classic rendition and a spirited, playful mood, illustrating her range of musical talent.

We here in Park Rapids extend our congratulations to Miss Jones and look forward to her and her sisters' next local performance. ~~~

How Ya Gonna Keep 'em Down on the Farm

After they've seen Paree ~~~

The new year brought a decision from Mary and Martin that changed things for the whole family. Lottie Lund spread the news via the *Hubbard County Weekly*.

~~~ January 20, 1926

This reporter has learned that one of our town's favorite families will be leaving us. Mr. and Mrs. Martin Jones and their four daughters are relocating to San Antonio, Texas. Mr. Jones suffers from asthma and has been advised to give up farming and seek a warmer climate. We bid this family a fond adieu. We shall miss them, personally, as well as the entertainment the Jones Quartet provided the community. Our loss is San Antonio's gain.

No doubt the talented girls will soon be performing under the city's bright lights. The quartet will play Saturday night at the auditorium, beginning at eight. Don't miss being there to give this family a warm sendoff. ~~~

Martin crabbed, "Lottie could've just said we're movin'. Ain't nobody's business why. Next thing you know over-the-fence talk will have me in a sanitarium with TB."

A warm sendoff, or any kind of sendoff, was not what the youngest Jones daughter had in mind. While the rest of the family prepared to move, Evelyn lapsed into an extended pout about having to move before the school year ended. "Why can't we wait until school's out?" she asked too many times to suit Mary.

"Let me repeat, we're moving now because farmers like to move in March before time to put in crops."

"Pa's not going to farm."

"I've answered that, too. The man taking over this farm wants to get started putting in his crops."

"And I want to finish the school year. I could live with Aunt Alice. Or Grandpa. He needs a housekeeper."

"Alice has a houseful of little ones and it looks as if Pa will be moving in with her. Since Anna died, there's no one to keep house for him. I'd take him with us but he doesn't like hot weather."

"Then I could help Aunt Alice take care of the kids and Grandpa."

"Her house is crammed to the rafters. I'll not add to that by asking if you can stay there."

"I'd be more help than nuisance. I'll ask her."

"Don't you dare."

"I'll bet I could stay with Shirley's family. Or rent a room at the boarding house where some of the teachers live. I'd be in good hands."

"Stop being bullheaded. We can't afford to pay rent. And you'd be lonesome before we were ten miles out of town."

"Piffle. I wouldn't be lonesome."

"Besides, you'll go to Catholic school in San Antonio. I've always wanted my girls taught by nuns. There'll be museums, the Alamo, those wonderful old missions. So much history. One of the first things I want to do is see a talking movie, and the opera and ballet. The Jones Quartet will have more opportunities to play than you have here. Think about that."

On that note, Evelyn stomped off and up the stairs.

Let A Smile Be Your Umbrella

On a rainy, rainy day ~~~

Gladys encountered the steaming Evelyn on the landing. "It'll be all right, Kiddo," she soothed. "I'd like to graduate with my friends, too, but I'm making the best of it."

"Bully for you." Evelyn stalked into her and Dorothy's room.

Gladys followed. "Want help packing?"

"Nah; I'm sorting books. Aunt Alice's kids can have *The Bobbsey Twins* set but I'm taking *Anne of Green Gables* to read on the long boring drive to Texas." Evelyn picked up the homemade cloth doll Santa had brought her the Christmas Robbie died. "Antonia's going along but she's not happy about moving either."

Gladys's eyes roamed over the room, the faded wallpaper, the worn rag rug next to the bed, and a cobweb crocheted from door to window. She moved to the window and watched sleet stitch an icy pattern on the glass. "Remember the stage we built out by the barn? We practiced dancing; hours on end in the blazing sun."

"Yeah; that was fun; pretending we were in vaudeville. Mama sat on a bench as our audience, or pretending to be our manager."

"The manager role was Hazel's. She always wanted to be boss."

"Still does."

"Remember the time Mama was on stage pretending to be an opera star? She was making up words to sound Italian. Pretty soon someone applauded, and it was the Watkins agent. Mama looked surprised and then she just took a bow and sat down with the agent to look at his products."

"Pretty funny," Evelyn said.

"We've had good times here. Playing in the haymow, running in the pasture, swimming in the creek, feeding baby piglets. I won't miss feeding the pigs, though." Gladys pinched her nose for emphasis.

"Me neither, and I won't miss Mama killing chickens for dinner, or butchering day." Evelyn pinched her nose, too, and released it. "Did you ever watch the men do that? I didn't. It made me sick thinking about it. I'd bury my head in a pillow but I could still hear the pigs or cows squealing." She stretched out on the bed. "Know what else I hated? Gathering eggs. I'm afraid of chickens."

Gladys giggled. "Afraid of chickens?"

"They're mean. They come charging at you with their beaks and claws and that red flappy thing. That big rooster with patchwork feathers was a terror, strutting around like he owned the place."

"That reminds me of a story. When Hazel and I were little there was a hen that laid her eggs on the roof of the henhouse. In summer, Mama always sent us out first thing in the morning to collect eggs, before it got hot. One day she told us to leave those that were in the sun. When they were hard boiled she'd use them for potato salad."

"Ha, ha, yolks on you."

"You and Dorothy weren't any smarter. One time Mama and Aunt Julia were papering the kitchen. They weren't sure they'd have enough paper so she told you and Dorothy to go tell Pa he needed to go over to Grandpa's and borrow the paper stretcher. She and Aunt Julia sat on the porch watching you two walk off. They let you get halfway to the field before she sent Hazel to bring you back."

Evelyn cracked a smile. "I kind of remember that."

"You know, we can take along the good memories."

"Oh, now you're Pollyanna again. Look for the silver lining and all that piffle."

"Well, Evie, you can sit here and be a sourpuss all you want but we're still moving. Get used to it. I'm going to see what Hazel and Dorothy are doing."

"Wait for me. I'll pack later."

They found Dorothy advising Hazel on what to take along and what to leave behind. "That frock's out of style. Give it to the church rummage sale."

"Horse feathers. I bought it at a rummage sale." Hazel packed the pastel green voile dress with a beaded bodice. "I'll wear it when we play concerts. And, listen, all of you, from now on when we play, no five and dime rhinestones. We're going to the city. We'll wear pearls. Coco Chanel says women should wear ropes and ropes of pearls."

"Which rich uncle died and left all his money to us?" Dorothy asked.

"Not real ones. Coco says pearls should be very fake and very beautiful."

"Now it's Coco, is it? Maybe you can get your good friend to send us some of her beautiful pearls. Fake, but beautiful."

Evelyn dug into Hazel's hat collection, trying on one after another. "I wish we didn't have to wear hats to church. They mess my hair."

"What hair?" Gladys asked. "With that bob of yours you could be a nun."

"Oh, come on. In case you haven't noticed, women have been bobbing their hair since the start of the Roaring Twenties."

Gladys tossed her head, allowing her shoulder-length curls to dance against her rouged cheeks. "I've had bobbed hair and spit curled bangs but I prefer long hair. It's a woman's crowning glory."

"If Mama heard you say that she'd make you go to Confession for being vain."

"She still has long hair. She just twists it up in back."

"Well," Evelyn argued, "if you and Hazel update your style maybe you old maids will find husbands in Texas."

"I'm hardly an old maid," Gladys argued.

"Me, neither," Hazel added. "I'm glad I haven't married. Then all of you would be leaving and I'd be here by my lonesome."

"You wouldn't be lonesome. You'd have that Viking who's taking over the farm. He can't keep his eyes off you when he's here. Play your cards right and you could marry him and live here on the farm forever."

"You're the one who wants to stay here. You marry him. It would give folks something to talk about; Evelyn Jones, child bride. Nope, not a chance my staying here. I'm excited about finishing high school. Mama says I'm going back if she has to scrub rich people's floors to pay my way."

"Won't you be embarrassed going to high school at your age?" Evelyn asked.

Their mother answered the question from the doorway. "Young lady, no one should ever be embarrassed about getting an education, no matter her age. Now, go to your room and finish packing."

Within a week the farmstead stood empty. With Pa and Mama leading the way in the Model T truck, and Hazel at the helm of Grandpa McLaughlin's old Essex sedan, the family headed south.

Wiping mist from the car window, Gladys swallowed a lump in her throat and bid a silent farewell to the familiar landscape that had been home for eighteen years. Bony tree arms and fingers stretched into the half-lit morning sky. The new owner's nanny goat, her udder swollen, bleated into the wind. One side of the weathered barn had long ago collapsed off the stone foundation. She recalled years earlier when a sign painter came and she and her sisters watched a message form on the side of the barn: Chew Mail Pouch Tobacco. Mama disliked the advertisement, saying the tobacco company people had probably never scrubbed tobacco stains out of shirts or scoured spittoons with lye water.

Just past the covered bridge over Beaver Creek, the wind carried the stench from a pig farm into the car. "That's something I won't miss," Gladys said.

Still obstinate, Evelyn mumbled, "You think there's no poop in Texas? It's a big state with lots of cattle and horses and swine. They must have mountains of manure."

Deep In The Heart Of Texas

The stars at night, are big and bright ~~~

Mary's weary eyes widened when Martin eased the truck onto Marshall Street and idled in front of a two story Spanish style house. A sign in the shape of a horse's head, hanging from a hitching post in the yard, identified the property as the residence of Frank J. Walters, D.V.M. Entrance around back.

"Here we are, Lass. The old horse made it." He patted the dashboard as if it were a horse's rump.

"I never dreamed the house would be this swell. Come on, let's go in."

"Wait, I'll park out back." He guided the truck into an alley and parked next to the carriage house where Doc Walters lived and had his office. Widowed, childless, and in his late fifties, Doc had told Martin he preferred the cottage to the big house he had shared with his wife. His practice was mainly horses owned by ranchers and breeders or those stabled at racetracks and rodeos. He'd hired Martin to tend the office and as groundskeeper and maintenance man for the property. The family also had a rent-free furnished house. Manna from Heaven, Mary called it.

The girls' car rumbled into the alley, with Gladys honking the horn to herald their arrival. Evelyn jumped out, hitched up her knickers and gaped upward. "Can't get over the sky. It must stretch for a thousand miles."

"You're not in Park Rapids anymore," Martin said.

"Or Kansas. You know, like in *The Wizard of Oz.*"

Gladys stretched her arms back and forth. "It's deliciously warm."

"I told you we wouldn't need our coats anymore," Dorothy said.

"It gets cold here now and then," Mary said.

All four girls looked at Dorothy, and Gladys spoke for them. "We gave away our coats."

"You what? Evie, your coat was practically new."

"I know, but…yesterday, when we stopped for breakfast, I don't know where it was, we saw this mission with a sign saying they needed warm clothing. Dorothy suggested we leave our coats there instead of carrying them with us down here."

Mary shook her head. "Well, that was a wonderful thing to do. May the memory of your generosity keep you warm during the first cold snap."

Laughing, Martin changed the subject. "How'd the car run?"

"Great," Hazel answered. "But, boy, the roads are awful here. They're more like trails. I expected to meet a herd of cattle."

"What kind of mileage did you get?"

"Gosh, I have no idea. When we ran low on gas, I stopped at a filling station, told the boy to fill 'er up, check the oil and tires, wash the windows. We'd go to the biffy, get a bottle of pop, and stretch our legs."

"Just asked about mileage, Hazelbon, not the entire trip."

Evelyn grabbed her mother's hand and pulled her away to explore the grounds. "Pa," she soon yelled, "you didn't say there was a swimming pool."

"If you can call it that," Mary said. Stagnant rainwater stood on the bottom; moss covered the sides and ragged grass rambled along the foundation.

"It's small," Evelyn said when her father joined them.

"Doc calls it a lap pool, just for swimming back and forth. I didn't mention it 'cause he was fixin' on coverin' it over. Maybe I can repair it."

"Yowza, wait'll my friends back home hear we have a swimming pool. They'll think we're rich. Doc must be rich."

"I reckon he makes a fair livin', but this place belonged to his wife's family. They're the ones with money. Old money."

"Who cares how old it is? Wow, a swimming pool."

Pleased to see Evelyn enthusiastic again, Mary said, "Come on everybody. I haven't seen the house yet and we're looking at a hole in the ground."

"You go ahead," Martin said. "I'll mosey around a bit and then start unpacking the truck." He dodged a birdbath and cut a beeline toward Doc's carriage house.

Entering the kitchen ahead of her mother, Evelyn stopped in her tracks. "Well, I'll be darned. Cement floors."

"Your pa says it's Mexican tile. I wonder how I'll keep it clean."

"With soap and water, I guess. You can't hurt cement." She pushed a button on the wall, bringing on an overhead light. "Pa never said the house has electric."

"Electricity, not electric. He told us all about the house; you just weren't listening because you were put out about moving. Your sisters are probably upstairs choosing bedrooms."

"Story of my life; little sister gets the leftovers and hand-me-downs. Hey, look; there's a set of stairs back here and another set in the front hall."

"Servants used the back stairs."

"Doc had servants?"

"Well, maybe not, but that's what the stairs are for. You'll probably find an attic room upstairs where a maid might have slept."

"I'm gonna explore." Evelyn took the back stairs two at a time.

Mary explored, too, beginning in the kitchen. A closet held mops, brooms, a dustpan, an ironing board and electric iron, a carpet sweeper and a vacuum cleaner. Doc's wife had everything. All these electric appliances. Back home, windmill generated power was unpredictable and Alice's house had not yet been hooked up to rural electric. I won't tell her about my electricity until she gets it, too, Mary decided.

In the cupboards she found a silver tea set wrapped in flannel, two sets of china, one fancy, one plain for everyday use; the same with eating utensils, one an ornate silver design and one utilitarian with bone handles. Drawers were filled with kitchen linens of all kinds. "This is all so nice," she said to Martin when he came in the door and glanced around. "It's as if people were living here one day and then just up and deserted it."

"That's pretty much the way it was, according to Doc. His wife died suddenly, and he moved out back."

"Sad," Mary said, and wandered into the other rooms.

Within days, the girls were back in school, enrolled at Blessed Sacrament Academy, run by the Sisters of the Incarnate Word and Blessed Sacrament. Mary learned that the sisters had recently moved their motherhouse and novitiate from Halletsville to San Antonio. They had not intended to open a school, but once they took in a few private students, demand increased. Soon they welcomed boarders and day students, elementary and high school. The academy brought back dear memories of her schooling in Iowa; now it thrilled her to have her daughters studying at a Catholic academy. She made a mental note to write and tell Sister Pius about the move.

By July, Mary faced a conflict. Martin had already decided that the Texas heat was unbearable and that Washington would suit him better. Mary argued, "Eddie's wife says it rains every day. The doctor didn't suggest a rainy climate for you."

Martin only shrugged, and Mary continued. "I've lost track of how many times we've moved. One farm to the next, county to county, because the rent was a dollar cheaper a month or the pasture was greener down the road."

"Had to make a livin'. I even worked day labor when farmin' was bad."

Mary softened her tone. "I know. You worked hard. But you're lucky to have a steady salary now. It's not risky like farming. You don't know what kind of work is available in Washington. And the girls have summer jobs, and we can't afford another trek across the country."

Martin ended up going by himself, to check things out. Mary handled Doc's office, assuring him that Martin would be back soon. After three weeks of endless rain out there, he had the Northwest out of his system. Mary silently took credit, her secret weapon had worked; a novena that her husband wouldn't like Washington. Confident they wouldn't be moving, she accepted a job teaching third grade at Stephen F. Austin Elementary, an easy walk from home to the Victorian two-story limestone building built in the last century.

When the girls returned to school in September, Hazel, Dorothy and Gladys were invited to join the one hundred member Incarnate Word College Orchestra. Mary had been right when she told Evelyn that more opportunities would present themselves in San Antonio, although Evelyn was peeved that she hadn't been asked. "You will be when you're a junior or senior," Mary assured her.

The Jones home once again became a gathering place for friends. When the house grew too noisy, Martin took refuge at Doc's bungalow, where the two sat outdoors under the vast starlit sky, smoking, visiting, and enjoying the music drifting toward them across the lawn.

Doc came to consider the Joneses his family and the girls called him Uncle Doc. He told Mary and Martin, "From what I've seen and heard, your daughters have the potential to become professional entertainers."

His opinion was golden with Mary and Martin; him being an educated man. And three of them were already playing in a professional orchestra. More and more, they encouraged their daughters' love for music and for sharing their talent with the public.

Ain't Misbehavin'

I don't stay out late, don't care to go, I'm home about eight ~~~

Doc's comment about the girls' potential prodded Mary into contacting Professor J.B. Tremblay. He had taught music in Park Rapids and he and his wife, Louise, moved to San Antonio last year. The professor had an inside line to talent scouts and booking agents, so Louise soon found engagements for The Jones Quartet. Doc Walters kept his ears open for word about wealthy Texans having parties for which they liked to hire local entertainers.

Although Mary and Martin were reluctant to let the girls go on the road, Louise had her way and arranged a summer on the Texas Theater Circuit based in Dallas. On a whirlwind tour, the Quartet, chaperoned by Louise, played theaters across Texas, as well as at rodeos, tea parties, debutante balls, cotillions, and private parties.

Mary wasted no time getting to the mailbox each day, hoping for postcards from the girls. She went directly to Doc's office to read the mail aloud to Martin. Squinting at Hazel's scrawl on a picture postcard of the beach at Corpus Christi, she read:

~~~ Dear Mama and Pa. Having a wonderful time. We miss you. The lady at the boarding house treats us like we're her girls. She lets us do laundry and ironing and take bubble baths. Last night a cowboy was giving Dorothy a line a block long, but we're not letting her or Evie associate with the rough element. Louise keeps a sharp eye on "the kids." And on me and Gladdie. Ha. Louise is strict, but she's a good egg. I know you worry about us going to Sunday Mass. We never miss. Sometimes we go right from the dance and then go home (wherever that is) and sleep. Speaking of sleep, I should be in dreamland. Evie said to tell you hi. I think that's what she said—her mouth's full of bobby pins. She's setting her hair and Gladdie is polishing her toenails pink. That's her current favorite color. Love, Hazelbon ~~~

That card was the first of many that would go into Mary's scrapbook.

Puttin' On The Ritz

Pants with stripes and cutaway coat, perfect fits, puttin' on the ritz ~~~

Sleep deprived and her neck stiff, Gladys stepped out the door of Hotel Rita in Brownsville, wishing the band made enough money to afford decent rooms. It was clean, but she had tossed about on the sagging mattress, equally disturbed by a toilet running in another room. "Count your blessings," Evelyn had mumbled. "At least this hotel has toilets."

Gladys scanned the horizon, and then motioned to the others to come outside when a sleek black automobile approached the hotel.

"It's a Doozy," Louise said, nonchalant, as if she saw one every day.

The driver of the Deusenberg bounced out and darted around to the passenger side nearest the sidewalk. "Afternoon, ladies. Hudson Wanamaker at your service. Manuel will be along shortly to pick up your instruments." Just then a pickup appeared; Wanamaker waited until the instruments were loaded and the music makers were settled inside before starting the Doozy.

"Not much out here except a lot of Texas," Dorothy commented after they'd passed miles and miles of brush and cotton fields. "Oh, look." She pointed to a sign, and she Evelyn read together. "His tenor voice/She thought divine/Till whiskers scratched/Sweet Adeline/Burma Shave."

Louise said, "Did you know the first of those was in Minnesota? That's where Burma Shave is made."

"Nope, didn't know that," Evelyn said, and yawned.

Finally, up ahead, there appeared a wrought iron gate, at least ten feet tall, with the letter K in the center of each door. A brown-skinned man wearing a sombrero opened the portals to King Ranch and Wanamaker sailed the Doozy through, followed by Manuel in the truck.

The limo glided along a gravel lane lined with pecan trees and mesquite shrubs. Enormous cattle grazed in herds of a dozen or fewer, while white cowbirds rode astride the bovines' backs or on their outstretched horns. In other areas, the land lay blanketed with sagebrush, cactus and chaparrals of dwarf shrubs, interspersed with columbine, salvia, verbena, and primroses.

"Uncle Doc knows the people here," Gladys said. "He told me its history."

"Tell us," Hazel said, "it'll break the monotony."

"He said it was started in 1853 by Captain Richard King and some other fella, a Texas Ranger. I think his name was Lewis."

"Lewis and Clark?" Evelyn asked.

"No, not that one. He was shot dead by the husband of a woman the ranger was running around with. King bought Lewis's share of the ranch at auction. When King died he left the place a half-million bucks in debt. His wife took over running the ranch and paid all the bills."

"Good for her," Louise said. "Women are always, well, usually, good managers. But today's Mrs. King is a generation or two removed from that one. Still, it appears that she or someone is managing things properly."

Gladys pointed ahead. "Look, there's the house." Atop a grassy knoll, the sprawling white mansion boasted front pillars thicker around than rain barrels, doors and windows accented with etched glass, wraparound galleries, and second and third floor balconies from which one could look out over the King empire. In the circular driveway leading to the house stood another car.

"That's a Pierce-Arrow," Louise said.

"How do you know so much about cars?" Gladys asked.

"The professor is an automobile buff. He keeps me informed."

On the lawn, four mariachi band members strolled, seemingly making music for their own enjoyment. "Competition," Hazel said.

"No, they'll be greeting guests," Louise explained. "We'll be in the ballroom."

Mr. Wanamaker opened the car door and helped each woman step out. He and Manuel unloaded the instruments while a maid ushered the musicians inside. "Mrs. King instructed me to show you to the salon," she said. "This way, please."

She led them under a crystal chandelier suspended from a sparkling white ceiling that seemed a mile away to Gladys, and then through a hall awash in thick Oriental carpet runners embossed with a fancy scrolled K every few feet. Peeking into rooms, Gladys noted one that appeared to be for men only, with leather-covered furniture and a gun collection on one wall. The opposite wall held a stuffed deer head, several pair of steer horns, and a floor to ceiling oil painting of Captain King, she guessed, surrounded by cattle. In the dining room, the table was set for perhaps fifty people. Across the hall, a parlor looked somber and uninviting with its dark Victorian pieces, while a sitting room offered wicker tables, and sofas and chairs upholstered in flowered chintz.

The salon, a glass-enclosed area off the ballroom, provided the perfect niche for a small band. The corner overlooked a well-groomed garden of yellow roses, whose perfume wafted in through open windows. The maid instructed, "Make yourselves comfortable. I'll be back with food and drinks."

When she returned, rolling a cart, Mrs. King appeared, too. Her cobalt blue taffeta gown rustled as she moved; diamond studded combs held her black upswept hair in place, and chains of diamonds encircled her taut neck and slender wrists.

She spoke to Louise. "I'm Lourdes King. Delighted that you accepted my invitation to play. Doc Walters speaks highly of the young ladies."

"Thank you. Allow me to introduce Hazel, Gladys, Dorothy, and Evelyn."

The hostess acknowledged each name with a nod and turned again to Louise. "The dining room doors will be open while we dine. I'd like background music, not loud, mind you, just background."

"I understand. I've planned classics."

"Perfect. After dinner the men will adjourn to the library for a cigar and we ladies will freshen up. When we come to the ballroom, a mix of music will do. We have an eclectic group of friends. Perhaps eccentric would be a better word for some of them." Smiling at her last comment, she added, "If you run out of beverages or food, summon a waiter. Oh, and we won't be sitting down to dinner for a while, so feel free to wander outdoors. The maid will summon you."

"Thank you, Mrs. King. That's kind of you. I hope you like our program."

"I'm sure I shall. Now I must leave. My guests are arriving."

As the hostess swished away, Evelyn said, "She didn't order that dress from the Sears catalog. Did you see her jewelry? She looks like she had an accident with the hall chandelier."

"Evelyn, control yourself," Louise said with an impish grin.

Dorothy lifted the linen cloth covering the food and popped a morsel in her mouth. "Not bad. Wonder what it is."

"Rattlesnake," Evelyn said.

Gagging, Dorothy drew a handkerchief from her sleeve and coughed the bite into it. "You brat, that is not rattlesnake."

"Then why'd you spit it out? Try that black stuff. Rich folks call it caviar but it's fish eggs. Those slimy things are snails but they call them by some French name."

"Icky. You're spoiling my appetite. I'll starve before the night's over."

"With all those sandwiches? Of course there's no telling what's in them, maybe armadillo. Look out for shell. It'll break your teeth."

Shaking her head, Gladys said to Hazel, "You can take the girls out of the country but you can't take the country out of the girls."

The evening progressed as Lourdes King had said: dinner, a break, and then dancing. The glittering ballroom lights were no competition for the women's emeralds, diamonds, rubies, pearls, and jade adorning their fashionable gowns.

By contrast, the men's attire ranged from black tuxedos and patent leather slippers to western suits, string ties, and colorful boots.

During a break, a lanky, red haired man with a glamorous woman on his arm approached Louise. "Ma'am, could y'all play our song? *It Had To Be You.*"

"We'd be delighted, Governor Moody."

"We're playing for the governor," Gladys whispered to Hazel.

"I know. I caught that."

"Imagine, the little Jones girls from Minnesota."

Lourdes King asked Louise for an encore of the governor's requested song, and Gladys handled the lyrics. *"I wandered around and finally found, somebody who ~~~"*

On the starlit ride back to Hotel Rita, while Louise, Evelyn and Dorothy fell asleep on cushioned leather seats, Gladys and Hazel discussed plans for their next engagement. It wouldn't be as lavish as the King's party, but it was closer to home and dearer to their hearts.

By The Light Of The Silvery Moon

I wanna spoon, to my honey I'll croon ~~~

Sipping the first glass of champagne she'd ever had, and not much liking it, Mary watched folks mingle at her and Martin's Silver Wedding Anniversary party. Martin had, by himself, gone shopping and picked out her dusty rose chiffon dress, telling her it looked fetching on the store manikin so he knew it would look even more fetching on his wife.

Father Beck, a young priest from St. Mary's Parish, commenced the event with a blessing of the couple, and Mary's friend, Sister Mary Joseph, offered an anniversary toast. After the barbecue dinner, eaten at tables around the lap pool, Dorothy wheeled out a two-tiered cake replicating the wedding cake from years ago. While everyone enjoyed dessert and coffee, Gladys and Evelyn harmonized through a medley of old tunes, opening with one of their father's favorites, "*Oh, the object of my affection can change my complexion, from white to rosy red ~~~*"

Later, Hazel broke through the din of conversation and called for attention. "Dearest friends. I hope you're having as good a time as we are. Now, Pa has always been outnumbered by gender in this family so we give him his due whenever we can. He requested a song and I told him we'd play it if he'd dance with his bride. That took some persuasion because he's an oddity among Irishmen. He doesn't dance. Well, he claims he doesn't, but I've seen him step out a time or two and he can hold his own. Pa, grab your lovely lady and let's get started."

Mary let Martin escort her to the plywood dance floor, where he awkwardly wrapped his arms around her and waited for the music. Dorothy vocalized this time: "*Peg o' my heart, I love you, dear little girl, sweet little girl, sweeter than the rose of Erin ~~~*"

"Good thing it's dark. I'm blushing," Mary said loud enough for those close by to hear. Soon others joined the anniversary couple on the floor. Doc Walters cut in for a dance with Mary, while Martin waltzed with Sister Mary Joseph, her habit swirling above her black high-top oxfords.

Later, halting the music, Dorothy announced, "Now we have a surprise for Mama. When she and Pa were married, a schoolmate wrote a poem for her. I found it while snooping around upstairs and decided to read it today."

~~~ Eight years have come and gone, since first I saw the bride-to-be.
A little, dark-eyed girl she stood, just verging into womanhood.
Her First Communion she made, her mind so true and bright,
then Confirmation followed, her soul washed pure and white.

Again before us then she stood, while honors crowned her head,
her graduation then took place, in that year's class she led.
Years of teaching now are o'er, her schoolma'am's trials past.
She's engaged to teach a school of one, perchance a primary class.
May the blessed angels be with you, all through your married life,
and guard you as they have done, thru this cruel world of strife.
And may the man to whom this day, your heart and love betroth,
be ever kind and true to you, tho the journey's long and rough.
And when dark hair has turned to gray, last earthly blessings given,
may you both enter into the pearly gates of Heaven.
Is this wish of your sincere friend, Elizabeth Gassman ~~~

On the last line, Dorothy guided her parents back to the dance floor, while Gladys led the Jones quartet into the next tune: *"Just a song at twilight, when the lights are low, and the flickering shadows, softly come and go ~~~ "*

Top Hat, White Tie, And Tails

I'm dudein' up my shirt front, polishin' my nails ~~~

Although occupied with engagements, Gladys had not failed to notice that San Antonians were abuzz about the opening of the Majestic Theater.

Uncle Doc stopped her in the yard one evening to discuss it. "I hear the owner aims to provide wholesome programs that'll erase the stigma of vaudeville," he said. "You know, some religious groups call vaudeville the gateway to hell."

Gladys raised her eyebrows and grinned. "Yes; the devil's playground."

Uncle Doc smiled, too. "I heard that opening night's star will be Rudy Vallee, but the owner wants local acts to warm up the audience. Perfect venue for the Jones girls."

"It sounds like a possibility. I'll have Louise look into it."

Louise followed through and, after a brief audition, the Jones Quartet landed a plum spot on the program. Opening night would mark the beginning of Prosperity Week, with guests Governor Dan Moody, and General Jose M. Tapia representing the president of Mexico, Emilio Portes Gil.

The Majestic had an ordinary brick facade, but the inner decor was rumored to be as majestic as its name. The Chamber of Commerce boasted that "The Queen of Houston Street" had nearly four thousand seats, the largest theater in the south and second largest in the country. When the Quartet was allowed inside to practice, even the world traveler, Louise, dropped her jaw. "Fabulous," she exclaimed. "It's like a picturesque village in Switzerland or Austria."

Gladys sighed, remembering a neighbor who struggled to provide for his six children. "With so much poverty around us, the money spent on this place is sinful," she said. "What was it Will Rogers said? 'Ten men in our country could buy the whole world and ten million can't buy enough to eat.'" She was preaching to herself; the others were exploring the theater's splendor.

She wandered off, surrounded by lighted balconies and towers, tapestries, turrets, columns, statuary, and arches wrapped with fragrant greenery. Stuffed doves and peacocks perched on elaborately carved balcony rails. Baroque-style sconces adorned gaily-painted walls; bright Oriental carpets splashed color on the floors, and the velvet seats were plush enough to serve as thrones for royalty. Stars spattered the darkened ceiling and wispy clouds created by a machine trailed below. A cave-like alcove in the lower balcony lobby featured stalactites whose water dripped into a pond alive with golden fish. A balcony above the projection booth seated black audiences, who had a separate entrance, box office, and elevator, all behind the theater.

Gladys stepped onstage, from where the size of the theater became a reality.

"I've got stage fright," Dorothy said. "And there's not even an audience."

"There will be," Louise reminded her. "We must make this performance special. High society will be here."

Evelyn presented a soft shoe shuffle at center stage. "We've been in high society before. Even met the governor."

Dorothy scoffed. "Your bony knees will be knocking when you see all those important people."

Gladys sided with Evelyn. "High society is no more important in God's eyes, or mine, than Mama and Pa and Professor Tremblay and Uncle Doc."

Hazel's voice echoed from a box seat. "Start practicing. I want to hear how we'll sound from up here. I'll move around as you play."

Evelyn cupped her hands around her mouth and yelled, "Who died and made you director?"

Louise called to Hazel, "You need to practice with the band. Come on down."

Gladys watched, amused, as Hazel took her sweet time joining them. It was often evident that Hazel resented Louise taking over as leader of the group and telling Hazel what to do.

Secondhand Rose, I'm wearing secondhand clothes ~~~

Although Gladys insisted that the high society folks expected for opening night did not impress or concern her, what to wear did. Hazel solved the problem when she came home elated about a black rayon dress she'd bought at a secondhand store.

"It's a Chanel," she raved to Gladys and Mama, "an honest-to-gosh little black dress. I'm sure it's never been worn, or maybe once. I paid two dollars for it. Who on earth would give away a Chanel?"

Mama inspected the dress. "What's so special about this? No waistline or bustline. Not surprising. I've seen pictures of that woman where she's dressed like a man. A man's hat, baggy trousers, a loose sweater. And she encourages people to get a suntan, says it's good for them and they look better."

"She never said that," Hazel argued. "I read that she accidentally got too much sun while on someone's yacht, and when reporters saw her they thought she was making a fashion statement. Anyway, that has nothing to do with her designs.

She believes the simpler the better and that women's clothing has always been too confining."

"I won't argue with that, but this is too plain."

"Mama, simplicity is the beauty of it. When Chanel introduced her little black dress a few years ago she called it the most essential thing in a woman's wardrobe. *Vogue* magazine likened it to the Model A. They called it the Chanel Ford, a uniform for all women of taste."

"A uniform for a funeral if you ask me. A lace collar or some sequins wouldn't hurt a thing."

Hazel rescued the dress. "Don't you dare. But listen, how about making one like it for each of the others. We've all been stumped about what to wear. This is perfect."

"I could sew a dress that simple in an hour."

"Good. We'll buy the material and you can get busy."

"If I do say so myself, no one will know who's wearing a Chanel and who's wearing a Mary Jones."

The dresses took shape in Mama's capable hands, with Hazel watchful that her mother didn't add sequins or lace collars. "Worse yet, rickrack," Gladys said with a grimace. "Mama loses all good taste when it comes to rickrack."

A pretty girl is like a melody, that haunts you night and day ~~~

Mary knew her pride in the dresses was justified when Louise saw Gladys being fitted, and raved, "I can't see a thread of difference between this one and the Chanel."

She zeroed in on Gladys's hair, braided atop her head. "I hope you aren't trying out the Swedish peasant look for the performance. Listen, I have an idea. I'll make appointments for all of us to have our hair done. That includes you, Mary. My treat."

Mary removed pins from her mouth. "No, I can do my own hair."

"I insist. Maybe some highlighting, like I do. It'll be fun. Ricardo will get a kick out of all of us coming in. He dotes on his clients."

"Ricardo?" Gladys asked. "A male beauty operator?"

"Stylist. And it's not a beauty shop. It's a salon."

"La de dah," Mary sang. "Too fancy for me."

"Not another word. It's final, you're going."

From the living room, Martin asked, "What about me?"

Louise called back, "Ricardo's good but he can't work miracles. He needs some hair to work with."

"I get no respect," Martin complained.

For the first time, the Jones women went to a hair salon. Mary copied Louise's elegant French twist; Gladys and Dorothy opted for tight curls and finger waves, while Hazel and Evelyn wore their hair parted in the middle and pulled behind the ears.

"We're more sophisticated," Hazel observed to Evelyn when they stood side by side in front of the hall mirror at home.

"Kind of old-ladyish," Dorothy said. "Gladys and I have a softer, younger look."

"You all look like movie stars," Mary gushed.

"Prettier than movie stars," Martin added.

Mary continued, "You're like two sets of twins. Really, I never noticed before but with identical hair styles, Evie and Hazel look alike and Dorothy and Gladys."

Doc tapped on the door and stepped in. "How about I take a picture of this handsome group?"

Mary checked her hair in the mirror. She had borrowed an emerald green taffeta gown from Louise, with rhinestone earrings, necklace and bracelet as accessories.

Martin had rented his first tuxedo, and his last, he declared now. "We look like a pair of old penguins," he told Doc as the camera gaped at the group.

"Speak for yourself. I'm thinking I should dress up more often."

Mary took the camera and directed Doc to stand with the group for a picture. Then it was time to head for the theater.

The opulence of opening night awed Mary, but her daughters' performance exhilarated and chilled her. Tears tickled her powdered and roughed cheeks when Dorothy sang two solos: *Look for the Silver Lining*, and *Always*.

"My heart's palpitating like a metronome," she whispered to Martin. "Good thing Doc is here. And doesn't Dorothy sound better than usual?"

"She always sounds like an angel to me. They say this place has perfect acoustics. Maybe that pipsqueak Rudy Vallee won't need his megaphone."

During an extended applause for the Quartet's performance, Doc whispered to Mary, "For my money, tonight is the start of bigger things for your daughters."

Mary dabbed her nose with a lace handkerchief. "Oh, Doc, I can't even imagine anything better or bigger than this."

THE TEXAS RANGERETTES

This Could Be The Start Of Something Big

You suddenly realize, this could be the start of something big ~~~

The opening of San Antonio's Sunken Garden Amphitheater, set among limestone cliffs that offered extraordinary acoustics, loomed as another high class venue for the Quartet. When Gladys learned that the Civic Opera was presenting the first show, *The Pirates of Penzance,* she insisted that the group audition to provide the music for the outdoor show.

The telegram announcing they had won arrived minutes after the family recited grace at a dinner celebrating Evelyn's eighteenth birthday. "We have Gladys to thank for this," Evelyn said after Hazel read the message aloud. "Gladdie is familiar with the music. Remember when you starred in *Pirates of Penzance* in Park Rapids. Oh, wait a minute. I think you played in the band instead."

Gladys narrowed her eyes at Evelyn, but then grinned. "Very funny, Sis."

"Thank you, thank you. Now, let's get back to my birthday party. Please pass the spuds," Evelyn said in a baby voice, and earned a laugh from around the table. The spuds request had been her first sentence as a baby and she dragged it out now and then to see if anyone still found it amusing.

Heaping mashed potatoes next to the roast beef on her plate, she said, "Good old Midwest food. After being a Texan for three years, I still can't get used to the food. Those refried beans. When they say they cooked a mess of beans, they mean a mess. And tamales, or whatever they are, wrapped in corn husks. In Minnesota we threw corn husks to the pigs. And what's with that chicken fried steak restaurants are offering? Which is it, chicken or steak?"

Gladys clamped a hand over her sister's mouth. "Ev-e-lyn, please be quiet. Don't you remember? Hazel has something to tell the folks." Gladys had willingly agreed to let *the boss* handle the announcement.

While Hazel gulped a glass of water, Mama asked, "What's going on?"

Hazel grabbed a deep breath." Well...we didn't know we'd hear about the audition tonight, but we have other big news. Some time back we met two swell gals, Willeen Grey and Jerry McCrae. They're billed as 'Swing and Sway with McRae and Grey.' We ran into them last night and they want the six of us to form a band."

"A band? What about the Quartet? What about Louise?" Mama asked.

"She's hinted that she wants to quit touring so she and the professor can travel."

Pa jumped in. "If that's the case, maybe that'd be a good time for you to quit the road show. Bet you can find plenty of work here in town. You've done the Juneteenth celebration for a couple of years. And that big show at the Majestic and now the Sunken Garden wants you."

"Those are wonderful places, but this sounds like a barrel of fun."

"And one of these days I'd like a son-in-law or two, some grandkids. Evelyn, is that boyfriend of yours a good prospect?"

Mama tapped her fork on Pa's wrist. "Hold your horses. You're off the subject. Hazel, are these girls Catholics?"

"With the name Jerry McCrae? As Irish as Paddy's pig."

"There are Protestant Irish. Surely you've read about the fighting going on between them and the Catholics in Ireland."

"Sure; I studied that in history class. They've been fighting since time began. Yes, Jerry and Willeen are Catholics. Willeen's a convert. Come to think of it, Jerry might be, too. But what does that have to do with our forming a group?"

"Because you'll be of like minds about playing in decent places and going to church on the road, that sort of thing."

Gladys opened her mouth to speak but Pa was a step ahead. "Now that your mother knows everyone's religion, let's talk about the places you'd play. Since Prohibition, lots of nice clubs have become gin mills with gangsters hangin' around. I don't want you gals gettin' caught up in a raid and thrown in jail. Evelyn's underage, not even out of high school."

"I will be before we go on the road."

"You'll be out of school; still underage. You wouldn't be allowed in clubs."

Noting concern on Pa's face, Gladys said, "I talked about that with Jerry. She'll be our leader and she doesn't want any trouble. Until Prohibition's over, and there's talk it will be soon, we'll play at family places, like we do now on the theater circuit. You'll like Jerry and Willeen. They're both my age. Jerry's mother died years ago; she lives with her dad and I think she has two brothers. Willeen was raised by an aunt and uncle. Don't ask me why."

"Wasn't goin' to. But young women on the road? Folks will talk. Even men musicians have a reputation for bein' wild."

"Folks always find someone to talk about. We drove here from Minnesota by ourselves. And we've been on the road."

"With Louise as chaperone. There are desperate men out there these days."

"There are desperate men here in town. A guy pulled a knife on my friend Ida and reached for her purse. She screamed and he ran off."

Mama sputtered, "Gladdie, you never told me that. Where did that happen and when? Were you with her?"

"No, I wasn't with her. It happened along the river."

"Dear me, what's this world coming to? A girl can't take a walk by herself?"

Evelyn punched her fists in the air. "Don't worry. We'll have safety in numbers. Let's see anyone take on six tough Irishmen. Women."

Mama continued, "With times so bad, who'll be your audience? Who has money for dances?"

"We'll have an audience," Hazel assured her. "People need entertainment now more than ever. You've seen the lines at movie houses."

Gladys recalled the pep talk Jerry had given them last night. "We're not going to make a fortune doing this. It'll cost money roaming all over the country. Jerry has connections with a network of small bands. One bandleader tells another. We'll be competing with others, but Jerry says there's room for all of us."

"Gypsies," Mama scoffed. "I suppose you'll travel by train."

Dorothy shook her head. "No; Jerry says it's easier getting around by car. We'll be more independent; not at the mercy of train schedules. That's a problem sometimes when we travel with the circuit."

"It's not exactly a car," Hazel added. "Well, it is, but it's a professional car."

"What in the world does that mean?" Mama asked.

"Jerry's uncle retired and made her a good deal...practically gave her, his funeral service vehicle."

Mama's fork chimed on her plate as it fell. "For crying out loud, if you're talking about a hearse, say so. We all know what kind of vehicle is used for a funeral."

Hazel slipped into a giggle, through which she rambled, "Jerry said that's what her uncle called it. A service...vehicle. It's a Packard...almost new...big enough for all of us and our instruments and luggage."

"There aren't any leftovers in it," Evelyn added, earning a laugh from Pa and a look of reprimand from Mama.

"A hearse, of all things. They make me think of gangster cars."

"Think of it as a limousine," Gladys said, and changed the subject. "We'll be called the Texas Rangerettes. That's respectable. We'll wear western costumes, chaps, ten gallon hats. With hats, we won't have to worry about our hair being perfect for every show. And with pants, no having to keep ourselves supplied with expensive stockings."

"Pants? I don't mind seeing them on women around the house, but in public? On stage?"

"Oh, Mama," Gladys chided with a laugh, "you always claim to be up-to-date on fashion. Besides, this would be a costume, not street wear."

Hazel kept things rolling. "Speaking of costumes; would you make them? No one sews better than you do."

Mama batted her eyes at her oldest daughter. "Blarney will get you nowhere."

"It's true. You could've been a professional seamstress."

"None of you liked me making your clothes when you were girls. You wanted store-bought."

"We've learned to appreciate quality. Will you make the costumes?"

"I suppose. It sounds as if you've made up your minds to do this. The Texas Rangerettes, of all things, riding around in a hearse."

"I guess we could ride horses," Evelyn said. "Would you like that better?"

"You're kidding, I hope. I don't know what you girls are thinking anymore." Mama rested her chin on her hand. "All right; I'll let you do this Rangerette business. You're good Catholic girls and I trust you."

While Hazel and Gladys carried dishes to the kitchen, Hazel mumbled, "She'll let us. I'm twenty-five, for Pete's sake. She couldn't really stop me."

"I suppose not, but it's nice to have her blessing. This all went better than I thought it would."

Back in the dining room, Gladys said, "Jerry wrote a theme song for us. It's called *We're All Pals Together*. Come on Rangerettes, let's sing it for the folks."

"*We're all pals together, sisters, pals and friends, singin' gals, swingin' gals, rootin' pals, tootin' pals, rain or shine, we do fine, 'cause we're all pals together.*"

Mama clapped her hands. "I like it. Maybe try a lower key."

"Pa, do you like it?" Evelyn asked.

"Shoot; the only thing I know about music is what you lasses tell me. If you say it's a good song, it's good enough for me." He raised his water glass and offered a Gaelic toast, "*Slainte.*"

Evelyn responded, "How about a toast to me? My birthday party has run amok. Where's my angel food cake?"

"Your mother can bring the cake. I've got the toast: May brooks and trees and singing hills, join in the chorus, too. And every gentle wind that blows, send happiness to you." Pa added, "That goes for all of you, the Texas Rangerettes."

From that night on, the household buzzed with more activity than a nest of riled hornets. The six women spent hours studying road maps, planning the logistics of travel, and practicing as a sextet. "Mother Hen," Evelyn teased Mama as she clucked around the musicians, urging them to eat or rest or advising them on tunes.

With all the hullabaloo going on, Gladys suffered from insomnia. As soon as her head hit the pillow, images and thoughts of life on the road emerged. Sure, they'd been out there for several years, but not to the far-reaching places Jerry had in mind. Not even praying the rosary quelled her fears and anxiety.

Let's Call The Whole Thing Off

You say either, I say eyether, you say neither, I say nyther ~~~

"Why so glum?" Mary asked Evelyn, who sat slumped at the table with a cup of coffee in front of her. When Evelyn failed to respond, she offered an explanation. "Tired. You were out late last night."

Evelyn shrugged. "Yeah, with Paul. He wants us to get married."

"Married? Well, a proposal usually calls for celebration, not a long face."

"Proposal?" Gladys called from the dining room.

Evelyn ignored her sister. "It's just that, we've been going out for a year and I like him, but I don't know if I love him or want to marry him. How do you know when you're in love?"

Mary pondered the question. "I can only compare it to what Sister Pius told me about a vocation. You just know. With falling in love, there might not be a lot of fanfare, fireworks going off, bells ringing, but one day you simply know. It sneaks up on you. At least it did for me, with your pa. It felt right." She patted Evelyn's hand. "It sounds as if this thing with Paul doesn't sound right to you."

"I guess that's it. And even if I were certain I was in love, I know I'm not ready to get married. For one thing, I wouldn't be able to tour with the Rangerettes."

"Oh, we need you," Gladys said, now in the kitchen. "You have to go."

"Aside from that," Mary continued, "you're only eighteen, Evie."

"Lots of girls marry right out of high school. Most of them, in fact. Only two girls from my class are going to a real college and one to nursing school. But it's not only about my age. Paul's been acting anti-Catholic, skipping Mass, eating meat on Fridays. I think he's rebelling against his parents. His mom is really, really religious. That's all she talks about. It's annoying to me so I can imagine how tired he gets of it. And Paul doesn't want to work in his dad's business. He doesn't know what he wants."

"Then it's not a good time for him to think about marriage."

"That's what I told him. Even if we don't get married, he doesn't want me going on the road. He says it'll ruin my reputation. I told him I've been on the road for several years and I'm not a fallen woman. I don't know if the Rangerettes will work out but I want to give it a try. It really sounds like fun."

It did to Mary, too. Often lately she felt downright envious of the new path the girls were taking. "I always say a novena for guidance," she offered.

"I will, but I've pretty much made up my mind to break up with Paul. I don't want things hanging over my head while I'm away and he needs to figure out what he wants to do with his life. I do, too, but for now I want to be a Ranger-ette."

Evelyn took her cup to the sink. "Well, life marches on. I guess I'll swim a few laps. That always clears my head."

"When you finish swimming, I want help on those costumes. You promised to hem the blouses."

Gladys laughed. "I'll do that. Have you seen her stitching? She'd never make it as a surgeon."

Green, Green Grass Of Home

Down the road I look, and there comes Mary ~~~

Using triangular photograph holders, Mary placed three postcards and two brochures from the girls into a new scrapbook titled: The Texas Rangerettes. It hardly seemed possible almost three months had passed since they took off in that awful hearse. Evelyn had sent a newspaper picture of the group standing beside the big old Packard, and an entertainment critic's brief review.

~~~ Topeka, Kansas: The Texas Rangerettes, that swell new all-girl sextet, will set your toes a'tapping and your lips a'smacking in a frenzied beat that has swayed dance audiences across the country. ~~~

The picture postcards showed swanky places: The Colonial Club in Augusta, Georgia; the Edgewood Gulf Hotel in Mississippi, a resort in Wisconsin, and a motion picture house in Ohio that was part of the string of theaters belonging to Publix Theater Corporation. Dorothy wrote on the back of that card:

~~~ The Publix Theaters were built by Hollywood's Paramount Studio. They're Art Deco style like the Majestic. They were built to show "Talkie Movies" but they also present live entertainment. Just think, we're sort of working for Hollywood. Ha, ha. Love, Dorothy ~~~

"Thank goodness they're playing in reputable places," Mary said when Martin walked into the room. Noticing a telegram in his hands, her heart caught in her throat.

"It's from Alice," he said. "Your pa died this morning, in his sleep."

Expecting this news any day, Mary's eyes pearled with tears while Martin stood behind her, caressing her hair, then rubbing her shoulders. "I'm sorry, Lass. Real sorry. He was a good man."

The old hometown looks the same, as I step down from the train ~~~

On the drive through Park Rapids and then to the McCarren farm, Mary and Alice huddled in the back seat, sharing family news. While they talked, Mary peered out the open window at the familiar countryside. The pastures lay strewn with stubble and haystacks. Above, set against a deep green background of Norway spruce and pine, the flaming foliage of birch, aspen, poplar, maple, and oak sparkled yellow, red, and gold as the sun filtered through. Thickets of scarlet sumac blazed like fireplace flames.

The pungent scent of bonfires reminded her of wienie roasts with the girls and of potatoes baked on a pile of rocks among the smoldering leaves. After the outdoor supper there might be a hayride, with Papa driving the wagon. Her eyes clouded as she recalled the struggling farmer who had somehow managed to scrape together the money to send her to Catholic school; the father who told bedtime stories to his motherless children, and had given her in marriage to Martin.

Alice squeezed Mary's hand. "What are you thinking, dear sister?"

"About Papa. Do you remember when we moved to Minnesota? We'd sit on the porch and watch the Northern Lights." Mary's mind sought scenes of the rundown farmhouse where her mother lived briefly, then died, and then of her own duties caring for the family.

"I don't specifically remember that," Alice said. "I was only seven when we came here. But I've seen the lights many times. The red and green smoky swirls make me think of ghosts."

"I can picture you and Eddie, Anna and Robert, jumping around in the yard."

"Probably trying to get away from mosquitoes. Never can enjoy a summer night around here what with flies and mosquitoes. God's plague on Minnesota."

"Maybe, but Mother always said the lights were God's blessing shining down from Heaven. A few months later, she went to Heaven."

"I barely remember her. Sometimes it seems I recall something about her but it's usually a story you older kids told." Alice paused. "Have I ever thanked you for taking over the household when Mother died?"

"Oh, my, I'm sure you have many times, but there's no need. It was really Julia and Anna who handled things. I married a year later."

"You weren't far away. I remember staying with you and Martin for a few days at a time. Shall we drive by your old farm tomorrow, and the one where Papa lived?"

"Oh, yes; I'd like that."

"There's a swell new house on that first farm of Martin's and yours."

"I'll want to take flowers to Robbie's grave."

"I've got plenty of mums and a few zinnias."

Mary leaned against Alice. "Thanks for taking care of Robbie's grave since we left. And Mother's, Victor's, Julia's and Anna's. Goodness, both Julia and Anna gone. Just the two of us sisters left now."

"Just the two of us. Ah, here we are now at my place."

Mary sat up. "It looks wonderful. I feel at home again."

Yes, they'll all come to greet me, arms reaching, smiling sweetly ~~~

Stepping off the car's running board, Mary watched a skein of Canada geese flutter south, listened to insects clicking in the pasture, loons warbling on the lake, and a mourning dove crooning a melancholy dirge as if to take part in this solemn occasion. Arm in arm, the sisters fell into step, crisp leaves eddying at their feet. A cluster of adults huddled on the porch, while children romped in the yard. Eddie broke from the adults to greet Mary with a bear hug. "Hiya, Mum. Gosh, it's great to see you. C'mon, I'll take you to the parlor to see Pa. He looks real good."

Grasping his hand, Mary thought: I don't want to do this. But once inside, viewing her deceased father was not as traumatic as she expected. He appeared rested, peaceful. "He looks more like Grandda than he did when he was younger," she told Eddie, who knew his grandfather McLaughlin only from photographs and others relatives' memories.

That night, settled in bed under one of Alice's quilts, Mary read her father's obituary from the *Park Rapids Enterprise.*

~~~ September 28, 1930: Larry McLaughlin, Resident 27 Years, Succumbs Tuesday. Lawrence McLaughlin, for the past twenty-seven years a resident of this community passed away Tuesday morning at 9 o'clock at the home of his daughter, Mrs. James McCarren of Osage township. Mr. McLaughlin was 78 years of age and had been afflicted with kidney trouble and the infirmities of old age for the past two years. The past four months he had been confined to bed. Funeral services were held Friday morning at 9 o'clock at St. Peter's Catholic Church of this city. Rev. J.P. Funk officiated and burial will be made at the East Catholic Cemetery.

Lawrence McLaughlin was born in the state of Massachusetts on January 1, 1852, where he spent his early life. Later he moved to Cottage Grove, Wisconsin, where in 1872 he was united in marriage with Miss Martha Burke. Thirteen children were born to the union, six have preceded their father in death. They were Catherine Grace, William Leo, Michael, Anna, Victor, and Julia (Mrs. Victor Olson). Mrs. McLaughlin died August 15, 1903, shortly after the family moved here.

The year 1880 the family moved to Dougherty, Iowa and the year 1903 came to Park Rapids, Minnesota. Mr. McLaughlin was a member of St. Peter's Catholic Church of this city. He was a kindly gentleman, a devoted husband and father. Of late years he had been making his home with his children. Those who survive are seven children: Joseph of Mason City, Iowa, Mrs. M.L. Jones (Mary) of San

Antonio, Texas, Robert of Flaxville, Montana, Eddie of Everett, Washington, Mrs. Jas McCarren (Alice) of Osage township, John of this city, and Clem, whose whereabouts are unknown at this time. There are fifteen grandchildren. ~~~

It's good to touch the green, green grass of home ~~~

At the depot, Mary clung to Alice. "Leaving you all behind again is as hard as it was when I moved to Texas. It's as heart-wrenching as when the girls left on tour in that awful hearse."

"I know, I know," Alice soothed, tightening her plump arms around Mary.

"Please come visit us, you and Jim. We'll show you our city."

The train stampeded toward them spewing soot and ashes, then gradually slowed, the wheels spitting molten fire like from a smithy's anvil. Screeching to a standstill, the engine heaved a final whoosh of energy.

Mary hugged James, then a final embrace for Alice, and more reminiscing until the conductor shouted, "All aboard." She paused on the train steps to call goodbye, then rushed to her seat for another look at Alice and Jim. While the train chugged away, she waved until her loved ones were specks in the distance.

And there's the old oak tree that I used to play on ~~~

Reliving the past few days, Mary didn't tell Martin that while visiting places the girls had played and gone to school and church, she felt their presence. Like the swirling Aurora Borealis, the ghostly forms of children danced around her, laughing, bickering, playing, making music. In images as crisp and colorful as autumn leaves she watched them deliver May baskets and Valentines to friends, saw them playing jacks on the porch, taking First Communion, being Confirmed, splashing in the washtub out back on Saturday nights. "Don't let Pa see us bare naked," they begged.

Last night when the western sky became a sea of fiery red, orange, and gold waves and ripples, the kind of run-together colors that she described to herself as a child's watercolor painting, she whispered the words she once called aloud to her little girls. "Come to the window and see the sky. Santa Claus spilled his paint." She felt them with her, their hands tugging at her skirt as they oohed and ahhed.

Speeding through miles of farmland, Mary wondered: What would the girls be doing now if we hadn't moved to Texas? Would some or all of them be married, or nuns, or teachers? Would they still be playing for local occasions?

She reached for Martin's hand. "I miss the girls."

He looked up from a magazine of western stories. "Me, too, Lass. It would've been nice if they could've been here."

Mary couldn't explain that it was the little girls she missed most, the ones she had conjured in Park Rapids. She had glimpsed Robbie, too, but her store of visual memories of him were limited, and ended at the cemetery.

That was the saddest moment of the past few days; the realization that she had so few images of her dear baby's short life. Although saddened by her father's death, his time had come. She accepted that; but after all these years, her arms still ached for Robbie.

's Wonderful, 's Marvelous

That you should care for me ~~~

The phone rang one long, two shorts; Mary grabbed the receiver and handed it to Martin. "Doc Walter's office. Martin Jones speaking." He paused. "Hey, Gladdie, good to hear your voice." Mary leaned in to listen.

"How're you and Mama?" Gladys asked through the crackle of static.

"I'm in fine fettle, but your mama caught a cold in Minnesota and has laryngitis. Her not bein' able to talk ain't all bad from my point of view, but she's throwin' a fit."

Mary bared her teeth at Martin; he returned a Cheshire cat grin. "Is everythin' okay with you gals, you callin' long distance and all?"

"We're hunky-dory, but you don't need to holler. I can hear you."

"Well, you speak up. Your mother's leanin' next to the earpiece so she can hear. First time she's gotten that cozy with me since Fido was a pup."

"Just wanted to say we're sorry we couldn't get away for Grandpa's funeral."

"We understood. It was a fine service and a good turnout. Everyone asked about you girls. Your female cousins envy you travelin' all over while they're home raisin' kids. Aunt Alice said to send her a postcard from somewhere interesting."

"I mailed one today."

"Say, you got a letter. Return address says Larry Jergens."

"Oh, him. We called him Jerkens. He's a club manager who was trying to make time with Hazel. Thought he was the reincarnation of Valentino."

"The letter's for you, not Hazel."

"If he can't get one woman, he tries another. Throw it away."

"Will do. You girls watch out for scoundrels. Use Irish diplomacy on them."

"What's that?"

"The knack for tellin' somebody to go to hell so's he looks forward to it."

"That's a good one. Jerry came close to saying that to a club owner who didn't like our costumes. He wanted his girl entertainers to be provocative; said his audiences look first and listen second when it comes to canary bands."

"Canary bands?"

"Girl musicians. Jerry asked him if the term Texas Rangerettes brought an image of chiffon and ruffles. He said no but he thought we'd at least wear skirts and show off our gams. She said we were leaving but he said he really needed a show for two nights. We needed the money, so we stayed. Another manager said we play like men. He thought that was a compliment."

"You run into a lot of that kind of thing?"

"All the time. Men musicians think this is their job; that women are too emotional to be consistent. Remember the teacher in Park Rapids who said Hazel couldn't possibly play the sousaphone, or Dorothy the trombone? He said wind instruments are for boys. And lots of men think women on the road are easy or, well; let's say they question our femininity. Women are paid less than men, too. Aww, don't get me started; I'm running up a phone bill here. The reason I called is to tell you what a theater critic wrote about us. I'll read it. He said, '*Variety* and *Billboard* find the Texas Rangerettes to be the hottest copy going. They've promised readers at least one headline story a month about this popular all-girl band. These girls can take off.'"

"Take off?"

"Improvise, kick out. I haven't seen the actual papers but the important thing is, they're writing about us. Girl bands are rarely recorded or reviewed. If they are, it's about how they look, what they're wearing rather than about music. Ask Mama to pick up some copies at that big newsstand downtown."

"She'll know who this is, *Billboard* and *Variety*?"

"Pa, they're the bibles of the music world. And they're writing about us. People all over the country read those publications."

"That's swell. We'll get several copies."

"Great. We'll be home soon. We all send our love. Say hi to Mama for us."

"She's listenin' and heard you. Thanks for callin'."

"They'll be home soon," Mary rasped when Martin hung up. But it wouldn't be soon enough to suit her. She couldn't decide which she enjoyed most, actually seeing them, or hearing about their adventures. Well, there was no need to choose; it was all of a piece.

Way Down Yonder In New Orleans

In the land of the dreamy scenes ~~~

Gladys wiped her face with a flowered handkerchief and dabbed at it again a minute later. "Whew, it's easy to believe New Orleans is below sea level. My dress shields are soaked and I'm clammy all over."

"Clammy," Evelyn said. "Pun intended? Clams, clammy, sea level?"

"Yeah, I got it. I meant it's muggy. And don't come up with a pun for that."

Despite the humidity, the streets teemed with life. Folks ambled along as if they had not a care in the world, fanning themselves with newspapers or cardboard fans. A cacophony of music oozed from a warren of streets, alleys, balconies, garden courtyards, and the open doors and windows of bars, nightclubs, and honky-tonks. Multi-colored neon lights surged and buzzed with electrical musical notes and names of clubs. A man wearing dark glasses and holding a white cane collected coins from those who stopped to listen to his hurdy-gurdy music.

Gladys dug in her handbag and found an unwrapped stick of gum and a hankie with a lipstick imprint on it. And a dime, which she dropped in the musician's cup.

The Rangerettes paused at a seedy joint where Jerry read from a poster out front. "La-La dancing to the music of Creole Floyd's Zydeco Band. Anyone know what la-la or zydeco is?"

Hazel leaned close to the door. "I hear fiddle, piano, maybe accordion."

Evelyn stretched her arms out and in as if playing a squeeze box. "Pa says the definition of a gentleman is a man who knows how to play an accordion but has the good sense not to. I told that to a Norwegian kid in Park Rapids who had a cor-deen. He shot daggers at me."

"You're awful, Evie," Hazel said, and turned to Jerry. "Are we going in to listen to that zydeco band?"

"We can't afford six admissions. Not on our coffee and toast wages."

"How about a couple of us?" Willeen asked. "We could flip a coin."

"Nope. We're all pals together. Until we get paid for that dance tomorrow night we've got just about enough for rent and food."

"Shoot, I'd rather listen to music than sleep or eat." Willeen sidled up to a popcorn vendor and listened to him draw a bouncy tune from his harmonica. He motioned for her to cup her hands and poured a scoopful of popcorn into them. He did the same for Gladys; the two women thanked him and wandered off to catch up with the others, standing in front of another club.

Hazel read from the billboard. "The Dew Drop Social Club, established 1885. Appearing this week, Louis Arm...."

Her voice faded beneath the blare of a trumpet, followed by, *"shark has, pret— ty teeth dear, an' he shows them pearl—y white."*

On the sidewalk, Sunday morning, don't you know ~~~

The women parked their fannies on the curb outside The Dew Drop Social Club into early morning, while Satchmo meandered through *Alexander's Ragtime Band, Basin Street Blues*, and dozens of other tunes.

The sleepy sextet barely made it to ten o'clock Mass. Gladys had chosen St. Patrick's after reading that it was built by Irish immigrants who had been snubbed at St. Louis Cathedral. They'd been made to sit in rear pews, and when they requested a Mass said in English, were told that God spoke only French. St. Louis Cathedral, with triple steeples rising higher than any building in the French Quarter, called itself a minor basilica. But when Gladys saw St. Patrick's white stone Gothic edifice with a single spire, and then stepped inside, she couldn't imagine anything grander. Stained glass windows glistened in the sun and the golden sanctuary featured murals that looked as if they replicated those in the Sistine Chapel.

After Mass, while the others made a beeline to their modest rooms for a nap, Gladys set off to visit other churches. She particularly hoped to hear the music at a Negro service. She found what she wanted at St. Augustine's, a simple white clapboard church. From up front, a tawny-skinned woman in a red choir robe watched Gladys slip into a pew, but she didn't miss a beat leading the congregation in a song that was at once plaintive and invigorating: *"I'll fly away, when I die hallelujah by and by, I'll fly away ~~~"*

Gladys didn't know the hymn and couldn't make out some of the words sung in a mixed patois, but the singers' spirit inspired her to tap her foot and hum along. Glancing down the row, she caught the attention of a petite girl of about five. Wiry black pigtails poked from beneath a white straw hat not unlike Gladys's. The girl's mother elbowed her to attention and they both continued singing.

During the dramatic sermon, a man behind Gladys repeatedly intoned, "Amen, brother," to the minister's exhortations.

Outside after the service, the rotund minister greeted Gladys as if she were one of his flock. Men tipped their hats, and the little girl waved her white-gloved fingertips. A woman whose gray complexion and hair reminded Gladys of ashes struck up a conversation. "I usta go to First African Baptist but I come here cuz the music's betta. Church gotta have good music."

"Yes, my Irish mother would say it was *ceol binn*, sweet music."

"Sweet music, sweet Jesus, hallelujah," the woman sang as she drifted away.

On the streetcar back to the hotel, Gladys reflected on the sin she had committed by going to a Protestant church. All right, she told her conscience, I'll confess it next time I have a chance. But it's not as if I skipped Mass and chose another church. Must I say it was a colored church? White, black, Protestant, Catholic, don't we all have the same God? Pondering these mysteries, she stepped off the trolley and found herself in the midst of a funeral parade led by a brass band playing a mournful tune. Garlands of fresh flowers and strands of beads hung from a casket borne by six hefty pallbearers.

Next to her, swaying to the rhythm, stood a man dressed to the nines in a blue and white seersucker suit, a white shirt and navy blue tie, and white crepe-soled shoes. He waved his index finger as if it were a conductor's baton.

"Excuse me," Gladys said, "could you explain this to me?"

He turned, doffed his straw plantation hat, and laid it back on his head of white curls. "Splain what, *Cher*?"

"Is this the way you hold funerals here? I mean, are they held in the street?"

"Ah, that. Not all, but leastways those for musicians. His friends givin' 'im a sendoff. On the way to the cemetery they play sad songs. When the deceased's been left behind for burial, the tempo picks up, celebratin' *joie de vivre*. Then the second liners join the parade."

"Second liners?"

"Dem what follows along wavin' dew rags and stoppin' to dance. Folks throw a nickel at 'em. The music and dancin' gives the dearly departed a joyous journey to the great beyond." He waved his arms upward, as if delivering a fire and brimstone sermon. Then he sang, "*Gonna join that grand procession, when the saints go marchin' in,*" while the band played a different tune.

His *joie de vivre* invigorated Gladys. Saluting him with two fingers to her brow, she thanked him for the information.

"*Bienvenue, Cher.*" He swayed down the street to catch up with the procession.

At the hotel, Gladys found the others gone. A note from Evelyn read: Gone to Joe's Lounge to tune up for the show. Practice! Be there!

"Practice?" Gladys asked her mirror image. "I'm ready to swing." The mile or so walk to the club, in the heat and humidity, dampened only her hair and clothes, not her enthusiasm.

That night, her spunk and animated gestures kept the others on their toes. During a break, Jerry remarked, "If I didn't know better, I'd think you'd been drinking all afternoon. The rest of us could've called in our parts and let you solo."

Do you know what it means, to miss New Orleans ~~~

Watching the Crescent City's skyline disappear from view, Gladys decided that its main charm was the music and the churches. The religious houses provided a welcome respite from the city's seamy side; its voodoo magic atmosphere, the hedonistic life style, the excess of everything, the decadence.

Willeen seemed to tap into her thoughts. "There were some strange characters in New Orleans. Men holding hands; others I couldn't tell if they were men or women."

Jerry drawled, "They don't know either, Willie." She dragged out a yawn. "I'd kill for a cup of *café au lait* right now."

"I like the chicory coffee and begnets."

Dorothy corrected Willeen. "It's pronounced ben yeah, spelled b-e-i-g-n-e-t."

"Well, thank you Miss spelling bee champion of the state of Minnesota."

To squelch a possible argument between two tired women, Gladys changed the subject to the music they'd heard. They all agreed it would be hard to beat.

Crossing a bridge, Willeen shrieked, "What's that awful smell?"

"The bayou," Jerry said. "Centuries of dead stuff out there in the swamps. Did y'all know they bury their dead above ground here?"

"You mean coffins out in the open?"

"No, goofy, in crypts." Jerry came alert at the wheel. "Whoa, I gotta pay attention. Did anyone see that road sign? Are we going the right way?"

"We're okay," Gladys answered.

"Listen, don't y'all go to sleep on me. I need a navigator. I'm not sure of this route and one of you has to spell me after an hour or so."

Willeen offered, "Let me sleep for an hour and then I'll drive."

"You got it. The rest of you, at least one of you, talk to me, keep me awake, sing with me. *Oh, the shark has pearly teeth, dear* ~~~ "

Gladys sang along while she began a letter:

~~~ Dear Folks: We just left New Orleans. It's Monday but I'll be darned if I know what date it is. Mama, you'd like the music and the churches here, especially St. Patrick's. Tell you about it later. Pa, the food is great, especially the weenies cooked by street vendors. Juicy and hot. The big news is, we heard Louis

Armstrong play and sing from box seats. Ha; outside on the curb. Wish you'd been there, Mama. I'll continue this later or have one of the girls add to it. Till then, oodles of love, Gladdie ~~~

Breezin' Along With The Breeze

The sky is the only roof I have over my head ~~~

A celluloid statue of Saint Christopher toppled off the dashboard into Gladys's lap. Bad omen, having the saint fall. Chiding herself for believing in omens, bad or good, she repositioned the patron saint of safe travel that Mama had given them. If Mama trusted Saint Christopher, that was good enough.

From the pilot's seat, Willeen said, "This is a swell route for scenery but the road's rough in places. Guess that's why it's called a Trace; there's hardly a trace of real road."

"It's more like a trail. Like there might still be pioneers and Indians trudging through the wilderness. I read that the government is making this road into a parkway." Gladys shrugged. "I'm not sure what a parkway is. Maybe places to pull over and park and get a better view. That'd be nice."

She had suggested a few stops to read the signs marking Civil War gravesites and Indian trails, but Hazel complained they'd never get anywhere if they stopped every ten minutes. They'd been on the Natchez Trace for an hour, winding past sprawling horse farms with pillared white houses cushioned between soft green hills, cotton fields that stretched from the road to the horizon, and swampland with stands of cypress whose tenacious roots grasped the shorelines of rivers and streams.

Gliding through a sun-dappled tunnel of trees, Willeen leaned over the steering wheel and peered through the bug-spattered windshield. "Our sightseeing's about over. Fifteen minutes or so, we'll hit heavy rain."

Within minutes, drops of water bubbled on the hood like it does on a hot pancake griddle. A few miles down the road, sheets of wind-driven rain pelted the Packard from all sides. Gladys yelled, "The wipers can't keep up. How in the world can you see where the road is in this gully-washer?"

"I can't, and I'm thrashed from trying." Willeen pulled off the road and cut the engine. "I could use a nap anyway."

"Oh, keep going," Jerry said. "This old horse can plow through anything. Sleet, ice; remember the time she outran a tornado? Whoo-eee, that was fun."

Willeen rattled the car keys over her head. "Be my guest. I'll switch places with you and you can have yourself some fun driving."

"Nah, we might as well stay put a few minutes. A nap sounds good."

Gladys, too stimulated to sleep, watched the storm instead. Mesmerized and awed by nature's power, she recalled her mother's stories about lightning strikes and deadly cyclones and blizzards. She fixed her eyes on a lone dogwood bent low from the unrelenting wind and rain. The dainty tree looked as if it were being punished, like a boy cringing from a schoolmaster's whip.

The scene reminded her of the dogwood legend. Supposedly it had once been a big tree, but after its limbs were used to make Jesus's cross, God stunted its growth so it could never again be used for a crucifixion. The cross in the cup of the flower served as a reminder of the crucifixion.

She turned her attention to the other side of the road, where a white convertible had pulled off for a moment. Then it took off again.

Resting her head on the seat back, she focused her eyes on the hearse's hood ornament draped in wind borne Spanish moss. Hazel called the Goddess of Speed image a heathen symbol and said she couldn't think why a funeral director would have a winged, naked woman leading mourners to the cemetery. Jerry said it was to give them confidence that the deceased was being carried quickly to the great beyond. As a joke on Hazel, the Rangerettes often clothed the woman with whatever they could find: crepe paper, elastic garters, a doll dress Evelyn bought in a used clothing store. Gladys's favorite was a tuft of feathers that made the goddess look like Sally Rand, the popular fan dancer.

The sky still loomed heavy and dark, but the rain had nearly ceased. Eager to see more of the Trace, Gladys tapped Willeen's arm.

"Wha...what?" Willeen groped with coming awake.

"It's stopped raining. Want me to drive?"

"No, I'll do it. That was some storm."

"You were dead to the world. Everyone was except me."

"I've been awake," Jerry said. "Off and on."

Yawning, Willeen turned the ignition key, stepped on the starter, and put the hearse in low gear. It groaned but didn't budge.

"Whoa, cut it," Jerry yelled, "the wheels are spinning. Lemme take a look."

While Jerry piled out on the other side Gladys opened the front door and looked down. "Oh, boy. Come on everybody, up and at 'em; we need elbow grease. Take off your shoes or they'll be ruined." She shucked off her straw sling pumps, stepped into muck up to her ankles, and slogged to the rear of the hearse.

Willeen shifted gears again, splattering Gladys and Jerry with slime.

"No, Willie, not yet," Jerry shouted. She scanned the terrain. "We need traction. A board or a gunny sack."

"And lacking that?" Gladys lifted a hank of damp hair off her neck and wiped away perspiration with her other hand.

"We got any newspapers?"

"Nope, I tossed them last time we stopped."

"We might have to use some of our clothes." Jerry put two fingers between her lips and whistled through her teeth. "Evie, Dorothy, Hazel, scout around for twigs, brush, anything like that."

Evelyn and Dorothy walked along the road, then crossed and paced that side, looking in the ditch. "They must've had a chain gang cleaning up," Evelyn called. "The only thing I found is a fence post with barbed wire around it. Don't think we wanna use that and poke a hole in a tire."

"Bring it. Maybe I can unwind the wire."

"It's tightly wrapped. How about I pull a board from that fence over there?"

"No," Gladys yelled, "those split-rail fences date back to the Civil War."

"Oh, go on. They'd have fallen apart by now."

Jerry swatted a plump mosquito on her arm, then another. "There has to be brush and twigs. We're in a forest, for gosh sakes."

Dorothy grimaced. "I won't go traipsing in the woods with snakes and critters. And look at the mud in there."

"You'd rather sit here and file your nails?"

While Jerry argued with Dorothy, Gladys watched a convertible approach; the one she'd seen earlier, but now the top was lowered. The radio blared static and a raccoon tail fluttered from the antenna. Animal parts hanging on cars always disturbed her, made her certain the person displaying the trophy killed the animal, maybe with his bare hands. Well, never mind that, maybe the two teenaged boys had something to use for traction.

The driver stopped several feet behind the women, on the road itself. Smart, Gladys thought, he doesn't want to get stuck. The boys jumped out of the convertible without opening its doors and swaggered forward, each alternately swigging from a beer bottle and dragging on a cigarette.

"Oh, oh," Gladys said to Jerry, "They might be more trouble than help."

"Nah, they're just kids. Most likely more bullshit than bull. Six of us, two of them. It's daylight, what harm can they do?"

Good question, but their drinking made Gladys wary. As they edged closer, she moved backward. Hazel, Evelyn and Dorothy moved, too, until the three of them were huddled by Willeen's open window.

The driver wore khaki pants and a green shirt with the sleeves rolled above his elbows. The wind whipped his dishwater blond hair across his forehead and he kept finger combing it into place. The other boy's looks and manner disturbed Gladys. He wore only a dingy sleeveless undershirt and baggy jeans that seemed about to fall off his slim frame. Dark hair straggled almost to his shoulders and he sported a goatee.

Gladys caught a whiff of underarm odor, and beer on his breath. She didn't want to appear alarmed by his presence, so she moved away and pretended to check on the wheels and how badly they were embedded. Standing in mud, she figured the boys wouldn't get close enough to touch her and risk filling their loafers with slush.

"What the blazes y'all doin' drivin' a funeral wagon?" the driver asked. He eyed the logo on the side of the hearse. "A girlie band. Do you wear cute little costumes, short skirts, maybe? Can't say's I ever heard of the Rangerettes. You, Donnie Bob?"

"Nope, but I like to dance." Donnie Bob reached across the mud chasm, grabbed Gladys's arm and pulled her onto the road. "C'mon, Tex." While he twirled Gladys, Jerry moved in and pulled her free.

Jerry propped her hands on her hips. "I'm right sorry we can't play games with you little boys, but we'd be grateful if you'd give us a boost with the car. In other words, hop on the train or get off the tracks."

Donnie Bob winked at Jerry. "I'd like to get on the train with you. One of those bed compartments."

Jerry sputtered a laugh. "Aw, jeez, you're not even dry behind the ears."

The boy didn't seem to catch the unflattering comment; his eyes were on a decrepit car coughing to a stop across the road. He mumbled something to his friend, and both boys tossed their bottles into the ditch and steadied themselves against the hearse.

In the other lane, the car door squeaked open; the driver unloaded his frame and the car's chassis lifted. He barreled across the road, hitching up his brown whipcord trousers, steam rising where his boots collided with pavement.

"Is he a mirage?" Gladys asked Jerry, who raised her eyebrows and shrugged.

"Well, let's pray Goliath is on our side, not theirs." Gladys watched Hazel cross herself, obviously thinking the same thing.

"Ladies," he huffed, nodding their way while steering his girth toward the boys. "Donnie Bob, Gordy."

"Hey, Uncle Ernie. Whatcha doin' out this way?" Donnie Bob's voice cracked in an obvious attempt to be nonchalant.

"Well, it's like this. I stopped by to see yer mama. She said you never come home last night so I figgered you was out joy riding. Ah don't like my baby sis frettin' so I said I'd round ya'up and send you home. Furst, we got some work t'do." With his paw on Donnie Bob's neck, he propelled him to the back of the hearse. Gordy hustled into position without assistance.

Goliath turned to the women. "The boys wanna he'p me git you outta this rut. You ladies stand away. Mud's apt to spit in every direction."

"We'll help push," Jerry offered.

"Preciate it, but there won't be much room back here when I'm one of the pushers." He plowed forward and leaned over to Willeen. "When I get in place, you start the engine, put it in low, and let out the clutch, very slow. Got that?"

"Gotcha."

After a couple of wheel spins the Packard sailed onto the road, leaving the smell of burning rubber before Willeen gained full control.

Gladys couldn't contain her relief; she applauded. Sauntering past the boys she noted the mud on their trousers. She couldn't tell if Goliath's pants caught any muck; they were already soiled when he arrived. "God bless you," she said.

"You ladies have a safe trip. Nice travelin' vehicle."

Jerry saluted him with two fingers to her forehead. "It's pretty dependable. Thanks for your help."

"Pleasure. Wasn't it boys?"

"Yessir," they chorused.

With everyone aboard, Willeen tooted the horn in thanks and the Rangerettes hit the road. Gladys inhaled a long breath of rain-freshened air through her open window. "My, my, those boys are in trouble with Uncle Ernie. I hope he's not too hard on them. They're probably nice kids, most of the time."

"They scared me," Hazel said. "I don't trust anyone who's drinking."

"Me neither," Dorothy said. "I doubt they're nice boys."

Evelyn raised her barbed wire post. "I was prepared to come after them with my shillelagh. I'm glad I didn't have to beat off the giant, too."

That was just like scrappy little Evelyn. Dorothy had reacted in her usual way, quiet, staying low, but Hazel surprised Gladys. The bossy older sister hadn't been evident. She really had been frightened.

"Aw, heck," Jerry scoffed, "I still say we could've handled it ourselves, the boys and getting out of the mud."

Gladys allowed Jerry her bravado. "Sure, but you have to admit it got more interesting when Goliath came along."

"Well, interesting, sure; that's a whole different breed of cattle."

Gladys reached under the seat and found the letter she'd started after they left New Orleans, whenever that was. Time flies when you're having fun.

~~~ Here we are, breezing along on the beautiful Natchez Trace, heading for Nashville and Memphis. We'll tell you more about the Trace when we get home. We ran into some heavy rain and were delayed, but no serious problems. This postcard I'm enclosing shows how rich folks live here. We saw lots of mansions, mostly Civil War era, but there's more poverty than riches. Along the railroad tracks everywhere we go there are stretches of "Hooverville."

I talked to a woman who said the Depression isn't even noticeable here, that Miss. is always the poorest state, for whites and coloreds. She's a photographer for the WPA, name's Eudora Welty. One day Hazel and I met a father and son named Lomax, from Austin. They have this machine that makes recordings. They travel around recording songs of different cultures. Negroes, Cajuns, Creoles, railroad workers, men on wharves, in cotton fields, turpentine camps, even convicts. An article in the local paper said the men call it "giving a voice to the voiceless." When these fellas go into Negro areas they paint their faces black because if white people saw them mixing, they'd be in trouble. We wanted to hang around and talk, thought maybe they'd record us. Ha Ha. But we had to get rolling. That's life on the open road. Love, Gladys and the gal pals. ~~~

Am I Blue

Ain't these tears in my eyes telling you ~~~

Gladys slouched in her seat, readjusted herself again and sighed. "My bones ache. I'm more than ready for this stop." They had passed a road sign that claimed Memphis was the birthplace of the blues and the home of W.C. Handy, and decided to pull in for the night.

Next to her, Hazel sorted through a mess of papers and read silently for a minute. "Listen to this," she said, "Handy supposedly wrote the first blues tune in Memphis in 1909. It says: He and his band were asked to play for the campaign of political boss Edward H. Crump. One of the songs, *Mr. Crump*, was not flattering, but Boss paid little attention to the words. What interested him was the positive way people reacted to Handy's music, which became so popular that Crump won the election. Later, new words were added to the song and it was renamed *The Memphis Blues.* He later described the blues as primitive, disturbing, and monotonous."

Willeen called, "All very interesting, but we can we stop? I need a potty break."

Jerry said, "Hold on a few minutes and we'll be at our hotel."

"Better not be more than that or I won't be responsible for my actions."

I'll be shoutin' hallelujah all the day ~~~

Registering at Chez Jay, Gladys asked the desk clerk where to go to hear some good blues. "We're musicians," she added, as if that might make a difference in what he suggested.

Tugging on his ear, he considered the question. "Wouldn't advise y'all go over to Beale Street. Sure, there's good music but it ain't a proper place for ladies such as yourself. Seedy characters, easy money and liquor. Lot more going on over there than music, if you know what I mean." He wiggled his overgrown blond eyebrows.

Jerry said, "We drove through that area on our way here. Didn't look that much worse than a lot of places we've been."

"Suit yourself, but the woman we've got singing in our lounge, she's every bit as good as that Bessie Smith folks rave about. Most of our guests stay here and see our show. No cover charge."

The women agreed to stay; the price was right and, as Hazel said, "It would probably cost a pretty penny to get into a decent club on Beale Street."

Floor fans stationed around the lounge did little to alleviate the humidity and the odor of tobacco and perspiration. A white-haired man with chestnut colored skin sat on a piano bench under a halo of smoke, playing a silent tune on his outstretched leg.

Gladys knew the feeling; she sometimes awoke at night with her hands moving on an invisible instrument. One morning Dorothy told the others, "Gladys elbowed me in the shoulder with her sax. She was really taking off."

The lights dimmed, and a robust woman emerged from behind a faded curtain. She wore a chartreuse caftan and a rope of white beads that coiled around her plump neck several times. Her grayish hair, twisted into rows and rows of tiny braids, reminded Gladys of the corrugated tin roof Pa once put on the hen house.

"Evenin' folks. I'm Seraphim. Piano man's Freddie." Acknowledging the trickle of applause with a nod, the songstress began her program. "This song's called *Wasted Life Blues*." Her face already perspiring, she sang, "*I've lived a life, but nothin' I've gained, each day I'm full of sorrow and pain ~~~*"

She went directly into *Down Hearted Blues*, followed by *Nobody Knows You When You're Down and Out*, and a string of other tunes pairing hope and melancholy.

"Powerful voice," Gladys whispered to Dorothy, "but I can't say much for the blues. Give me a more upbeat tune."

At intermission, most of the audience disappeared and within an hour only the Rangerettes remained. Finishing a medley, Seraphim squinted at the women and pleaded, "Gals, ahm runnin' outta gas. Mind if I sit a spell with y'all?"

While Jerry dragged over a chair, Seraphim sashayed to the table and eased her plump frame onto a chair. "Desk clerk says you's a band of some sort."

Jerry made introductions while Seraphim motioned to the waiter to bring a round of soft drinks. "Smoke makes my throat dry and scratchy. Reckon you gals knows that feelin'. Some blues singers like that scratchy sound. Not me." She sipped from a glass of ginger ale. "So, this your first time in Memphis?"

"Yes," Gladys said. "We wanted to hear the blues. But to be honest, the songs make me sad."

"Why you think they's called the blues?"

"Of course, but I didn't expect it to affect me this way. I feel sort of…drained."

"Could be the weather, not the music." Seraphim poured water on her handkerchief and wiped her face. "Fats Waller tole some woman, 'If you don't know what jazz is, I caint tell you.' I reckon that's the same with the blues. But lemme see if I can 'splain. The blues is 'bout what's goin' on in somebuddy's mind. And lots of folks are feelin' low these days. Real low. You caint sing the blues iffen you don't feel it here." She tapped her cushiony bosom. "It's like gospel, ya gotta feel it."

Gladys recalled the gospel singers in the church in New Orleans. They seemed to have been lost in the music, absorbed in what they were singing. Like Seraphim.

"Some years back in *Variety,* I think it was, somebuddy said only Niggrahs can do the blues justice. I don't agree. They's lots of folks what are depressed and oppressed, colored, white, ever' shade in between. The blues is about hard times, bad times, hurtin' and cryin'. I 'spect they's even some rich white folks these days singing the blues. Another fella I heard 'bout says anybody can sing the blues if he can play the role of the down and out." She swayed her head from side to side. "I think ya gotta know hard times to sing the blues. Ya hadta have a hard row to hoe. Ya gotta feel it."

Gladys wondered what hardships, what obstacles Seraphim had encountered on her road to the same kind of places the Rangerettes played. Given her skin color, the road most likely had more potholes than the ones they traveled.

"You listen some more. You'll see the blues is not all 'bout grief and bad times. A blues song ain't no good 'less it's got hope, too."

The Rangerettes talked music with their hostess for another hour before the manager came to say he was closing. In the lobby, as they said goodbye and watched Seraphim leave, Evelyn said, "She sings here but she doesn't stay here."

"She lives in Memphis," Hazel said. "Why would she stay here? Anyway, this is a whites only hotel. Didn't you notice? The audience was all white."

"I wasn't checking people's color. I was listening to the music."

The next afternoon, as they traveled through Tennessee's green rolling hills, Evelyn and Dorothy harmonized, "*Bye, bye, blues, bells ring, birds sing, sun is shining, no more pining ~~~*"

Yeah, bye, bye, Gladys thought. To take her mind off the blues she propped a tablet on her knees and wrote a letter to the folks.

~~~ Dear Ma and Pa: Here's a brochure from the Peabody Hotel in Memphis. We walked over to see it because everyone said we should. It's high falutin' all right. In the lobby there's a fountain with ducks in the water. We were going to eat at the hotel, but Jerry took a look at the menu and said it was too rich for our pocketbook. Evelyn said there might be duck feathers on the salad. Ha.

We didn't play in Memphis; just stopped to listen to the blues. Seems to me it just makes sad people sadder. I want my music to make people happy, to lift their spirits, not add to the misery. We stopped in Nashville to see the Grand Ole Opry. It cost a quarter to get in. It used to be free but they thought charging would keep the crowds to a manageable size. It didn't. We saw the Delmore Brothers, Zeke Clements and the Bronco Busters. That's more my style than the blues. Guess I'm just a hick at heart. Oh, by the way, try to find a radio station that's playing Bill Monroe music. It's called Blue Grass. He plays mandolin and sings duets with his brother. You'd like it, Mama. Love, Gladys ~~~

Lazy Bones

Loafin' thru the day, how you spec to make a dime that way ~~~

After touring Savannah's lush parks, its Georgian mansions and its massive churches, the Rangerettes stretched out on lumpy beds at the modest Peach Blossom Hotel. "We can have a three hour nap," Gladys said, setting the alarm clock. No one responded; they were dead to the world. The next thing she knew the alarm jolted her awake, and six women rushed to get into costume.

Entering the Peach Blossom Pavilion, Hazel did a double take. "Well, if this isn't peachy," she said, sending Gladys into an undignified fit of giggles.

Peach-colored cloths draped the tables, on which sat a peach-shaped candlestick and ashtray. Fake windows were framed in ivory colored material with a pattern of luscious peaches smattered throughout. The waiters wore black trousers and peach colored jackets; a rotating ceiling light cast peach circles on the dance floor, and above the bandstand an oversized photograph of Georgia's Peach Blossom Queen demanded attention. "Mah only granddaughter, Charlotte Sue," the club owner boasted to Gladys and Hazel as they set up their instruments.

During the first set, Gladys watched a statuesque cigarette girl, scantily clad in peach satin, thread her way among the tables carrying a tray under her uplifted bosom. "Cigarettes, cigars, chewing gum," she warbled.

A man stepped forward and handed her a slip of paper. She nodded to something he said, and he dropped a coin on her tray. Tucking the note into her cleavage, she wandered toward the band, dropped the paper in Gladys's lap and moved on singing, "Cigarettes, cigars, chewing gum."

At break time, Gladys drew in the slide on her trombone and placed it in its stand. Opening the note, she expected it to be from a Stage Door Johnny wanting to meet her after the show. Instead, the signature was a familiar name, and the message asked her to come to table seven. As she stepped off the bandstand, the man came forward to meet her. "Miss Jones; I'm Johnny Mercer."

"Yes, I'm pleased to meet you. I'm Gladys."

Mercer's wide grin revealed front teeth parted in the middle. He offered his arm and, at his table, introduced his wife, Ginger. She presented a soft, dainty hand to Gladys. "Delighted to meet you."

Her voice oozed charm and hospitality. When she patted perspiration from her nose with a lace handkerchief, Gladys recalled Jerry's observation that women sweat, ladies perspire, and Southern ladies glow. Ginger Mercer glowed.

"Would you like a drink?" the songwriter asked Gladys.

With Prohibition repealed, she assumed he meant hard liquor. "Just water, please," she said.

Ginger drew on a cigarette in an ivory holder, exhaled, and waved her hand at the smoke. "Johnny says y'all have been written up in *Variety.*"

"Yes, luckily we've been mentioned a time or two."

"Don't be modest. From what I've heard so far, it's well-deserved. You gals look precious in those costumes."

Feeling the dampness under her arms, Gladys felt as if she'd just come in from the bunkhouse and Ginger Mercer, in her chic gown, was the lady of the manor.

"I'm a dancer, you know," Ginger said.

Before Gladys could respond, Mercer said to his wife, in a southern gentleman tone, "Sweetie, I need to speak with Miss Jones and I expect she needs to get back to her music."

He turned to Gladys. "To get to the point, I have copies of a song I wrote with Hoagy Carmichael. Maybe you've heard of him. Anyway, it's had a bit of play on radio and I'm pluggin' it wherever I go. I wonder if you and the Rangerettes might play it." He handed Gladys the sheet music and pulled more copies from a briefcase at his feet.

"Play one of your songs? Gosh, you bet. It'd be a pleasure."

Ginger nudged her husband.

"Ginger thinks I should sing it. If you don't mind."

"We'd be honored. Let me talk to my partners and we'll study the music a bit. If you'll excuse me. Nice meeting you both. And thank you." Gladys backed away, then turned and wove her way back to the bandstand.

"Where is he?" Evelyn asked when Gladys finished her story.

"At that table to the left. Don't stare. Okay, he's not looking this way."

"He is now. Say, he's cute. Not much older than we are."

Jerry said. "Let's take another five to look over the sheet music."

Five minutes was all they got; the audience grew restless for the show to continue. On a drum roll from Willeen, Jerry called for attention. "Okay folks, settle down and we'll get back to business." She waited for conversation to subside.

"We've been handed a new tune to play. And the man who wrote it is here. He's been around the music business a while and he's agreed to sing his song. Let's hear it for Savannah's own, Johnny Mercer." She cupped her hand above her eyes and peered out at the tables while a burst of applause brought the composer front and center.

She gave the band a thumbs-up; Mercer leaned into the microphone and crooned, "*La-zy bones, sleepin' in the sun, how you 'spec' to get yo' day's work done.*"

The audience at the tables stood for a better look at the celebrity. Those who'd been itching to dance crowded around the band instead, swaying to the music of the Texas Rangerettes backing up Johnny Mercer.

Brother Can You Spare A Dime

Why should I be standing in line, just waiting for bread ~~~

A cotton candy sunrise haloed the Blue Ridge Mountains; dew sparkled on weeds in the ditches, reminding Gladys of the flickering candles on childhood Christmas trees. The white gossamer fog lurking in the lowlands looked as if a theater scrim had been dropped on the valley.

In the backseat, Evelyn raised the curtain on the window and peered out. "Mama used to say that spider webby stuff in the pasture was spun by fairies."

"Leprechauns," Dorothy corrected.

"There's no such thing."

"But there are fairies?"

"Oh, I don't know. Leave me alone. I'm going back to sleep."

"You started it. And move over, you're almost on top of me. Close your window, too. The breeze is chilly."

"Feels good to me. Put on a sweater."

"Girls, girls," Hazel chided.

"You sound like Mama," Dorothy scolded back.

"When you behave like children, I feel as if I am your mama."

Gladys stayed out of the tiff, but she agreed with Dorothy; the older Hazel got, the more she leaned toward motherliness, or was it bossiness? Then again, Hazel was right, too. Dorothy and Evie often behaved like children, bickering over nothing.

Needing a break from driving, Gladys pulled alongside a row of dilapidated buildings that appeared to have once been the center of a village. "Anyone for a bite to eat?"

"Where?" Dorothy asked. "You gonna perform a miracle and turn that Royal Crown Cola sign into loaves and fishes?"

"Oh, ye of little faith. There must be a café around here somewhere." Gladys tumbled out and rubbed her back.

Jerry landed on her feet outside the hearse and looked around. "I think this is what mountaineers call a holler."

Evelyn asked, "If we holler loud enough will someone bring us food? All we have is a box of damp soda crackers, a black banana and three squished Moon Pies."

"I'll have a Moon Pie," Willeen said.

"They look more like cow pies."

"In that case, I'll pass."

"Me, too," Gladys said. "I need to stretch my legs. Be back in a few minutes."

"Are you going to find the ladies' room?" Willeen called. "Let us know which tree it's behind."

Gladys marched off through a stand of redbuds, moving quickly to exercise her legs but not so fast that she missed the profusion of chicory, Queen Anne's lace, and black-eyed Susans. Clumped together they made a cheerful bouquet of faded blue, delicate white and golden yellow. Squirrels scampered at her feet, insects whispered in overgrown grass, two blue jays scolded each other, and a praying mantis perched on a branch of a fallen tree, like a gargoyle on the corner of an ancient building.

Hearing music, Gladys moved in its direction. Around a bend, she encountered a gray-bearded man seated on a weathered pew outside a ramshackle church with nothing to indicate denomination. Clad in overalls whose patches had been patched, he glanced up as she came through the trees, but didn't seem startled to see a stranger. He tipped his stained straw hat and offered an almost toothless smile. "Mornin'"

"Hello. I heard your music. I'm Gladys Jones."

"Laddie MacFergus, here."

"Pleased to meet you, Mr. MacFergus. What's that instrument you're playing?"

"Dulcimer."

"It's beautiful. What kind of wood?"

He inspected it as if he weren't sure. "Made this'un from curly maple."

"You made it?"

"Jest a mountain dulcimer, for pluckin'. Small, fits on yer lap. There's fancy ones, called hammered dulcimers. Got more strings. You play 'em by strikin' the strings with a wood hammer."

From along the path, came Dorothy's voice, "Gladys. Where are you?" She stepped through the trees. "What are you up to? We need to go."

"Come over here." Gladys waited until she and the others gathered around. "This is Laddie MacFergus. He makes dulcimers. Like this one. Laddie, these are my friends. Some are my sisters, but they're friends, too." Realizing she sounded giddy, she sat beside the old man. "I don't think I mentioned that we're musicians? We'd love it if you'd play for us."

Eyes closed, Laddie brought forth a gentle tune. Finishing with a flourish, he then laid the instrument across Gladys's knees. Her fingers touched the strings and picked out a melody as if it were waiting for her. Laddie reached under the pew and pulled out a fiddle and bow. Without a word, he and Gladys found their stride as a duet.

Two women appeared seemingly out of nowhere, one of them jiggling a baby on her bony hip. Then a young boy joined them, and a scraggly mutt whose tail wagged in time to the music.

The other Rangerettes hurried back for their instruments. By the time they had set up next to Gladys and Laddie, more villagers had emerged from a copse behind the church. Before long they were clapping, singing, and dancing some sort of reel Gladys had never seen. Two teenaged girls captured everyone's attention with a clog dance, not unlike an Irish jig.

An hour of rollicking music and dance flowed before Jerry could convince the audience that the band must leave. Back at the hearse, the men talked about the size of the tires and ran their calloused hands across the sleek surface of the hood. The women stood apart, seemingly in awe. Gladys wondered if any of them had ever seen an automobile. Did they even know the original purpose of this touring car?

A woman sidled up to her. "Wait jist a minute," she said before shuffling across a dirt road to a weathered shack. Returning, she handed Gladys a loaf of unwrapped bread and a corked jug. "Fresh baked this mornin' That's buttermilk in the jug."

"Thank you kindly," Gladys said. "I haven't had buttermilk for years."

Willeen tooted the horn. "Let's go. Where's Dorothy?"

"She went back to the church to offer a prayer," Gladys answered. "You know it's Sunday and we never did get to Mass. I hope the Lord accepts good intentions."

"She better pray we find a filling station soon. Here she comes. All aboard that's comin' aboard."

Back on the road, Hazel broke off chunks of crusty bread and passed them around. "You know," she said, "sometimes I get tired of this gypsy life, living in a funeral wagon, rude people, bad food or no food, then a day like this comes along. This was pure fun."

Gladys nodded her agreement. "These people have almost nothing but the worn clothes on their backs and yet they're happy."

"When it comes down to it, we don't have much in the way of earthly goods either. Just our instruments and our music. We're happy, aren't we?" Hazel waited a beat, then another. "Hey, I said, we're happy, aren't we?"

"Is every—body happy?" Jerry called, impersonating Ted Lewis.

"Hush," Evelyn yelled. "Willeen, stop the car."

Willeen jerked her foot off the gas. "What? You sick off that buttermilk? It stinks to high heaven."

"No, just pull over and listen."

From deep in the valley, bouncing from hill to hollow, the skirl of bagpipes reached them. Hazel and Dorothy picked up the tune, "...*the pipes, the pipes are callin', from glen to glen, and down the mountainside.*"

The plaintive whine of the instrument and the somber song gave Gladys's upbeat spirit a setback, like those darn blues in Memphis had done. Then, recalling the discord earlier this morning between Dorothy and Evelyn, and Hazel putting in her two cents worth, she realized everyone was calmer now. She credited the tunes played with the villagers and the music now echoing off the mountainside. "Music hath charms to soothe the savage breast," she murmured.

Home On The Range

Where the deer and the antelope roam ~~~

With school out and summer days long and languid, Mary relished the freedom of spending an hour or two reading a book, revisiting the Alamo, or, like today, sewing new curtains for the kitchen. Listening to the radio while she worked, she learned that *Lazy Bones* had become the first solid hit for the Mercer/Carmichael team.

Turning to Martin, she repeated what she'd heard on the radio, and added, "Those two songwriters owe their success to the Rangerettes."

Martin raised his eyebrows. "Because they played his song, one time?"

When he stretched his laughter too long to suit Mary, she came after him with a broom and chased him outside.

At noon, Martin waved a white hankie through the kitchen door. "Can I make it up to you with these cards from the girls? I picked up the mail."

"Well, all right. I'll feed you dinner if you behave yourself."

"You dish up the food; I'll read to you. This one's from Dorothy."

~~~ Dear Mama and Pa: It was good to be home with you. Now here we are in the Midwest, our old stompin' grounds. Mount Rushmore is something to see. It's not finished yet, but looking at those huge faces carved on the side of a mountain is hard to describe. Especially under the moonlight. President Coolidge called it a National Shrine. Love, Dorothy ~~~

"Let me see the picture," Mary said, while Martin took a bite of meatloaf and then began reading another note.

~~~ Dear Folks: The Badlands are a desolate area of rocks and craters that seem endless. Deathly quiet. Like another planet might be. I can't do it justice trying to describe it. Will bring home postcards. Oh, we saw lots of buffalo. Time to skedaddle. Yours till the whipped cream peaks and sees the salad dressing. Hazel ~~~

Mary laughed at the silly rhyme. "Gosh, they sure are seeing the country."

"You should go with them sometime. They've asked, you know."

"I can't be away that long. Read the next card. I peeked; it's from Gladys."

~~~ Here's a picture of the Corn Palace in Mitchell. I remember Pa always wanted to see it. It's one of the strangest sights I've laid eyes on. The murals are replaced every year and are made from thousands of bushels of corn, grain, grasses, wild oats, blue grass, rye, straw and wheat. A-maize-ing! Ha Ha. The rea-

son the pioneers built it was to prove the fertility of South Dakota soil. Lit up at night, it does look like a palace, maybe the Taj Mahal. Love, Gladys ~~~

Martin slit open an envelope with his table knife and unfolded two sheets of paper. "We hit the jackpot. One letter from Evie and one from Hazel. Here's Evie's."

~~~ Dear Mama and Pa: You'd have died laughing at the roadhouse we played. Happy Jack's Chicken Shack. We stopped there to eat and Happy Jack O'Malley asked us to play. We had extra time, so we did. Good food. I ate so much chicken I cackled. Happy Jack plays fiddle on WNAX radio. Their sponsor is Gurney Seeds. Pa, bet you've used some of those. Mama, too, in the garden.

He invited us to tour the station. We met the Sunshine Coffee Boys, Harmonica Dutch, and Herbert Lemke. He sings religious songs in German. And a guy named George B. German, a cowboy singer who reads the farm news. And a sweet little girl only eleven who sings up a storm. Margaret Gramm.

The Rosebud Kids is a family of comic entertainers led by the father, Oscar Kosta. In the act he uses the name—okay, are you ready? Oscar Fiddlepoop. I about cracked a rib laughing. Have you heard of a bandleader named Lawrence Welk? He was there. Big guy with a German accent. We had a swell time in Yankton. Cluck, cluck, from the hens. E.D.G.H.J.W. ~~~

"Cluck, cluck," Mary mimicked, and urged Martin to continue reading.

~~~ Dear ones: We saw a wonderful sight today, just by chance. We were driving near the little burg of Jefferson when we saw two huge crosses in the ground. One was in a field, the other a few miles away by the Catholic Church. It was so odd that we stopped. They're called Grasshopper Crosses. I'm copying this info from the brochure. In 1874, grasshoppers devoured all the crops in sight, within an hour. It happened the next year and the next and many settlers had to move or give up farming. One Sunday, the priest led the congregation in prayer, asking for God's protection. He organized a pilgrimage of hundreds of people, not all Catholics, who traveled all day by wagon to set up three crosses in different locations. Grasshoppers did come again, but the area within the perimeter of the crosses was spared that year and ever since.

I was reminded of Grandpa. I always squirmed when he described "hoppers" eating crops. I imagined they had big teeth like a dog. He warned us to stay away from hoppers because they'd spit poison tobacco juice on us. One time I asked, why tobacco juice? There's no tobacco growing around here, is there? He said I was a smart little girl, but that hoppers do spit brown juice that looks like what men spit after they chew a wad of 'bacca. He told great stories. I miss him. Stay well, Hazel ~~~

Mary sighed. "I miss Pa, too. And my daughters. Sometimes I wish they'd settle down here. But they're happy and that makes me happy."

Nice Work If You Can Get It

And you can get it if you try ~~~

"SOS," Gladys called. Watching a ribbon of steam curl from under the hood, she prayed that whatever the trouble was it wouldn't delay their travel; or worse, be the end of the road for the Packard.

"There's a town just ahead," Jerry said. "I see the water tower."

The streets leading to the business district of the county seat town were lined with two-story houses with front and back porches, manicured lawns, and American elm and box elder trees along the curbs. Gladys steered the smoking vehicle into the repair bay at Hank's Auto Shop.

While the others stretched their legs outside in the balmy air, Gladys and Jerry watched with trepidation as the mechanic checked under the hood. "Nice engine," he said, patting it as if the hearse could hear and feel the compliment. Wiping his hands on his striped coverall on which the name Hank was stitched in red, he gave his diagnosis. "Radiator hose is shot."

"What's that mean in dollars?" Jerry asked.

"Aww, not much, but I gotta get a hose somewhere. I'll call Sparky, up the road a few miles. His boy can bring it, maybe late afternoon." Wiping dust from the side of the vehicle, Hank read aloud, "Texas Rangerettes. We're All Pals Together." He stood back for another look. "Think I read about you in a magazine."

"We get some ink now and then. I'm Jerry McRae; this is Gladys Jones."

"Hank Halton. Tell you what, you gals better plan on spending the night. I recommend the Garberson Hotel, block and a half south of here."

"Is that the best hotel or the only one?" Gladys asked. "Not that we're used to the best."

"The only one, but it's nice. There's Maude's Tourist Home, but there's how many of you?" Hank glanced out the window. "I doubt Maude's got room for six. I could call her."

"The hotel is fine," Jerry said. She and Gladys stepped outside to tell the others.

"Oh, great," Willeen grumbled, "we have to tote suitcases and instruments a block down the street?"

Jerry rubbed her eyes and peeked through her fingers. "I'm sure'nuf sorry the hotel isn't above this garage, with an elevator to your room. For cripes sake, if Hell was across the street and Heaven was a block away, you'd choose Hell."

"Whoa, someone got outta bed on the wrong side. Or do you have the monthlies? You're owly."

"Owly? What the Sam Houston does that mean?"

"Out of sorts."

"Yeah, well, transportation problems do that to me. Leave the instruments and take what bags you need for the night. See what kind of rooms you can get, on the cheap. Don't know what this repair will cost. I'll hang around and see what Hank hears from his friend."

While Hazel rummaged for her bag, she said, "You know what, Mama has relatives in this town. I'll ask at the hotel for a phone book; see if I can find them."

"We're not here to socialize," Jerry said.

Hazel planted her hands on her hips. "We're here because we can't go anywhere. If I want to look up relatives instead of sitting around a hotel all afternoon, that's my choice."

"Yeah, yeah, you're right. Sorry. Go on, get outta here."

Gladys stayed behind with Jerry, while the others loped off toting baggage. Willeen and Evelyn walked side by side, each wearing a peasant blouse, shorts, saddle shoes and anklets. Trailing them, Hazel and Dorothy wore dirndl skirts, sleeveless blouses, and sling back shoes with no stockings. They held their valises close to their bodies to keep the wind from whipping their skirts around the waist. Hazel's straw hat lifted off and floated along the gutter. She dropped her bags and gave chase until a man scooped it up in front of the Ben Franklin store and presented it to her.

It amused Gladys when he simply strolled off, as if four pretty women, strangers in town, parading down the street carrying suitcases, was something he saw every day.

Inside, she thumbed through an old *Reader's Digest* magazine while Jerry churned around the room, chewing on her thumbnail. Before long, Hank popped in, as if he were the doctor and they were the family waiting for news about the patient. "I rang up Sparky in Bigelow. The hose'll be here in a couple of hours. His boy is on another errand."

Jerry nodded. "Okay. We'll go over to the hotel and take a nap. I've been accused of being owly."

Hank grinned; he seemed to understand the term. "Where you gals headed?"

"Roof Garden at Arnold's Park."

"Sure, Lake Okoboji. I seen Big Tiny Little play there. And the Six Fat Dutchmen. They're a polka band. And Whoopee John, the daddy of the concertina."

Hank nodded at a poster on the wall showing the Whoopee John band, and read from it, "John Wilfahrt and his band will play."

Gladys hid a smile and waited for Jerry's reaction. She read the lines from the poster and placed an imaginary comma after the bandleader's name, "John Wilfarht, and his band will play. Powerful music. Wish we had a catchy slogan like that."

Hank chortled, dragging it out until it waned to little more than a hiccup. "That's his real name, I swear." He dipped his hand into the melting ice of a metal cooler and came up with three bottles of Nehi pop hanging from his indelibly grease-stained fingers. "Name your poison. Orange or root beer."

"Orange, please, I'm driving," Jerry said.

"Not right away, you ain't." He wiped the moist bottle on his pant leg, snapped off the cap on an opener on the wall, and handed it to Jerry. He repeated the routine for another orange, gave it to Gladys, and opened his root beer. "You know, if you gals wanna put on a show t'night, I could pull some strings; get somebody to open the Legion hall." He grinned. "We call it our civic center. Wouldn't take long to spread the word and you'd have an audience."

Gladys watched Jerry pretend to ponder the idea. The truth was, they were always eager to find extra work. Like that gig at Happy Jack's Chicken Shack. Maybe playing tonight would pay for the repair.

"What would the traffic bear for admission, if we did a show?" Jerry asked.

"Umm, hard to say. Times are tough."

"I heard that," Jerry drawled.

"Local bands usually put a hat on stage and folks toss in what they can afford."

"Just so you know, we wear ten-gallon hats. I'll be satisfied if we make enough to pay the hotel and your repair bill."

"I'll keep it as low as I can."

"Thanks, but don't cut yourself short. So, what kind of music do folks around here like? We play most anything."

"Most anything should do it. Old-time or polka. The kids like jazz, swing, big bands. Hey, whatta you think of Benny Goodman?"

"That cat plays a mean licorice stick."

"Sure does."

"Are you a musician?" Gladys asked.

"Self-taught. I play guitar. Say, maybe before the show you'd let me sit in with you, warm up on a few tunes."

Jerry dropped her bottle into a slotted wooden crate. "Hank, you're a man after my own heart. You bribe us with soda pop, then proposition us. Okay, you arrange for that civic center of yours and you can warm up with us. I'll check back with you later. Just don't get so worked up anticipating your break into show biz that you forget about that radiator hose."

"I'm on it. Meanwhile, introduce yourself to folks on the street and by tonight we'll all be cuttin' a rug. You got some posters, hang 'em on the light posts. Tell you what, I got a megaphone. I'll have Sparky's boy drive through town announcing the dance, even up in Bigelow. Folks come from miles around for a dance."

Roll out the barrel, we'll have a barrel of fun ~~~

In the morning, after breakfast at Clara's Palace Café, the rehabilitated Packard was back on the road. "Despite the trouble, that was a good time," Gladys said.

"Sure was," Jerry admitted. "I always thought Iowans were sober folks, like that dreary couple in the famous painting. You know the one I mean?"

"Whistler's Mother," Willeen said.

Jerry groaned. "Willie, sometimes I wonder about you; bless your heart. I said couple, not somebody's mother."

"American Gothic," Hazel offered.

"Yeah, that's the one. Anyhow, these folks had a high old time. I had a heck of a time keeping up with Hank on the polka. He was cute once he cleaned the grime off his face. Darn cute."

Among those cutting a rug at the dance was Vonnie Woodward, social reporter for the local paper. She had told the group her write-up would be in the next issue, and she'd send a copy to their home address.

Zing, went the strings of my heart ~~~

Mary's cousin Aggie's envelope beat Miss Woodward's to the San Antonio mailbox. Finding mail from Aggie alarmed Mary; the two exchanged Christmas cards every year but rarely anything more. This had to be bad news about family. Seated on the front steps, her heart racing, Mary tore open the envelope and shook out the contents. Her fingers fumbled when she picked up a newspaper clipping that fell from between a folded letter. An obituary, she thought, and closed her eyes for a moment. Peeking, she noted it wasn't a death notice. The first line about bad luck concerned her, but reading further allayed her fears.

~~~ *Osceola County Clarion*, June 15, 1934
Entertainment Troupe's Bad Luck, Our Good Luck
A broken radiator hose was an unlucky happening for a troupe of entertainers, but their misfortune was none of our own. Local residents enjoyed a treat last Thursday evening when the Texas Rangerettes hosted an impromptu show at the American Legion. The all-girl band staged a fabulous show, playing their regular program as well as requests.

The popular musicians, who travel in an old Packard hearse, had engine trouble and were forced to stop for repairs. From here, they will play at the Roof Garden at Lake Okoboji, then on to Wisconsin for a tour of resorts.

During the show's intermission, this reporter was granted an interview. Two of the musicians, Jerry McCrae and Willeen Grey, are life-long Texans. The other four, sisters Hazel, Gladys, Dorothy and Evelyn Jones, are originally from Park Rapids, Minnesota. The eldest sister, Hazel, commented, "I knew we had relatives here, but we'd never met any of them until tonight. We visited with our mother's first cousin, Agnes Guertin, and her daughters, Goldie Foley and Maybelle Dries."

Mrs. Guertin told this reporter, "It was wonderful meeting the Jones girls. I have fond memories of their mother. As girls, we attended dances together, and Mary played with my brothers in their little band."

Until next week, dear readers, I am, Vonnie Woodward ~~~

Mary hurried out back where Martin was pulling weeds in the vegetable garden. "Listen to this," she said, waving the clipping. "The girls met some of my cousins and I'm even mentioned in the article."

After Mary read the piece aloud, Martin said, "I've always told you those gals can take of themselves. They have car trouble and they end up doing a show. You worry too much about them."

Recalling a Gaelic word meaning rubbish, Mary sputtered, "*Raimeais.* You worry as much as I do." She looked into the distance. "I wonder where they are now, what they're doing. They sure have some adventures."

"I keep tellin' you to go with them."

Mary swatted Martin's arm. "Yes, you do. And I keep wondering why you're so danged eager to get rid of me."

South Of The Border

Down Mexico way; she was a picture, in old Spanish lace ~~~

Back home for a respite, Gladys pushed open the back door and nearly stumbled over Jerry, seated on the stoop. "Whoa, you startled me. What are you doing here?"

"Too early to knock. I wasn't fixin' to wake anyone."

Gladys tugged up the legs of her cotton slacks and sat beside Jerry. "What's on your mind?"

"I think we should do a gig or two in Mexico. Then we can bill ourselves as international stars."

"I never think of Mexico as international."

"It might be a stretch, but it'll look good on our posters."

"If you say so. South of the border sounds like fun to me. Let's round up the others; see what they think."

The opening show at Cantina Maria in Piedras Negras had a small audience; there wasn't room for anything more. The simple adobe building held a tantalizing aroma of fried food, ancient spices, and fiery sauces. Between sets, the entertainers enjoyed snacks from Maria's kitchen. Like a mother urging her children to eat, Maria called out the names of the foods: chorizo, paella, tortilla, frijole, burrito, sopapillas, enchildala, chalupa. The performers ate everything in sight, followed by flan for dessert and bottles of pop brought from home. "Don't drink the water," Mary had warned.

The next night, the Cactus Lounge of the Laredo Hotel in Nuevo Laredo had a full house. "They seem to be tourists," Jerry told the others. "I'll introduce the opening song in English and see what happens."

She stepped forward to greet the audience. "Good evening. We'd like to open with a song that's been around so long no one seems to know who wrote it. We know it as *The Streets of Laredo.*"

Hearty applause indicated the crowd understood English. "It's sometimes called *The Cowboy's Lament,* or *The Dying Cowboy,* but its roots are in Ireland, where it was known as *The Bard of Armagh.*"

She sang a line, "*Oh, list to the tale of a poor Irish harper, and scorn not strings in an old withered hand; remember these fingers could once move more sharper, to waken the echoes of his dear native land.*

"It was also a sea chanty called *Over the Sea to Skye,* and another one called *The Unfortunate Rake,* about a young sailor named Rake who was cut down in his prime. *So beat the drums lowly, and play the fifes slowly, there goes an unfortunate boy to his home."*

That familiar line brought a rousing reaction. "Okay, enough music history," Jerry said. She nodded at the band, and they began the song with Jerry and Evelyn doing the vocal. *"As I walked out in the streets of Laredo, as I walked out in Laredo one day, I spied a young cowboy all wrapped in white linen, all wrapped in white linen as cold as the clay ~~~ "*

The next morning, confident that the show had been a success, Gladys bought a newspaper and searched for a review. Finding one in *Las Noticias de Piedras Negras,* she handed it to Evelyn to read aloud over breakfast.

When Evelyn began in Spanish, Hazel requested, "Translate, please."

"When in Rome, do as the Romans do."

"We're not in Rome."

"No, we're in May-he-co. And this is a good time to practice Spanish. Sister Carmelita used to say, 'Use it or lose it.' *El Tejas Rangerettes famoso trajeron recientemente su sur de la musica de la frontera para dos compromisos. Un desempeno por el todo banda de baile de mujer se jugo en Cantina Maria en Piedras Negras; el otro estaba en el Hotel de Laredo en Nuevo Laredo."* Evelyn paused to sip coffee and scan the review.

"Oh, this is just swell," Hazel griped.

"Costumed en el traje occidental, las mujeres mantuvieron un paso rapido, conmutacion entre el columpio occidental, el jazz, y los aires populares. Cuatro de los miembros del banda son hermanas: Hazel, Gladys, Dorothy y Evelyn Jones. Los otros dos seres de Rangerettes Willeen Gris y Jerry McRae."

Dorothy feigned a yawn. "Gosh, this is interesting, Evie."

"You took Spanish. Figure it out."

"I figured out the word costumed, and our names."

"A la delicia de las muchedumbre, Senorita McRae y Senorita Evelyn Jones cantaron varias canciones en el espanol. El fallo McRae dijo ella crecio en Tejas tan espanol es su segundo idioma, mientras Senorita Jones lo aprendio en preparatoria despues de mover a San Antonio del Minnesota. Este revisor espera que el Rangerettes haga otro vist abajo nuestra manera verdadera pronto."

Evelyn caught her breath. "Okay, translation for you grumpy gringos. In a nutshell, he mentions our western costumes, the music, western swing, jazz, popular tunes, gives our names, says the crowds were delighted when Miss McRae and Miss Evelyn Jones sang in Spanish. Having grown up in Texas, Miss McRae's second language is Spanish while Miss Jones learned it in high school after moving to San Antonio from Minnesota. The other girls should have learned it, too, but they had a habit of cutting Spanish class."

Hazel grabbed the paper. "It doesn't say that."

"So I made up that part. Anyway, the reviewer hopes we visit again real soon. *Comprende?*"

"*Si,*" came a chorus of five. Evelyn took a bow.

My Bonny Lies Over The Ocean

My bonny lies over the sea ~~~

On the trip home, Gladys did a double-take when Jerry said, "Now that we've debuted outside the U.S., I'd like to set up some shows in Hawaii."

"The Hawaiian Islands?"

"Unless there's a Hawaii I don't know about. I got a letter from a booking agent who suggested we do a tour."

Hazel waded into the conversation. "Can we afford sailing to Hawaii?"

"Okay, here's the deal. Everybody listening? Cruise lines are touting Hawaii as an antidote to the Depression blues. They're looking for entertainment on the way over and back."

"So we sing for our supper?" Hazel asked.

"Of course. There's no fare. What more do you want? And hotels over there are clamoring for entertainment. Same deal; we get a free room or a cheap rate in a luxury hotel."

"I'm packing my bags," Hazel said.

"We can't drive there, can we?" Willeen asked.

Jerry hooted. "No, dear heart, we'll put the Packard in her stall for this trip."

Back home, after Jerry had secured the cruise booking, Gladys suggested to her sisters that the folks should go with them to Hawaii. When Hazel proposed the idea, Pa pulled forward in his platform rocker, turned off the Bob Hope Show, and asked, "You want us to go where?"

"Hawaii. Jerry is booking us at the Royal Hawaiian Hotel on Waikiki Beach."

"Oh, my," Mama said, "I saw pictures of that place in *National Geographic*. It's called the Pink Palace of the Pacific."

"Hold on, Lass. Have you gals got money for that kind of travel? I sure don't. Money doesn't grow on trees here."

Gladys answered, "For us, there's no fare, in exchange for performing on the ship. Maybe we can finagle a reduced fare for you and Mama, as our managers. We get free or reduced rates at the hotel, too."

"Managers. I like that," Mama said. "How much is the fare?"

"A little over two hundred dollars round trip from San Francisco."

"Two hundred?" Pa shook his head.

"Martin, let's go. I can get a substitute to teach my classes."

"Have you gone mad? You know I don't like being on water. When I was a kid I heard tales about trips from Ireland, coffin ships and burials at sea. Scared me silly."

Evelyn, playing Scrabble with Dorothy, dismissed the comment. "Both grandpas used to tell those stories but that was eons ago. Ships are better now."

"Don't forget about the Titanic not so long ago."

"The Titanic? Don't worry, there won't be any icebergs on the way. Anyway, I read in the brochure that this ship has cork insulation. You've seen the way a cork floats, haven't you?"

"Yeah, I've seen corks do that a time or two, but I don't float. Why do you think I shower at Doc's instead of using the tub here?"

"Come on, this trip will be good for you. Get you away from a Texas winter."

"I came to Texas to get away from Minnesota winters. Are you gonna keep movin' me? February's near perfect here."

Dorothy weighed in. "The ship has that new-fangled air-conditioning. We'll be comfortable no matter the weather."

Pa nodded at the open window, where dimity curtains ruffled in and out on the breeze. "There's air-conditionin' for you. You gals go ahead and have a good time. Your mother and I'll stay put and hear all about it when you come home."

Mama laid aside her tatting needles and a doily. "Martin, we should go. You haven't seen the Rangerettes perform since we went to Galveston two years ago."

"Lass, you know I'm their biggest fan, but I hear and see them perform all the time, right here. Like I said, I don't cotton to being on water."

"Okay, then. You're always saying I should travel with the girls. Well, I'm going to Hawaii."

A cheer erupted from the girls.

"I have a little money saved," Mama added.

"You do?" Pa asked. "Holdin' out on me, eh? Okay, spend your egg money."

Mama laughed. "Egg money? I haven't heard that since we were on the farm."

"Pa, please go," Dorothy begged.

"With all you women. Lordy, I'd be a thorn among roses."

"Professor Tremblay's going."

"Then we'd be two thorns among roses. End of discussion. Godspeed."

Mama wagged her finger. "Don't complain later that you weren't invited."

"Well, dang, that takes all the fun out of it if I can't complain."

In the morning, Gladys found her mother at the kitchen table earlier than usual. "Could hardly sleep," she said, "worrying if I have enough money, and proper clothes for a sea voyage. Is Mass available on a ship?"

"Yes; Mass and a Protestant service. These ships are as big as…probably the town of Park Rapids. Main street, anyway."

Mama yawned and rubbed her eyes. "Never dreamed I'd go to Hawaii. What's next, Ireland? Oh, that would be grand. But it won't happen."

Gladys winked at her. "Don't be so sure. Mention it to Jerry and see what happens."

California Here I Come

Open up that Golden Gate ~~~

Roosting on the edge of her train seat, Mary paid little attention to her fellow passengers. She kept her eyes on the western vista; the majestic Rockies, the canyons and deserted mining camps, the cowboys on horseback. "It's like watching a movie," she told her daughters before reluctantly leaving her seat for her sleeping berth. "Thank you for this wonderful trip."

With a two-day layover in San Francisco, Louise guided the group on a tour; she and the professor had been there before. The Texans rode cable cars to view Nob Hill's mansions, the Mark Hopkins hotel, the Alamo district's Victorian homes, and Mission Dolores dating back to 1776. Along the wharf, they lunched on crabs out of the shell, and clam chowder served in edible sour dough bread bowls. "Martin would love this," Mary said. "He likes sopping up soup or gravy with a piece of bread. So do I," she confessed with a grin.

The Golden Gate Bridge glistening in the sun dazzled Mary. On an island visible from shore, the new Alcatraz Prison housed some of America's most dangerous gangsters and racketeers, including Al Capone and Machine Gun Kelly. Closer in, on a strand of rugged rocks, hundreds of sea lions produced an overpowering odor. Mary sputtered a laugh when Evelyn pinched her nose and said, "Not exthactly conduthive to *bon appetit.*"

"Let's get out of here," Louise said, and spirited them off to tour the Gold Rush Museum and a photographic exhibit of the 1906 earthquake. Then, as Irish luck had it, they entered Chinatown through Dragon's Gate and found themselves entangled in the midst of the New Year's parade, led by an undulating, smoke-snorting, multi-colored dragon with human feet. A children's band provided tinny music and resounding gongs, while firecrackers popped and sizzled, so alarming Mary that she took cover in the doorway to a laundry. From there, she listened to the workers' sing-song, exotic language. Every sight and sound of San Francisco intrigued her.

Exhausted from their day, the troubadours agreed on an early dinner in the hotel dining room, after which they would retire. While finishing dessert, a spotlight came on in the corner of the room, and the hotel manager basked in the glow. "Ladies and gentlemen; may I have your attention? We're honored to have with us some special guests. Of course, all of you are special guests, but I hope I won't be intrusive by introducing the Texas Rangerettes." The light swung to the table; other diners looked up and a few applauded.

"They never heard of us," Evelyn said to Gladys. "Surely he's not going to ask us to play."

"Are you kidding? Of course he will."

The manager addressed the musicians. "We don't usually offer music with dinner, but I wonder if you'd honor us tonight. I'd be happy to have a bellboy fetch your instruments."

Gladys nudged Evelyn. "What did I tell you?"

After a quick discussion at the table, Jerry responded. "Thank you for asking. We'd be delighted to play a few tunes."

The diminutive manager drifted over to the table. "You'll find a reduction on your bill when you check out," he said to the group in general while he ogled Dorothy and patted her hand.

As Dorothy pulled away, Evelyn shimmied toward Romeo, her hips swaying while she crooned, "*Ten cents a dance, that's what they pay me, come on big boy, ten cents a dance.*" She looked into his eyes and he squirmed backward.

Surprised by her youngest daughter's seductive performance, Mary watched the befuddled manager run his hand across the cheap toupee askew on his head and then nervously lick his lips, above which a mustache appeared to be drawn on with a mascara pencil.

"Like I said, there'll be a reduced room rate," he hemmed and hawed, and scurried away like a fugitive.

Mary chided Evelyn, "Shame on you," before breaking into laughter that had more people staring at her than had paid attention to the announcement that the Texas Rangerettes were in town.

Suddenly Mary found herself lifted to her feet by Hazel and Gladys and propelled toward the corner where the band would perform. "What…what are you doing?"

The girls sat her on a piano bench. "You're playing with us," Gladys said, her hand planted on her mother's shoulder so she couldn't rise.

"No, no, I can't."

"Don't make a scene," Hazel ordered as Jerry and the others arrived with their instruments. "You've played with us hundreds of times."

Jerry raised her eyebrows at Mary. "We'll go easy on you."

Trapped between six young women, Mary willed herself to relax throughout the hour long performance that kept diners lingering. Finally, she whispered to Jerry, "I'll need toothpicks to keep my eyes open if this goes much longer."

"I'll wrap it up," Jerry said as a slurred voice requested *Melancholy Baby.*

She waved in the man's direction. "I knew you were here somewhere. That's a request we never fail to get." She started the group off with "*Come to me my melancholy baby. Cuddle up and don't be blue ~~~* "

After they completed the song she announced, "Time to call it a night. In closing, we'll do our theme, *We're All Pals Together.*"

A few minutes later, collapsing into bed, Mary said her prayers, adding a litany of thanks for her daughters and their accomplishments and for their generosity in taking her with them on what was already an unforgettable trip. What an evening this turned out to be. I did pretty well, all things considered, if I do say so myself. If only Martin were here it would be beyond perfect.

She worried for a minute that he might not be eating properly. Who knew what he and Doc were concocting for meals. One day Doc had cooked and served mashed potatoes with sardines on top, and Martin came home raving about it. Mary refused to prepare it, telling Martin, "Once you open a can of sardines in the house, the smell is there forever."

She thanked God for her family's good health and that they all had steady jobs during this bleak time for the country. With tonight's music ringing in her ears, she left it at that. She had told God many times she was grateful for all her blessings. If He didn't know by now, well, what more could she say?

Dreamy Honolulu Moon

Shining above, oh what a Heavenly sight ~~~

Waiting to board the S.S. Lurline, Mary studied its brochure and learned that it was launched in 1932 and was the most popular of the four cruise ships run by Matson Navigation Service. The Lurline traveled outbound from San Francisco to Honolulu, homebound to Los Angeles, and then back to San Francisco.

The liner could carry more than seven hundred passengers plus a crew of four hundred. Sleek and white, with blue smoke stacks and glossy teak decks, it boasted a formal dining room and the casual Verandah Cafe and Dance Pavilion with wicker and bamboo furniture and palm-filled nooks. Mary planned to use the library with its plush leather chairs and well-stocked shelves, and spend time in the Writing Room, sending letters and postcards on Lurline stationery to Martin and to friends and family. She wondered if using the embossed paper might look boastful, but she hadn't brought stationery so the letterhead would have to do.

She and Gladys and Hazel shared a giggle when they overheard Evelyn and Dorothy discussing the two plunges on the ship. "We might be swimming alongside other celebrities," Evelyn said.

"For gosh sake, Evie, we're not celebrities."

"Well, we're not as popular as Ginger Rogers, but...."

"Ginger Rogers? We're a million miles from that gal."

Mary interrupted them. "Girls; it says here that among the ship's notable passengers have been Bing and Dixie Crosby, Jeanette McDonald, and Edgar Rice Burroughs. Amelia Earhart and her plane sailed on the Lurline in December of 1934, and just a month ago she flew the plane from Oahu to Oakland, California."

"See," Evelyn taunted Dorothy, "look around. I'll bet you'll see familiar faces."

"Sure, and they'll recognize us, too. You bet."

"Come on," Mary called. "It's nearly time to embark." The last word sounded strange; a word she never thought she'd use in a sentence pertaining to herself. This whole experience was more like a dream than reality.

While some passengers hosted private bon voyage parties in their rooms, the Texas group mingled at the ship's party, nibbling at the buffet of cheeses, deviled eggs, fresh fruit, pigs in blankets, chocolates, and fruit punch. Mary's eyes widened when a steward explained that five hundred bottles of champagne and fifty pounds of caviar would be consumed today. She told the young man, "I could easily lose sight of the Depression if I allowed myself to do so."

In costume, the Rangerettes strolled about and introduced themselves as the featured act in the Dance Pavilion. Their competition, playing in the dining room, would be Peggy Gilbert and Her Metro-Goldwyn Girls, who had appeared in Hollywood musicals. When the glamour gals paraded around wearing sophisticated evening gowns, Mary studied them closely, then said to Louise, "Classy, but the Rangerettes are more down to earth. More fun."

She jerked to attention at a blast from the ship's horn, warning non-passengers to leave. Fifteen minutes later, when two blares warned stragglers to leave the ship, she found the rest of her party at the railing, where they dropped streamers to people below. Finally, after three gentle toots, the ship eased away, passed under the Golden Gate Bridge and slipped into the calm blue-green Pacific.

Mary tried to soak up the new images so she could write to Martin, but at the moment she had no words for the grandeur. She simply lifted her head to the sky and enjoyed the mist on her face. So this is what the sea smells like, she thought. Clean and salty and…fishy. The next time I open my trunk I'll recognize the smell I only imagined before.

They're wearing 'em higher in Hawaii ~~~

Five days later, on Boat Day, the staff from the Royal Hawaiian Hotel rowed out to Diamond Head and boarded the Lurline. To the music of the Royal Hawaiian Band, young girls wearing grass skirts swayed and swiveled across the deck, wrapping leis around passengers' necks. "I hope they're wearing something under their leis," Mary said, lifting her gardenia necklace for a whiff.

"Don't count on it," Evelyn said. "Nor under the men's loin cloths. Him Tarzan, me Jane." She eyed a bronzed young man who had been diving for silver dollars.

"Behave yourself," Mary scolded as he approached her.

"Aloha," he cried, wrapping an orchid lei around her neck.

"Aloha," Mary answered as he moved on with his armful of garlands. "I don't know if that means hello or goodbye," she added.

"Both," Dorothy said.

"Oh, well, that's simple enough to remember."

"Aloha," came another welcome, and the Texans were whisked away by car to the hotel. Mary rubbernecked out the window at the stately palm trees, the pristine beaches, the villages where women strutted about wearing colorful sarongs, and brown children played in the sun.

Ahead sprawled the Royal Hawaiian Hotel, one of the "jewels of Waikiki," their driver explained in his spiel. "The Spanish-Moorish architecture is unique to this part of the world. It's partly a tribute to Rudolph Valentino, adding mystery and romance to the island. The ground on which the hotel stands is sacred; once the home of King Kamehameha and the queen."

Mary's breath stopped when she entered the lobby, aglow in pink décor and lush with tropical greenery. When Jerry scurried off to greet someone she knew, a poster told Mary that he was Del Courtney, and his band, comprised of a dozen young men who looked about the same ages as the Rangerettes.

During the next few days, the Tremblays flew off to another island and the girls spent their free time with the Courtney band, discussing music, sightseeing, or relaxing on the beach and listening to Hawaiian music. Mary strolled along the shoreline, letting the foamy surf caress her feet, and sifting shells through her fingers. One afternoon she watched in awe as two boys plowed into the crashing surf, only to emerge standing atop their colorful wooden boards. That night she wrote to Martin.

~~~ Dear Martin: The hotel's beach is private; roped off, and they actually rake the sand daily. Can you imagine? Today I watched boys "surfing." They take these big boards into the water and ride on the waves. It's hard to describe. The hotel has a group of musicians called the Waikiki Beach Boys. They never leave the sand from sunup to moon glow. One of the men, Chick Daniels, is known for his pants-dropping hula, leaving himself in only comical underwear. Our hostess told us that he once dropped his pants and had forgotten to put on his drawers.

The girls have a suite with three double beds, and I have a small adjoining room that's rounded because it's in a tower. I feel like Rapunzel (a fairy tale story I used to read to the girls). I keep the window open and fall asleep listening to music and laughter from the beach. We went to a luau last night—that's a Hawaiian picnic. The food was "ono" (delicious), but I could hardly enjoy myself for thinking about all the hungry people in our country. I took only a bite of everything because there was too much to eat large portions. Here's some of what we had: Kalua pig (baked in an oven in the ground), kim chee (spiced cabbage), lomi lomi salmon, mahi mahi (white fish) poi (a kind of paste that you dip things in), stuffed taro leaves and ti leaves, corn chowder, lots of rice, chi (pork stew), char sui (spare ribs), banana bread and mango bread. For dessert, haupia, a coconut pudding. I couldn't sleep; my stomach was too full. Say hi to Doc for me. I sent him a card. I miss you. Love, Mary ~~~

In addition to the Royal Hawaiian performances, Jerry had booked the band at the Alexander Young Hotel, as well as on the other islands. Mary had a front row seat wherever they played, and wrote Martin:

~~~ Dear Husband: My two favorite shows were the one at an Officer's Club near Pearl Harbor, and an outdoor show where the audience was sailors from the warships anchored nearby. It gave me an odd feeling to see those ships, prepared to go to battle. I pray that never happens.

You should've seen the girls, in their costumes, but instead of western hats they pranced around wearing sailor caps. They looked as cute as can be. The sailor boys went wild. It's so much fun here. I'll have to do penance for all the pleasures I've been afforded. But tomorrow we leave for home, and I'm happy about that, too. I'm eager to see you and to tell you more. Love, Mary ~~~

For the return voyage, Mary armed herself with a journal, a sketchpad and a box of colored pencils. It had been years since she had taken time to draw, but now she would scratch out scenes of the harbor and of Diamond Head as they became distant mirages. There was so much to tell Martin; she didn't want to forget a single detail.

Back in the states, Del Courtney posed his friends for a photo. Leaning against the ship's rail, windblown and smiling, leis around their necks, were Gladys, Hazel, Dorothy, Willeen, Louise, Jerry, Evelyn, and Mary. Crouched in front, wearing a woman's hat and draped in flower neckpieces, Professor Tremblay held a life preserver lettered: S. S. Lurline, San Francisco.

When Del's photo arrived, Mary placed it on the piano where she could see it every day. Each time she looked at it, she thought: That's me standing there aboard ship. I really took that trip.

When Martin first saw the photo he said, "See there, the professor was a thorn among roses, even with that flowered hat on his head."

"He had a wonderful time. You would have, too. If I go again, you're going with me if I have to put you in a straightjacket and a life preserver."

"That'll be the only way to get me there, Lass. The only way."

"It could be arranged," Mary said. "Your daughters have clout."

What Is This Thing Called Love

Oh, who can solve, this mystery ~~~

"*Ain't nobody's business if I do,*" Billie Holiday sang. Gladys had been reading, but laid aside her book to listen to the radio. It didn't get any better than Billie Holiday, even if she sang the blues. It was the voice, not the lyrics.

Dorothy showed up in the doorway and listened, too. When the tune ended, Gladys turned down the radio. "You're out late. Where've you been?"

"Went to a movie. James Cagney. It was boring." She dropped onto the bed. "I see enough corruption and disregard for others when we're on the road."

"Then why'd you pick that one?"

"Keith picked it."

"Huh? Who the devil is Keith?"

"My boyfriend."

Speechless, Gladys waited, watching Dorothy pick at a tuft of lavender chenille on the bedspread. "I'm not going on the next tour," she finally said.

"Whoa; back up to the part about your boyfriend."

Dorothy quieted the tangle of Bakelite bracelets clanking on her wrist. "His name is Keith Foss. I've been writing to him while we were away, and seeing him since I got home. I met him before we left on the last tour, on a blind date, arranged by Nina. Well, by her boyfriend. He's an F.B.I. agent."

"Nina's boyfriend is an F.B.I. agent?"

"No, Keith is."

Gladys let this sink in. "Pa will be impressed. But what's he doing here? Why not Washington?"

"There are F.B.I. field offices all over the country."

"Oh. Well, why hasn't he come to the house for you? It's only proper."

"I don't need a lecture on proper manners. We meet at the cafe where Nina works. Her boyfriend hangs out there until she gets off work."

"Okay, start at the beginning and tell me about this mystery man. And what does he have to do with you not going on tour?"

Dorothy flipped onto her side and faced Gladys. "He's dreamy. Kind of reminds me of Gary Cooper. He has dark hair, wears glasses, and he's thirty-four."

"What? That's nine years older than you."

"I can add. So what if he's older? I'm not getting any younger. We're all old maids, as far as that goes. None of us has had a personal life. Keith's the first man I've dated more than three times."

Gladys knew all too well; she hadn't been on a date since—well, who knew? "Is he Catholic?"

Dorothy nibbled a cuticle. "You sound like Mama. I don't know."

"You don't know?"

"The subject hasn't come up."

"That's an important subject."

"Sure, but it'd be embarrassing to come right out and ask. Anyway, that's why I need to stay here, to get to know him better. Sometimes I don't even know myself. I'm either a Rangerette or a Jones girl. Evelyn hated that when we were kids, never being just herself. When I'm with Keith and my friends, I'm plain Dorothy Jones."

"Not so plain, in case you haven't looked in a mirror lately."

"Oh, you know what I mean. I need to do something on my own, something my sisters aren't doing. I need to stand on my own two feet and decide what I want to do."

"Does Keith want you to stay here?

"He hasn't said so. I know for sure he likes me."

"How could he not? You're talented, beautiful."

"You have to say that because you're my sister."

"I wouldn't say it if wasn't true. You have to invite him over to meet us."

"That's scary."

"Are we that bad?" Gladys crossed her eyes and stretched her mouth with her fingers, making light of the situation but concerned just the same about her innocent little sister being involved with a worldly F.B.I. agent nine years her senior.

"Mama would say, keep that up and your face will freeze that way."

Gladys relaxed her face and laughed. "When I was a kid I wondered how long I'd have to hold it until it froze."

"Yeah, well, anyway. If I bring Keith home, wouldn't he think I'm pushing him into, you know, something serious, if I ask him to meet the family?"

"Something tells me you're already serious. Tell you what, have him pick you up here next time. Introduce him and then scram. You know Mama, before you leave she'll invite him for a meal. Then you suggest Sunday dinner. That way you might find out if he's Catholic. You could say something like, 'Come about noon, after Mass,' and see what he says."

"Jeepers, now you're writing a script for me. Okay, next date, he picks me up here. Then you tell me if you think I should stay here instead of going on tour."

"No, no, like you said, this is your decision. I'll miss you like crazy if you stay here, but this is up to you."

I want a Sunday kind of love, I want a love that's on the square ~~~

Gladys agreed with Dorothy that Keith resembled Gary Cooper, but she noticed right off that he lacked the actor's shy "aww, shucks," attitude. He came armed with yellow roses for Dorothy and a double layer box of Whitman's chocolates for Mama. When Willeen and Jerry arrived for dinner, he roped them in with, "I've had some dealings with the Texas Rangers but I didn't know they had women in their ranks. Especially six pretty ones."

Under the cover of nine people chattering and dishes clattering, Gladys nudged Dorothy and whispered, "He made the sign of the cross when we said grace."

"I know. Mama was looking, too."

Later, while Hazel filled coffee cups and Gladys served pecan pie, Pa slipped out of his suit jacket and invited Keith to do the same.

He stood and shucked off his blue blazer, revealing a holstered gun strapped across his blue and white striped shirt. With a disarming glance, he said, "Don't worry, Mrs. Jones, there's only one of me and you've got six Texas Rangers on your side."

Mama waved her hand as if she hadn't given the gun a second thought, but she kept her eyes on the holster after he sat down.

"So," Pa said to Keith, "tell us more about your work."

"Tell about the impersonator you're after," Dorothy suggested, her eyes aglow.

"Ah, yes, slippery George." Keith plucked a cigarette from a bronze case with F.B.I. engraved on the lid and Dorothy pushed an ashtray toward him.

"This Hungarian has been a thorn in J. Edgar's side for years. We don't know where he is right now but he'll pop up under another alias. He's pretended to be an army colonel and a famous aviator and a dozen other people. Claims Louis B. Mayer, from the movies, is a friend, but he lies outta both sides of his mouth. Back in the twenties, he toured the country impersonating the son of Baron von Krupp, the German arms maker. He met with governors, politicians, even duped Henry Ford, who supposedly loaned him a touring car."

Keith gestured at a picture of Pope Pius on the wall. "Believe me, this swindler would've had an audience with the pope if he lived here."

Gladys mumbled to Dorothy, "He knows who the pope is. Another good sign."

All eyes were on the G-man, waiting while he dragged on his cigarette and exhaled, directing the smoke out the open window beside him. "The guy was finally caught and deported, but he's a sly fox and returned using a stolen passport. Before long he was flashing phony credentials as an ambassador's son. Back and forth across the country, pretending to be someone important, hanging paper every step of the way."

While Keith crushed out his cigarette, Pa explained to the women that hanging paper meant writing bad checks. I knew that, Gladys thought; the Rangerettes have been handed a rubber check or two.

"This bum has served time, been deported more than once, yet he keeps coming back like a boomerang. His file's as thick as that stack of sheet music on the piano bench." Keith glanced across the table. "Can you play all those tunes, Mrs. Jones?"

Gladys contained a laugh when Mama blushed and said, "Oh, after a fashion."

"I'd love to hear you play sometime, and the Texas Rangers, too. Anyway, my favorite story about George is when he was staying at a YMCA in Illinois. He'd told the manager he was an ambassador's son and the manager had no reason to doubt him. One day the impostor told the manager he had to go to Chicago on business and needed cash. The manager cashed a twenty dollar check for him, and our man left a couple of suitcases behind, indicating he'd be back.

"Before long, the manager learned from another clerk that the man was a scam artist and that he'd gone to Bloomington. Off the manager went, determined to find the bum who'd cheated him. As luck would have it, the manager ran into George on the street in Bloomington and told him he'd have to make good the double sawbucks or he'd have him arrested on the spot. Mister Bigshot maintained he was the ambassador's son and that he would pay back the money when his father's check arrived. Then, you'll love this, he asked the manager to loan him five bucks, which he would pay back, plus the twenty, when he returned to Springfield in a few days. To show he was on the up and up, he offered his suitcase as security."

"Don't tell me the sucker bit on that one?" Pa asked.

"You betcha. The dimwit handed over five bucks and went home with another piece of shabby luggage. Of course the impostor never returned and the manager was out twenty-five bucks instead of twenty, plus what it cost him to drive to Bloomington."

"My word," Mama sputtered. "Like the saying goes, Fool me once, shame on you. Fool me twice, shame on me."

"This guy has fooled the best of 'em, Mrs. Jones, including the Bureau."

Keith stayed well into the afternoon, spinning yarns about the cases he'd worked. After he left, Dorothy surprised everyone except Gladys by announcing that she was staying home from the next tour to keep company with Keith.

Mama and Pa fussed over Dorothy, delighted with the idea of having her home. "I'll fatten you up," Mama promised. "All you girls need some meat on your bones."

"I'm lookin' forward to seein' that agent again," Pa said. "His stories are better than the ones in Doc's detective magazines." He glanced at Dorothy. "Maybe one of you girls will get married after all."

Dorothy flushed and lowered her eyes. "We're only dating."

"That's how it begins."

Gladys and Willeen agreed that Dorothy needed time off to see how things would work out with Keith. Hazel and Jerry huddled in a corner discussing who among the musicians they knew might sit in with the band, while Evelyn said more than once, "He's definitely a dreamboat."

Now into their sixth year, the Texas Rangerettes left San Antonio as a quintet.

Who's Sorry Now

Whose heart is breaking ~~~

Four months later, when the band checked into their hotel in Tulsa, the desk clerk handed Gladys a postcard. The message read:

~~~ Gladdie, call me in the morning. Mama will be at school and Pa will be at Uncle Doc's. Love, Dorothy ~~~

The switchboard operator placed the call. "Hey, what's up?" Gladys chirped when her sister answered, certain there would be an engagement announcement.

Dorothy's monotone voice told another story. "I'm ready to join the band."

Gladys hesitated. "Well, great, but what about Keith?"

"He's divorced. That's the end of that tune. He didn't have the decency to tell me. Nina's boyfriend mentioned the ex-wife in conversation. I guess he thought I knew." Dorothy blew her nose. "When I asked Keith about it, he said he didn't think his ex was relevant, that he wasn't planning on knotting himself to my apron strings. And besides, he said, divorced Catholics can't remarry."

"He said that? How rude."

"I'm such a dope."

"No; he's a heel; the cad."

"At least I dumped him, not the other way around. But it hurts. I love him."

Having never been in love, Gladys searched for comforting words but came up with only, "We miss you. The band needs you. Come to Tulsa."

"I miss you all, too. Well, this is your dime so I won't keep you. Tell the others what happened and that I don't want to talk about it. I'll see you tomorrow night, or the next morning, depending on train schedules."

"Come straight to the hotel. I'll leave word where to find us if we're not here."

"Guess I can't stand on my own two feet after all. Anyway, I didn't tell the folks about Keith's divorce. I said he's been assigned elsewhere, which is true, and that I'm going back on the road."

"Keep your chin up, Honey. See you soon." Gladys hung up, and shed a few tears for her little sister before going to tell the others.

Who's sad and blue, who's crying, too ~~~

When Dorothy arrived, Gladys promised she would urge Jerry to put some melancholy ballads on the program, because that's what Dorothy felt like singing and playing. Jerry went along with it until one evening when Dorothy could barely finish singing *Little White Lies*, and then choked on the opening line to the next song: *Love me or leave me.*

Jerry called an intermission and wound her arm around Dorothy. "Honey, we all feel bad for you, but that's enough dramatics. Leave the torch songs to Ruth Etting. You turn even upbeat ditties into dirges." She mimicked Dorothy's somber rendition of *Happy Days Are Here Again.* "Happy is the keyword in that song."

While Dorothy escaped to the powder room, Hazel advised, "Go easy, Jerry," and Gladys backed her up.

Evelyn said, "Torch songs are popular. Why not let her do one or two a night?"

"Willeen," Jerry called, "you're the only one who hasn't voted."

"Sure, give the kid a break."

Jerry threw up her arms. "The majority rules. She sings torch songs."

Dorothy worked though her broken romance and gradually became her old self, on and off stage. One night while she and Hazel were harmonizing to *"Blue skies, smilin' at me, nothing but blue skies, do I see,"* Jerry leaned toward Gladys and sang, *"Dorothy's back in town,"* to the tune of *Lulu's back in town.*

"We're all pals together," Gladys replied.

I'm An Old Cowhand

From the Rio Grande, but my legs ain't bowed, an' my cheeks ain't tanned ~~~

Gladys awoke with her head against the window and a crick in her neck. She swiveled her head from side to side hoping to relieve the ache.

"Finally someone's alive," Jerry said. "It's been so quiet I thought I was driving this hearse on business."

Gladys swatted Jerry's arm. "That's creepy. Where are we anyway? For some reason, it seems as if we're going south instead of toward Texas."

"We crossed the Georgia and Florida line a few miles back. I decided we need a vacation in the Sunshine State."

"Florida? Jerry, I'm ready to go home."

"Me, too," Hazel called from the back. "The best place for vacation is at home."

Dorothy's head popped up. "What's all the yelling about?"

Evelyn surfaced, too. "Did someone say we're in Florida?"

"Florida?" Dorothy asked. "Did we get detoured?"

Willeen laughed at all the confusion, and sang, *Moon over Miami, shine on my love and me."*

"Sorry to disappoint you, Willie," Jerry said, "Miami's on the Atlantic. We're going to the Gulf of Mexico. Okay, listen everybody; here's the deal. We've been driven hard and put away wet. My cousin Aidan wants us to visit him in Sarasota, relax for a day or two. He owns a club there. Well, calling it a club is stretching a tad. Actually, stretching it a lot. It's called the Packing House Café. He wants us to play there a couple of nights."

"Ah," Hazel said, "so this isn't a vacation; it's a busman's holiday. When did you and your cousin make these plans, unbeknownst to the rest of us?"

"I called him about a family matter; a week ago. I didn't know if we'd have time so I didn't mention it to y'all. I'll call him tonight and tell him we're on our way. He owns land on a key, with some bungalows and sleeping cots."

"What's a key," Dorothy asked.

"An island."

"Why didn't you just say so?"

"Because they call them keys."

Evelyn tapped Jerry's shoulder. "You said packinghouse. You mean it's near some of those butcher houses like in Chicago? I'll never forget that rancid odor. Like bones burning."

"No, no, celery packinghouses. They grow tons of celery in Florida."

"Celery is an aphrodisiac," Willeen offered.

"Celery?" Jerry asked.

"Yep. I read it somewhere."

"Well, look out pals, the boys here are gonna be swarmin' around us."

And I come to town, to hear the cowboy band ~~~

At mid-afternoon the next day Gladys scanned road signs as the Packard sailed past palm trees, directions to Gator farms, and long stretches of nothing. Jerry had said to watch for Cattlemen Drive or Bee Ridge Road or trail or something. "Nice to have specific directions," Gladys heckled Jerry.

"Yeah, well, I've been in bigger places than this. We'll find it."

"Just follow your nose. Whew; I never thought celery had much smell but it's overpowering."

"Look at those fields over there. That's a whole lot of celery. Oops, here's my turn." Jerry veered onto a shell driveway and within a few yards stopped in front of a frame building with a handmade sign: Packing House Café. Alongside, stood a pickup and a mud-spattered boat with a sign reading: Chartered Fishing Trips and Gator Hunts.

"Your cousin's a busy man," Gladys said.

"Even as a kid he had his hand in more than one pot at a time. Hey, there's the man himself."

Aidan pulled Jerry out of the driver's seat and into a bear hug. "Well, if you ain't a sight for this ol' cracker's sore eyes." Over his shoulder he whistled as each of the other women stepped off the running board. "You travel in fine company, cousin."

"You should see us when we doll up."

Evelyn whispered to Gladys, "He's cute, and a flirt."

Jerry punched Aidan on the arm. "Well, aren't you gonna ask me?"

"Ask you what?"

"What you always ask. When you gonna settle down and get married?"

A sly grin preceded Aidan's query, "What do you always answer?"

"When I get durn good'n ready."

"Yeah, I ain't in no hurry neither. Say, Uncle Finn's old hearse looks great."

"Yep; runs like a two-bit gangster on the lam."

"Guess we both like Packards." Aidan swung his head toward the customer parking area.

Jerry smacked her forehead. "Whoa. Did you come into a family inheritance I got cheated out of? You've got beach property, a truck, boat, a new car."

"You know me; lotta irons in the fire. Bought an interest in a citrus grove last month. One hand feeds the other. Hey, let's go inside; I'll buy y'all a beer, or lemonade, whatever you fillies drink."

Gladys paused inside the door to look around. The glossy white walls featured murals of palm trees and beaches, orange groves and pink flamingoes. A dozen or more tables, covered with orange oilcloth, held bouquets of celery stalks with delicate leaves.

The mixed odors of fried onions, cigarette smoke and beer, stirred by rattan fans suspended from a stamped tin ceiling, forced her to stand next to an open window for a breath of outdoor air. The window sported curtains tied back at the sides to let in light, but the cotton material did not match any of the other curtains.

Over the bar, a sign promised: Nude girls—tomorrow. Neon lights flashed beer names, each touting itself as the finest: Miller High Life, the Champagne of Bottled Beer; Budweiser, the King of Beers; and Haven's Pilsner, 5 cents a glass, claimed not a burp in a barrel. Behind the bar, a simple sign for De Soto Beer boasted only that it was brewed in Tampa.

Two customers lounged on barstools, a youthful cowboy with a lariat hanging from the belt loop of his jeans, and a silver-haired woman wearing a blue chambray shirt, riding pants, chaps and boots.

Evelyn nudged Gladys. "Her face is as leathery and wrinkled as a catcher's mitt. That's the way we'll look in a few years if we stay on the road."

"Hope not. We aren't out in the weather like she is."

It didn't take long for the cowboy to leave the aged cowgirl. He had Willeen pinned in a corner, giving her the once-over, especially her legs, displayed in tan shorts.

"Hey, Buck," Aidan called, "the little woman's comin' around the bend. Reckon she's looking for you?"

"Shee-it, you ain't seen me." Buck slithered out the back door.

Glancing out the window, Jerry said, "I don't see anyone."

"No, but I got your pal out of a jam."

"A jam? She seemed to be enjoying herself. Must be the celery."

"The celery?"

"Never mind; just something Willeen told us earlier." Jerry ambled over to inspect the stage, with the other women close behind.

"I know it's cramped," Aidan said. "I rarely have a six-piece band."

"We'll fit if we starve ourselves for a couple of days." Jerry bounced on the platform, testing the knot-holed boards.

"Hey, take it easy," Aidan said.

Above, strands of red Christmas lights glowed, and on a corner of the stage sat a wooden well bucket with "Tips" painted on the side. Aidan explained, "Local entertainers play here to get started in the business. Their only pay is tips, but you gals, you're a big name, I'll reach into my pocket if we come up short."

"Nah; all we need is a place to rest our bones."

Gladys covered a yawn with her hand. "And I'm ready now."

"You'll like my place on the beach. The Casa-not-so-Grande. It's not quite the *Ca d'Zan* but you'll sleep good."

Jerry cupped her hand behind her ear. "Cadeewhat?"

"House of John. John Ringling's palace on the bay."

"He lives here? Ring-ling, the circus king. Remember that rhyme?"

"He ain't king no more. Millions of bucks worth of art but he's broke, in debt up to his armpits and in poor health, t'boot. Owes everybody and his dog. Wife died, no kids. Talk is the house will be seized to pay his debts."

"You know him personally?" Gladys asked.

"Nah; seen him around. He's got an old Rolls I'd like to have. He owns a hotel where famous folks stay. Surprised you gals haven't rented rooms there."

"Pfft," Jerry sputtered, "you're the one with money. Besides, how could we turn down free room and board at that casa ain't-so-grande of yours?"

"Well, that way I can keep an eye on you. It's a sleepy town. Not much crime, to speak of, but you never know. There's a casino on the beach and folks get rowdy. I'll sleep in the cottage next door, shotgun ready to dispense cowboy justice." Aidan aimed a pretend shotgun at the door. "Shoot first and ask questions later."

"Be still mah heart," Jerry drawled, "don't know how we've gotten along on the road without you."

Gladys wandered around studying the clutter displayed on the walls. There were license plates from around the country, lanterns, a stuffed fish entangled in a net, a celluloid carnival Kewpie doll, a calendar featuring Betty Grable's pin-up picture, a yellowed newspaper headline announcing the 1929 stock market crash, and a picture of a white hen with a sign around her neck that read: No fowl language, please.

Hanging from the ceiling were more artifacts: animal traps, a pelt of some kind, an array of faded piñatas, a roller skate, a Confederate flag, farm implements, and hundreds of miniature seashells strung together like popcorn on a Christmas tree.

Aidan pointed to a snapshot of himself and another man. "You heard of Ernest Hemingway? That's Papa. His autograph is scribbled on the front of my boat."

Before Gladys could respond, Dorothy squealed, "Icky. Look at those huge roaches." She climbed onto a barstool and wrapped her feet around the top rung.

Aidan laughed. "They're just palmetto bugs. Throw a saddle on one and take a ride. You should see our skeeters." He held his hands a foot apart.

"I've seen skeeters that big in Minnesota," Dorothy countered.

That launched Jerry into a monologue about how everything is bigger in Texas, until Dorothy stopped her with, "What about Babe the Blue Ox?"

"In Texas he'd be the runt of the litter."

Aidan broke up the competition. "I'm takin' drink orders. Then I'll fetch some boiled peanuts and gator meat for a snack."

"Is that peanuts and gator together in one dish?" Gladys asked, making a face.

"Nope. Each stands on its own merit. Later, we'll stop by The Smack for a burger. Best in the state."

She propped her elbows on the bar. "Sounds good. I'll pass on peanuts and gator and save room for a burger."

Yippee yi yo kayah ~~~

Aidan had described Sarasota as a sleepy town, but with the restaurant packed from door to door and out onto the porch, things were anything but quiet. The boisterous crowd and the Rangerettes dug into plates of food that would have satisfied a threshing crew. Aidan's cook, a Seminole Indian who wore his ebony hair in two braids, dished up heaping plates of barbecued spare ribs cooked outdoors in a pit, with sides of corn bread and swamp cabbage, all for four bits.

While folks sopped up the vinegary barbecue sauce with corn bread, Aidan took to the stage and waxed nostalgic about his relative from Texas, Miss Jerry McRae. Gladys finally mentioned to Jerry that most of the patrons weren't paying attention, so she elbowed the boss out of the way and the band took over. They opened with their theme, *We're All Pals Together*, followed by *Empty Saddles in the Old Corral*, popularized by Bing Crosby.

In response to several requests, the band settled into western swing. For several years, people across the country had clamored for this blend of hillbilly, cowboy, polka, folk, jazz, and blues. The Rangerettes' fellow Texan, Bob Wills, called it

Texas fiddle music, still others used the terms western jazz, hot string band, and hot fiddling. Whatever it was called, the women enjoyed playing it. Gladys and Evelyn stopped the dancers mid-shuffle with the Patsy Montana hit, "*I wanna be a cowboy's sweetheart, I wanna learn to rope and to ride,*" with Evelyn doing the yodeling.

When the song ended, Aidan sauntered over and took Gladys's hand. "That was mighty pretty, but they can do without you for a bit. Let's dance."

He didn't give her time to protest; he led her to the dance floor and opened his arms. She folded into them as if they were an old married couple. Gladys recognized the clean scent of Fels Naphtha soap on him, mixed with cigarettes and beer. Feeling lightheaded, she blamed it on the warm room and the crowd closing in. Or was it being in a man's arms? She couldn't remember the last time she'd danced with a man. Maybe last year at a Christmas party, and that had been Uncle Doc. This was a man her age, tall, blond and charming.

On the last note of the second tune, Aidan gave her a gentle twirl and brought her about face. "The lady can sing, play an instrument, and dance. A triple threat." He bent over and brushed his lips against hers.

Relieved that her blush didn't show in the dark, and trying to appear unaffected, Gladys said, "I enjoyed dancing. Now I better get back to work."

He escorted her to the stage, and while she picked up her trombone, he turned his attention to Hazel. "The band can do without you for few minutes. How about dancing?"

Gladys laughed out loud watching him lead Hazel away. He was nothing but a flirt, being nice to Jerry's friends.

As the hour grew late and the dancers' energy waned, the band switched to slow tunes. Couples swayed cheek to cheek to *I'll String Along With You; The Very Thought of You; The Way You Look Tonight;* and *Cuddle Up A Little Closer.*

Aidan had said earlier that he closed whenever he decided it was time. This night he shut down just past one when a ruckus broke out. It began after Dorothy stepped up to sing a request. "*Say, it's only a paper moon, sailing over a cardboard sea, but it wouldn't ~~~*" On that note, a blustering packinghouse foreman who'd been after her to dance with him lifted her off the stage onto the floor.

The band kept playing, except for Evelyn, who tried to whack the fella on the shoulder with her clarinet, but he ducked and the instrument glanced off Dorothy's cheek. She reeled and lowered herself to the floor, her back against the stage.

The music stopped; Aidan hauled the man away and dumped him outside. While Hazel dashed to the kitchen for a towel and ice, Aidan yelled, "Closing time," and herded the other customers out the door.

Returning to Dorothy, who had her head in Gladys's lap, he said, "I'm sorry about that. We better get you to the hospital. Your pretty little nose might be broken."

"Didn't hit my nose, but any closer and it could have put out some teeth or my eye." Dorothy angled a mean look at Evelyn. "What were you thinking? You could have brained that guy. If the gourd head had a brain."

"I didn't aim for his head. That would've broken my clarinet."

"So you aimed at my head."

"I did not. Hitting you was an accident. I said I'm sorry."

Aidan pulled away the ice-packed towel. "You need beefsteak."

"Not hungry," Dorothy said.

He reared back and laughed. "For your eye. You're gonna have one heckuva a shiner." He went to the kitchen and returned with a raw spare rib, which he held against her cheek.

Jerry leaned into his shoulder. "Nice sleepy town you got here, Cousin."

"I told you some folks get rowdy."

Dorothy grumbled, "Not to mention Evelyn and her lethal weapon. Wait until Mama hears about this."

"Keep Mama out of this," Evelyn snapped, and stomped off to the bathroom.

"Hush, Dorothy," Gladys soothed. "Evie will feel bad all the way to Texas."

Obviously trying to lighten the mood, Aidan offered, "I was thinkin' I'd take you gals gator huntin' while you're here. How about it? The night's still young."

Dorothy leaned on Gladys and pulled herself upright. "Not me, thanks. But take Evie and her clarinet along for protection. Come to think of it, she's got a billy club under the car seat, too."

"Billy club? Hey, Jerry was right; you gals don't need me or any other man looking after you."

Gladys, thinking of Goliath, said, "We make do, with a little help from friends and strangers."

On the way to Texas, Dorothy got over being perturbed at Evelyn, mostly so she would stop singing, "*What can I say dear, after I say I'm sorry?*"

When they reached San Antonio, and Hazel pulled the hearse into the alley by Doc's little house, Gladys rolled out the back door, massaged her butt and muttered, "Home sweet home. This cowgal has been on the trail too long. I've got saddle sores."

The little vacation Jerry set up in Florida had been no picnic. The second night they performed during a storm that knocked out electrical power. Lanterns and lightning strikes provided the only illumination and thunder rolling across the tin roof accompanied the music. Still, they had an audience, and the tips in the bucket were generous. Bad weather often brought goodwill from folks.

Dancing With Tears In My Eyes

Weeping for the memory of a life gone by ~~~

Gladys's spirit and body revived under Mama's tender loving care, but she and her sisters recognized that it was Pa who needed attention. Listless, pale, and unable to keep food down, he insisted he had a touch of flu. But it was the longest bout of flu any of them had seen.

"I'll get him to the doctor," Mama promised her daughters when they left in late January for another Lurline-Hawaii tour. From there, they went directly to the Ozarks. On opening night, a telegram arrived from Mama with the stunning news that Pa had incurable stomach cancer. Unable to cancel their contract, the Rangerettes completed the engagement with heavy hearts and little enthusiasm.

Back home, where they planned to stay for the duration of Pa's illness, the sisters found him depleted in energy. Never an imposing figure, he had been whittled to little more than a scarecrow's frame.

Hazel, having inherited Pa's knack for bookkeeping, took over running Uncle Doc's office. And she made a chart of household jobs for each of them.

"Put me down for making meals," Dorothy offered. "I'm a good cook."

Hazel narrowed her eyes. "Since when?"

"Since I stayed home for a few weeks, when I fell for a con man's line. Mama and I had fun cooking and Pa enjoyed sampling."

"Okay, you're chief cook. Who's the bottle washer?"

Evelyn raised her hand. "I don't mind doing dishes, but I won't scrub the toilet."

"You should be so lucky," Gladys said. "Until we moved to the last farmhouse with an inside toilet, Mama made Hazel and me scour the outhouse twice a week. Hot, soapy lye water for the seat and the floor. Right, Hazel?"

"Yeah; we had the cleanest outhouse in Minnesota."

As the weeks passed and Pa spent more time in bed, the sisters took turns reading Zane Grey westerns to him, reminiscing about the old days, and telling stories about their travels.

One day when Mama was at school, Gladys confided, "We didn't tell Mama about this, because Aunt Anna died from appendicitis, but in Hawaii this last time I thought I had it. Then the others started having bellyaches. When we told the hotel doctor we'd all eaten potato salad at a food stand on the beach, he said we had a touch of food poisoning. We finished the show with one of us toddling off to the bathroom every few minutes."

Pa managed a wan smile, while Gladys inwardly scolded herself: For gosh sakes, his pain is obvious, while I sit here babbling about a bellyache.

Watching him grimace and hold his breath, and then sigh when a pain passed, she recalled a musician who smoked weed and claimed it was good for what ails you. Relieved his rheumatism, he said. She doubted it back then, but now she wondered if there was something to it. Uncle Doc would know, but what would he think if she asked him about smoking dope?

"Here's a funny story, Pa. We stopped at a diner in Fort Worth. Right next door was a Washateria. That's a place where you can rent washing machines."

"Rent 'em, and take 'em home?"

"No, no. You use them there. They had four machines, a nickel a load. So we got our dirty clothes and washed them. Then, lugging them out to the car, we thought, where are we gonna dry them? Down the road, we found a nice green pasture so we stopped and spread our clothes on the ground and bushes. Evie was shaking out a red blouse when, all of a sudden, a bull entered the peaceful scene. We scrambled over the fence. The beast came and sniffed our laundry and finally strayed off. We stayed in the car until we thought the clothes were dry, then we grabbed them and high-tailed it out of there."

A spark of amusement flashed in Pa's eyes before he fell asleep.

Longing to know how her parents felt about this phase in their life together, Gladys often busied herself outside their open bedroom door to hear their conversations. Hazel scolded her for eavesdropping, but Gladys insisted it might be bad manners but there was no commandment saying thou shalt not.

She enjoyed hearing them reminisce about people they'd known in Park Rapids. They often had different stories about what, where, why, when or who, but she and her sisters were that way, too. Hazel always thought her version was correct because she was oldest, while Dorothy said that because Hazel's mind was several years older, she'd probably forgotten details. Senility, you know, she teased.

One afternoon when Gladys was weeding the flowerbed near the patio, Pa made his way out there and sat down with Mama. After discussing the warm weather for a minute, Pa said, "We've had it good here, haven't we?"

"My, yes," Mama said. "We've had steady jobs when times are rough for many people. Our daughters are happy, healthy, successful."

"Thanks to you. I pretty much left the upbringin' to you. I'm sure proud of 'em, though."

"I know you are. Have you ever told them?"

"That I'm proud of 'em? Oh, gosh, I must have."

"It wouldn't hurt to tell them again."

"Suppose not." Pa cleared his throat. "I wasn't always the best provider."

"Oh, go on; you did fine. Farming's risky. We had as much as most, more than some. I've always been grateful you didn't have the curse, spending money on beer and whiskey like so many men."

"Well, truth be known, that wasn't due to good character. I never really liked liquor so it was easy to stay away from it. If I had an extra dime I'd rather buy you some sheet music than me a drink."

"Aww, Martin; how sweet."

"Doc keeps brandy at the office. The good stuff. We have a nip now and then, but I can take it or leave it. Anyway, I'm thankful you can teach. I ain't left you nothin' but the cash under the mattress and that don't even make a lump."

"Don't worry about money. I'll get by."

"I always wanted to buy you a diamond to replace that cheap gold band."

"I'd never part with my ring. Besides, you gave me four diamonds. Our girls."

"They sure are that. Five diamonds countin' Robbie. Do'ya ever think about the lad? What he'd be like today?"

"Oh, yes, every day. And that's not all. You know, they say when a person loses a limb he sometimes feels as if it's still there?"

"Yeah, I've heard that."

"Well, a baby is as much an extension of a mother's body as an arm or leg. For a long time after Robbie died I could feel him in my arms. His weight, the way he squirmed to get down. I still remember how he felt, different than the girls. They were fragile; he was sturdy, solid, like a boy should be."

"I reckon his death was the lowest point in my life."

"Mine, too. Absolutely. And I didn't help you much. I'm sorry."

"No need for that. You had your hands full."

Conversation lagged for a moment before Pa spoke. "When my pain's bad I think about how he must've hurt and couldn't tell us."

"Don't dwell on his suffering. He's been with the Lord all these years. But in my mind I've watched him grow into a fine young man. He looks like you."

"You don't say? That's not so good."

"It's plenty good."

Gladys thought of her parents' wedding photo on the piano. Pa always said they look mad at each other. Next to it sat a framed snapshot of Robbie, taken with Mama's Brownie Kodak camera shortly before he died. Seated in his pram, heavily bundled in white clothing and a cap, only a round little face showed. Without the picture, Gladys wouldn't remember him at all.

"Do you think I'll see Robbie if I get to Heaven?" Pa asked.

"I know you will. And there's no *if* about it. You'll get to Heaven."

"All those rosaries you and the girls say, is that to get me through the gate?"

"I guarantee it. When you see Robbie, tell him hello from his mother."

When Pa didn't respond, Gladys thought he'd fallen asleep in his lawn chair. Then Mama asked if he was afraid, and he answered, "Not with you by my side."

"I'm right here. So is God. I love you, dear heart."

"Love you, Lass."

Gladys tried to think if she'd ever heard her parents say those words to each other, but it didn't matter. She'd never doubted their devotion to one another.

They sat quietly for a minute. Then Pa said, "Sing that tune I used to like; the one about the horse."

"You mean *The Strawberry Roan*? I remember how you'd come running whenever it played on the radio."

"I always liked it better when you sang it."

Mama sang, "*Down in the corral, a-standin' alone, was this old caballo, a strawberry roan, and a big forty-four brand was on his left hip ~~~*"

Peeking through a bush, Gladys choked up seeing her parents holding hands.

In The Gloaming

When the lights are dim and low, and the quiet shadows falling ~~~

From the window, Mary watched Doc approach the house. Doctor Sisle had stepped outside for a cigarette and seemed to be waiting for Doc. They were close enough to the house that she heard their conversation.

"How's Martin tonight?" Doc asked the medical doctor.

"Seems to be managing the pain right well. Better than I expected. I see you've got your little black bag with you."

"Shave and a bath. Martin would rather the ladies didn't have to do it."

"Men are shy about that." The doctor dropped a cigarette and rubbed the butt into the ground. "What I was getting at; I hope you aren't practicing medicine here. Human medicine. You being just a horse doctor."

Mary cringed at the deliberate insult, but relaxed when Doc answered, "Seems to me the humane thing to do is to help God's creatures when they need it. First do no harm, as you MDs like to say. Now if you'll excuse me, my friend is waiting."

Days later, after Mary realized that Martin had been sleeping peacefully at night, the conversation between the men ran through her mind. Was Doc giving Martin something to ease his pain, in addition to what Doctor Sisle gave him? She told Gladys what she'd heard and asked if she should confess it.

"Confess what?"

"Well, I don't rightly know."

"That you overheard a conversation? It's possible you misinterpreted what Uncle Doc said, or meant."

"I suppose. The radio was blaring right next to me and I was rattling dishes."

"Then don't let what you heard, or think you heard, trouble you."

"You're probably right." Sighing with weariness, Mary fixed her eyes on the pale orange sunset. "Mother called this time of day the gloaming. Haven't heard that word for ages. There was a pretty song called *In the Gloaming.* It came out after Mother died. I remember because I thought of her when I first heard Harry Lauder sing it. Martin said only a Scots-Irish, like me, could understand that man's garble. He bought me the sheet music so I could sing it in words he understood. Evie was a baby. She liked it, too."

"I'd like to hear it. Let's find the sheet music." Gladys took her mother's arm. "First, let's take a walk. In the gloaming."

Though I passed away in silence, it was best to leave you thus, dear ~~~

Martin died in his sleep, near dawn, not in the gloaming. Mary noticed that his gentle snore had stopped; then his breath slowed. She felt for a pulse, found a flutter, a whisper, and then nothing. Watching the clock measure off time, she continued checking, but there was no movement.

"Praise be, your suffering is over." She kissed his cheek, crossed herself, took a deep breath, and another, releasing months of tension. Then she woke the girls.

After breaking the news in a strangled voice, and being surrounded in her daughters' arms, Mary took a calm command post. "Hazel, please go tell Doc. Gladys, please call Father Dusseau so he can come and administer last rites. And call Doctor Sisle and ask him to stop by. I recorded the time of death, but he'll verify it and notify the funeral home. The viewing will be there, not at home. Your father didn't want people traipsing into the house at all hours like when Robbie died."

She twisted her uncombed hair into a knot at the back of her head and secured it with hairpins. "Gladys, when you've finished with the phone, I'll call Mother Joseph."

Later that morning, Mary told Mother Joseph, "I already miss Martin, but I'm at peace. I prepared for his death, knowing he'd be in a far better place. I've been thinking about which is harder to handle, a sudden death like my baby's, or an expected death like Martin's. The sudden death is far worse. I feel as if I've already done much of my mourning Martin for several months, since we heard the diagnosis."

Despite thinking she was prepared, or that she had finished mourning, a deluge of emotion overtook her the next day when Martin's obituary appeared in the *San Antonio Express-News*. Hands shaking, she handed the paper to Hazel. "It's like long ago when I read Robbie's death notice. I can't believe it's my loved one whose name is printed here. Please read it to me."

~~~ June 23, 1937, Jones, Died Tuesday, June 22, at the home, 421 Marshall, Martin L. Jones, aged 59 years. Beloved husband of Mrs. Mary Jones; father of Hazel, Gladys, Dorothy, and Evelyn Jones; brother of Mrs. Nellie Slack. Funeral services will be held at Riebe Undertaking Company Chapel Thursday morning, 8:30 o'clock, followed by services at St. Mary's Catholic Church at 9:00 o'clock, Rev. T. J. Kennedy officiating. Interment in San Fernando Cemetery No. 2. ~~~

Wringing her handkerchief, Mary said, "It's not much to sum up a man's life. I wish they'd called and asked for more information than just what the funeral home sent. I should have thought of it myself, to call the paper."

Gladys comforted her. "Those who knew him don't have to be reminded of who he was."

Breaking protocol, Father Dusseau allowed the Jones Quartet to play before the service, while parishioners gathered in the church. Then the four women took seats in the front pew with their mother and the rest of the family: Jerry, Willeen, and Doc.

Back at the house after the burial, bustling about making tea, trying to keep her mind and hands busy, Mary said, "That was a good turnout for Martin. You know, he often said he didn't have many friends."

"Pa said that?" Gladys asked. "Gosh, he had the whole Knights of Columbus group, the neighbor across the street who invited him over to play pool. And Uncle Doc. With a friend like Uncle Doc, he didn't need much more."

"Yes, we were blessed when we moved to Doc's place. I wish Martin could have grown old here. The two of us."

Mary sighed. "But that wasn't God's plan. Where will He lead me next?"

Git Along Little Dogies

We round up our horses and load the chuck wagon ~~~

Mary put her foot down when the Rangerettes insisted she join them on their resumed tour. "For one thing," she said, "I recently had a ride in a hearse. I'm not eager to get back in one."

That brought a somber silence until Evelyn argued, "We won't go unless you go. We'll up and quit."

"You'll do nothing of the kind. You've never run out on commitments."

"There's always a first time. Please come. We can use another Rangerette."

"A Rangerette? That's nonsense. I can't keep up with you kids. And I'd look silly in one of those costumes you wear."

Dorothy said, "Maybe Evelyn is right about quitting. With Pa gone, we should give up touring and play only locally, so you aren't alone."

"Nonsense again. I don't need a keeper. I have my teaching job, and Doc asked if I'd do his books for him. I expect he wants to keep me occupied and on the payroll. So, I haven't been turned out to pasture yet. Now git along little dogies and pack your saddlebags."

In the morning, Mary stood at the bottom of the stairs as her daughters straggled down toting luggage and wearing long faces. Evelyn grabbed her mother into a hug and then fled outside. Hazel and Dorothy said goodbye and skittered away like shy rabbits, while Gladys lingered in the kitchen.

Mary said, "Don't forget that box of food I prepared."

"Hazel carried it out. Listen, we'll be home before you know it."

"I know. I'll stay busy with fall housecleaning and lesson plans for school."

"Get some rest. Sleep till noon."

"I couldn't sleep till noon if I was a mummy. Go on; Jerry's honking the horn."

Gladys threw her arms around her mother, then darted through the door and across the yard without looking back.

Mary watched the Packard glide onto Marshall Street, with all six women waving from the windows. Dissolved in tears, an image emerged of Martin's old truck rattling into the alley on the day they arrived from Minnesota. Eleven years ago this past March. Eleven years is a long time, she thought, yet it seems like only yesterday. Now here I am, alone in this big house that smells like illness and stale bouquets and the girls' cologne and shampoo.

An empty feeling crept over her, draping her in loneliness that caused her to slump from its weight. She roamed through the rooms, straightening sofa pillows, picking up papers, Evelyn's nail polish, and Dorothy's book of Robert Louis Stevenson's poetry. It had been wonderful having the four of them home for several months, despite the reason they were there. Dorothy had talked about giving up travel with the band. Whatever would she do if she stayed home? What would any of them do without the band? Mary recalled overhearing a woman at the church bazaar say, "There come the old maid Jones girls." Were they really past their prime for marrying?

Her eyes trailed to the piano, its top covered with sympathy cards, Mass offerings, and letters. It seemed like an insurmountable effort to get started answering them, so she wandered off with a promise to herself to do it later. There were plenty of *laters* waiting.

Puttering in the kitchen at noon, she half expected Martin to come in for dinner. He had sometimes brought Doc with him, knowing she always prepared enough for a guest or two. She'd grown up preparing meals for a crowd and still found it difficult to cook for two. And now just one.

The telephone sputtered several rings. It was Doc's signal, not hers. Doc had long ago added a phone to the house and she and Martin enjoyed the convenience, but Martin was more apt to use it just for the heck of it than she was. Like calling to ask what was for dinner, or what she was doing. She remembered one silly conversation as if it were yesterday. Martin called and said, "It's five o'clock. I'm on my way home."

"Oh, how long do you think it'll take you?" she asked.

"A minute, maybe less."

"Good; I'll set the table."

Glancing out the window now, she watched Doc drifting in the yard. He must be as lonely as I am, she thought. I should invite him over to eat tonight. Not that I feel like eating, but having company would force me to cook and eat something.

Summoning strength from the trinity that had helped her through many times of sorrow, she opened the door and walked toward Doc's cottage.

There'll Be Some Changes Made

From now on there'll be a change in me ~~~

A trio of fuzzy brown ducklings splashing in a pond caught Gladys's attention from where she sat on a park bench. The little creatures brought momentary pleasure, something that had been lacking these past few months. Her faith had been tested during Pa's illness, waning when she watched his agony and decline, ebbing when she asked God for strength, guidance, and comfort and her request was granted. On the road, when not occupied with music, she sought seclusion, sometimes in church, other times in a park such as this one near the hotel where the Rangerettes were staying.

While she meditated, a man sat down, making her wonder why he chose this seat when there were several empty benches. About her age, he wore a suit and hat and was not bad looking in spite of a pockmarked face. Propping a bulging brief case at his feet, he scanned the front page of his newspaper for a moment before saying, "Nice morning."

She didn't feel like talking, but she responded, "Yes, warm and sunny."

Her response seemed to encourage him. He laid the paper in his lap and stretched his arm across the back of the bench, his fingers close to her shoulder. "I saw you in the hotel lobby. I'm staying there, too."

Apprehensive that he had followed her here, Gladys said no more.

"They're one of my customers. I'm in sales, office supplies. Name's Max." He drew a business card from his lapel pocket and offered it to her. She glanced at the card but didn't take it, so he withdrew his hand. "You here on business or pleasure?"

"Ah, business, with my family."

"Where you from?"

"San Antonio." This was already more than she wanted to reveal to a stranger.

"Dayton's my hometown. Ohio."

Gladys slung her handbag over her shoulder. "Do you have the time?"

He lifted his shirt cuff. "Almost ten. Say, I haven't had breakfast. There's a coffee shop around the corner. Will you join me?"

"Oh, thank you, but I must be going. I didn't realize it was so late." She rose and took a few steps.

"You don't have a few minutes for a cup of coffee?" He stood, and moved toward her, not in an aggressive way, but close enough for her to know he was making a move on her. His shaving lotion had a familiar fragrance. Bay rum, maybe.

Over his shoulder, she saw a cop walking his beat. Sidling around Max, she chirped, "Good morning, Officer. I wonder, could you direct me to the Royal Hotel? This gentleman is a stranger in town, too, and wasn't able to help me."

The officer tipped his brimmed cap. "Yes, Ma'am. It's on the next block. I'm going that way if you'd like to walk along."

"It'd be a pleasure," she said, and left Max holding his bag of stationery and envelopes and his salesman's lines.

Later, reflecting on the encounter, she realized she had been rude. At one time she would have been flattered by the man's attention. She might even have gone with him for that cup of coffee. Decent male company on the road was almost nonexistent, and he had been friendly, not menacing. She chided herself for using the cop as a shield, and for pretending to not know where the hotel was located. What it boiled down to, she finally decided, was that men, worldly men, no longer interested her. Only one man could satisfy the deep longing she'd had for…nearly all her life. The Lord Jesus.

By the time the band returned home, Gladys had made a decision that would alter not only her life, but those of the Rangerettes and Mama. How could she tell them what she was going to do? Especially Mama, after what she'd been through the past few months?

To her surprise, Mama seemed in good spirit, preparing for the opening of school. Perhaps there was no time like the present to reveal her secret. The next morning she joined her mother in the courtyard, where she was working on lesson plans. Gladys rested her head against her lawn chair and closed her eyes, steeling herself for the conversation she was about to initiate.

"Still sleepy?" Mama asked.

"Yes; I barely slept last night."

"I heard someone roaming about."

"Sorry if I woke you."

"That's all right. What's bothering you? You usually sleep well at home."

Looking directly at Mama, Gladys said, "I have something serious to tell you. I'm gong to apply for admission to Incarnate Word. I spoke to Mother Joseph yesterday."

Gladys saw Mama's hand tremble as she lowered her coffee cup to the table. She aligned the cup in a square in the design on the table cover, as if that were of utmost importance. Finally, she said, "I'm overcome. I don't know what to say."

"Listen to this, from Isaiah." Gladys opened her prayer book. "'I heard the voice of the Lord saying Whom shall I send? Who will go for us? Here I am, I said, send me.'" She closed the Missal. "That's how I feel. Send me."

She grasped Mama's hand. "I hope those are happy tears, because I'm very happy."

"They're happy tears. Oh, yes."

"Good. Now, will you help me tell the others?"

"Of course, but...."

A moment passed. "But what?"

"First I should tell you something."

Gladys waited, and waited. "Mama, what?"

"While you were away I went to a retreat at the convent, and...."

"And....?"

"I want to join the convent. If they'll accept me."

Gladys gripped the chair arms to steady her body.

"I guess you're as surprised as I was about your news. You're as still as Saint Francis over there in the garden. I'm surprised myself. But you know, as a girl I thought about being a nun."

"Of course. Have you talked to Mother Joseph?"

"She's been away on sabbatical. I wanted to ask what you girls think. I never imagined you'd be coming home with the same idea."

For months Gladys had seen Mama's eyes brimming with sadness; now they glowed with renewed life. "I think it's fantastic. But can you, having been married?"

"Have you forgotten that Louise became a nun after the professor died? She's now Sister Grace, a Carmelite in Oregon."

"Of course. I'm so flustered I'm not thinking. The worldly Louise, of all people."

"She needed a dispensation and I'm sure I will, too. Sister Pius told me a calling can come any time in one's life. I never expected Martin to die so young, but he's gone and you girls are away most of the time. I prayed for guidance. I told God that if he needs me, I want to serve. If they'll have an old woman, that is."

"You're not old. You're bright and talented and healthy. God needs women like you, no matter their age. I'm pushing thirty."

"Mother was only forty-nine when she died, God rest her soul. I'm older than that and I'm preparing to begin a whole new life."

"It's incredible. Listen, I have an appointment with Mother Joseph on Friday. We'll go together."

"Yes, we'll bolster one another. I'll call and let her know I'm coming."

Gladys grinned. "No; let's surprise her. She'll enjoy this."

"I don't know if we should spring it on her that way."

"It'll be fine. And when we finish our postulancy and novitiate, we'll apply to teach music."

"I suppose so. I'm in such a dither I haven't thought that far ahead."

"I know. I'm giddy, and humbled, even sad, that I'll be leaving the band, my sisters, Jerry and Willeen. But now I won't be leaving you behind. That would have been the saddest thing of all."

The screened door whined open and Hazel came out wearing felt mules and blue striped pajamas. Evelyn and Dorothy, still in their nightgowns trailed after her.

Gladys called, "Come here, all of you. We need to talk."

Side By Side

We'll travel along, singing a song ~~~

Silence followed Gladys's announcement. Evelyn circled the courtyard, then turned and faced her mother and sisters. "Gladdie, I always knew you'd do this someday, but Mama?" She wrapped her arms around herself. "I never thought I'd be telling someone that my mother is a nun. It gives me goose bumps."

Mama held out her hand. "Come sit on my lap. I'll warm you up."

Gladys stood in the half circle of chairs that held her mother and sisters. "This is what I've always wanted, but I've struggled with making the commitment. It means breaking away from my dear sisters and from the band. I'll miss that. I'll miss you all, terribly, but I'm ready to pledge myself to God." Emotion overcame her and she gave way to tears.

"I'm thrilled for you," Evelyn said from Mama's lap. "Really I am."

Hazel dragged a handkerchief from her pajama pocket, blew her nose and wiped her eyes. "Me, too, but the band won't be the same without you."

Dorothy raised her hand as if she needed permission to speak. "I mentioned this before; after Pa died, that maybe it's time we all gave up the band. Put some order to our lives instead of traipsing all over."

"You're quitting the band?" Hazel asked.

"I didn't say that, but I'm restless on the road, not entirely caught up in it. After my breakup with Keith, I realized that marriage is not God's plan for me. Maybe He wants me to be a bride of Christ."

Hazel reared up in her chair. "You're not only giving up the band, you're going with Mama and Gladys to the convent?"

"Calm down. I don't know. But think about it, all of you. Life with the band is fun but the glitz is on the surface. Like all of show business. We're small potatoes but we've still seen the adulation that audiences give entertainers. Gosh, look at this past summer, all the hullabaloo about Jean Harlow's death. A goddess, they called her. You'd think she'd found a cure for leprosy."

Mama broke in. "That's true, Dorothy, but she served a purpose if her talent made people happy. These are troubled times and folks need entertainment. Your music makes people happy, too."

"Sure, but bands like ours are a dime a dozen. We could be washed up any day. I say abandon the career before it abandons us, and think about a more stable future. I've heard Mother Joseph say there are never enough nuns to do God's work. The sisterhood would be a place where I'm needed. Where we're all needed. We don't have to give up music. We could teach, sing in the convent choir."

Astounded by this speech from the usually quiet Dorothy, Gladys added, "I've always admired the respect and support among nuns. For me, being with like-minded people will help keep me closer to God."

Evelyn knuckled a runaway tear, and Mama patted her hand. "Honey, don't cry. Be happy for us."

"I am happy. But this is strange. It takes some getting used to."

"Tell you what. Let's have breakfast. We'll continue this discussion later. Now get off my lap, you're heavy."

While they ate, Hazel confided, "When I was a kid, and the nuns talked about vocations, I thought a lot about it. But I expected a big booming voice telling me I'd been chosen. One day at school, a boy called my name, loud, and it startled me. I thought it was God."

Evelyn said, "If it was Cal Arness, you did think he was God." She sang, "*He isn't much at a dance, but then when he takes you home, you'd be surprised.*"

"Try being serious for a change. What I was trying to say is, I've waited for that special moment when I'd hear God calling. Maybe He's been calling and we've been making such a racket with our music that I couldn't hear the message."

"Guess it's okay for you to toss in a bit of humor."

"I didn't intend it as humor. What I mean is, I still don't know if I have a religious vocation. In spite of thinking about it for years."

"Then don't push yourself," Mama advised. "Sister Pius told me years ago that if you have a vocation, you'll know it. I know it and Gladdie knows. Dorothy seems to be considering it."

Evelyn draped a white dishtowel over her hair and forehead. "How would I look as a nun?"

"Wonderful," Mama said.

"Okay, that settles it. I'm in."

"You're in?" Hazel cried. "So it matters how you look? Is that the criteria?"

"Calm down. You're harping on everything I say. No, it doesn't matter how I look. I've thought about the religious life, just like the rest of you."

While Mama soothed Hazel, Gladys folded her arms around Evelyn. "Are you saying you want to go with me and Mama?"

"I think so. I'm scared. I don't know. Yes, definitely. It's now or never."

"Count me in," Dorothy said with no hesitation.

Mama placed her hand over her heart. "Oh, I don't believe this."

Gladys shivered; something mystical had happened this morning. "Mama," she said, "our decision seems to be contagious. Did you sprinkle holy water on the eggs?"

The comment broke the tension for everyone except Hazel. She whirled around and fled out the door.

Gladys started to follow, but Mama held her back. "Give her time alone. This is stunning news. I need to lie down and absorb what's happened here."

Hazel disappeared until late afternoon. Gathering the family around her, she announced, "I'm going, too. We've been band pals together and we can be nuns together. Best of all, we finally got Mama to travel with our group."

While the others swarmed around Hazel, Gladys stepped back. This morning she had been prepared to leave her entire family. The scene now unfolding before her eyes was beyond comprehension.

Overcome with emotion, she moved in and embraced her sisters and mother.

Have You Met Miss Jones

Miss Jones, Miss Jones, Miss Jones ~~~

Gladys cranked the metal doorbell wing alongside the frosted glass-paneled door at Incarnate Word Convent. Mama, dressed in the simple black suit and black hat she'd worn for her husband's funeral, stood beside Gladys.

A rosy-cheeked novitiate greeted them. "Good morning. I'm Audrey. May I help you?"

"Good morning. I'm Gladys Jones. I have an appointment with Mother Joseph. This is my mother, Mrs. Martin Jones." She glanced over her shoulder. "And my sisters."

Each woman identified herself.

"Hazel Jones."

"Dorothy Jones."

"Evelyn Jones."

They all wore dark clothing, as if already preparing for convent life. Only Hazel sported a tinge of color; a lilac and blue rayon scarf.

"I hope it won't be too much trouble if we all see Mother Joseph," Gladys said.

"Follow me," Audrey instructed, and led them through a hall where she tapped on a wooden door.

"Come in," came a familiar voice.

Audrey swung the door wide. "Mother Joseph, Gladys Jones is here, and her mother and sisters."

The nun straightened herself behind her desk and peered through rimless spectacles. "Good morning, friends." And to Audrey, "Please bring more chairs."

The young woman bustled away and quickly returned with three chairs. After unfolding them and placing them in a row, she retreated to the door but lingered there.

"Thank you, Audrey. You're excused. Please close the door." Mother Joseph pushed a stack of papers out of her way. "This is a pleasure. I was expecting only Gladys. Mary, how are you? I've been meaning to call but I was away."

"I'm well. I hope this isn't an imposition. I told the girls I should let you know we were all coming, but I was overruled by four."

"I'm delighted, and curious. What brings you here?"

Gladys spoke for the group. "We want to apply for admission to the order."

Mother Joseph leaned closer. "I beg your pardon. You said *we*."

"Yes, we."

"All of you?"

"The whole family."

Mother Joseph folded her hands atop her desk. "This is serious business. Gladys, when you called for an appointment, I was pleased to hear that you wished to join the order. At one time or another you've all spoken to me about the sisterhood in general terms. Mary, you've told me about your mentor who advised you about a vocation."

"Yes, long ago. I never thought the calling would still come."

"Ah, yes, the calling. That's a good to place to begin. I'll answer a question I hear nearly every day. Does the religious life choose me, or do I choose it? The answer to both questions is yes. The word vocation is from the Latin, *vocare*, meaning to call. God calls you, but within that invitation is free choice. You can say yes or no."

Evelyn raised her hand, as if in school, waiting for permission to speak.

"Yes, Evelyn."

"Saying no to God seems like something you don't do. I always found it hard to say no to even a nun in grade school. If she told me to do something, I did it."

Gladys watched amusement ripple across the nun's plump face. Leave it to Evelyn to bring in humor, even if unintentional.

Mother Joseph said, "This child will have no trouble with our obedience vow. But, to continue, you'll be learning about our founder, Jeanne Chezard de Matel, who experienced years of conflict about her vocation. She was a bright, attractive young woman who enjoyed parties with her friends. One day she received a message saying, 'I have destined you to institute a new order in Christ's name.' She responded, 'Praised be the Incarnate Word.' That was the beginning of our order."

All business now, Mother Joseph pulled a handful of brochures from a drawer and passed them around. "I want you to attend this program; Discernment Day. You'll hear sisters share stories about decision making and how they adapted to the religious life. Meanwhile, I want you to keep a journal. Set aside time each day to listen to God and to yourself. Write down your thoughts. When did you first consider becoming a nun? Was it in school, in church? When you're on the road, do you wish you were in the convent or at church? Another thing, we recommend that you don't tell anyone that you're considering the religious life."

Dorothy asked what Gladys intended to ask. "Why? I'm excited and want to shout my news to the world."

"Yes, of course. I'm confident none of you made this decision lightly, but some girls, the very young especially, are influenced by a grandmother, an aunt, a friend, someone with more authority than herself. She may want to please that person by joining the convent, or by not joining, whichever way that person advises."

Gladys recalled the day Hazel finally decided to come with them. Was she simply following her sisters, eager to please someone, Mama, maybe? She put aside the questions to listen to Mother Joseph.

"What you can do for now is ask friends and family to pray for you. Tell them you're facing an important decision. Light a candle for your special intention. There are other things you should do to prepare. Open yourself to God's presence and voice. Listen to your inner responses. Practice periods of silence. I think you'll begin to see the benefits of silence. Visit the sick, the elderly; feed the hungry, visit a monastery or some of our missions. Talk with the monks, the brothers. Write down how you feel when you're doing these things. Does it give you satisfaction, or do you become impatient? Make a list of questions to bring to Discernment Day."

Evelyn faked a pout. "Homework, back in school."

"Yes, back to school. I pray you'll all graduate with us. You certainly have the qualifications we seek."

"What are those?" Hazel asked.

"First, you must be a high school graduate, or continue your education here. You've all met that stipulation. Let me read from the list: Sound judgment, reasonably good health, emotional maturity, moral integrity, strength of character, a religious spirit that indicates a desire to thrive and grow through the religious life and be faithful to the commitment. And a family spirit which promises growth, esteem, and dedication to our order." She glanced up. "Of course, *family* in this instance refers to our community. But you're already a family, a small community, with a plenty of spirit."

Gladys watched Mother Joseph's eyes sparkle and the soft wrinkles around them deepen as she acknowledged each woman in turn. "I must say, I'm always happy to welcome applicants, but it's usually one at a time. Once we had twins who came together, but I've never heard of five members of one family applying on the same day. I'm sure it's a first. All I can think is that God loves you very much and doesn't want you separated. You've always been close and you'll still be together. Mary, as a widow, you'll need a dispensation. We'll appeal to Archbishop Drossaerts. I'll file the necessary papers."

"Thank you. I'm still overwhelmed. But if I could have a minute, I'd like to relate something that happened long ago. I remembered it the other day."

Mother Joseph nodded approval and Mama turned to her daughters.

"You probably recall that after my sister Anna died, I was terribly despondent. I spent days in bed feeling sorry for myself, worrying that all my loved ones would be taken from me, one by one. Finally, I forced myself up. As I was going downstairs, I felt a hand on my shoulder. I thought one of you had come up behind me but there was no one there. Then a peaceful feeling washed over me and I sensed a voice telling me that my daughters would always be with me. I thought that meant that none of you would die before I do, the way it's supposed to be, parents first. I became confident that I'd die before any of you do. I never imagined the message meant that I'd never be without you because we'd all be together here."

Gladys tried to speak but couldn't. Suddenly everything was beginning to soak in; they actually were doing this, together. It was real.

Mother Joseph stood with her hands under her scapular. "This is indeed a blessing on your family and on our order. As I said earlier, I suggest we keep this to ourselves for now. You women have a following, and the news could create a stir."

"I agree," Gladys said, "with one exception. We need to tell our band partners. But they'll keep our secret."

Let The Rest Of The World Go By

With someone like you, a pal good and true, I'd like to leave it all behind ~~~

Gladys held the back door ajar while Jerry pulled off her western boots and parked them and a dripping umbrella in the kitchen corner.

"This meeting better be important," Jerry said, "you're dragging me out in a monsoon."

"I promise good coffee. Not like Hazel's. She makes Midwest coffee; too weak." Hearing herself prattle, Gladys realized she was nervous about telling Jerry what was going on. She poured a cup of coffee and carried it to the table, where Mama and Jerry were discussing the rain, how they had needed it for the gardens and crops, but enough was enough.

When Dorothy came in and sat down, too, Jerry said, "You three look as sober as undertakers. What's wrong?"

"Nothing's wrong," Gladys answered, "but brace yourself for some news."

"Oh, oh; who's leaving the band this time?" Jerry glanced at Dorothy. "Not you again?"

Dorothy nodded. "Yes, and Gladdie, too."

Jerry's eyes blinked wide open and stayed lifted. "Both of you? What's going on? I go away for a few days and come home to find I'm losing two band members?"

My pal, Gladys thought, that's only half of it. "More than that. Hazel and Evelyn, too. We've all applied to enter Incarnate Word Convent."

Jerry opened her mouth to speak but nothing came out.

Dorothy said, "I know it's a shock."

"A shock? That's putting it mildly. Does Willeen know?"

Gladys realized she'd left out one Rangerette. "She knows. Actually, she's seeing Mother Joseph right now."

"Seeing Mother Joseph?"

"Willeen's applying, too. Hazel and Evelyn went with her."

Gladys felt Jerry studying her as if she were sorting through every minute they'd ever spent together and still didn't recognize someone she knew. "Willeen said she's thought about it for a long time but never had the nerve to take the step. When we told her our plans, she jumped right in."

"She's thought about it a long time? Willeen Grey? Willie?" Jerry's voice kept rising. "I've known her for years and never heard her utter a word. You all have at least mentioned it."

"Some people keep it to themselves," Dorothy offered. "Mother Joseph says it's best not to talk about it until you're certain. Willeen probably wasn't sure. She's a convert and might not have wanted to mention it."

"I know she's a convert. We were baptized together."

It occurred to Gladys that in all the time she'd known Jerry and Willeen, she'd never heard the circumstances of why and when they became Catholics. But she didn't dally on that now, even though silence had fallen over the table.

When Jerry rose and walked to the door, Gladys worried that she was so upset she was leaving without another word. But Jerry turned around, looking sadder than Gladys had ever seen her. "I'm a bandleader without a band."

"I'm sorry. At first I thought it would be just me but then the others decided to go with me."

"Unbelievable." Pausing, Jerry threw up her hands, and her wise-cracking personality emerged. Doing a Jimmy Durante double take, she muttered, "Stop da music. Every—body wants to get outta da act."

On the brink of tears anyway, Gladys laughed until she cried.

Jerry backed toward the door. "Okay, I'm coming in again and you can tell me I was dreaming the first time."

"It seems like a dream, but it's really a dream come true." Gladys felt Mama's hand on hers and realized she had left out another person. "Oh, there's one thing more," she told Jerry.

"More? What more could there be? Uncle Doc is becoming a priest?"

Gladys laughed. "You're close. Mama is going with us. To the convent."

Jerry wagged her finger at Gladys. "Okay, now you're putting the shuck on me."

Mama stretched a grin from ear to ear. "It's true. Isn't it wonderful?"

Jerry slapped the table with both hands. "Well, I'll be a monkey's aunt. I swear I've never seen a day to beat this one. Now that it's sinking in, I'm not all that surprised by Gladys's decision. But the whole shootin' shebang, including Willeen and Mama. I never saw that coming. I'm as bowled over as Joe Louis was when Max Schmeling trounced him all the way through twelve rounds."

Again, Gladys saw sadness on Jerry's face when she added, "I feel like the only girl in class who hasn't been asked to the dance."

Hoping to cheer her friend, Gladys said, "No, dear pal, by the first of the year, you'll be the only one going to the dance."

The comment backfired. Jerry wiped her eyes on her sleeve and murmured, "Going to the dance stag is worse than not being asked."

Here I Am, Lord

I have heard you calling in the night ~~~

Gladys tugged off her black gloves in the vestibule of St. Mary's rectory. "Good morning, Father Dusseau. I hope I haven't kept you waiting."

"Not at all. Good morning." The priest led her into his office, showed her to a chair and seated himself at his mission style oak desk. He glanced at some papers on his desk and then looked up. "I have a confession. I've known your family since you came to the parish, but I've never known for sure which sister I'm talking to. I had to check my notes to see which one you are. Not that you all look exactly alike. I just couldn't say for sure which name went with which face."

"You're not alone, Father. We've been *the Jones sisters* to most folks since we were kids. A unit, it seems, rather than individuals." She paused. "Come to think of it, if we're all admitted, when we're wearing our habits folks still won't be able to keep us straight. We'll still be *the Jones sisters.*"

"Yes, I suppose so." He referred to his papers again. "You are, age twenty-nine, I see. You wrote on the application that you've considered the sisterhood for some time. Mother Joseph told me that all of you have. You and your sisters."

"That's correct." While Gladys waited for the next question, she noted that the priest's jowly cheeks, pinched tight by his Roman collar, were like pockets, like the pliable bread Mexicans used for sandwiches. She couldn't think what it was called.

"I hope your joint decision isn't based on staying together as a unit, as you put it. We call that the colonial response, a desire for family members to stay together."

Gladys considered the comment, thinking of Hazel. Did she decide to join because she would be left behind? What about Willeen? She was like family. Father hadn't asked about Willeen so Gladys answered truthfully.

"That's not the case with my sisters and me. When I announced my decision, and then my mother, the others said it was the nudge they needed. My father's death created an upheaval, a crossroads where I knew I needed a change. I've experienced living in the world, but not with it. If that makes sense. I knew I wanted to dedicate myself to service to the Church. And I knew I wanted to be in Texas, closer to my mother. I never suspected how close we would be, if we're approved for the convent."

Father Dusseau tapped his finger on his closed mouth, which indicated to Gladys that she was on her own to make her case. "The most important things in my life are love for God, family, and music. If I'm allowed to teach music, I'll have it all right here. Mama always told us that God gave us the gift of music and that we must use that gift to the best of our ability. She stressed, 'For unto whomsoever much is given, of him shall be much required.'"

"Luke, chapter twelve, verse forty-eight," the priest murmured.

"So my sisters and I used our talents to entertain. We got caught up in it, playing at community events. It was fun. It was exciting. Then we moved to Texas and other opportunities arose. I don't think any of us ever imagined our little family band would become a career, but one thing led to another. Always, in the back of my mind, was the religious life."

Father Dusseau dipped a pen in an inkwell and scratched notes on the forms on his desk. Placing a blotter over the wet ink he looked up as if he had something to say, but when he didn't speak Gladys moved ahead.

"My sisters and I have been on the road for several years. There were times we barely had enough money to get to the next town. The school of hard knocks, if you will." She squirmed, hoping the rough life she'd led would not be held against her. "I think of those years as my apprenticeship. I come armed with knowledge about the world, the good and the bad."

"Indeed. I know that monasteries and seminaries hope for men who've seen the world, who understand what they're giving up."

Buoyed by validation of what she'd said, she added, "Yes, the world has a lot to offer but I find that I don't need, or want, a lot of what it offers." Having run out of thoughts, she put the conversation in Father's hands by staring at him as he had at her.

He complied with, "I'm sure my next question doesn't apply to you, but we always ask it of applicants. Are you simply seeking shelter, a place where you will be taken care of, a roof over your head?"

"Oh, no, Father. I've always worked for a living. I don't know any other kind of life. And I don't see sisters as being taken care of. The ones I know care for everyone around them. As teachers and nurses, they seem devoted to their work."

"You must understand that the religious life takes discipline and energy."

"I'm blessed with those traits."

"Your endurance on the road speaks to that. The religious life can be a daily struggle, adhering to the vows, to the choice you've made."

"Couldn't the same be said of other choices? Marriage, for instance?"

"Certainly. We all face a host of troubling situations. It's my duty to point out the reality of convent life. Play the devil's advocate, if you will. The decision to enter is often not as difficult as the decision to stay, when it comes time for final vows."

Grateful for this two-way conversation, Gladys said, "It was difficult on the road, too, practicing my faith, worrying about whether or not we'd get to Mass on Sundays and Holy Days. We succeeded, for the most part. I'm confident I'll succeed here, too."

The priest cleared his throat. "What I was getting at, and again, this is information I'm obliged to pass along, is that women come to us for many reasons, some of them very much misguided. As badly as we need sisters, we turn some women away. They might be fleeing a bad home situation from which they want to escape. Others see the religious life as a boost to their image. Sibling rivalry is a common factor. We have a sister here who, years after her final vows, confessed she had lied about her reason for entering the convent. I don't recall the reason she gave then, but she told me that she really joined because her brother was a priest. That he was so adored and favored by family members that she felt becoming a sister was the only way to earn their lasting love. Oddly enough, she's very dedicated, one of our best teachers."

He removed his glasses and rubbed his eyes. "Then there was the teenager who believed she was possessed by the devil and wanted to hide from Satan. Other women are afraid of having a relationship with a man and want a haven where they won't be confronted with their feelings about men. We've had women leave because they can't tolerate the male dominance in the community. As one put it, 'The constant kowtowing to men, from the pope on down to the parish priest.' She was an angry young woman."

His shrug made Gladys think he didn't quite understand the former sister's line of thought. Then, almost as if talking to himself, he said, "We also get women who have feelings toward other women. They see this as a place to foster such an arrangement."

Gladys sat motionless, grateful his eyes were not on her. She'd met women on the road who were obvious about their interest in females, but she'd learned to accept that they were different from most of the women she knew.

Sensing that the priest was uncomfortable with the subject he'd opened, she switched topics. "My hope is to teach music. I believe music is the thread holding society together. Immigrants who came here with little more than the clothes on their backs brought instruments. My great-grandparents couldn't read or write but they played fiddle and mandolin. The children had harmonicas and penny whistles. My mother's grandfather used to tell her that if you see an immigrant getting off a boat without an instrument, he probably plays the piano."

The priest acknowledged the comment with a grin, as if he'd heard it before.

"Music is the one constant in everyone's life. Rich or poor, at home or in school, in church or on the street, people are drawn to music. I'll never have children of my own, but I do love them. I hope to bring them the joy that music has brought me since I was in the cradle."

She caught her breath, hoping Father might speak again instead of sitting there like a doting uncle letting his favorite niece go on and on. Out of steam, she folded her hands in her lap and waited.

Pulling his watch from the folds of his cassock, he said, "Gladys, I've enjoyed talking with you. I don't think I need keep you any longer. Is there anything more you'd like to say?"

She thought a moment. "I suppose only that a teacher of Mama's used to tell her that God can call us into service at any age. Now God has chosen not only her, but her four daughters, too. I can't express how happy I am."

"The Lord works in mysterious ways. This situation is particularly mysterious."

"But I was thinking earlier about families with several nurses, lawyers, doctors, teachers, plumbers. Yet, people think it's odd when more than one member of a family enters the religious life."

"Oh, that part is not unusual. It's all of you entering at the same time that makes it a peculiarity."

"Yes, you're right. Well, as Mama often says, 'We'll let God settle that.' He settled this matter and called us all together instead of one at a time."

The priest rose and came around his desk. "I'm pleased to sign your application. I'm certain the others will be approved."

"Thank you, Father. May I have your blessing before I leave?"

While she knelt, Father Dusseau held a crucifix over her head. "Dear Lord, thank you for the gift you have bestowed on our community. I humbly ask your blessing on your child, Gladys Jones, and on her family as they embark on a spiritual journey. Please give them faith, strength, and courage to prevail in their ministry."

He added, "The Lord will guard your coming and going, both now and forever. Psalm twenty-one."

Across The Alley From The Alamo

Where the starlight beams its tender, tender glow ~~~

Gladys had never been inside the renowned Menger Hotel, but she knew its history. Situated across from the Alamo, the hotel had long been the home away from home for cattle and oil barons, presidents and ex-presidents, military commanders, and film stars. The guest registers gathering dust in storage were said to include the names of John Pershing, William Howard Taft, Warren G. Harding, General U. S. Grant, William Sydney Porter (O. Henry), Captain Richard King of the King Ranch, and Teddy Roosevelt, whose headquarters were at the Menger during the months when the Rough Riders were forming and training. Now, in the midst of the Depression, business at the posh hotel had declined, but it managed to stay afloat.

When San Antonio's Texas Rangerettes stomped onto the Rotunda bandstand on New Year's Eve, they pulled out all the stops for what would be their swan song, opening with *We're All Pals Together*. But the band took a backseat to dozens of teenage "shiners," those whose dancing was so outstanding and exuberant that others cleared the way and stood back to watch them perform the new sensation, the Big Apple. Done in groups and led by a caller, the shiners jitterbugged in combinations of the Lindy Hop, Charleston, Shag, Black Bottom, Virginia Reel, or other steps they improvised on the spot. *Variety* had written about the Big Apple, "It requires a lot of floating power and fannying."

Gladys and Hazel were in stitches watching Evelyn and Dorothy float and fanny with a circle of eight, following directions called by a lanky young man wearing a white sweater, Oxford bag pants, and saddle shoes. Planting his feet outward like a duck, he called, "*Truck to the right, reverse to left, stomp that right foot now the left, swing and sway. Wiggle, wiggle, wiggle. Big apple.*" The dance ended with all the dancers raising their arms and crying, "Praise Allah."

Back with the band, Evelyn wheezed, "Whew," and caught her breath. "I don't know who Allah is but I praise the Lord I'm not in the middle of that frenzy."

"Getting old?" Gladys teased.

"At least I tried it. Didn't see you out there."

The room gradually quieted as the revelers' stamina waned and the band played slow, nostalgic tunes. Shortly before midnight, Rotunda waiters distributed paper hats and tin horns. Willeen tap-tapped on a snare drum and Jerry led the crowd into a countdown, "Ten, nine, eight, seven, six, five, four, three, two, one, Happy New Year." The Rangerettes took off on *Auld Lang Syne*, the music smothered by singing, clapping, whooping, shrill whistles and horns.

The party ended with two songs. Jerry sang the lyrics to *For All We Know,* and on the line, "*We won't say goodnight, until the last minute, I hold out my hand and my heart will be in it,*" she lifted her eyes, her voice, and her hands to the five musicians she was losing to the religious life.

Then the group played and sang Irving Berlin's *The Best of Friends Must Part.* The significance of the final songs would not be known to anyone until a week later.

On that cool Texas morning blanketed by stars, the Packard carried the six pals away together for the last time. An end of an era, Gladys thought. With mixed emotions challenging her ability to speak, she glanced at Mama, who had watched the band's performance from off stage. Tonight she's had her first, and last, ride in this "awful hearse." And I'm taking my last.

She patted the worn cloth seat. It's been a wonderful ride, but I'm ready to take the road less traveled.

Among My Souvenirs

A letter wrapped in blue, a photograph or two, I find a rose or two ~~~

Gladys waved a creased photograph. "Anyone know who this is?"

Hazel studied the snapshot of a man standing outside a nondescript dance club. "Looks vaguely familiar," she said, and then sang, "*but who knows where or when.*"

Laughing, Gladys held the picture over a wastebasket. "Going once, going twice, gone."

Since New Year's day the women had been sorting their belongings, cleaning the attic, closets and cubbyholes. With poverty among the vows they would take, they had given away books, clothing, jewelry, and household items to the Sisters of Charity Bargain Center. Mama had filled her trunk with family mementos and shipped it to her sister, Alice. Jerry took the Rangerette scrapbooks, postcards, posters and photos; they were part of her past, too. She would store the instruments until they were allowed at the convent.

The Joneses had paid their dowry to the convent with the understanding that the money would be invested and never used by the community until after each sister's death. As required, they had set aside funds for board and clothing during the time between novitiate and profession.

Gladys and Hazel sat cross-legged on the floor, wrapping newspaper around collectibles from their travels. Into a charity box went salt and pepper shakers from the Corn Palace and Wisconsin Dells, a plaster replica of Mount Rushmore, ashtrays from Happy Jack's Chicken Shack and the Packing House Café, a miniature blown glass guitar from the Grand Ole Opry, a Golden Gate Bridge made of wire and a paper dragon from Chinatown. Each item evoked memories and chatter, but Gladys found the chore easier, emotionally, than expected. There was a kind of freedom in unloading material things, in simplifying life. Being on the road had been unsettling; she would finally put her feet down in one place and stay there.

Evelyn lingered in the doorway. "I packed Pa's things. Mama's been avoiding it but she told me to go ahead. And I cleaned out Fibber Magee's closet in the front hall. Nothing of value there. Oh, Dorothy, I found these." She handed her sister a strip of three photos taken at one of those carnival machines where people pull a curtain and pose for the hidden camera.

With only a glance at herself and Keith Foss, Dorothy tossed the strip into the wastebasket. "Right; nothing of value in the closet."

A wave of sadness washed over Gladys, for Dorothy, but it fled quickly. She had never seen Dorothy as content as she'd been these past weeks. That went for all her sisters and Mama. There seemed to be no second thoughts; no looking back.

Hazel had been digging in a box and now she wiggled across the room wearing a grass skirt, a lei, a sombrero, and, on her fingers, castanets chattering like teeth on a forty-below-zero Minnesota morning. Her sisters broke into a collective giggle.

Mama called from the kitchen, "Stop fooling around and get to work."

A chorus of "Yes, Mama," preceded more laughter.

"Go ahead, get it out of your system. Soon you'll be taking vows of silence."

"She'll be Mother Superior before we know it," Evelyn mumbled.

"I heard that. Don't be pert."

Gladys eased up behind Mama and massaged her shoulders, drawing comfort as much as offering it. Soon their positions would be equal, rather than mother and daughter, they would be sisters.

"I've been listening to you girls chatter," Mama said. "Before long, we'll all be in a long period of silence."

"We may have to tape Evie's mouth shut."

"Listen to the pot calling the kettle black," Evelyn called. "You even talk in your sleep. And play instruments."

Gladys patted Mama's shoulder. "We'll be fine."

"I know. But remember, we don't take final vows for years. None of us should be afraid to drop out if this isn't a true calling. We'll promise each other that. There's an old Irish proverb that a promise is a debt. We owe that to each other."

"I wonder what Pa would say about all of us becoming nuns."

"Well, for one thing, I wouldn't be going if he was still here."

"I hope not," Gladys teased. "I meant his four daughters."

"He'd have been proud to see you go off together. Like I would be if he was still here and I wasn't going. Maybe I'd be a bit envious. Like when you all took off in that awful hearse."

"You were envious?"

"Sometimes. You were doing something I'd once thought about doing. Mostly I was content to stay home. But that's in the past. We're all going to travel together now, on a more wonderful journey than the band ever took."

"That's for sure."

"I wonder what people will say when they hear what I'm doing. Martin's gone only six months and off I go. Leaving that life behind, almost like it never existed."

"People will always talk about something."

"Of course. It doesn't matter what others think. I'm content with my decision."

Gladys pulled herself up. "Hazel and I are going over to Jerry's. Wanna go with us? We plan to stop and see Uncle Doc. I think he's still in shock over our news."

"He sure is. I'll miss him. He's a good friend. No, I won't go along. I'll see Jerry and Doc later. But before you go, let me read you a letter I wrote to my cousin Elizabeth O'Brien. Tell me if it sounds okay."

"You write wonderful letters. I'm sure it's fine, but I'd love to hear it."

~~~ Dear Elizabeth: I can't remember if I wrote to you before and told you the good news. It is that the four girls and I are going to be sisters of the Blessed Sacrament, and want your prayers that we will persevere to the end. We are all happy, and knowing you, I know you will be happy for us. Now, I am letting you, and you are the only one I will write, tell the others, and ask their prayers for us. I know sometime you will come to see us. We will be postulants for six months, then novices for a year, and at the end of three years, we take final vows, which will erase all sins of life, like baptism does. I am so happy that the Lord has called and that we can try to serve him in our humble way. I know the world will think us foolish, but that is the world's view, and I hope more will enter to try and serve Him, for today, as never before, are his works chastised and criticized. Lots of love, Mary. ~~~

She scanned the page. "Does it sound too preachy? I never like it when people go overboard talking about their religion, wear it on their sleeve."

Gladys laid a kiss atop Mama's head. "It's wonderful. I'm sure Cousin Elizabeth will be thrilled to receive the letter."

SISTERHOOD

Oh, What A Beautiful Morning

I've got a wonderful feeling, everything's going my way ~~~

On the Feast of the Epiphany, a lavender blue sky filtered through a trellis entwined with blooms Gladys could not name, but its perfume dominated the morning air like incense in church. As Doc's Oldsmobile edged away from the curb, she took a last look at the house. Between her and Doc, Mama sat motionless. Behind them, Hazel, Dorothy and Evelyn were silent, too.

Knowing her world would soon be mostly black and white, she soaked up the colors around her: a newsboy's red bicycle, a woman wearing a gaudy flowered dress, a pair of pink flamingoes, and a street vendor's cart laden with fruits and vegetables. The tilted wagon reminded her of a box of crayons; the vibrant hues aligned in rows: apple, cherry, radish, rhubarb, raspberry, orange, peach, nectarine, apricot, pear, banana, squash, cucumber, celery, watermelon, and the exotic blue-purple family: blueberry, eggplant, turnip, and grape.

Parked at the curb in front of the putty colored convent, Uncle Doc slid out of the car and opened the trunk. "I'll carry these up for you," he said as the women huddled on the sidewalk.

Gladys lifted her bag. "Thanks, but that's not necessary. We've lugged around instruments heavier than this bag. We weren't allowed to bring much." She fought back an urge to hug him. Like Pa, Uncle Doc was not given to displays of affection. She tapped his arm and said, "Thanks for everything, Uncle Doc."

"You call or write, when you can." He quickly moved away to say goodbye to the others.

Her head high, Gladys marched toward the convent where Mother Joseph and Father Dusseau waited at the bottom of a flight of steps. Nearly there, she stopped to glance over her shoulder. Doc leaned against the car while her sisters scudded along the walk with Mama behind, like a mother hen shooing her chicks in the right direction. Yes, this is right direction, Gladys thought. She waved to Uncle Doc and then waited for the others to catch up.

Mother Joseph extended both hands and greeted them as a group. Father Dusseau said, "Good morning. Before we go inside, Mother Joseph would like a picture of us together, for our files." Posing alongside the building, the candidates' dark clothing and shoes fit the solemn occasion, with only Dorothy's pale blue coat for contrast.

Inside, Mother Joseph introduced the postulants' mistress. "Sister Mary Abraham will show you to your quarters where you'll change into your habit. You'll attend Mass, take Communion, and there will be a brief ceremony inducting you into the order. The other four applicants, including your friend Willeen, arrived last night. After Mass, you'll have breakfast in the postulant's refectory. Then Sister Abraham will take you to Study Hall to orient you on some of the house regulations. Everything is explained in detail in the Constitutions, a book you'll be given." She turned to her colleague. "Sister Abraham, the first class of nineteen-thirty-eight is in your hands."

With a courtesy nod, Sister Abraham thanked her superior. Escorting her group upstairs, she explained, "The first floor is for sisters who have professed their vows; the second for novices and, here we are, the third for postulants."

The dormitory looked to Gladys like a hospital ward. The walls were white, the floors tan linoleum, with one colorless rag rug running the length of the room. The only color was Sister's red scapular. As she moved about, an Al Jolson tune played in Gladys's mind: *When the red, red robin, comes bob-bob-bobbing along ~~~*

Snapping out of frivolity, she noted that windows on all sides provided natural lighting and a view of the tree tops. The quarters were not as confining as she had imagined, and certainly nicer than most of the hotels the Rangerettes had frequented.

Rows of desks and chairs lined one wall, and twelve beds with white coverlets were divided six on one side of the room, six on the other. Each cubicle had a two drawer dresser, atop which sat a white enamel water pitcher and wash basin, a drinking glass, two white towels and two washcloths. At the end of the room three sinks stood beside three commodes, separated like the beds, with sheets that could be pulled closed.

Mistress pointed to a door across the hall. "That's the hygiene room, with doors and walls around the tubs for privacy. You'll be assigned fifteen minutes for a Saturday night bath and hair washing. Be on time or you'll have to wait until the following week. If you feel, with good reason, that you need a bath other than on Saturday, you must request it. For modesty, you will wear a chemise in the tub and lather the soap through it, then change into a white cotton nightgown and black robe and tie a bandanna around your hair. At all times, we practice custody of the eyes, meaning giving each other privacy.

"As for personal items received from home, luxuries such as hand lotion and shampoo will be combined and dispensed among everyone, as will food, books, or stationery. You'll be allowed letters and pictures, but tell your family to keep it to a minimum. No mail will be given out during Lent and Advent. We inspect all incoming and outgoing letters and packages."

Sister Abraham paced to the sink. "At night, after you wash up and brush your teeth, you'll refill your pitchers here. Used water should be disposed of in the sink. Any questions?" She waited. "All right, then. Please dress in your habit. Hang your extra habit in the closet in the corner. I trust that you sewed name tags in your garments. Place your worldly clothes in your suitcase for storage. Your bag should have your name on it, too. I'll be back in a few minutes."

Gladys drew the curtain around her bed and quickly changed into what would be one of two dresses she would wear for the next six months. Placing the shoulder-length black veil on her head, she glanced to the wall, expecting a mirror, but there was none. She would have to assume the headpiece was on properly, with just a wave of hair showing in front. She knew how the habit looked on her; her mother had sewn the two dresses each required at entry, and they'd all tried them on to be sure they fit.

The ankle-length black garments had white Peter Pan collars, white cuffs on the long sleeves, and a removable short cape to be worn for formal occasions, such as today. The dresses had no pockets; instead, a cloth bag attached to the belt held a rosary, note paper, pencils, a handkerchief, and a small watch. Black undergarments, long stockings held in place by a garter belt, and black shoes completed the outfit.

She pushed aside her curtain and waited until Sister Abraham materialized in the doorway and crooked her finger for the newcomers to follow. Watching Mistress from behind, Gladys thought she seemed to glide rather than walk. Feeling exhilarated, she emulated the nun's gait, as if walking on air or floating on a cloud.

In the candlelit chapel, she stood next to Willeen. They passed a look of acknowledgment and then dropped their heads, already practicing custody of the eyes. During the ceremony, the candidates as a group asked to be considered for membership in the community. Mother Joseph accepted and welcomed them, and Mass continued.

After the postulants' had breakfast, Sister Abraham escorted them to Study Hall. From behind a podium she began, "I'll pass around copies of the Constitutions. You will study and learn all the rules pertaining to sisterhood. I'll hold classes to help you along."

Shuffling papers, she continued, "As you might know, the word postulant comes from the Latin *postulare,* meaning to demand. Yes, we'll make demands, on your time, your body, your mind and soul. Your days will be scheduled and rigorous. You will rise at five, attend Mass, have breakfast, do obedience, attend theology classes and lessons on how to live in the community, meaning here, not outside life. After lunch comes recreation, homework, afternoon break, chapel, dinner, recreation, Vespers and meditation. Bedtime is at nine, lights out by nine-thirty. You'll welcome lights out, I assure you. Oh, and there's choir practice twice a week."

Ah, Gladys thought, a chance to sing. She had heard long ago that if one doesn't sing, she loses the ability. And there was that old saying: To sing is to pray twice

"Each of you will have a personal director who will observe and evaluate your sincerity, disposition, and aptitude for embracing the religious life. All the professed sisters will be watching you, too. During postulancy, silence is observed at all times except during recreation and on designated days such as Sundays, Holy Days and holidays. Today you're free to speak. We'll begin in earnest tomorrow. We practice the Great Silence from a given signal in the evening to breakfast. You will speak to no one, not even in the dormitory, and you must never enter another sister's cell. Silence is a valuable tool. You'll discover for yourself what I mean by that."

Gladys fretted for a moment about the difficulty of being with her sisters and mother day in and day out and not being able to speak to them. She and her sisters had always walked in on each other in their bedrooms. Living as Rangerettes in cramped quarters, there had never been a suggestion of privacy.

"You are expected to be on time for meals. If you come in late, you will kneel and beg pardon of the mistress, then say grace and take your seat. While the body is being fed, the soul will be nourished by silent reading. The readings will be spiritual. For example, the history and martyrdom of female saints. Occasionally I'll allow talking in the form of a discussion. You might be asked to read aloud. If so, you will rehearse so your voice is pleasant to hear.

"We do not allow particular friendships. Becoming too friendly with another applicant can result in being sent away. At no time should you assemble in pairs. At recreation you may play cards, games, do crafts, read and visit. I know we have musicians here. You might want to prepare entertainment for Sunday evenings. We all enjoy the shows staged by postulants."

Sister Abraham sipped from a water glass and then continued. "Earlier, I mentioned obedience. That means chores. We rotate kitchen help, laundry, sewing, working on our little farm, and scrubbing floors and toilets. I remember as a postulant thinking that I spent more time on my knees scrubbing floors than I did praying. To get through toilet cleaning, I offered it up to God. A lesson in humility. And remember, in my postulancy, they were outdoor toilets."

Offer it up, Gladys thought with amusement. That was what the nuns from her childhood always advised, whatever the situation, good or bad. A scraped knee, offer it up. A good grade on a test, offer it up. Rain on the day of the class picnic, offer it up. And cleaning outhouses, she knew plenty about that.

"What you had for breakfast this morning will be the usual fare. Cereal, usually oatmeal or cream of wheat, sometimes canned or fresh fruit, maybe soft boiled eggs and toast. Coffee is served with warmed milk but no sugar. The milk from our farm is quite sweet as it is. Where you sat this morning will be your assigned seat. In front of you is a drawer in the table for your place setting. After each meal, novices will bring in pans of hot water, one for washing dishes, one for rinsing. Doing dishes must be accomplished in silence, no clanking dishes or utensils. When rules are broken, even one as minor as this might seem, we expect you to admit such lapses to the community at Chapter of Faults, held once a month. There, we recite the Confiteor as a group; then each sister kneels and admits her violations of the Constitutions, religious discipline, or rules of the house. Sisters are given a penance, based on the severity of the violation."

Sister Abraham offered an enigmatic smile before revealing, "One postulant often had to ask pardon for breaking the seriousness of Chapter. She liked to juxtapose her offenses. Once she asked pardon for crossing her legs and running down the stairs. Well, don't you know, we'd all like to have seen her do that."

While the postulants tittered as a group, Gladys decided she liked Mistress. She had a sense of humor and would most likely be easy-going with her fledglings.

"Let me see, where was I? Lunch is usually bread and hot soup: bean, lentil, pea, maybe vegetable with a soup bone. For supper, you'll have meat and potatoes. You're expected to clean your plate. Leftovers are served over and over, until gone. Some of our girls are willing to eat extra helpings of food for what they call 'the good of the order.' We rarely have dessert, except for Sunday nights when we might have ice cream, or fresh fruit from the orchard, perhaps a cobbler or shortcake. You will eat only at meal time, with the exception of cookies or crackers at recreation."

While Sister Abraham droned on, Gladys forced herself to sit erect and to keep her eyes from drooping. She had hardly slept last night and had arisen before dawn. Needing fresh air, she wondered how long it would be before she stepped outdoors again. That chance came after lunch, when the official photographs were taken.

"We all have our little black dresses now," Hazel said when the Jones quintet lined up for the camera.

"Bet you're wearing pearls underneath yours," Evelyn teased.

"I feel like a prim schoolgirl," Gladys said, and Dorothy agreed.

"You're all radiantly beautiful," Mama said. Quoting Apostle John, she added, "Beloved, we are God's children now; what we will be has not yet been revealed."

"I know what I'll be," Evelyn said. "Tired. I'm already reeling thinking about the schedule we'll have."

Gladys slipped her arm around her youngest sister's tiny waist. Even throughout the long silence coming, all she would need to do is look at one of her sisters or Mama to find the strength and inspiration needed to take the next step forward.

Let Us Sing To The Lord

Let us sing a new song, not with our lips, but with our lives ~~~

Surrounded by darkness within her curtained cubicle, Gladys awoke without benefit of the morning bell. She remembered a German nun at Sacred Heart Academy who opened her class with: *In der mitte der nacht, fangt der neue tag,* meaning: In the middle of the night, a new day begins. Having adjusted from night owl to day person, she relished each new day

Lying on her simple cot, she recalled life on the road, collapsing into bed about the time other hotel guests were rising. She often struggled to sleep through the cacophony of alarm clocks buzzing, toilets flushing, water running, hotel doors slamming, voices in the hall, street noises, and the previous night's music ringing in her ears. Here, in silence like nothing she'd ever experienced, sleep and rising came easily. Concentration and meditation were easier, too.

She silently recited a line from one of Saint Augustine's sermons, another phrase that helped her start each day. Anyone who has learned to love the new life has learned to sing a new song, and the song reminds us of our new life.

When the bell shrieked she slid out of bed and began her morning ritual. By the time afternoon break rolled around, her energy had flagged. She picked up a glass of milk and a graham cracker and chose a chair in the corner.

Mama bustled into the community room, a patina of dust in the folds of her habit, her face flushed, a blotch of soil on her nose. "What a lovely day," she announced to her colleagues. "Evelyn and I were at the farm. Old McDonald's villa, she calls it. I love being on a farm again; there's a rhythm to it. God, man, and animals working together. Or, in this case, women. So, what have you been doing, Gladys?"

"Dorothy and I had kitchen duty. My hands ache from kneading bread. Then I had a calligraphy class and we made prayer cards. I'll send one to Aunt Alice."

"She'd love that. Where's Hazel?"

"She'll be along. I saw her in the laundry. She won't be happy. She doesn't like using the Mangle ironer in what she calls the sweat shop. Says it's the devil's own invention."

"Oh, you girls. I realize that laundry is known as the worst job around here. All those heavy habits, bedding and towels, but none of the chores are any harder than what I did every day on the farm. And I had four little ones under foot. I suppose we've all become soft with modern conveniences. Ah, there's Hazel now. I'll go say hello to her."

Willeen rushed over and sat next to Gladys, "See that postulant over there. She says Mary's a spy. That she's too old to be a postulant, that she's a professed sister who'll report on us at Chapter of Fault if we misbehave and don't admit it."

"A spy? My mother?"

"That's what she said. I told her that the point of Chapter is that we admit our own discretions. Others don't tattle on us. I told her I know Mary from way back but she didn't believe it. She said posing as your mother is part of the cover. She said it's enough believing that all four of you are sisters. I don't think she's going to make it here. She's odd; whispers in her sleep, as if she's telling secrets to someone."

"Willeen, this is gossip. We're required to practice charity to others."

"Claire's not charitable about your mother."

"Nevertheless, at Chapter we'll need to beg pardon for this conversation. You know we're supposed to talk only about edifying matters, about something good."

"Oh, is that what edifying means?"

Evelyn joined the conversation. "Claire should be more worried about Captain Ahab reporting on her than Mama."

Gladys narrowed her eyes at Evelyn. "Her name is Sister Mary Abraham."

"She's like Captain Ahab. Only he hounded a whale instead of postulants."

Mistress spoke from the doorway, "Chapel in five minutes."

"Yes, Captain," Evelyn mouthed.

Gladys shook her head, wondering if Evelyn would remember to accuse herself of these unkind comments at their first Chapter of Faults assembly.

Take Me Out To The Ballgame

Let me root, root, root for the home team ~~~

Seated by an open window in the infirmary, Gladys sneezed twice, blew her nose, and wiped her eyes. On the grounds below, past the garden where two elderly sisters were hoeing weeds, a softball game had begun between the postulants and the novices. Gladys's cold and fever kept her sidelined, and Mama opted out due to her age, so several novices had been assigned to play with the postulants.

At recreation yesterday Evelyn had informed her team members, "The novices gave us their worst players."

"How would you know that?" Mama asked.

"Wouldn't you? The captain of their team is that novice who's built like Babe Ruth. No one argues with her. You know who I mean. Face as freckled as a pinto pony. And she puts on that honey-coated voice that makes her seem so sweet."

Gladys tskked to herself at the way Evelyn continued to amass indiscretions to confess at Chapter.

Evelyn demonstrated how to adjust their habits for easier movement. She pulled the back of her dress and petticoat through her legs and up the front and held it at her waist, so the skirt looked like britches. "We pin them like this. Our dresses are lighter weight than the novices' habits. I don't think they can adapt theirs like this."

Dorothy frowned. "Why would they want to? It looks unladylike. Irreverent."

"For Pete's sake, don't be stuffy. I'm twenty-six, not ninety-six. I'm becoming a nun, not a mummy. We need exercise and fun. Remember having fun?"

"Yes, I do. You don't have to be snippy. I'm just saying what I think."

"Me, too, and I think even sisters are allowed to have fun. Why else would we be having this ballgame?"

"Well, I'm not pinning my dress to my waist."

Now, watching the action on the field, Gladys got a kick out of the way Dorothy's unaltered dress whipped at her ankles as she skimmed the bases.

Gladys stretched out on a cot, listening to the voices outside. She wished she were either playing or cheering with Mama for their team. But there would be other games, other activities. Certainly the days here were not as much fun as life on the road had been, but they were predictable and less stressful. Early to bed and early to rise meant eight solid hours of sleep each night, something she had come to covet. And a nap right now wasn't an indulgence; it was just what the doctor ordered. Or at least the sister nurse in charge of the infirmary.

At recreation the next morning, Evelyn informed Gladys, "Despite Dorothy fumbling around in her long skirt, we won."

Dorothy eyed Evelyn. "And...."

"And? Oh, yeah. The pretty one smacked a home run. Clear across the field."

Hands on her hips, Dorothy urged, "And...."

"Oh, all right. You won the game for us. Don't let it go to your head."

They Didn't Believe Me

And when I told them, they didn't believe me ~~~

Back when the Jones women approached Mother Joseph about entering religious life, Gladys speculated that news about their career change would cause a stir. But inside the convent the former musicians had no inkling what had gone on following their enrollment. Not until the end of postulancy did they read articles Jerry left at the convent. Mother Joseph confided that she held back the clippings because she felt they might be disruptive or cause problems with decisions about continuing.

Mother Joseph now decided the articles would be of interest not only to the Jones family but to the other sisters. She asked the women to share some of the stories at recreation, after which the papers would be filed in the convent's archives.

Gladys read two headlines: "Quit Dance Halls for Convent Life; Four Texas Rangerettes and Mother Take Long Planned Step," and "Dance Band Members Turn From Torch Song to Psalms." The latter piece began:

~~~ San Antonio, Tex (INS) From a throaty torch song to the chant of the litany, from swing tunes to psalms. From, indeed, all the din and lively gaiety of a dance band platform to the ethereal, sedate calm of a convent. ~~~

Finishing that, she followed with a brief article titled "Entire Family Enters Convent," accompanied by a photo of the five women.

~~~ These four daughters and their widowed mother of St. Mary's parish, San Antonio, were recently admitted as postulants into Incarnate Word and Blessed Sacrament convent there. Originally from Minnesota, the four sisters were members of the Texas Rangerettes, an all-girl dance orchestra which toured the United States. Miss Willeen Grey, another member of the musical group, joined them in the convent. ~~~

While Gladys passed around the article, Hazel read excerpts from a San Antonio newspaper dated six months earlier, January 24, 1938.

~~~ Five Rangerettes, members of a widely-known girl orchestra are settling today into the routine of the Blessed Sacrament Convent. The step was taken by Mrs. Martin Jones and her four daughters, Hazel, Gladys, Dorothy, and Evelyn, along with Willeen Grey. The great contrast between their lives entertaining at fashionable centers as a swing band and their life in the convent is indicated by the fact that the taking of vows calls for six months silence. Fans said it would never last; that the women couldn't possibly prefer the glow of sanctuary lights to

the glitter of footlights. But without a qualm, they laid aside their boots and buckles, their wide-brimmed Stetsons and bright kerchiefs for the somber robes of a religious order. ~~~

Gladys, noting that Hazel's voice had strained with emotion, took the paper and continued reading.

~~~ Miss Jerry McRae, left a bandleader without a band by their decision, explained that her erstwhile followers had long planned the step. She said, "It was something they thought about for years, when the time was right. No matter where we were playing they insisted on going to Mass. Many a time we played all night and then went to church in costume. We must have looked a wild lot, in those big hats and clumping books with our makeup still on, but those Irish girls and their mother, and Willeen, too, were just as devout as any of the rest of them."

Miss McRae added, "When I last saw them they were as enthusiastic as they ever were over a swell new contract or hitting up a hot new number. I saw them after Vespers and I never saw such a happy lot. They'd been busy from daylight to dark but were as fresh as daisies and bubbling over with excitement. They were particularly pleased by being told they would be allowed to teach music after taking their final vows. Power to them all, they're a grand bunch of troupers. I guess even God can't ask for more than that." ~~~

Dorothy read an excerpt from another article.

~~~ Hollywood's Paramount Studio camped on the convent doorstep, wanting permission from Archbishop Drossaerts to make a newsreel of the women becoming postulants. The cameramen were denied permission; ecclesiastical censure forbade that type of publicity, but the archbishop told reporters that, to his knowledge, this was the first time in religious history that five members of one family entered a convent at the same time. ~~~

"That'll show Dorothy," Evelyn whispered to Gladys. "She used to make fun of me for thinking I was right up there with Alice Faye. I didn't think that at all, but now we find out Hollywood had an interest in us."

"Maybe for a fleeting moment. Paramount Studio is familiar with our work because of our Publix Theater tour. For me, those days seem like a dream. I don't miss that life one iota. Do you?"

Evelyn gave her sister's chin a tiny pinch. "Not even that much."

Hazel is another matter, Gladys thought. Her older sister, alone in a corner, wiped her eyes as Dorothy read aloud another piece about the former Rangerettes.

Come Haste To The Wedding

Ye friends and neighbors, forget all your sorrows, your cares and your labors ~~~

The bell summoning residents to arise and come to chapel had not yet broken the silence when Gladys awakened. Her eyes turned immediately to her bridal gown. Today she and her sisters and mother would become brides of Christ. She'd been surprised to learn that the Church considered nuns to be married women; she had always thought of them as single.

Mama and two other postulants had made the gowns for the nine novices. One postulant's father, a dry goods merchant, had donated the ivory tulle for the calf-length dresses with a cowl neck, fitted bodice, drop waist, and long-sleeves.

Gladys had enjoyed choosing a new name. Each postulant was allowed to list three choices, with no guarantee they would be accepted. The name could not be that of a living member of the community. She chose Clara, Genevieve, and Rose, with none a clear favorite. Mama had listed only one name, Pius, after her childhood music teacher in Iowa. "If I can't have Pius," she said, "I'll take what they give me. After all, none of us has a say in our name when we're baptized. It's the parents' choice." Dorothy picked Grace, Helen, and Catherine, while Hazel opted for Jude or Brendan.

"Why men's names?" Evelyn asked. "I've always wondered why many nuns have men's names."

"Saint Jude is my favorite saint, and I like Saint Brendan, too. He was Irish."

Evelyn shrugged. "Suit yourself." She flipped through a book of saint's names and recited a litany of exotic possibilities "Glyceria, Lelia, Sabina, Thais, Peregrine. Isn't that a bird? I don't know; maybe I'll make it simple and choose Dorothy."

Dorothy's eyes lit up. "You'd take my name? How nice."

"Sure, then I'd be the pretty one."

"Oh, not that again. What is it with you and that old song and dance about me being the pretty one?"

Evelyn ignored her sister and recited a few more names. "Raphael, Moses, Daniel. No, not a man's name. That just doesn't seem right."

Now the day had come; they would all learn their new names. While washing her face, Gladys felt warmth radiate across her cheeks. With no mirror, she imagined looking aglow with excitement. But did the glow come from soap and water or from what Mama called inner happiness and peace? Or had the stifling July heat caused her face to flush? She recalled one of Pa's jokes, that Texas summers were so hot the birds used potholders to pull worms from the ground. Thankfully, the summer he died, a year ago, had been relatively cool and he hadn't suffered from the heat. As he lost more and more weight, he sometimes needed a blanket.

Offering a prayer for Pa, she added: "We miss you. Please pray for us."

She slid a comb through her hair but didn't fuss; her veil would cover her curls and soon they would be gone. After shedding her nightgown and putting on fresh underwear, she stepped into her gown. It fit perfectly. Using hairpins, she secured the headpiece in place. Now the phrase "taking the white veil" had meaning.

Perspiration dripped on her brow and her heart raced. I'm like an adolescent waiting for her first date to arrive, she thought. Who was my first date? Was it the banker's son, the boy Pa didn't trust? Or Lyle Forbes, the shy boy who sat next to me in band and finally passed a note asking me to a school dance?

Both boys were lost in time when her advisor, Sister Paul, parted the curtain around the cubicle and nodded for Gladys to follow. Last in the line of postulants moving down the stairs, single file, straight as soldiers, she couldn't be sure which of the women ahead were her mother and sisters. How odd; Mama was seeing all four daughters dressed as brides at the same time. Odder still, four daughters were seeing their mother dressed as a bride.

The chapel overflowed with sisters of all ages and the postulants' families and friends. Out of the corner of her eye, Gladys saw an iridescent pheasant feather she knew adorned Jerry McRae's favorite rust fedora.

After the gospel, Sister Abraham nodded at her class. In perfect harmony, they rose from the front pew. Bishop Sloan stepped forward and asked the group as a whole, "Do you manifest a true vocation and a sincere desire to be received into the Incarnate Word and Blessed Sacrament order?"

"We do," the candidates replied.

"Granted," the bishop said.

The women followed their guides to a room, where each knelt and removed her headpiece. At rehearsal, Gladys thought she wouldn't mind having her hair cropped, but now, when the snipping began, it seemed as if she could actually hear the auburn tresses hit the floor. She wanted to reach up and feel the stubble before Sister Paul covered it with a net coif, but she dared not move. Tonight in the privacy of her room she would run her hands over her shorn head, like a blind person touching someone's face to get to know its features.

Enough about hair, she scolded herself. The cutting symbolizes a willingness to renounce the vanities of the world. Hair has no importance.

The guides dressed the candidates in their habits. Identical to a professed nun's with the exception of a white veil instead of black, the uniform consisted of a long white robe with cuffed sleeves, a crimson scapular embossed with a blue crown of thorns and the IWBS logo, a red leather cincture with a black rosary attached, a starched guimpe around the neck and shoulders, the coif, and a stiff white bandeau across the forehead.

Feeling faint, Gladys worried that she might pass out from the heat and from the weight of the new garments. To take her mind off the possibility, she stole a glimpse of her mother and sisters. They looked grander, and happier, than she'd ever seen them.

Sister Abraham led her class back to chapel, where Bishop Sloan awaited them in the open doorway of the Communion rail. While the nine new sisters prostrated themselves at his feet, he prayed over them for what seemed to Gladys to be fifteen minutes. "Rise," he finally said, and she got up as gracefully as her cumbersome garments allowed.

He took a lighted white candle from a wrought iron stand and handed it to the first sister. "You shall no longer be known as Ruth Marks, but as Sister Mary Agnes Marks, your new name in religion."

He moved sideways. "You shall no longer be known as Willeen Grey, but as Sister Mary Thomasine Grey, your new name in religion.

"You shall no longer be known as Claire Stone, but as Sister Mary Francis Stone, your new name in religion.

"You shall no longer be known as Doris Mills, but as Sister Mary Thomas Mills, your new name in religion.

"You shall no longer be known as Mary Jones, but as Sister Mary Pius Jones, your new name in religion.

"You shall no longer be known as Hazel Jones, but as Sister Mary Jude Jones, your new name in religion.

"You shall no longer be known as Gladys Jones, but as Sister Mary Genevieve Jones, your new name in religion.

"You shall no longer be known as Dorothy Jones, but as Sister Mary Catherine Jones, your new name in religion.

"You shall no longer be known as Evelyn Jones, but as Sister Dorothy Jones, your new name in religion."

The bishop addressed the novices. "The significance of the name change stems from biblical times. When he gave himself to God, Abram became Abraham, Jacob became Israel, Simon became Peter, and Saul became Paul. Each of you has taken a new name as a bride of Christ. Congratulations."

Each novice placed her candle in the stand, distinguished the flame, and accepted a plain gold band from the bishop. He looked out on the congregation. "It is my extreme pleasure to give your community nine new Sisters of the Incarnate Word and Blessed Sacrament."

That evening, twirling a gold band on her ring finger, left hand, a high-spirited Sister Genevieve wrote to her aunt in Minnesota:

~~~ July 25, 1938: My dearest Aunt Alice: I am sending you this holy card in remembrance of our Clothing Day. It was beautiful and we are very happy. May God bless you. Pray for us. Your niece, Sister Mary Genevieve, IWBS (Gladys) ~~~

After the ink dried, she ran her fingers over the signature.

Sister Mary Genevieve. No classic song, no note of music, no dainty stroke of a violin bow had ever produced such an exquisite resonance as did those three words: Sister Mary Genevieve.

In the silent dormitory, a new tune, the Jones Symphony, thundered in her ears: Sister Mary Pius. Sister Mary Jude. Sister Mary Genevieve. Sister Mary Catherine. Sister Mary Dorothy.

Come All Ye Who Are Weary

And I will give thee rest ~~~

On her knees cleaning the choir loft floor, Sister Jude said, "Gladys, I need to talk about something."

"I'm Sister Genevieve."

"Sorry. I still think of you as Gladys. And since Evelyn became Sister Dorothy I can't keep her name straight in my mind."

"Leave it to Evelyn to create confusion. But listen, we shouldn't be talking. We're supposed to maintain silence, except for important matters."

"This is important. For one thing, I have trouble sleeping. I have confusing dreams all mixed up with nuns and musicians. Sometimes all of you are nuns except me. I wonder if that means I don't want to finish what I've started."

Sister Genevieve wiped perspiration from her brow with the back of her hand. "I've never believed that dreams mean anything in particular. I think we go to sleep with our minds filled with thoughts and images that carry over into sleep. We remember snippets of more than one dream and it seems like one so it doesn't make sense."

"Do you ever question if you made the right decision, coming here?"

"I can't say I do. I've never been happier. I love studying church doctrine, singing in choir, and the Gregorian chants. Don't you love the chants? I can't wait to start college courses. Honestly, I feel like a schoolgirl."

Sister Jude sighed. Must Sister Genevieve always be so cheerful?

"You're not thinking of leaving, are you?" Sister Genevieve asked.

"I've considered it. Sometimes I feel stir crazy, in spite of the hectic schedule, the reading and studying and chores." Sister Jude leaned on her haunches. "This will sound petty, but when I'm struggling to get all the pieces of my habit in place, I think how nice it would be to simply put on a blouse and skirt instead."

"I'm with you on that. I hope in my lifetime they make habits even somewhat simpler. Look at my sleeve dangling in the scrub bucket."

Sister Jude cast a sideways smile at her sister. "Count your blessings. At least your hair isn't falling in your eyes."

"What hair?"

"Exactly my point. I miss my hair. Isn't that silly? And here's something else that troubles me. Before we came here I never thought much about being a wife and mother. Now I wonder what I might be missing. One night I dreamed I was holding a baby."

"Like I said, I don't put stock in the meaning of dreams. Try exercise before bedtime, maybe walking up and down the stairs. You might sleep better."

"Wouldn't it be nice to walk to the neighborhood store for Blue Bell ice cream, like we used to when we returned from a road trip?"

"Gosh, that would be good. Now you've made me hungry. Anyway, have you talked to Mistress or your counselor about your doubts?"

Sister Jude lowered her head. "I'd be ashamed to. I'd feel like a failure."

"No, that's what this time is for, to ask questions, to talk about doubts."

"I feel as if my counselor is geared toward talking me into taking final vows, not with being concerned with whether or not I'm suited for this life."

"How about talking to Sister Pius? She's still your mother."

"I don't want to bother her. She's deliriously happy."

"How about Mother Joseph?"

"No. That's why we have personal guides. She has other duties."

"But we have a friendship that goes back before the convent."

"I would never impose on that relationship. You know, I've been thinking about what Father Dusseau said about the colonial response. I remember that day when we all discussed the convent. I was the last to decide. Maybe I gave in because the rest of you were doing it."

"I don't think so. When we were kids you talked about being a nun."

"Yes, well, kid talk is one thing. This is actually doing it." Sister Jude ran her fingers silently across the organ keys. "It's been a long time since I played an organ. Or cello. I wish I could play my cello. It soothes me."

"I know what you mean. When we finish our training we'll play again."

Sister Jude slid off the organ stool. "Don't tell Dorothy or Evelyn about this talk. I mean, Sister Catherine and Sister Dorothy."

"Silence is golden, dear sister. You can count on me."

That night at Vespers, Sister Jude began a novena for guidance. The following day she took her sister's advice and sought counseling.

Her crisis of faith passed and, in July, 1939, with her head, heart and black oxfords planted firmly in religious life, she stood with her sisters and mother to take her first temporary vows. Father F.O. Beck officiated at the ceremony.

From that day forward, the Rangerettes' music dimmed to a distant note for Sister Jude. The band would always be in her heart, but there was room for new songs; those dedicated to service to God.

Blowin' Down The Road

My children need three square meals a day ~~~

Tumbleweed bounced alongside the convent's Plymouth and pebbles spit at the windshield as the car jostled over a dusty country road. "Now I know what they mean by the Dust Bowl," Sister Pius said to her colleague, Sister Helga, at the wheel. "We can't even have the windows open."

Until two months ago, Sister Pius had not been off the convent grounds for a year. Now, with only six months left before taking final vows, she had an assignment teaching Catechism to children living in a migrant worker's camp. Although she found her mission rewarding, the plight of these needy people, especially the children, frustrated her. Her schoolroom, a shack with a table for her desk and produce crates for the students to sit on, represented the conditions under which the families lived, often with a dozen people in two or three rooms. Yet, the children were eager to learn, and with her fair grasp of Spanish, she enjoyed conversing with them in their native tongue while at the same time teaching them English.

Whenever Father Alveraz dropped in to check on the children and ask questions, little brown hands fluttered for attention. Sister Pius stood back and let her students demonstrate that they would soon be prepared to receive the holy sacraments.

At the end of each session, she rewarded them with a song fest. Sometimes she taught them English tunes, other times she listened while they serenaded her with Mexican folk music and danced in the dirt yard. One afternoon while watching them romp in the December sunshine, she heard a commotion in one of the nearby huts and recognized the wailing as that of a woman in labor.

"*Adios, manana,*" she called to the children. Lifting her skirt above her ankles she sprinted across the lane and stopped at the house's open door. When her eyes adjusted to the dimness inside, she saw only a young girl, no more than thirteen or fourteen.

Sprawled on a dingy sheet on a cot with one meager pillow, the girl mumbled, "My sister she go for help," before lapsing into a stupor.

Sister Pius thanked God that help was on the way. Her five children were delivered by a doctor and she realized that, at age sixty, she had never helped deliver a child nor seen one born.

Her eyes roamed the room. The windows had no screens or curtains; above the cot hung a metal crucifix with the Christ figure loose and leaning to one side.

Two double beds sagged in the corner, but how many people lived in this hovel? Were there any adults in the camp or were they all in the field, leaving children on their own? There must be someone, the girl's sister had gone for help.

"Thirsty," the child mumbled.

Sister Pius stepped into what amounted to a kitchen, where a trail of cornmeal straggled from an open bag onto a table. Nearby sat a sprung rat trap, with nothing in it. She imagined rodents lurking in the corners, waiting for a feast of grain.

She ladled water from a bucket and raised the girl's head to help her drink. Then she dribbled water on her handkerchief, wiped the girl's face and placed the folded cloth on her brow. "Where's your mother?"

"On the truck. To the field. My sister she go for Senora Paloma." The girl placed her hands on her stomach and pressed down. "It hurts, oh, it hurts."

"I know; I know, little one. Try to relax between the pains. I'm Sister Pius. What's your name?"

"Charita." She fingered the Incarnate Word medallion around Sister's neck.

"Pretty name. It means Little Charity." Quite likely, the girl did not understand the meaning of the word charity.

Charita's face distorted in pain as a contraction began. Sister released the child's grip on the medallion and held out her hand. "Squeeze as hard as you can." With her other hand, she dabbed perspiration from Charita's face, and prayed silently: Suffer the little children to come unto me. Blessed Mother, help this child bear her cross of suffering. Let no harm come to her or her baby.

A plump woman burst into the room carrying a black satchel and a paper bag holding towels. "Out of the way," she ordered Sister Pius.

Charita's sister, who didn't look much older than the girl in bed, stayed in the doorway, an anxious frown on her pretty face, a baby balanced on her hip. Sister Pius guessed the baby was a boy, but was he the girl's child or was he her brother? Noting a stain on the girl's blouse, across her full breasts, Sister felt certain it was milk. Two children, and both were mothers.

"Rosa," Charita cried. The older girl swung her baby to the floor and went to hold her sister's hand.

The brown-eyed infant peered at Sister Pius, seemingly unafraid. Picking him up, she tried to recall the last time she'd held a baby. Perhaps one of Alice's grandchildren. Memories of Robbie suddenly overwhelmed her. She was holding him...cradling him...singing a lullaby...then he cried, screamed.

No, that was Charita crying. She focused on the present.

"Push, *nina*," Senora Paloma ordered, "once more, push, there's the head."

Sister Pius wanted to give Charita privacy but she couldn't help looking at the emerging baby, this God-given but misplaced child.

"A *nina,*" Rosa announced.

After swatting the baby's wrinkled brown butt, Senora cut the cord and wiped its face and scrawny body with a wet towel. Then she swaddled the infant in another towel and placed her beside the child-mother.

Sister Pius hovered near the bed, enthralled with the miracle of a newborn. She'd forgotten how tiny they were, how perfect, how beautiful. The baby's delicate fingers fluttered and her unfocused dark eyes seemed to take in her surroundings. "May I hold her for a moment?" she asked Charita.

The sleepy girl nodded, and Sister lifted the baby. "You're beautiful," she crooned. "Charita, have you chosen a name for her?"

Charita shrugged, as if she'd never considered names. "I like Anjelica."

"Ah, yes; she's an angel."

"Anjelica Josephina."

"Very nice."

A car horn tooted, and Sister heard her name called. She laid the baby next to its child mother and kissed her on the cheek. "I'll pray for you and Anjelica, and I'll visit you next time I teach. I hope you'll come to my class. You can bring the baby."

Charita yawned, and closed her eyes.

Sister Pius trotted off to the car, while a passel of children called, "*Adios.*"

Sister Helga waved her arm at the youngsters. "Out of the way, please, out of the way." Shifting car gears, she asked, "How're they doing with their lessons?"

"Very well; very well indeed." Sister Pius leaned back in her seat, her mind on Charita and Rosa and their babies. At supper, she would try to hold back some food, tuck it into her book bag to bring for the young mothers.

Would that be stealing? Yes, her conscience said. No; not really, her other self rationalized. She would be depriving only herself of that food. Still, it was stealing.

After telling Sister Helga about what happened today, Sister Pius added, "I'll talk to Mother Joseph. There must be an agency to help these young girls and their babies. Still, there are so many needy families these days; how does one decide the order in which they will be assisted?"

Sister Helga had no answer. Two days later, Sister Pius's concern for the children was momentarily set aside when the serenity of the convent was shattered by world events.

Praise The Lord

And pass the ammunition; we're on a mighty mission ~~~

Sister Pius fingered a sign of the cross over her water glass, a simple thank you for the lunch set before her, and then broke her slice of white bread into three pieces to honor the Holy Trinity. As she reached for her soup spoon, she saw Father Cozad enter the room, his face as hard and gray as a tombstone, and a radio tucked under his arm. This was clearly not a social call.

As he spoke to Sister Abraham, she stepped backward, shaking her head as if he had said something so shocking she needed to distance herself from him. She lowered herself to a chair and covered her face with her hands.

"Sisters," Father Cozad said, "if I may have your attention. There's no easy way to say this. About a half hour ago, the Japanese bombed Pearl Harbor."

While a collective gasp rose, he found an electrical outlet, plugged in the radio and adjusted dials.

Breaking the rule of silence, a young novice whispered to Sister Pius, "It's another Orson Welles hoax. Remember when he announced that Martians had landed? I was petrified."

Yes, she remembered, but now, listening to the nervous radio announcer relay bits and pieces of news, she knew this attack was real. Between the static she picked out key words: Battleship Row explosion, about 8 a.m. Hawaii time, USS West Virginia, destroyers, cruisers, USS Arizona, sinking."

Mother Joseph had come in; now she crossed herself as she said to Sister Abraham, "One of our postulants has a brother on the Arizona. His letters come from there. I must go to her."

"Our prayers are with her, Mother Joseph. We'll go to chapel." Sister Abraham addressed the novices. "I know you would like to stay here glued to the radio, but we have work to do. We must pray as we've never prayed before. For our country, for our president, for all the young men who will be called into service, and women, perhaps, for all those whose lives may have been lost this morning." Her voice faltered on those last words.

Sister Pius flashed to a memory of a starlit night in Hawaii when she watched the Rangerettes perform for a cheering throng of youthful sailors. They, and all those monstrous ships anchored in the harbor, had seemed indestructible. What would Martin say about this horrific event? Before his death, reading newspaper accounts of what was called "the gathering storm in Europe" he'd been concerned about Hitler, Mussolini, Stalin, Hirohito. The war years ago had not been "the war to end all wars."

On her way out of the room, surrounded by her daughters, Sister Pius heard the radio announcer suggest that America's west coast might be vulnerable to attack. With her youngest brother, Eddie, living in Washington, she prayed for his and his family's safety.

The following day, while the sisters huddled around the radio, President Roosevelt announced that he had asked Congress to declare war on the empire of Japan. In a halting voice he called December 7, 1941 "a date which will live in infamy."

While the country geared up to fight, overseas and on the home front, the sisters felt the same concerns and fears of all Americans. But life remained much the same. Accustomed to a meager diet, food rationing caused no problem, nor did blackouts; the community simply retired when the practice air raid siren blared.

"Our ammunition is prayer," Sister Pius advised her daughters. "We know that's a powerful weapon. God will do the right thing for the world."

No Other Love

Can warm my heart, now that I've known the comfort of your arms ~~~

As senior member of her class, Sister Pius was first to recite her perpetual vows. This required making a total commitment to God; to follow His invitation to *go sell what thou hast, and come follow me.*

Reading from a card, she spoke with no trepidation. "At last Jesus will be mine and I will be His. What more can I desire? The whole world could not satisfy my heart, for it belongs to Him whom the angels adore and the moon and sun stand in wonder. I will espouse Christ, my beloved, King of Heaven and earth and wish to remain His bride forever. Therefore, I, Sister Mary Pius Jones, vow and promise poverty, chastity and obedience to Almighty God in the presence of the Blessed Virgin Mary, the angels and saints, the whole Heavenly court, to all my superiors and their successors according to Our Holy Rule and Constitutions, and I hope with God's grace to persevere faithfully until death. Amen."

She removed her white veil, and her spiritual guide placed a black veil in its place. Mary Loretta McLaughlin Jones was now and forever Sister Mary Pius Jones.

Her heart pounded with admiration as she listened to her daughters recite their vows and watched them exchange the white veil for black.

Hazel, Gladys, Dorothy, and Evelyn stood side by side as Sister Mary Jude Jones, Sister Mary Genevieve Jones, Sister Mary Catherine Jones, and Sister Mary Dorothy Jones.

I'll Be Seeing You

In all the old familiar places ~~~

Sister Pius relaxed in a cushioned lawn chair under an umbrella of pecan trees. Fanning her face with the *Victoria Advocate,* she watched her daughters skitter about visiting with colleagues. After taking final vows sixteen years ago, the siblings had been separated, assigned to various schools in the archdiocese. Now they were reunited for the first time, spending the summer at the motherhouse in Victoria.

Last night, the proud mother had listened to them discuss their own lives as well as catching up on news about friends. They all knew that Sister Thomasine Grey had left the religious life after twelve years. Because such matters were private, they didn't know the reason for Willeen's request to be relieved of her vows. Sister Pius reported that Willeen was now teaching music at a private school in San Antonio.

Sister Genevieve kept in touch with Jerry McRae Collins. She and her husband purchased Uncle Doc's property years ago and lived in the house with their two sons. Uncle Doc stayed on in the carriage house and died recently at eighty-seven.

Over the years, Sister Pius had come to believe that her daughters' separation from each other had prompted them to develop individual interests that complemented their common interests: God, family, and music. Sister Jude's college degree, a major in history and a double minor in business administration and sociology, allowed her to teach those subjects in high school. Sister Genevieve had majored in history and minored in political science, of all things, and taught elementary students. Both stayed involved in music. The two younger sisters had teaching degrees and rotated from school to school, wherever needed.

Sister Pius had spent time on her knees when her oldest daughter, Hazel, had, as a novitiate, struggled with uncertainty about whether or not she had a vocation. After overcoming her crisis of faith, she often assured her mother that she was happy and fulfilled as Sister Jude.

As for Gladys, the first to make the decision to enter the convent, Sister Pius could not remember a time when she worried about Sister Genevieve. She was the epitome of what nuns called a "true religious."

Dorothy, the quiet one as a child and young adult, still had that trait. Enveloped in serenity, Sister Catherine had an almost angelic demeanor.

Spunky Evelyn; well, she might not always act devout, but Sister Dorothy was as dedicated to the religious life as were her older sisters. She was still a character, though. There she went now, her skirt hiked to her knees as she darted across the lawn to catch a sheet of newspaper that had floated away from an elderly nun.

When Sister Dorothy returned to her sisters, the quartet huddled together talking, absently swaying toward each other as they might have on the bandstand years ago. Sister Pius noted that her middle-aged daughters were not the slim-waisted lasses they'd been as Rangerettes, but they still moved with the agility and inhibition of musicians. Her seventy-seven-year old hulk creaked and ached and badly needed a tune-up. Still, despite the infirmities of old age, she could not imagine how life could have been better. She'd been blessed with everything she ever wanted: a dependable family, education, marriage to a good man, a vicarious fling in show business through her daughters, and the honor of serving God in the sisterhood. To the best of her ability she had been a good daughter, sibling, wife, mother, teacher, and sister.

My cup runneth over, she thought as Sister Genevieve approached. "Sister Pius," she said, "some of the nuns have asked us to go inside and give a concert. Will you play with us?"

The elderly nun flexed her arthritic fingers as best she could. "Sister Genevieve, I thought you'd never ask. Help me up, please."

I've Heard That Song Before

Please have them play it again, and I'll remember just when ~~~

Sister Catherine greeted the reporter from *Mary Immaculate, the Oblate Monthly* at the front door of the motherhouse. Although the Jones women had long ago removed themselves from the limelight, eager journalists periodically resurrected their story for new audiences. The sisters did not seek publicity; nor did they shun it; they granted interviews and enjoyed reviving memories of their show business career.

"I see this as a 'keeping up with the Joneses' story," Jane Meskill said to the five nuns in the parlor. "Some background on your early days, and then, by comparison, what your life is like now."

At the end of a spirited and free-wheeling hour of reminiscing from five nuns, Meskill said, "That was the easiest interview I've ever done. I'm not sure I even asked any of my prepared questions. But now I will. Are you at peace with your decision to enter the convent?"

Sister Pius said, "I could speak to that, but I've heard Sister Catherine answer the question in a way that sums it up nicely. Sister Catherine, you have the last word."

"Thank you, Sister Pius." Sister Catherine turned to her guest. "I always say that after traveling throughout the United States, we came to our religious home only a hundred miles from our earlier home in San Antonio. Had I known the advantages and joys of religious life, I would've entered the convent sooner than I did."

In closing the article, Jane Meskill wrote, "The five Jones Sisters have given everything they have to serve the King of Kings and His Immaculate Mother, and the peace they have found in that service can be seen on their faces and in the calmness of their ways."

Reading her quote in the paper reminded Sister Catherine of an old tune: *You'll find your happiness lies, right under your eyes, back in your own backyard.*

It's most certainly been true in my case, she thought.

You've Got To Be Carefully Taught

To be afraid, of people whose skin is a different shade ~~~

Sister Jude raised her classroom windows at San Antonio's Blessed Sacrament High School. The dry November breeze drifting in did nothing to alleviate the stuffiness, nor did the electric fan that whirled manufactured air in only one direction.

Seated at her desk, she raised the skirt of her habit to her knees, but that, too, offered little relief. Rumor had it that habits were going to be modernized, but such changes developed slowly and she didn't expect to wear the more comfortable garb for several years.

Fanning her face with a sheaf of papers, she went to the door to greet her eleven o'clock class of girls. A few boys had taken her Commercial Course, but most of them considered it for girls, especially those who were not college bound and would work as secretaries.

"G'morning, Sister Jude," the teenagers chorused.

"Good morning, Gwen. Good morning, Joyce. I like your necklace."

"Thank you, Sister Jude."

It amused her how the girls used accessories to individualize their uniforms, be it a large piece of jewelry, a bright scarf, beads dangling from a ponytail, or a white blouse with a pointed collar instead of a Peter Pan. Having once been fashion conscious, she sympathized when they complained about uniforms, explaining that she had dressed in conformity most of her life, from school uniforms to cowgirl costume to nun's habit. She once brought a grainy black and white photo of the Rangerettes to prove her story.

A student pointed to one of the musicians. "I'll guess this is you."

Sister Jude shook her head and tapped her image with a pencil.

"Gosh, you were pretty," the girl said. Covering her obvious embarrassment, she added, "you still are."

"Sister Jude thanks you, and so does my alter ego, Hazel Jones."

"Your name was Hazel?"

She didn't confuse things by saying it was actually Hazelbon.

"Why did you give up the band and become a nun?"

"Let's say it's a greater calling." She ran her finger across the photo. "These three are my sisters. They entered the convent at the same time I did, as well as this girl, Willeen, and my widowed mother."

"Your mother? I didn't know mothers could be nuns."

"In some cases they can. Sister Pius taught here for many years and is retired."

"I can't imagine my mother as a nun. No way."

Knowing the girl's mother, Sister Jude couldn't imagine it either.

On this Friday morning, she dictated a letter and the girls scribbled shorthand characters on steno pads. After they transcribed and typed their letters, she had them cut a stencil, and showed them how to attach it to the mimeograph cylinder, and how to ink the machine.

She paused when Sister Ingrid tapped on the open door and motioned with her eyes for Sister Jude to come into the hall. After a brief conversation with the principal, she returned to her students.

She froze for a moment, remembering the day Father Cozad announced the bombing of Pearl Harbor. Then her body temperature rose; she thawed, and trembled. "Girls, please be seated." Hearing a tremor in her voice, she offered a silent prayer to stay calm.

"President Kennedy has been shot in Dallas." She breathed deeply, a technique she had used years ago to overcome stage fright.

The students reacted as she expected; they stared open-mouthed, screamed, or wailed. Questions flew too fast for her to catch them all. "Who shot him? Was it the Communists? Is there going to be a war? Is he dead?"

She clapped her hands to quell the commotion. "We don't know who did it. The president is alive, but it's a serious injury to the head. Governor Connally is also wounded. They've been taken to a hospital."

"What about Jackie?" a student asked.

Sister tried without success to rein in her impatience with this girl who often seemed to have no respect for elders or position. "Lois, Mrs. Kennedy is not a personal friend of yours. Please call her Mrs. Kennedy or the first lady. To answer your question, Sister Ingrid said nothing about Mrs. Kennedy so let's assume she's all right. Come everyone, we'll go to chapel and pray."

"But it's almost lunch time," Lois argued.

"Until the noon bell rings, we'll be in chapel."

"Will school close early?"

"You'll be informed if that's the case."

From somewhere in the chaos of the halls, Sister Jude heard a boy's voice. "My dad will be glad if the president dies. He hates Democrats, especially the Kennedys. He hates rich people, too."

She couldn't be sure who spoke the words, but as the day passed she heard similar remarks on the radio in Sister Ingrid's office. The opinions on who shot the president ran the gamut. It was an ignorant southerner, a Republican, a Catholic hater, Fidel Castro, a Communist conspiracy, a right wing conspiracy. Someone suggested that Vice-President Johnson might have instigated the murder.

Prior to the trip, Sister had read that advisors warned the president he should skip the Dallas appearance because he was unpopular there. But had anyone imagined it would come to this?

Secluded in her classroom after the students were sent home, she struggled to understand why people made these dreadful accusations. Where had they learned such deep hatred? A song about bigotry, from *South Pacific*, played in her mind: *It's got to be drummed in your dear little ear, to hate all the people your relatives hate, it's got to be carefully taught.*

She had witnessed racial segregation and other discrimination on the road, including bias against women musicians and women in general. She'd read that, even today, women in South Carolina, Alabama, and Mississippi were excluded from jury duty. She'd read the compelling new novel, *To Kill A Mockingbird*, in which a Depression era black man is unjustly convicted of raping a young white woman in a small town in Alabama. And somewhere along the road one night, the Rangerettes had seen white robed men on horseback, burning crosses in a field.

Sister knew that today in Texas, Mexicans were segregated as effectively as were Negroes, but her travels had taught her that prejudice did not confine itself to the South. She'd seen it rear its ugly head in Iowa years ago when the owner of a café refused to allow a black family inside. The cook protested, saying she'd quit and leave him with a room full of diners. He relented and told her she could feed them at the back door. "Throw their plates in the garbage when they finish," he'd said. "We won't want to use them again." The cook, on her way back to the kitchen, muttered that she would save the plates and serve her boss's supper on them.

Those had been difficult times, but thus far the current decade had been equally turbulent and unsettling. Recalling how people during the Depression were forced to live on the streets or in their cars, it appalled Sister Jude that today's rebellious young people chose to live that way. She'd read about the civil rights march on Washington earlier this year, about walk-outs and sit-ins across the country, church bombings that killed children, firemen blasting demonstrators with water hoses, knocking some unconscious and bloodying others. Dr. Martin Luther King, Jr. had been in solitary confinement in a Birmingham jail without a mattress for his cot. *Life* magazine had recently published an article about the United State's military involvement in Vietnam. Now President Kennedy had died at the hands of a sniper. Could things get any worse?

She had seen the candidate on the campaign trail and had fallen for his good looks and what folks called "charisma." She admired his intelligence and wit when he debated Richard Nixon. When he became the first Irish Catholic president, she recalled stories her mother told about her immigrant grandparents. "It validates their struggles," she said to Sister Pius. "One of their own is in the White House."

She supported the president's stand on civil rights and medical care for the aged, and openly displayed her pride when space exploration became a reality under his administration. She cheered young Americans who envisioned an ideal world and heeded President Kennedy's call, "Ask not what your country can do for you, ask what you can do for your country." Willeen Grey, who left the convent, joined the Peace Corps. Last year, Willeen died from untreated malaria while posted in South Africa. Deeply saddened, Sister found comfort in her memories of Willeen and in knowing she aided suffering human beings during her service abroad.

Sister Jude held no illusions that Mr. Kennedy was perfect as president or in his personal life. Rumors about his infidelity with a movie star and other women dismayed her. During his first months in office he recklessly brought the country to the brink of nuclear war, but then successfully forced the Soviet Union to dismantle its missile bases in Cuba.

Burdened with sorrow over what seemed like a country gone mad, she recalled her sadness earlier this year when Pope John died. But it hadn't been overwhelming like today's grief. The religious community's Masses for their beloved leader had been celebratory, not mournful.

What of the young man who allegedly shot the president? The radio reported that Lee Harvey Oswald, from New Orleans, had defected to Russia and later moved to Texas. He had a Russian wife and a baby. Sister offered a prayer for the accused and his family. If he had done this traitorous deed, and he repented, God would forgive him. And she must, too. But would others?

She prepared herself to go back to the convent. Together, the community of sisters would hover near their one television set, viewing and reliving every moment of the tragedy until President Kennedy was laid to rest.

He would rest, but what about the millions of Americans, the billions of people around the world, feuding over a host of differences? Would they ever rest? Would there ever be peace on earth? Discord within the Church had forced the papacy to examine what many faithful Catholics called outdated ideas about birth control and abortion. There were so many arguments and changes that Sister Jude's head sometimes ached from trying to keep up with current doctrine.

She closed her classroom door and stepped into the deserted corridor. The smell of wax and sawdust, a blend used to dust the wooden floors, accompanied her to the front door, where she found the janitor slumped in a corner next to his buckets, brushes and brooms.

He rose in her presence, his fleshy black cheeks stained with dried saline and his raisin brown eyes gone liquid. Swiping away dampness with his sleeve, he murmured, "Terrible day, Sistuh Jude. Terrible."

"Yes, Mr. Williams. We can only pray that things will be right again." Recognizing a lack of conviction in her voice, she invoked strength from Saint Jude. Placing her hand atop the janitor's; hers dainty and pale, his rough and black, she added, "Never give up hope. Someday things will be better. For your children, and their children."

"I reckon you's right. I pray you's right." He opened the door. "I lowered the flag earlier. Should I should bring it in?"

She took a moment. "No. Turn on the front lights and leave the flag in place. If anyone calls you on it, tell them I said to keep it flying."

"Yes, Sistuh Jude."

Lifting her head, she watched Old Glory flutter in the breeze. Although the day had held its heat, a chill spread through her body. The flag always did that to her, but the patriotic chill was always followed by warmth and comfort, as if she were actually wrapped in the Stars and Stripes. This time warmth and comfort eluded her.

Sister Jude became aware of an eerie silence. There were no people outside, no moving cars, no bikes, and no children playing games. Quite likely it was the same across the country. A shooting on the streets of Dallas had brought America to a standstill.

Try To Remember

When life was so tender ~~~

"I declare, I never thought I'd see this day," Sister Pius said to her daughters.

"Here I am, eighty-two and celebrating my silver anniversary in the sister-hood."

"You're eighty-three," Sister Genevieve reminded her.

"No, I'm not. Oh, yes, you're right. Nevertheless, I was married to Martin for more than thirty years and now I've been married to the Lord for twenty-five."

Sister Jude raised her water glass. "As Pa used to say, *slainte.* And here's to another twenty-five."

"Oh, my, not for me. For you girls, yes. You'll see another twenty-five."

Monsignor F. O. Beck said the anniversary High Mass for the Silver Jubilee. As a young parish priest, he officiated at the ceremony when the five women took their temporary vows. Although the daughters were being feted, too, they wanted the focus on Sister Pius. At the reception, Sister Dorothy read a poem into which they had all put their thoughts and come up with a verse that satisfied them.

~~~ Jubilee Greetings to Our Dear Mother, Sister Pius

The air is filled with music; our hearts are filled with song, for this glad day brings memories, which to you alone belong. We offer you best wishes, congratulations and a prayer, that the joys of this day may linger, and be with you everywhere. God love you! Your loving daughters, Sisters Jude, Catherine, Dorothy, and Genevieve ~~~

The celebration brought another excuse for reporters to retell the Jones story from long ago. Prior to the occasion, under the *Victoria Advocate* headline: Mother, Four Daughters Looking Back As Sisters, journalist Pat Witte began:

~~~ Most nuns come from gentle, sheltered backgrounds and are not particularly experienced in the ways of the world. But four good Sisters, and real sisters to each other, who will celebrate their Silver Jubilee Saturday at the Incarnate Word Convent motherhouse in Victoria, were once members of an all-girl band, the Texas Rangerettes, which played the nightclub and theater circuit from Hawaii to Mexico and all over the U.S. What's more, their mother will celebrate her silver milestone as a nun at the same time as her daughters. ~~~

The Rev. Father George Elmendorf related their story in *The Word of God Catholic Weekly.* Headlined: Memories Of A Priest; From Music Hall to Cloister, he stated that he wrote the piece "in the hope that this may bring others into the convent to become teachers in our Catholic schools where there is a great need for more sisters."

Except for relatives, Sister Pius never entertained the notion that anyone in Park Rapids, Minnesota, remembered the Jones family. She was taken by surprise when her sister, Alice McCarren, sent a clipping from the *Park Rapids Enterprise* headlined: Whatever Became of the Jones Girls?

The article recapped their career from the early days in Minnesota to life on the road and to the convent. It concluded with an explanation that the information had come from a Park Rapids resident who read about the women in *National Student Musician* magazine. He brought it to the newspaper's office, asking, "Does anyone remember the Jones girls?" The editor stated that none of the current staff knew who they were, but an inquiry in the paper brought a host of responses.

Along with the clipping, Alice wrote:

~~~ Sister Pius, I'll tell you, for two days my phone didn't stop ringing after that item came out in the paper. Everyone wanted to talk about the Jones girls. I made a list of the people who called but I can't find it right now. I'll send it next time. Gilbert Dell said to say hi to Gladys. He said, holy mackerel, they all became nuns. Iris Tuttle asked to be remembered to you. Said she was your piano student. She has an illness called lupus and gets real sick from time to time. Do you remember that brother of hers who was homely as a bullfrog? Still is, come to think of it. One time Evelyn said he couldn't help being homely but he could at least stay home so she didn't have to sit next to him in band practice. That tickled me. She was just a kid.

I'll write more later. Wanted to get this clipping off to you. Love to the girls from all of us here. Your little sister Alice ~~~

Swing Low, Sweet Chariot

Comin' for to carry me home ~~~

While a nurse bathed Sister Pius, Sister Catherine wandered down the hall at Huth Memorial Hospital in Yoakum. Through the windows, early morning loomed gray and dreary, in tune with her mood. Since 1954, when Sister Pius suffered a heart attack, her health had declined. She continued teaching music until 1963, when her memory and eyesight began to fail. Now, nearly a decade later, her time had come to go home to God. Sister Catherine and Sister Genevieve had been at her bedside for a week, and Sisters Dorothy and Jude would arrive today.

In the cafeteria, fortifying herself with scrambled eggs and toast and waiting for Sister Genevieve to join her, Sister Catherine watched a nurse approach. Although Sister Catherine didn't feel like talking to anyone, she offered a gracious smile when the woman said, "I hope I'm not bothering you, but I wanted to say that it's a pleasure caring for your mother. She's a wonderful woman."

"Thank you for your kindness to her. I'm Sister Catherine. Oh, and here's Sister Genevieve."

"I'm pleased to meet you both. Sister Catherine, you were my teacher. I was Grazia Cortes. I'm Grazia Paneta now."

The name rang a bell, but Sister couldn't place the student; there had been many over the years. "Please join us," she said, thinking that perhaps chatting for a bit would take her mind off her bedside vigil. "Which school did you attend, and when?"

"Halletsville, early fifties."

"Of course. It's coming to me now. You have a brother, Carlos?"

"That's right. You probably remember me as your worst music student. I had, still have, a tin ear. Never could read music, couldn't even play that simple recorder. I remember that gadget you used for drawing lines on the blackboard. It held pieces of chalk to make lines and then you drew notes and other symbols. It was as if you were teaching a foreign language."

"Music does have a language all its own."

"I remember once you brought pictures of you and your sisters and told us about your band. I was fascinated, but mostly I was glad you used time for that and we didn't have to perform that day. The worst was when we had to solo so you could put us in groups, as sopranos or whatever. You rolled your eyes when I sang the scale."

"Oh, my, was I that obvious?"

"One time we had a concert for our parents. I didn't sing the words to the songs. I just hummed."

"Well, I knew that."

"You did?"

"Your lips didn't move during the whole song."

Grazia laughed at herself. "How dumb of me."

Sister Genevieve tapped into the conversation. "Do you have children?"

"Two teenaged boys. The oldest plays in a rock band."

"Yes, rock. Well, I've seen a lot of music styles come and go."

"I think today it's not so much about the music as it is the spectacle, the lights, noise, the yelling. I tell myself at least he can read music." Grazia turned to Sister Catherine. "I remember once someone asked if you liked Elvis Presley. You thought a minute and said 'He has a unique style.'"

Sister Catherine couldn't help smiling. She remembered the boy with side-burns who asked the question.

Sister Genevieve said to her sister, "You were more tactful than I'd have been."

"Elvis seemed like a nice boy. Something happened along the way. Drugs, among other things. I feel sympathy toward him."

Sister Genevieve nodded. "Reminds me of the time a student asked if I'd seen the Beatles on the Ed Sullivan show, *The Toast of the Town*. I said I knew he featured animal acts but I didn't know he'd started having insects. I was having a bit of fun. I wasn't always up to date on current music but I'd have had to be tucked away in a backyard bomb shelter to have missed hearing about the Beatles."

"My, yes," Sister Catherine said. "My students went for those boys. Like all the fuss the bobbysoxers made over Sinatra in the forties."

"Sinatra was someone to fuss over. At least he could sing," Sister Genevieve offered. "I'm astonished at the number of young people in the music business today. When we began as a group in the twenties, oh dear, is it that long ago? Anyway, we were the exception, not the rule. Now it seems there are more youngsters than adults making records. I like to see children succeed in music, but some of them are barely out of diapers."

Sister Catherine patted her sister's hand to interrupt. This particular spiel often went on and on, and Grazia most likely needed to get back to work. But when she made no move to leave, Sister Catherine said, "If it makes you feel better, not all my students were promising musicians. My classes were about music appreciation, about enjoying music, all kinds, having fun with it."

"Fun? Well, that part escaped me."

"I'm sorry I couldn't reach you."

"Oh, I was kidding. You did reach me. I admired your dedication, your enthusiasm. You were good with music, and seemed to enjoy it. That inspired me to do well in subjects I liked. Science, and here I am, a nurse."

"A noble profession. I considered becoming a nurse."

Sister Genevieve leaned forward. "You did? I never heard a word about that."

"If you'll recall, we weren't allowed to share many words those first years in the convent. I decided music was a better route for me. I should say the easiest, since I knew my way. And there isn't much call for nurse musicians."

"Oh, dear, time for rounds," the nurse said. "I've enjoyed talking to you both. I admire your family, and all the nurses have deep respect for your mother. For her courage and faith. It's an honor to have her with us. Well, I mean, I wish she wasn't with us, but...."

Sister Catherine saved Grazia from further explanation. "Please come see us when you have time. You can meet our other sisters. They're coming today."

"I will. Bless all of you, and your mother. I'm happy I ran into you."

"I'm glad, too." Sister Catherine watched Grazia walk away, her rubber-soled white oxfords squeaking against the waxed linoleum. Sister removed her glasses and rubbed her eyes. "She lifted my spirit."

"Yes; it's fun seeing former students. But now we should get back to Sister Pius."

When they returned, Sisters Jude and Dorothy were there. Sister Jude stood beside her sleeping mother, holding her hand, while Sister Dorothy ran her fingers through Sister Pius's parchment thin hair. "It's so white, and soft, like soap foam."

"Her face has gotten round since I last saw her," Sister Jude said. "From drugs, I suppose. Still, despite the extra weight, she looks frail, fragile."

"Does she wake up and talk?" Sister Dorothy asked.

Sister Genevieve answered, "Yes, but most of what she says doesn't make sense. Yesterday she mumbled that a man put a ladder up to the window and came in."

Sister Dorothy blinked back tears. "Maybe it does mean something. That God is coming to get her. A stairway to Heaven; something like that."

Sister Catherine recognized that her sister needed to find meaning in the words. "You could be right. I'm sure it meant something to Mama." The word Mama sounded unfamiliar to her ear, but she let it go at that.

Toward evening, Sister Pius clearly spoke the word *peace*. Positioned around the bed, the four sisters crossed themselves. Sister Jude said, "Peace be with you, dear mother. We love and honor you." Each daughter kissed Sister Pius's pale brow.

A priest who had earlier administered last rites to Sister Pius entered the room. "Good evening, Father Rowe." Sister Catherine introduced her sisters. "We were about to say the rosary. Will you lead us?"

While the group recited the prayers, their eyes on Sister Pius, she moved her fingers on the brown beads twined in her gnarled hand. Her parched lips moved and her faint, halting voice led them. "Holy Mary…mother of God, pray…for us sinners, now…and at the hour…."

They paused when she did, waiting for her to continue. Several moments passed before Sister Catherine spoke. "Mama used to say if you fall asleep praying, the angels finish for you. Sister Pius is with the angels. Let's continue our rosary."

The sisters recited the line that had been left unsaid. "Now and at the hour of our death," and began another round of beads.

A band of angels, comin' after me ~~~

Reading an article in the *Victoria Advocate,* Sister Genevieve thought: This was supposed to be about Sister Pius, not about her daughters and their former career. Well, I suppose it doesn't matter; the five of us are forever entwined in a single story.

Written by Mary S. Hanley, Women's Editor, the piece was titled: Musical Nuns Recall Days on Stage.

~~~ The four sisters reminisced about their musical career and their mother's talent yesterday in the parlor at the Incarnate Word motherhouse on Water Street, where they had gathered to make preparations for their mother's funeral. They recalled that their father was not musically inclined but enjoyed hearing their mother play for him every night after dinner.

Sister Genevieve recalled their mother's reaction when her daughters adopted the new, more modern garb for nuns. "Sister Pius liked it. She was progressive and had always been aware of fashion. She was a talented seamstress as well as a musician and artist. Even she, finally, wore a more comfortable collar and headpiece."

"Mother was elegant in her manner," Sister Catherine said. "She endeared herself to the nurses during her recent confinement before her death."

Also present for services will be Sister Joseph Gosse, Superior at Blessed Sacrament in San Antonio when the Jones family entered the congregation. Sister

Dorothy recalled Sister Joseph saying at the time, "I had prayed to get two or three new sisters but I was overwhelmed when I got the five wise men!" ~~~

Sister Genevieve recalled the photo of the five of them in their first full habits, their faces pinched between the white starched guimpe. They had looked like the robed Magi often depicted on Christmas cards.

That night in the receiving line at the wake, she noted that Sister Jude, now the matriarch, wore the mantle with grace and dignity. Sister Dorothy's demeanor was one of resignation, the mischief faded from her eyes, the animation gone from her body. Sister Catherine's composure and stability impressed Sister Genevieve. She told herself they should all be at peace, knowing the beauty and happiness that now surrounded Sister Pius. But this was also a time for grief; they should not deny those feelings. They had lost their mother.

She gave way to emotion when an old friend entered the room and knelt at the casket before coming to the receiving line, where the five former Rangerettes embraced in a circle. "Your mother is as lovely in death as she was in life," Jerry said. "I don't need to tell you how much she meant to me."

"She loved you, too," Sister Jude said. "And dear Willeen. You were her fifth and sixth daughters."

Sister Catherine added, "After becoming a nun, Mother saw death as the beginning of life, not the end. We had her for ninety years, now it's God's turn to enjoy her wonderful company."

Sister Genevieve pulled herself together. "I know that, intellectually, but, oh, my, I'll miss her. Her guidance, her strength, her wit."

Reminiscing ceased when other visitors stepped up to speak to the sisters. Sister Genevieve slipped away after a few moments to find Jerry.

During their conversation, Jerry dug into her tooled leather tote bag and pulled out a photo. "I had to bring this."

The image of four little girls in cowgirl outfits enchanted Sister Genevieve. "These are the Jones sisters. You need two more for Rangerettes."

The proud grandmother shook her head. "There'll never be another set of Rangerettes."

"You're right. As the kids say today, we were something else."

Being with Jerry remained a bright spot for Sister Genevieve during the following somber days. Close friends were one of life's greatest blessings, second only to her sisters.

Sentimental Journey

Gonna take a sentimental journey, to renew old memories ~~~

Seven, that's the time we leave, at seven. The old tune drummed through Sister Genevieve's mind, but it was closer to six o'clock. She and her sisters were headed for the Rice Hotel in Houston to entertain at the reception for the National Assembly of the Leadership Conference of Women Religious.

This marked only their second public appearance since leaving the stage on New Year's morning, thirty-one years ago. The first had been a Christmas concert during a time when Sister Pius was hospitalized. The headline in the January 7, 1969 issue of the *Yoakum Herald-Tribune* read: The Nuns Once Played Jazz; Famous Jones Sisters Entertained at Huth Hospital.

Sister Genevieve fastened her seat belt. "Thank the Lord for air-conditioning," she said to Sister Jude. "It beats the hearse. Remember how we sweltered?" She waved her hand under her armpits. "On stage wasn't any better. Suffocating heat, the smoke choking us. How did we survive?"

Sister Jude crooned, "*Thanks for the memories,*" and they shared a laugh.

"I'm excited we're back on the road again," Sister Genevieve said.

Her comment evidently reminded Sister Dorothy of a popular song. Across the aisle, she encouraged the busload of nuns to join in a sing-along. "*On the road again, I can't wait to get on the road again ~~~*"

She segued the group into a Bob Wills tune, "*Deep within my heart lies a melody, a song of old San Antone ~~~*"

"With all due respect to the vocalist," Sister Jude said to Sister Genevieve, "no one sang that song better than Patsy Cline. For that matter, no one sang any song better than Patsy Cline. Especially melancholy tunes."

"What about Dorothy when she was pining for her G-man?"

"Not even young Dorothy; bless her heart."

For their performance at the hotel, the quartet wore calf-length black habits with white dickeys, and short veils trimmed with white. Sister Genevieve played violin; Sister Catherine, piano; Sister Jude, cello, and Sister Dorothy, flute. Their program mixed old songs and new: *Amazing Grace, Battle Hymn of the Republic, Edelweiss, It's a Grand Night for Singing, Moon River, Morning is Broken, Somewhere My Love, The Song of Rain, The Sound of Music,* and *A Time For Us.*

Sister Genevieve offered a silent thank you when dinner was announced. Performing had made her weary and famished, but at the table, everyone wanted to talk rather than eat. On the way home, when her stomach growled from emptiness, she couldn't recall what had been on her plate or how much of it she had eaten. She took the edge off her hunger with peanuts and mints saved from her nut cup.

Sister Jude held out her hand. "Don't mind if I do. Just a candy or two; peanuts make me cough. Whoa, that's enough." She popped a mint in her mouth. "You know, the performance today was fun, but the spotlight is not my cup of tea anymore. I'm not as young as I used to was, as the saying goes."

"You and me both. We're pushing seventy."

"I am. You've got a few good years yet." Sister Jude eased off her shoes. "Oh, my aching feet and legs."

"You and Sister Catherine at least got to sit. Sister Dorothy and I had to stand the whole time."

"Sitting too long is hard on leg circulation. Besides, you and Sister Dorothy could sit. No one said you had to stand."

"It's proper to stand when one plays the violin."

"Well, then that's your choice."

"If I sit, the violin seems more like a fiddle. More old country."

"An old fiddle plays a fine tune. Itzhak Perlman sits when he plays violin."

"He has leg problems from polio back in the forties. But, my, I think I'd give up my legs if I could play the way he does."

"He surely has the gift." Sister Jude yawned and closed her eyes.

Sister Genevieve yawned, too. "Today sure took me back to the old days. Only it was a much nicer place than some of the joints the Rangerettes played in. You know, we've been pals for a long time, haven't we?"

When no response came, she turned to her pal, who had already slipped into slumber. "You could go out like a light as a kid and you still can," she mumbled. And those two kids behind me, Evie and Dorothy, were always last to fall asleep out on the road. Whispering and giggling until Willeen sat up, her hair wrapped in those awful metal curlers, and yelled, "Quiet in the bunkhouse."

Sister Genevieve's mind rambled, weaving together images from the past. The next thing she knew, the bus ground to a halt. She opened her eyes and watched the forms of sleepy nuns lurch from their seats and silently fall into place in the aisle.

She nudged her sleeping sister. "We're home, Sister Jude, wake up."

The Last Roundup

I'm heading for the last roundup ~~~

Sister Dorothy slid into the front passenger seat of the convent's Ford station wagon. She and her sisters were going to the new Theatre Victoria to see and hear one of her former students perform.

Lark Pruitt began making a local name for herself at age eleven, the same age as her idol and fellow Texan, Barbara Mandrell. About the same age, too, as Evelyn Jones, now Sister Dorothy, had been when she and her sisters first performed in Minnesota. Lark, now twenty-two, had cut three albums and been given some attention on radio. The petite blonde admitted she borrowed her style from "the princess of steel," the name given Mandrell for her talent on guitar.

On the ride to the theater, Sister Dorothy evoked a memory of her first meeting with Lark. Taking roll on opening day of a new school term, Sister called, "Lucille Pruitt."

A voice from the back of the room answered, "Lucille Pruitt couldn't make it. She's my grandmother. My daddy calls me Lark. You can, too."

Sister Dorothy advocated teachers taking control from day one. Fixing her eyes on the little girl, she instructed, "The word *can* assumes I'm physically able to call you Lark. *May* means you're giving me permission."

"Huh?" the teenager asked.

"Lesson two. I'm Sister Dorothy. Please address me properly. If you didn't understand what I said, don't say, Huh? Try, Excuse me, Sister Dorothy."

"Yes, Sister Dorothy."

"And please give my regards to your grandmother. Now, where was I? Ross, Charles? Are you or your grandfather here?"

Amid a classroom filled with giggles, a boy called, "Yo! I mean, yes, Sister Dorothy. Present, Sister Dorothy."

She had the upper hand from then on.

Sister Catherine parked the car in the theater's lot and the four women bustled inside. An hour later, at intermission, Sister Dorothy asked her sisters, "Well, what do you think?"

Her expectant smile turned downward when Sister Jude reached under her veil, wiggled her finger in her ear and shook her head, as if trying to rid herself of swimmer's ear. "I couldn't hear the lyrics for the noise."

Sister Catherine said, "Maybe if Lark sang alone, but with the backup singers, I can't make out the words to anything."

Sister Genevieve poured salt on the wound. "I feel as if I've been run over by a steamroller. The flashing lights, the musicians jumping around. I'm all keyed up."

"Well," Sister Dorothy huffed, "are there any *good* reviews?"

She felt a motherly hand on her shoulder. Sister Jude said, "Your protégé plays guitar very well. Most of the young folks I see on television just move their fingers up and down on the strings. They use the guitar as a prop more than an instrument. I'm enjoying the show, really."

Sister Catherine added, "Yes, there's a wonderful energy onstage," and Sister Genevieve nodded her agreement.

Somewhat assuaged, Sister Dorothy sauntered back in and relaxed in her seat, despite the onset of a headache and numbness in her left leg. Too much sitting, and, maybe the music was a tad loud, but she was not about to admit it to her sisters.

Lark romped onstage and raised her arms to accept the applause and whistles. Wearing form-fitting white jeans tucked into white boots, a red blouse and a red western hat with the edges curled back, she let the noise roll for a minute. Then she quieted the audience and squinted into the dark. "There she is, a few rows down. Okay, folks, I'm taking a minute to pay tribute to a special guest. My former music teacher, Sister Dorothy Jones."

"My stars," Sister Dorothy whispered to Sister Genevieve, "I didn't expect this."

Lark paced the stage, tossing her mane of crinkly curls across her shoulders. "Sister Dorothy is somethin' else. She's the best. I have many fun memories of her. Okay, here's one. You don't expect nuns to do crazy things, do you? But she did. Wait, I have to back up. Before she was a nun she was a Texas Rangerette."

Several whoops interrupted Lark. "Aha," she said, "we have folks from Kilgore here. Welcome. But I'm not talking about the Kilgore Rangerettes drill team. I'm talking about an all-girl band, back in the old days. I guess about the thirties."

"On with the show, Cutie-pie," a male voice yelled.

"Hey, Bubba. This is the show. This is where I talk, and you listen."

Spunk, Sister Dorothy thought. Maybe I taught her that, too.

"On the day before Halloween a boy asked if we could wear costumes tomorrow. Some of us moaned; we were in high school, for crying out loud, but Sister Dorothy said, 'Sure, why not?' Next day, when we came to class, there she stood in her Texas Rangerette outfit. Even chaps. You know what they are…those kind of bloomers for cowboys. And boots, and a hat with a round top, like, you know, that huge guy on *Bonanza*. Hoss, is that his name?"

"Hoss Cartwright," someone yelled.

"Anyhow…." She riffed a bar or two on her guitar for effect. "Sister's outfit reeked of moth balls. Didn't quite fit either. Guess she was skinny in those days. Well, she's still thin, but I mean, well, not one kid came in costume, not even the boy who asked if he could. Remember that, Sister Dorothy?"

"I sure do." She doubted if her voice had been heard, but it didn't matter; Lark didn't wait for an answer.

"Sister Dorothy is amazing. She can play any instrument she lays her hands on. And yodel. Man, I love yodeling. Don't y'all? But I can't get the hang of it. Luckily, we have someone here who can."

Sister Dorothy shot a worried look at Sister Genevieve and whispered, "Oh, no, I'm not going up there." But Lark introduced her sister, Amy.

Amy line-danced across the stage and Lark reached for her hand. Looking into the darkness, she said, "This one's for you, Sister Dorothy. The song you used to sing with your sister Dorothy." She held up her hand. "Wait another Texas minute. I better explain. See, Sister Dorothy's real name was Evelyn but she chose Dorothy when she became a nun. Her sister, who used to be Dorothy, is Sister Catherine. I think."

"Whatever," an impatient man called. "Enough already about nuns. This ain't Sunday school class."

My sentiments, exactly, Sister Dorothy thought. Get on with it, Lark.

As if the student heard her teacher, Lark caressed the mike and sang, "*I wanna be a cowboy's sweetheart, I wanna learn to rope and to ride.*" She pretended to twirl a lasso overhead while Amy came in on the yodeling segments.

Sister Dorothy wanted to dance in the aisle, but if she did she would've missed the fun on stage. Two sisters having a great time together, like the Jones sisters and the Rangerettes.

Gonna saddle old Paint and ride, to the faraway ranch of the Boss in the sky ~~~

Less than a week later, Sister Dorothy found herself in a San Antonio hospital bed, diagnosed with heart arrhythmia and a valve problem. With Sister Genevieve in Victoria, Sisters Jude and Catherine hovered over their kid sister, plumping pillows and straightening blankets.

"It looks as if I inherited Mama's heart disease," Sister Dorothy said. "Now we have cancer and heart disease in our line. I want all of you to take care of yourselves when I'm gone, have regular checkups."

Sister Jude fussed, "Foolish talk. You aren't going anywhere. Doctors can easily treat the problems you have. Sister Pius was ninety; you're only sixty-eight."

"Sixty-seven. But who's counting? Nevertheless, don't avoid seeing a doctor like I did. They want to keep me here a few days to get my heart beating like a metronome. Tick, tick, tick." She swayed her head back and forth. "Ooh, that makes me dizzy."

Sister Catherine said, "With a few pills you'll be teaching in no time."

"Right, now you two go on back to your duties and let me rest up for when they spring me from this place."

And The Angels Sing

The prettiest song I ever heard ~~~

Sister Catherine had just bid someone goodbye at the parlor door when Lark Pruitt entered, wearing a simple black dress and a somber face. Sister Catherine said, "Lark, thank you for coming."

"Oh, yes, of course. I didn't think you'd know me."

"My sisters and I saw your show. I'm Sister Catherine, the other Dorothy."

"The other...oh, I understand. I'm so sorry for your loss. I was floored when I saw Sister Dorothy's obituary in the paper. I had no idea she was sick."

"Neither did we. The heart problems developed, and then a stroke. Her death came as a shock but we thank God she didn't suffer long. Just about four months."

"I wish I'd kept in touch."

"Don't let that burden you. I should have called you." Sister Catherine touched the musician's elbow and steered her away. "Please stop by the convent when you have a chance. After your show that night, Sister Dorothy mentioned that she wanted to give you something."

"Something for me?"

"Yes, an old guitar. She got it at about the age you were when you started playing. Our father gave it to her for Christmas, or maybe her birthday. He liked swapping things, making deals. It's more than fifty-years-old, and small, kind of a cross between a fiddle and guitar. The label reads: The Gibson."

"An antique Gibson? Awesome."

"Well, not quite antique. And it needs new strings."

"I can string a guitar blindfolded. That's cool she wanted me to have it."

Sister Catherine arched her eyebrows. "It may not be as cool as you think. I'd forgotten this, but when I took it out of storage, I saw that painted on the front of the guitar, in red nail polish, are the words, The Singing Kid. Pa had a fit when Evie did that. He said she'd ruined a perfectly nice instrument. It's true; it probably doesn't have the value it should."

"It's way valuable to me. She sometimes called me The Singing Kid. What a hoot. She was the original Singing Kid."

"Yes; and now I understand why she wanted you to have it."

"Will tomorrow be all right, to pick it up?"

"Are you coming to the funeral?"

Lark nodded. "I called some others who were in her classes."

"Wonderful. There's a luncheon at the convent after the burial. My sisters and I plan to play some music. Sister Jude on cello, Sister Genevieve on violin. I'll play piano. Sister Dorothy usually played clarinet or flute. Do you, by chance, play either of those instruments?"

"Both. Clarinet better than flute."

"Then will you fill in for Sister Dorothy?"

"Fill in? Oh, gosh, are you serious?"

"Yes. It would be sad for the Jones sisters to play as a trio."

"It would be an honor to play with you." Lark wiped her eyes with the back of her hand. "Is it okay if I go see Sister Dorothy now?"

"Of course. Say hello to my sisters before you leave."

"I will, and thank you, Sister Catherine."

After Lark viewed the body and slipped away to speak to the others, Sister Catherine knelt on the prayer bench at the casket. "Sister Dorothy," she whispered, "Lark is going to sit in for you tomorrow."

Later, she told her sisters, "When I told Sister Dorothy about Lark playing with us tomorrow, I could have sworn her mouth twitched in that impish smile of hers."

Off We Go

Into the wild blue yonder, flying high, into the sky ~~~

From the moment Sister Genevieve watched an eerie television image of a man bouncing out of Apollo 11 onto the moon's surface, and heard astronaut Neil Armstrong say, "That's one small step for a man, one giant step for mankind," she had been captivated with the space age. From more miles away than she could comprehend, she watched three astronauts leave a plaque reading: Here men from planet Earth first set foot upon the moon—July 29, 1969 a.d. We come in peace for all mankind.

It had both amused and irritated her that some of the nuns watched the television program with doubts. They said a man on the moon couldn't possibly be true, that the government wanted to fool other nations with propaganda about how advanced the United States is. Sister Pius argued with the skeptics, but Sister Genevieve didn't bother; they wouldn't change their minds.

Her longing to fly dated to childhood when Mama read aloud from a biography of the Wright brothers. One summer when a barnstormer pilot came to the county fair, Gladys begged Pa to let her fly. "Sorry, Lass," he said, "It's five bucks a ride. Don't know who he thinks has that kind of money around here." She learned the answer when a boy she knew climbed aboard the plane with his father and waved to her. After that pilot soared out of her dreams, the dashing Lucky Lindy stole her affection; then Nellie Bly and Amelia Earhart garnered her admiration, and astronauts simply awed her, especially Sally Ride, the first woman in space.

Although many people these days were blasé about space travel, Sister Genevieve strove to see every launch and landing, or at least a rerun on the evening news. The Challenger liftoff this sunny January morning particularly interested her. Aboard with the crew, teacher Christa McAuliffe planned to instruct students around the world from her unique classroom. Sister's second grade students would view the liftoff, as well as tune into Ms. McAuliffe's classes. In assembly, the children and teachers counted along with the clock on the television screen and echoed the words coming from Houston. "We have liftoff."

Trembling with excitement, Sister Genevieve thought of a friend in Florida who witnessed a launching and said the earth rumbled beneath her feet. Sister could almost feel that sensation now, thousands of miles from the eastern seaboard.

In little more than a minute, her exhilaration turned to disbelief when the craft disappeared, leaving a trail of fire and sparks and smoke not unlike a Fourth of July fireworks finale. In the classroom, and on screen, wide-eyed spectators screamed, cried, or stared slack-jawed. Cameras zoomed in on the astronauts' families, even children, and on Christa McAuliffe's parents. Sister Genevieve couldn't bear looking at them. No one should have to witness loved ones blown apart and dissolved by the atmosphere, and have that agony shared with the world.

A little girl with thick black pigtails tugged on Sister's habit, wailing, "What happened? What happened?"

Attempting to keep her face and voice free of emotion, Sister Genevieve cooed, "God took them to Heaven, Chloe. Their souls are in Heaven."

"But, but, I don't want to go Heaven like that."

Kneeling beside her, Sister said, "I promise you won't go to Heaven like that. You'll be a very, very old woman when you go and it will be quiet and peaceful and you'll be happy." But her inner voice asked: How can I promise that? Violent things happen to children every day. Even in this small town there are parents who won't let their children walk alone to school.

Sister Genevieve and the other teachers escorted their students into chapel, a moving sea of navy and white uniforms. There, a guidance counselor spoke to the children in a calm voice, answering questions about what they had seen.

While the televised image replayed across Sister's mind, a scene from the past bubbled to the surface. Pa lay in bed, ill, listening to the radio. "Come quick," he called, and she and Dorothy ran from opposite directions to see what he needed. Spellbound, they listened to a hysterical radio announcer attempt to describe the horror of seeing the Hindenburg dirigible explode and its fiery skeletal carcass drift to the ground. She and Dorothy and Pa had shared that experience, and she longed to call her sisters, to hear their voices. But Sister Catherine was at her own school and Sister Jude, now retired, had gone to the theater with other nuns to see the comedy Nunsense. She, too, would be devastated; she loved the space program.

That evening at the convent, Sister Genevieve's emotions spilled over when a grim-faced President Reagan spoke to the nation. "We will always remember them as we saw them this morning as they prepared for their journey and waved goodbye and 'slipped the surly bonds of earth to touch the face of God.'"

She fell asleep with that heartbreaking line echoing in her mind, and she awoke wanting to know its origin. At the school library, the librarian pulled a volume from a cart next to her desk. "It's right here, Sister Genevieve. I was curious about it myself."

In a quiet corner, Sister read the poem written by RCAF pilot John Gillespie Magee in 1941, shortly before he was killed in action. She copied it on notebook paper and slipped it into her prayer book. During the following days, she read the poem instead of her prayers. No, she thought one morning at Mass, not instead of; this is a prayer.

~~~ Oh! I have slipped the surly bonds of Earth, And danced the skies on laughter-silvered wings; Sunward I've climbed and joined the tumbling mirth of sun-split clouds, and done a hundred things you have not dreamed of, wheeled and soared and swung, high in the sunlit silence. Hov'ring there, I've chased the shouting wind along, and flung my eager craft through footless falls of air....up, up the long delirious, burning blue, I've topped the wind-swept heights with easy grace, where never lark nor e'er eagle flew. And, while with silent lifting mind I've trod, the high, untrespassed sanctity of space, Put out my hand and touched the face of God.~~~

Outside in the amber sunshine, she lifted her face and watched gauzy clouds entangle themselves in the branches of towering live oaks. With the words to the poem still in mind she wondered: When will I soar? When will I touch the face of God? I'm prepared. I'm seventy-eight and about to retire.

Then, skimming along the sidewalk, she thought: Meanwhile, I have a job to do. The children are waiting.

On Eagle's Wings

And He will raise you up, on eagle's wings, Bear you on the breath of dawn,
Make you to shine like the sun, and hold you in the palm of His hand ~~~

Sister Genevieve tucked a knit blanket around her sister's form and stood back to watch her sleep. Sister Catherine's pallor marked the years of congestive heart failure that had culminated with her being hospitalized for double pneumonia.

"Pretty one," Sister Genevieve murmured.

"She is pretty," Sister Jude said, "and a wonderful person."

"Oh, my, yes." Sister Genevieve sat down close to Sister Jude so their talk wouldn't disturb Sister Catherine. "But when I said pretty I was thinking about how Sister Dorothy always called her the pretty one."

"What was that all about anyway? If I ever knew, I've forgotten."

"As I recall, Evie was upset about some boys at school calling her spunky."

"She surely was that. I miss the little rascal."

"Me, too; every day. It doesn't seem possible it's two years she's been gone."

"Remember the time she called from the bedroom, 'Oh, Gladdie, I'm so sorry; I spilled indelible ink on your new white blouse.' We tore in there; you started to cry, and we finally realized it was a fake ink blot and an empty bottle. You chased Evie out to the barn and grabbed her by the shoulders and shook her."

While Sister Genevieve smiled at the memory, Sister Jude asked, "But you were telling me about Evie being upset because someone called her spunky. What does that have to do with Dorothy being pretty?"

"Oh, you didn't let me finish. One boy said he couldn't keep us Jones girls straight; that we all looked alike. The other boy said no we didn't, and explained that you were, I believe, the cute one with dark red hair. I was sweet, or had a sweet smile or some such thing, and Dorothy was the pretty one. Evie didn't think it was a compliment being called spunky. She was just a kid, maybe twelve. Anyhow, she began taunting Dorothy about being the pretty one but I don't think Dorothy ever understood how it all got started. It used to rile her, though."

"Those two used to go at tooth and nail. The next minute they'd be giggling and singing; the best of friends."

A small sound from Sister Catherine brought the two sisters to her bedside.

"Can we do something?" Sister Jude asked. "Would you like water?"

The patient wheezed, "I saw angels."

"Oh; that's wonderful," Sister Genevieve said.

"Singing…Mama. Sister Pius and Sister…."

"Sister Dorothy," the eldest nun prodded.

"They were singing."

"I can hear them now," Sister Genevieve said.

"Said…it's all right for me…to leave you. Come home…to the Lord."

Sister Jude kissed her sister's forehead. "Yes, dear one, if you're ready; go in peace. We'll miss you but we rejoice that the Savior awaits you."

"Greet our loved ones for us," Sister Genevieve added. "We love all of you."

"Love you…."

Those were Sister Catherine's last words, spoken while her sisters held her hands and prayed.

Three days later at the gravesite, with everyone else gone to their cars, the two nuns leaned together with their shoulders touching, each with an arm around the other. Sister Genevieve tugged a pink carnation from a cascade on the mahogany casket and offered it to Sister Jude, then plucked another blossom for herself.

"You know," she said, "I always thought of us as a pair, because we're the oldest, and the younger two as a pair. But I was closer in age to Sister Catherine than I am to you."

"We're a pair now," Sister Jude said. As they approached the car waiting to take them back to the convent, she added, "Thanks for holding me up during the burial service. I felt wobbly; thought the wind would carry me away."

Sister Genevieve paused, and patted her sister's hand. "I thought you were holding me up. Well, I expect we'll each need an anchor now and then. There's just the two of us."

Sunrise, Sunset

One season following another, laden with laughter and tears ~~~

"We're twins," Sister Genevieve said, "very old twins."

She and Sister Jude each wore a calf-length white dress topped with a burgundy scapular, and a short, dark blue veil with a band of white linen across the hairline. Today they were celebrating their Golden Jubilee, along with ten other women celebrating twenty-five, fifty, sixty, or seventy years as Incarnate Sisters. The Mass had been said by Bishop Charles Grahmann, once Sister Genevieve's third grade pupil. Now it was time for the reception and lunch.

Sister Genevieve lifted a white carnation tied with gold ribbon from a florist's box and approached her sister. Sister Jude tilted her head to the side and raised her chin. "I don't trust you with that hat pin. Your fingers aren't as fine-tuned as they once were."

"I'm steady as she goes, thank you." Squinting, Sister Genevieve poked the pin into fabric and through the corsage stem. "Sorry I can't say the same about my eyes. I need new glasses. Okay, hold still, got it."

Sister Jude peered into the mirror and adjusted her wide framed, round glasses. From behind, Sister Genevieve studied her own image. "My face looks as if it's been seamed together by Evelyn. She couldn't sew a straight line to save her life."

"Oh, you have barely a wrinkle, thanks to clean living for fifty years."

"Imagine that. Fifty years here. And they said it wouldn't last." She pulled her corsage from a box. "Would you please pin this on me?"

"Sorry, my arthritic fingers are stiff this morning."

"Ah, so it's your fingers that aren't fine tuned anymore. Well, like I said, we're very old twins. Doddering old sisters."

"Speak for yourself. I do not dodder. Whatever than means."

They locked arms and shuffled down the hall. "Listen," Sister Jude said. "It's that new string quartet."

Sister Genevieve paused, halting them both. "What's the song they're playing?"

"I have no idea. They're young novices."

"So were we once. As musicians and as nuns."

"I just hope they don't play that, what do you call it? Rap?"

"Oh, my, say a prayer we're spared that *raimeais*."

"The what?" Sister Jude asked.

"*Raimeais,* as Mama used to say. Rubbish. Don't you remember?"

"Can't say I do." Sister Jude lingered at the door. "I wish Sister Catherine had lived another year for this. She almost made it."

"She and Sister Dorothy died way too young. They should be here instead of us old-timers. But they're having a grand jubilee up there, without us. Sister Pius, too. Come on, old-timer; let's go in and celebrate."

After You've Gone

And left my crying, you'll feel blue, you'll feel sad,
you'll miss the dearest pal you ever had ~~~

For Sister Jude's funeral, Sister Genevieve wore a navy vest and a long-sleeved, white, street-length habit, with a short navy veil trimmed in white. She chose the same style habit for Sister Jude's burial garments. While Sister Genevieve rarely thought of her older sister as Hazel, she recalled that the young woman had been stylish and liked hats, so Sister Jude would meet her maker in style, complete with a veil, although some nuns no longer wore them.

At the service, Sister Genevieve and her good friend Sister Marian Oleksik presented the communion gifts. Sister Marcella Srubar escorted Sister Genevieve out of the chapel, and under a tent at the gravesite, she sat next to General Superior Sister Stephana Marbach.

That night in her room, watching lightning lace the sky, Sister Genevieve realized she had barely been alone since Sister Jude was diagnosed with colon cancer and, mercifully, died quickly. Like their mother, she had lived to age ninety, and had, during her last days, said that life as a bride of Christ had been one of contentment and satisfaction. The two eldest Jones siblings had enjoyed nine years side by side since their Golden Jubilee.

Despite constant attention from her friends, Sister Genevieve felt profoundly sad and distraught. Why had God called her sisters home and left her behind? Even Jerry McRae was gone. Following a kidney transplant, she lapsed into a coma and died a few days later.

Sister Genevieve allowed her friends to dote on her because it seemed to make them feel useful. Sister Marian encouraged her to participate in activities: quilting, boxing CARE packages, decorating for convent parties, tutoring students, and taking Communion to shut-ins and prisoners.

"How times have changed," Sister Genevieve said as Sister Marian drove them to a nursing home. "Imagine, sisters distributing the Holy Sacrament."

"Amazing, isn't it? We've come a long way in our careers."

One day General Superior Sister Stephana called on Sister Genevieve for a special job. "Sister Kathleen McDonagh is coming from Corpus Christi to give a talk. She recently fell and broke both wrists, so I'd like you to look after her. She's been here before and said you were especially warm and thoughtful."

Sister Genevieve knew it would take all her energy to be cheerful, but mindful of her vow of obedience she accepted the assignment, whose purpose, she knew, was to focus on someone other than herself. It did that and more; she came away from the weekend with renewed energy and spirituality. Sister Kathleen's seminar reawakened and reaffirmed her devotion to the order and its foundress, Jeanne Chezard de Matel. Sister Kathleen had updated the Victoria community on her recent travels to Rome and France, where she'd done research toward the Canonization of Mother Jeanne. Sister Kathleen was also translating Mother Jeanne's 17th century writings from French to English and Spanish.

"It's a worthy endeavor," Sister Genevieve complimented her guest as they parted. "It would be wonderful if our foundress became a saint."

"It would, indeed. Many thanks for your hospitality. I hope to see you again."

Sister Genevieve waved goodbye and then headed for breakfast, where she greeted everyone with an enthusiastic good morning.

"You're looking bright-eyed and bushy tailed," Sister Marian replied. She removed a pair of waffles from the microwave oven and dribbled blueberry syrup on them, while Sister Genevieve selected a bagel and a packet of cream cheese.

When both were seated, Sister Marian suggested, "Come with me to computer class this morning."

"Computer? Oh, thanks, but I don't think so."

"It'll be fun. You can look up anything on the World Wide Web. Just type in a subject, say, giraffes, and up pops information." She snapped her fingers.

Sister Genevieve licked cream cheese from her finger. "Giraffes. Lovely animals. One should never stop learning, but I'll stick to books. I have letters to write today. I've neglected my correspondence. I must tell people about Sister Jude's death."

"You can write letters on a computer and send them by e-mail. That means electronic mail. I'm going to have my own e-mail address."

"I'll stick to my quill pen and scrolled papyrus."

"Very funny. Okay; I'll see you at lunch. Maybe I can talk you into sitting in on the next lesson. A computer's mind is a terrible thing to waste."

Sister Genevieve laughed. "Now who's being funny? Have a good time."

In the solitude of her room, she reclined on her bed against two plump pillows. With Sister Kathleen's seminar fresh in her mind, she wanted to reread a magazine published by the convent commemorating the 400th anniversary of Mother Jeanne's birthday.

The photos delighted her, showing sisters from earlier eras wearing the traditional habit, then the various modernized dresses, and finally today's young women whose clothing would not identify them as nuns. She preferred those who wore at least a veil with their suits and dresses. Why not be recognized as a nun if that's what you are?

Pictures of Incarnate Word sisters in Kenya brought memories of early teaching days, when she urged children to donate pennies and nickels to the missionaries in the Belgian Congo. One youngster handed her a dime and said, "The tooth fairy left this but I'm giving it to the pagan babies." She could still see his dear face and that gaping hole in his gums. Big brown eyes, dark hair, what was his name? Nice family. Emilio, that's it. Little Emilio.

Included in the magazine were comments from former students: housewives and mothers, a former mayor of Victoria, a poet laureate of Texas, an English professor/poet laureate/playwright, the editor of a Catholic magazine, and a doctor who thanked her first mentors for the training, the rigor, and the discipline that helped her take a place in society. Numerous former students had returned to the diocese as lay teachers; others had entered the religious life as priests, bishops, brothers, and sisters.

She remembered colleagues who had gone the extra mile to help children with special needs; those who didn't fit into the mold of public school but thrived under Blessed Sacrament's nontraditional approach. Sister Catherine had taught some of these children, and Sister Pius's special cause had been migrant children.

In Sister M. Emiliana Grafe's article, The Mystery Of Vowed Religious Life, she wrote: "For many people the life of a Religious, as vowed persons are often called, is a bewildering mystery. Members of the Catholic faith may have learned to respect this calling, but perhaps have very little understanding of it. To others, it makes no sense at all, or even worse, they have serious misunderstandings of it."

She added, "Religious are on the same journey of faith with the rest of us; they have just taken a less traveled path. Theirs is a different approach, but one they feel is best suited to them and one to which God has called them."

Well said and simply put, Sister Genevieve thought. She'd always found it difficult explaining to others why she joined the convent. She removed her glasses and rubbed her eyes, then closed them for a minute, thinking of those early days.

When she awoke her digital clock showed she had slept through lunch. Well, she wasn't hungry and Sister Marian hadn't stopped by. Or had she? Maybe there had been a knock at the door and she'd slept through it.

She resumed her reading. An article about the days when the order kept a small farm where they raised vegetables and kept chickens and cows reminded her that her mother had always enjoyed going to the farm. One anecdote told about a nun who couldn't find the guimpe she had hung on the clothesline. Then a cow wandered by and regurgitated the collar, as if to say, "Too much starch."

Another sister, remembered by others as the first to drive a car, was described as speeding down the street with her veil flying out the window. Students who rode with her said their prayers before entering the car. Police often looked the other way when they saw Sister coming. But one time she hit the sheriff's horse and had to appear in court. This story evoked a memory of the silly television show, *The Flying Nun,* and that led to Sister Dorothy and her silly antics. She had always been able to make folks laugh. That was a special gift. Sometimes these days it was difficult finding something to laugh about.

Reading about two nuns with the same name who took their vows together, died the same day and were buried side by side, she thought: Not even the Jones family went that far with togetherness.

One story took her back to World War One. As a child she'd been unaware that the German language was banned from schools, but the teacher in this piece wrote about government agents coming to school to remove German text books. That sparked a memory of Pa explaining that Germans in America were not responsible for the war. Her mind drifted to that dreadful flu and her aunt's and uncle's deaths; then to Uncle Clem's disappearance. According to Clem's daughter, they never learned what happened to him.

Sister Genevieve read an article called: Vocations; Where Do They Come From? Sister M. Andrea Hubnik wrote that it has become a fairly common occurrence to have blood sisters join the convent, or cousins, or aunts and nieces, and that at the present time in the Victoria community there were blood sisters from nine families. She added, "Perhaps one of the most unique familial combinations in this community is that of a mother and four daughters. Though from this relationship, only one daughter survives, the richness of the experience remains one of tremendous love and dedication."

It took a second for her to recognize herself. "My goodness, that's me," she said aloud. "I suppose it is a unique story. And there's only me left to tell it."

She scooted off the bed. Who was that cousin who wrote to Sister Dorothy asking for information about the Jones family? The letter might be among Sister Jude's things. I'll write to the cousin and tell her about Sister Jude's death. See if I can offer any other information.

She found a pencil and notebook and sat at her desk. A cache of memories surfaced, her mind working faster than her hand as she jotted notes. Was it Hazel or Evelyn who put on a blonde wig and stuffed a pillow in her blouse and did a Mae West impersonation onstage? Had to be Evelyn; Hazel was not given to such tomfoolery. Although she always loved a good joke. Or a corny joke.

While Sister Genevieve reminisced and worked she hummed an old tune from *The Pirates of Penzance.*

I have a song to sing, O, I have a song to sing ~~~

CODA

Getting to know you, getting to know all about you ~~~

My correspondence with Sister Genevieve began with her letter telling me about Sister Jude's death. Over the years, the letters and pictures chronicled for me her family's early story, as well as her life in the convent. Here are excerpts from some of the letters.

~~~ August 15th, 1995: Dear Madonna: Good to meet you. I have some news for you. I'll send the write-up of Sister Mary Jude, who became 90 years of age on July 30th. My mother was also 90 when she died. Sr. Jude had cancer. She was in the hospital for a week taking tests. Thanks be to God she went quickly to Heaven. They kept her medicated to avoid the pain. God's will be done. Sr. Jude loved to tell jokes and to read. I miss her but I know she's at rest now in Heaven. I must stop now and answer some letters in the name of Sr. Jude. Please excuse all the mistakes I make. I am 88 yrs. but people can't believe it. Love you, Sr. Genevieve Jones ~~~

~~~ February 20, 1996: Dear Madonna: I got telephone calls and letters praising you for the article you wrote [about us] for *Catholic Digest*. I felt so proud of you. Many thanks and prayers. In my next letter I will tell you more. At times I forget how to spell words but that's because of age and my hearing isn't good. God said, "It wouldn't be life without crosses." So I trust and know that Jesus always keeps his promise. Wishing you love, peace and joy in the Incarnate Jesus, Sr. Genevieve Jones ~~~

~~~ September 9, 1996: Dear Madonna: Just a short note to tell you that I have been very ill. All of a sudden back in August I felt sick and dizzy. So I'm in the infirmary recovering. I'm getting great care and lots of prayers. Thank God for all his help. I couldn't walk or move my body but now from all the pills I take I'm doing real good. I can use a wheelchair and get around by myself. I was so weak they even had to feed me. I hope it will never happen again. Just keep praying for me as I do for you. I miss your letters, they are interesting to read. I can say the Office now, which I love. Sr. Marian, whom I call my earthly Godmother, helps me so much. Write when you can. With love and peace and joy in the Incarnate Word, Sr. Gen Jones ~~~

~~~ April 5, 1997: Dear Madonna: I must get this letter off to you today. We have Adoration later and I need to go downstairs for it. On April 27th I'll be 89 yrs of age. Time goes by so fast. Two more years will be my Jubilee 60 yrs, if I live, that is. I used to tell my mother that I didn't want to live that long but I've changed. Mother used to say, "You will have to do whatever the Lord says." So I want to live because I'll get more graces from Jesus. God bless you and all your family. Love you, Sr. M. Genevieve Jones ~~~

~~~ August 29, 1997: Dear Madonna: I'm doing pretty good now but for awhile my hand was shaky. The weather is very hot outside but inside I wear a sweater. You can never tell about Texas weather. It's like me. Ha! Keep writing to me and I'll try to answer sooner. With love, peace and joy in the Incarnate Jesus, Sr. M. Genevieve ~~~

There came a time when Sister Marian Oleksik stepped in to help her friend cope with illness. Although the letters were written by Sister Marian, the words were Sister Genevieve's.

~~~ March 29, 1998: Dear Madonna: Thank you for your letters and for your personal interest in the Jones girls and for your story [about us] in *Reminisce*, which everyone liked so much. Please forgive me for taking so long to acknowledge all. I have not been well. My hands are shaky. I am not able to write and sometimes my thoughts are disconnected. Sr. Marian, a dear friend, is writing this for me. I am getting stronger and use my wheelchair to get around. I walk behind it, and ride in it sometimes. I will probably not be able to answer all the letters I receive but Sr. Marian helps me a lot. She is 82 and I will be 90 on April 27. God is good! Thanks again, Madonna. I do enjoy hearing from you. You are in my prayers. May the peace and joy of the Risen Christ remain in your heart today and always. Happy Easter! Love, Sister Genevieve ~~~

The next letter came directly from Sister Marian.

~~~ May 14, 1998: Dear Madonna: Thanks for all you've done for Sr. Genevieve. She is appreciative of every act of kindness. She is the same smiling nun regardless of how she feels. We celebrated her 90th birthday and she enjoyed every minute of her party. Her poor hearing is her biggest problem but she never complains. Parkinson's has slowed her down and has limited some action. There are always nurses on the job around the clock if she needs help. She is under the doctor's care and takes her medication faithfully. Keep us in your prayers. One of these days I'll send you pictures and perhaps some articles or letters she has here. I'm not sure who her closest relative is but since you have been writing magazine stories about the Jones family, I thought you might want them. Sr. Genevieve sends her love for your thoughtfulness. God bless and keep you in his care. Gratefully, Sr. Marian ~~~

~~~ Christmastime, 1998 [a letter to Sister Genevieve's friends and relatives.] Greetings: I know you must be wondering why you haven't heard from Sr. Genevieve for some time. I shall explain. Sr. Genevieve and I have been close friends for many years. She is not able to write or function as well as she did a year ago. She cannot care for herself and is confined to the Infirmary where she is able to get 24-hour care. Some days are better than others for her. She is still pretty alert and would be more so if her hearing were better. Since she is not able to write, I am using this form letter in order to reach all of you. She loves all her dear friends and relatives and delights in hearing from you. Please keep us in your prayers, as we do you. May God bless you. We wish you a Merry Christmas and a New Year filled with the peace and love of the Christ child. We send our love and prayers, Sister Marian and Sister Genevieve ~~~

~~~ February 23, 1999: Dear Madonna: I'm sorry I haven't written sooner. Days fly quickly into weeks and months. Thank you for keeping in touch. Sister Genevieve's condition has worsened. The tremors and muscular rigidity caused by Parkinson's disease have become stronger and leave Sister weaker. She eats less and sleeps more. We have a beautiful example of a "patient sufferer." Only once in a while do I hear her say, "Please help me." When I ask what I can do, she never answers. Sometimes she calls for Mama and Papa. The nurses keep her in bed part of the day and sitting up other times. Keep her and all of us in your prayers. Most of us here are elders, retired nurses and teachers. I know Sr. Genevieve appreciates your notes. God bless you in this holy season of Lent. With our love and prayers, Sr. Genevieve and Sr. Marian ~~~

I was away from home when Sister Genevieve died on March 11, 1999. A message on my answering machine from Superior General Stephana Marbach related the news. In July of that year, Sister Genevieve would have celebrated 60 years in the sisterhood.

In my mail, I found a letter and a small box from Sister Marian. The box contained pictures, Sister Jude's Saint Jude medal, the silver medal won by Gladys Jones in a 1926 high school music contest, and a simple white bud vase holding a pink silk rose. Sister Marian wrote:

~~~ Dear Madonna: Thank you for the love you've given Sr. Genevieve throughout the years. All you did meant so much to her. I didn't have much to send you from Sr. Genevieve's treasures. She practiced poverty well. She treasured the little vase and pink rose. I thought in Florida you could have a fresh rose in the vase each day to remind you of her. She was such a dear and I miss her so much. I'm sure she's smiling down upon us from Heaven. She was a lovable person. You couldn't help liking her. Everyone did. I loved her very much. We spent a lot of time together. It would be nice if you were near; we could have a chat. Keep us in your prayers. You are in ours. God bless you always, with love and prayers, Sister Marian ~~~

I also received a letter from Sister Stephana M. Marbach:

~~~ Dear Madonna: Sister Genevieve died peacefully in the early hours of the morning on March 11th. There were many of us with her at the time of death; likewise, there were sisters who kept a 24-watch for the last few days before Sister's death. Sister Genevieve and her mother and three sisters were wonderful people. They brought so much to religious life; they were a joyful catalyst to all with whom they came in contact. We already miss Sister Genevieve but we know that her reunion with her parents and sisters and one brother is a harmony of love and joy. Gratefully in the Incarnate Word, Sister M. Stephana Marbach, Superior General ~~~

Sifting through my letters, I found one from ten years earlier from Sister Perpetua Hawes, Superior General. She had replied to a request from a relative seeking information about the Jones family, and that cousin shared the note with me. Sister Perpetua wrote:

~~~ This remarkable family has been a great source of inspiration and joy not only to our religious community, but to those they taught and now associate with in our area. ~~~

It has been a pleasure telling their story.

You and the song are gone, but the melody lingers on ~~~

REPRISE

May I always laugh and sing, beneath God's clear blue sky ~~~

Like all women who traveled with bands in the 1920s-1930s, the Texas Rangerettes were pioneers, rebels if you will, who challenged chauvinistic views of women and changed social attitudes about gender. These troubadours shared a spirit of adventure, determination, and enthusiasm. Coming of age in an era when most women were housewives, the musicians instead ventured into a competitive and unpredictable arena where, against all odds, they proved they were capable of navigating the open road and handling themselves in a man's world. They paved the way for hundreds of female bands to flourish during World War Two, when men musicians were overseas.

In 1940s slang, all-girl bands were Swing Shift Maisies, substitutes for the real thing (men). They were not viewed as professionals, but as temporary, patriotic groups, entertaining at dance halls and USO clubs on the home front. After the war, the musician's union pressured bands to hire veterans, and most female orchestras disbanded. Road weary anyway, the women chose to take other jobs or to marry and raise families. Men's big bands gradually disappeared, too, as more and more people stayed home to watch television.

The Texas Rangerettes made enough of a splash to be recognized by *Billboard* and *Variety*. Then, in a career change that made history, the Jones sisters enjoyed the best of both worlds. Without forsaking music, they found a new audience among school children. Decades ahead of the time when many women returned to school, the sisters furthered their education in the 1930s, enabling them to enter the teaching profession. Admired by colleagues and respected by students, Sisters Jude, Genevieve, Catherine, and Dorothy were every bit as successful as Hazel, Gladys, Dorothy, and Evelyn Jones had been. In highly diverse roles, as swinging, singing musicians, and as teaching sisters, they inspired and endeared themselves to those who knew them.

Sister Pius (Mary McLaughlin Jones) spent her music teaching career at Blessed Sacrament Academy High School in San Antonio. She died on January 26th, 1972.

Sister Jude (Hazel) received her Bachelor of Arts degree from Our Lady of the Lake College in San Antonio with a major in history and a double minor in sociology and business administration. She received numerous certificates and awards in the business field. For 37 years she taught music, shorthand, typing and bookkeeping at Blessed Sacrament Academy High School in San Antonio. After retiring, she served as the Academy's records clerk for seven years. Retired from active ministry, she resided at Incarnate Word and Blessed Sacrament Convent in Victoria, assisting wherever she was needed as long as her health allowed. She died at age 90 on August 7th, 1995.

Sister Genevieve (Gladys) received her Bachelor of Arts degree from Our Lady of the Lake College in San Antonio, with a major in history and a minor in political science. She held a Teacher's Permanent Elementary Certificate of the First Class for grades one through seven. She taught at Blessed Sacrament Academy High School in San Antonio, at Sacred Heart School in Halletsville, Praha Public School in Praha, and Nazareth Academy and Our Lady of Victory School in Victoria. She also served as a library aide. After retiring in 1986, she resided at Incarnate Word and Blessed Sacrament Convent in Victoria, where she devoted herself to prayer, hospitality, and helping others. She died at age 90 on March 11th, 1999.

Sister Catherine (Dorothy) taught music in San Antonio, Halletsville, Shiner, and Ganado schools. Retired in 1983 after 44 years of teaching music, she resided at Incarnate Word Convent in Victoria. She died at age 78 on June 21st, 1988.

Sister Dorothy (Evelyn) received a special award from the Modern Music Masters Society in May, 1972. In addition to teaching music in various schools, she twice served as president of the San Antonio Unit of the National Catholic Music Educator Association, and was on the Liturgical Commission of the archdiocese. She died at age 67 on April 24th, 1979.

Combined, the five women gave 237 years to their ministry. Together through earthly life and eternal life, mother and daughters lie side by side in Victoria's Catholic Cemetery in an area dedicated to all religious.

In response to my inquiry about why the Jones women entered religious life at the same time, Sister Marian Oleksik said, "We cannot answer that question. We know God initiates the call, and in their case they all responded. No one who knew the Jones sisters would say they were unhappy in the life they chose. The case was, indeed, quite unusual; the Lord had His reasons for keeping them together. He loved them, I think, and did not want them separated."

We're all pals together ~~~

My information about Jerry McRae and Willeen Grey is scant, so my depiction of them is mostly fictitious. Willeen did leave the convent after twelve years, but I don't know what happened to her or to Jerry.

After my article about the Rangerettes appeared in *Reminisce* magazine, a reader found my telephone number in the directory and called me. He said his mother had known Jerry McRae, and he gave me the name and address of another woman who had played with the Rangerettes. I was puzzled, as neither her name nor picture appeared in the many articles I have, nor had Sister Genevieve ever mentioned her. I wrote to the woman, but her terse reply did not confirm or deny that she had been a Rangerette or that she even knew Jerry McRae. She said she was sorry she couldn't help me; she was busy with volunteer work for the symphony, and all her clippings and pictures were pasted in scrapbooks, making it impossible to remove them and make copies.

Using search engines on the Internet, I found that this woman played with two bands in the 1930s and 1940s, but there was nothing to indicate an association with the Rangerettes, either before or after they disbanded.

And the band played on ~~~

Whose story is this? The Jones daughters' or their mother's? Both, really, but credit must go to Patrick and Mary McLaughlin, impoverished immigrants who brought with them to America a love of God, family and music, as well as a work ethic that blossomed in their granddaughter, Mary Loretta. She passed those traits and her talent to Hazel, Gladys, Dorothy, and Evelyn, who used their musical gift to bring joy and relaxation to audiences during an era of great need.

Then, fulfilling a personal dream, they applied their expertise and spirituality to leave a legacy of music and religious education to children in the San Antonio archdiocese.

That legacy and heritage thrives within the McLaughlin family. Alice McCarren's granddaughter, Diana Robertson Craig, holds a Bachelor of Arts degree in Music Education, as does her husband, Jim Craig. Like the Jones girls, Diana and Jim started their careers by playing in junior high and high school jazz orchestras and groups. They met in college, where they were involved with performance groups. Today, they both teach music in elementary and middle schools, and their four sons play in bands.

And the music goes 'round and 'round ~~~

FAMILY ALBUM

[on group photos, names are listed left to right]

Photo 1~~~Uncle Pat Drew, Martin Jones, circa 1898
Photo 2~~~School Orchestra, Park Rapids, Minnesota, circa 1924, front: Dorothy, Evelyn, Gladys, back, third from left: Professor J.B. Tremblay
Photo 3~~~Declamation Team, Park Rapids High School, 1926, back, second from left: Gladys
Photo 4~~~Dorothy, circa 1927
Photo 5~~~Gladys, circa 1927
Photo 6~~~ Gladys, circa 1928
Photo 7~~~Evelyn, circa 1928
Photo 8~~~Jones girls playing in an unidentified all-girl band, circa 1928: Hazel, Gladys, Evelyn, Dorothy
Photo 9~~~Rangerettes: Dorothy, Gladys, Evelyn, Hazel, circa 1930
Photo 10~~~Evelyn, Dorothy, Gladys
Photo 11~~~Lurline tour, circa 1934: Gladys, Hazel, Dorothy, Willeen Grey, Mrs. J.B. Tremblay, Jerry McRae, Evelyn, Mary, in front, Professor Tremblay
Photo 12~~~Lurline tour: Hazel, Gladys, Dorothy, Evelyn, Mrs. Tremblay
Photo 13~~~Dorothy, Gladys, Mary, Evelyn, Hazel (front), circa 1937
Photo 14~~~Before entering convent, January 1938: Hazel, Gladys, Father A. C. Dusseau, Evelyn, Mary, Dorothy
Photo 15~~~Before entering convent, January 1938: back, Evelyn, Dorothy, Gladys, Hazel; front, Father J. Wayne Cozad, Mary, Father A.C. Dusseau

Photo 16~~~January 1938, postulants: Hazel, Evelyn, Gladys, Mary, Dorothy

Photo 17~~~Headlines

Photo 18~~~July 1938, novices: Sister Jude (Hazel), Sister Catherine (Dorothy), Sister Pius (Mary), Sister Genevieve (Gladys), Sister Dorothy (Evelyn)

Photo 19~~~Silver Jubilee 1964, back: Sister Genevieve, Sister Dorothy, front, Sister Catherine, Sister Pius, Sister Jude

Photo 20~~~Poem written by daughters for their mother on Silver Jubilee

Photo 21~~~Sister Dorothy, Sister Jude, Sister Catherine, Sister Genevieve, Reception for National Assembly of the Leadership Conference of Women Religious, Houston, Texas, 1974 ~~~

Photo 22~~~Sister Pius

Photo 23~~~Sister Jude

Photo 24~~~Sister Catherine

Photo 25~~~Sister Dorothy with music award

Photo 26~~~Sister Genevieve

Photo 27~~~Sister Genevieve and students, Nazareth Academy, Victoria, Texas

Photo 28~~~Sister Marian Oleksik, Sister Genevieve Jones, Golden Jubilee, 1989

Uncle Pat Drew and Martin Jones (18 years old).

3

4

5

6 7

8

9

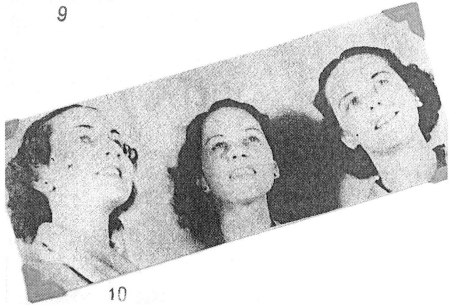

10

11

S. S. LURLINE

12

13

14

15

16

QUIT DANCE HALLS FOR CONVENT LIFE

Four "Texas Rangerettes" and Mother Take Long Planned Step

(N. C. W. C. News Service)

SAN ANTONIO.—Four blood sisters, members of an all-girl dance orchestra, and their mother have been admitted as postulants into the Incarnate Word and Blessed Sacrament Convent here. The four girls and their mother are the sole surviving members of their family, the father having died here last summer.

The young women are the Misses Gladys, Hazel, Dorothy and Evelyn Jones. Their mother is Mrs. Mary Jones. The girls were members of the "Texas Rangerettes," a dance orchestra of which Miss Jerry McRae, herself a convert to the Catholic Faith, is the leader. The only other member of the group—Miss Willeed Gray—became a postulant in the same convent a week after the Jones family was admitted. The Misses Jones and their mother were admitted with the proper recommendation from the Very Rev. A. C. Dusseau, O.M.I., who had known them in St. Mary's parish here for 12 years. The Misses Jones had long considered the step of entering the convent, the Rev. Alois J. Morkovsky states, writing in "The Southern Messenger" here. They played their last dance engagement with the "Texas Rangerettes" on New Year's Eve. The organization had toured the United States and the Hawaiian Islands.

JANUARY 28, 1965

MEMORIES OF A PRIEST
BY REV. FATHER GEO. ELSINORE, ALA.

From Music Hall To Cloister

Last Dance for the Jones Girls

They went from the stage to the convent with enthusiasm

PARK RAPIDS Enterprise

Whatever Became Of The Jones Girls?

"THE JONES SISTERS"
They all became nuns

Nuns Once Played Jazz

17

18

19

Jubilee Greetings
To Our Dear Mother, Sister Pius!

The air is filled with music,
Our hearts are filled with song.
For this glad day brings memories
Which to you alone belong.
We offer you best wishes,
Congratulations and a prayer,
That the joys of this day
    may linger
And be with you everywhere.
    God Love You!

Your loving daughters,
Sisters Jude, Catherine,
    Dorothy and Genevieve

20

Amazing Grace . . . . Early American

Battle Hymn of the Republic . . . . Howe & Steaffe

Edelweiss . . . . Rodgers and Hammerstein

It's a Grand Night for Singing . . . Rodgers and Hammerstein

Moon River . . . . Mancini

Morning is Broken . . . . Farjeon and Stevens

Somewhere My Love . . . . Dr. Zhivago
                                    (Laura's Theme Song)

The Song of Rain . . . . P. Durand

Sound of Music . . . . Rodgers and Hammerstein

A Time for Us . . . . (from Romeo & Juliet)

and

many others

21

22

23

24

25

26

27

28

0-595-33186-6

Printed in the United States
26422LVS00004B/48

9 780595 331864